How Green Was My Valley

"Full-flavored, full-bodied . . . like the pull of a strong tide."
—SATURDAY REVIEW

"Brilliantly seen and told . . . tender . . . often violent . . . intuitive and passionate." —SPECTATOR

"Superb . . . A book to restore one's faith in human life." —NEW YORK SUN

"Magical." —LOS ANGELES TIMES

"The reader emerges aglow with sharing the happiness of the characters."
.—CHICAGO TRIBUNE

LAUREL
EDITION

RICHARD LLEWELLYN

How Green Was My Valley

LAUREL
EDITION

To my father and the land of my fathers

A LAUREL EDITION

Published by
Dell Publishing Co., Inc.
1 Dag Hammarskjold Plaza
New York, N.Y. 10017

Laurel ® TM 674623, Dell Publishing Co., Inc.
Previous Dell edition #3923—Eleven Printings
First Laurel printing—November 1976
Printed in U.S.A.

Chapter One

I AM GOING TO PACK MY TWO SHIRTS with my other socks and my best suit in the little blue cloth my mother used to tie round her hair when she did the house, and I am going from the Valley.

This cloth is much too good to pack things in and I would keep it in my pocket only there is nothing else in the house that will serve, and the lace straw basket is over at Mr. Tom Harries', over the mountain. If I went down to Tossall the Shop for a cardboard box I would have to tell him why I wanted it, then everybody would know I was going. That is not what I want, so it is the old blue cloth, and I have promised it a good wash and iron when I have settled down, wherever that is going to be.

It has always seemed to me that there is something big to be felt by a man who has made up his mind to leave the things he knows and go off to strange places. I felt the same for the rose cuttings I took from the garden down to the cemetery. But men are different from flowers for they are able to make up their own minds about things. And that should make the feeling bigger, I think.

But all I have felt this past hour since I made up my mind is an itch between my shoulders where a piece of wood got threaded in my shirt while it was blowing on the fence to dry. I felt very badly just now, mind, when I said good-bye to Olwen, but since I did not actually say good-bye to her, and she has no notion I am going, it does not seem the same as saying good-bye properly, so I am feeling perhaps better than I should in false pretences.

This old blue cloth is a worry to me now, for I keep having thoughts that it might be torn or lost and I would have it on my conscience for the rest of my life. Even when I was very small I can remember my mother wearing it. Her hair was fair and curly, thick to choke the teeth of the comb and always very pretty even when it turned white.

My father met her when she was sixteen and he was twenty. He came off a farm to make his way in the iron works here, and as he came singing up the street one night he saw my mother drawing the curtains upstairs in the house where she was working. He stopped singing and looked up at her, and I suppose she looked down to see why he had stopped. Well, they looked and fell in love.

Mind, if you had said that to my mother she would have laughed it off and told you to go on with you, but I know because I had it from my father. They were married in six weeks after that in the worst winter for years. We have had terrible winters since, but my father always said there would never be another winter like that one when my mother and him were married. They used to get up in the morning and find their breath had frozen to thin ice on the bedclothes.

Things were very rough in those days. There were no houses built for the men and married people were forced to live in barns and old sheds until enough houses were built. There was a lot of money made over houses, too. My father was paying rent on this one for more than twenty years before he bought it outright. I am glad that he did, because if he had not, my mother would have had nowhere to go these past few years.

But in those days money was easily earnt and plenty of it. And not in pieces of paper either. Solid gold sovereigns like my grandfather wore on his watch-chain. Little round pieces, yellow as summer daffodils, and wrinkled round the edges like shillings, with a head cut off in front, and a dragon and a man with a pole on the back. And they rang when he hit them on something solid. It must be a fine feeling to put your hand in your pocket and shake together ten or fifteen of them, not that it will ever happen to anybody again, in my time, anyway. But I wonder did the last man, the very last man who had a pocketful of them, stop to think that he was the last man to be able to jingle sovereigns.

There is a record for you.

It is nothing to fly at hundreds of miles an hour, for indeed I think there is somehting to laugh about when a fuss is made of such nonsense. But only let me see a man with a pocketful of sovereigns to spend. And yet everybody had them here once.

When the men finished working on Saturday dinner-time, my mother would hear the whistle and run to put the old stool outside the front door to wait for my father and my brothers coming up the Hill.

I have often stood outside the door looking down the Valley, seeing in my mind all the men coming up black with dust, and laughing in groups, walking bent-backed because the street is steep and in those days it was not cobbled.

The houses, of course, are the same now as they were then, made of stone from the quarries. There is a job they must have had carting all those blocks all those miles in carts and wains and not one road that you could call really good, because the land was all farms, then.

All the women used to dress up specially in their second best with starched stiff aprons on a Saturday morning, for then the men were paid when they came off the midday shift.

As soon as the whistle went they put chairs outside their front doors and sat there waiting till the men came up the Hill and home. Then as the men came up to their front doors they threw their wages, sovereign by sovereign, into the shining laps, fathers first and sons or lodgers in a line behind. My mother often had forty of them, with my father and five brothers working. And up and down the street you would hear them singing and laughing and in among it all the pelting jingle of gold. A good day was Saturday, then, indeed.

My father and my brothers used to go out in the back to the shed to bathe in summer, but in winter they came into the kitchen. My mother filled the casks with hot water and left wooden buckets full of hot and cold for sluicing. When they had finished and put on their best clothes they came in the kitchen for the Saturday dinner, which was always special.

Sunday, of course, there was no cooking allowed unless my father was going down to the pit to see into some matter or other, and even then my mother was very careful.

But Saturday was always good with us. Even I can remember that, but only when I was small, mind.

We always had hams in the kitchen to start with, all the year round, and not just one ham, but a dozen at a time. Two whole pigs hanging up in one kitchen, ready to be sliced for anybody who walked through the door, known or stranger. We had a hen house for years in the back yard, here. Fine white and brown hens, and you should have seen the eggs they laid. Brown, and dark speckly brown, and some almost pink, and all as big as your fist. I can just remember going out and crawling in the straw to the nests while the hen was shouting and flapping her old wings at me, and laying hold of one, very warm, and so big for my little hands that I had to hold it to my chest to carry it back to Mama in the kitchen. Hens have got a funny smell with them, one that comes, I think, from their feathers, just as a man will have his own smell about him. That smell of hens is one of the homeliest smells it is possible to put your nose to. It makes you think of so much that was good that has gone.

But when we used to sit down to dinner on Saturday, it was lovely to look at the table. Mind, in those days, nobody thought of looking at the table to keep the memory of it living in their minds.

There was always a baron of beef and a shoulder or leg of lamb on the dishes by my father. In front of him were the chickens, either boiled or roast, or ducks, or turkey or goose, whatever was the time of the year. Then potatoes, mashed, boiled and roast, and cabbage and cauliflower, or peas or beans and sometimes when the weather was good, all of them together.

We used to start with Grace, all standing up and Mama holding me in the crook of her arm. My father used to close his eyes tight and look up at the stain on the ceiling, holding his hands out across the table. Sometimes when he opened his eyes he would catch me looking at him and shake his fist at me and say I would come to a bad end, in play, of course. Then Mama would tell him to go on with him and leave me alone.

But indeed, so far my poor old father has been so right I have long thought he must have been a prophet.

When we sat down, with me in Mama's lap, my father would ladle out of the cauldron thin leek soup with a big lump of ham in it, that showed its rind as it turned over through the steam when the ladle came out brimming over. There was a smell with that soup. It is in my nostrils now. There was everything in it that was good, and because of that the smell alone was enough to make you feel so warm and comfortable it was pleasure to be sitting there, for you knew of the pleasure to come.

It comes to me now, round and gracious and vital with herbs fresh from the untroubled ground, a peaceful smell of home and happy people. Indeed, if happiness has a smell, I know it well, for our kitchen has always had it faintly, but in those days it was all over the house.

After my mother had taken out the plates with my eldest sister, my father carved the chickens or whatever was there.

My mother was always on the run from the table to the stove to cover the plates with gravy and she was always the last to start her dinner.

"Eat plenty, now," my father used to say, "eat plenty, my sons. Your mother is an awful cook, indeed, but no matter. Eat."

There was never any talk while we were eating. Even I was told to hush if I made a noise. And that way, I think, you will get more from your food, for I never met anybody whose talk was better than good food.

After the plates had been polished clean with bread that my mother used to cut holding the flat, four-pound loaf against her chest, the pudding came out, and let me tell you my mother's puddings would make you hold your breath to eat. Sometimes it was a pie or stewed fruit with thick cream from the farm that morning, but whatever it was, it was always good.

And after that, then, a good cup of tea.

My father never smoked his pipe at table, so while my sister was washing in the back, he and my brothers went in the next room, and sometimes I was allowed to sit on his knee.

If he and the boys were going in to Town to buy something, there was a wait while my mother got ready to share out the spending money.

My mother kept all the money in the tin box on the mantelpiece over the fire-place in the kitchen. Every Saturday for years she put her little pile of sovereigns in with the others, until the box was so heavy they had jokes helping her to carry it, and sometimes my biggest brother, Ivor, carried her and the box and all.

When she had it on the table, she would open the lid and sit back, looking at my father.

"Well, Gwilym?" she would say, in her deep voice.

"Well," my father would say, and take the pipe out of his mouth to sit up and blow his nose. That was always how it was when there was money to be spent over the usual housekeeping.

My father always said that money was made to be spent just as men spend their strength and brains in earning it and as willingly. But just as they work with a purpose, so the results of that work should be spent with a purpose and not wasted. So in our family, since all the grown-ups were earning except my sisters and my mother and me, there was always thought before the tin was taken out of the kitchen.

If my father and the boys were going over to the Mountain to see a rugby match, they would want a few shillings extra between them and my father would take half a sovereign and share it out. Their spending money was fixed because there was little to spend money on.

They had their beer down at the Three Bells at the bottom of the Hill, and my father paid all the dues once a fortnight. Sometimes there were outings with the choir and now and again a visit to a match over in the next valley or an International in Town. But when that happened the whole Valley, you might say, except those in bed or on crutches, would be going. Very few of them ever saw the match, mind, but they would all go to Town, and that was the main thing. They would know about the match from their friends on the way home, so they could argue as well as the next. So what was the odds if they saw the match or not.

I had my Saturday penny when I was quite small, and I used to buy toffee with it from Mrs. Rhys the Glasfryn. She made the toffee in pans and then rolled it all up and threw it soft at a nail behind the door, where it stuck. Then she took a handful with both hands and pulled it towards her, then threw the slack back on the nail again. That went on for half an hour or more until she was satisfied it was hard enough, and then she let it lie to flatten out. Hours I have waited in her front room with my penny in my hand, and my mouth full of spit, thinking of the toffee, and sniffing the smell of sugar and cream and eggs. You could chew that toffee for hours, it seems to me now, and never lose the taste of it, and even after it had gone down, you could swallow and still find the taste hiding behind your tongue.

The first time I had real spending money was when Ivor got married. Bronwen came from over the mountain where her father was a grocer. Ivor met her when he went there to a choir competition and went in the shop for some eggs for his voice. Bronwen served him and I suppose they started talking about one thing and another, but whatever it was, it must have been very interesting because he missed the competition by hours, and he was well cursed for it. A grand tenor he had from my father, see, and trained beautiful. So he was a sad loss.

Dai Ellis the Stable, who took the choir over and back

in the brake, told my father about it. Ivor must have walked every step of the way over the mountain home because he only got in about an hour before my mother got up to get the breakfasts. My father only laughed.

"Beth," he said, "we will be losing Ivor before long now, you will see. He will be the first."

"Well," my mother said, and she was not exactly smiling, but as though she was wrapping a smile inside a thought, "it is quite time, indeed. I wondered how long. Who is she?"

Nobody knew, then. And nobody would dare to ask, even my father. He said everybody had their own thoughts and likings, and it was the business of nobody else to go about asking questions and poking their snouts. He never did.

Poor Ivor had it very badly too. He was off his food for days. Coming in after the shift, he had his bath and went up on the mountain-side to lie in the grass and think. At least, he said he was thinking, when I went up there one day to him.

"Thinking," he said to me. "Go from here, now, before I will sling you head first in the river."

He used to go over the mountain twice a week after that, week in and week out in snow and all, and if he missed Dai Ellis, he walked back all those miles over the mountain in the pitch black. It must be real love that will have a man like Ivor doing all that just to see a girl for a few minutes with her father and mother in the room.

One Saturday afternoon after dinner when Ivor had almost driven my father silly with walking up and down and sighing and going out to the door to look down the Hill, and coming back to pick up the *Christian Herald* and give it a shaking and put it down, we heard a trap pull up outside the door.

My father got up knowing he had a visitor, and my brothers stood up too. Ivor was at the door being very polite to the father of Bronwen who had come over to see the family. My father sent me from the room as they passed in.

"Dada," said Ivor, as white as lilies, "this is Bronwen's father."

"O," said my father. "How are you, sir?"

"I am very well, indeed," Bronwen's father said, looking at all of them and the room too in one single look. "There is cold it is."

From then, of course, they got on fine, and by the time my mother had made the tea, they were like old friends indeed, and Bronwen's father got drunk as a lord down in the Three Bells before he went home that night. My father had had a couple, too, mind, but he always knew when enough was going to be too much, and you could not get him near another pint after that.

Then my father took my mother over the mountain to meet Bronwen's mother.

But one Saturday before that, Bronwen came over by herself before the men came up the Hill.

I will never forget Bronwen as she was when I saw her coming up the Hill with the double basket held on her hip.

She had on a straw bonnet with flowers down by her cheeks, and broad green ribbons tied under her chin and blowing about her face. A big dark green cloak was curling all round her as she walked, opening to show her dress and white apron that reached below the ankles of her button boots. Even though the Hill was steep and the basket big and heavy she made no nonsense of it. Up she came, looking at the houses on our side till she saw me peeping at her from our doorway, and she smiled.

Indeed her eyes did go so bright as raindrops on the sill when the sun comes out and her little nose did wrinkle up with her, and her mouth was red round her long white teeth, and everything was held tight by the green whipping ribbons.

"Hullo, Huw," she said.

But I was so shy I ran in to Mama and hid behind the wall bed.

"What is the matter with you?" my mother asked me, but I only pushed my face in the blankets.

And then Bronwen called softly from the front.

Mind, my mother had never seen Bronwen or heard her voice, but I am sure she knew who it was. She put her head on one side, and put down the fork she had been cooking with, and went to the little looking-glass to take off this old blue cloth and do something to her hair.

"Is that you, Bronwen?" she asked, while she was still looking at herself.

"Yes," Bronwen said, though indeed you could hardly hear.

"Come in, my child," my mother said, and went out to

meet her. They looked at each other for a little time without speaking, and then my mother kissed her.

In five minutes my mother knew all there was to be known, and Bronwen had been told most of the little tricks Ivor had got up to when he was small, and what sort of things he liked to eat, and how he would never drink his tea hot and things like that. Indeed, talk got so warm that Mama nearly missed sitting outside and my father was shouting a chorus with my brothers almost at the door when she screamed, and ran to push out the stool, sitting down quick, and putting her hands tidy to wait.

"There is something radically wrong here," said my father, coming in. "You have never been late before, my girl."

Then he saw Bronwen behind the door and he laughed.

"Wrong?" he said. "No, indeed. Right, that is what it is. Ivor."

My father put his fingers down the back of my neck and pulled me out of the kitchen just when Ivor, coal and dirt and all, was going to kiss Bronwen.

"Those things are not for you, my son," he said, "you will have your turn to come."

My sisters came back from the farm just then and my brothers were bathing out in the back, so the house was full of noise and laughing, and the smell of the cooking made you so hungry you would have pains inside.

Bronwen came over plenty of Saturdays after that, but I was always shy of her. I think I must have fallen in love with Bronwen even then and I must have been in love with her all my life since. It is silly to think a child could fall in love. If you think about it like that, mind. But I am the child that was, and nobody knows how I feel, except only me. And I think I fell in love with Bronwen that Saturday on the Hill.

Still, that is past.

Chapter Two

A GRAND TIME we had at Ivor's wedding. There was nearly a fight about where the wedding was going to be. Bronwen's father wanted it done in the Zion chapel over the mountain, but my father was sure our chapel would be ready in time.

Every man in our village had been helping for months in

the evenings to build our chapel. I used to play in the bricks and blocks and plaster with the other boys while the men were working, and fine times we did have.

Indeed, the Chapel looks the same now as the day it was opened by some preacher from Town. We had no preacher of our own for a long time because the village was not rich enough to pay one, so the grown-ups took turns to preach and pray, and of course the choir was always there.

Ivor got married to Bronwen in our new chapel as my father wanted, and you should have seen the fun after.

For a miracle, it was a fine day. My father wore his top-hat, my mother had a new grey dress and bonnet, all the boys had new black suits and bowlers, and I was in a new black overcoat with a velvet collar. There is a swell I was.

But you should have seen Ivor and Bronwen. He had a new black suit too, but my father lent him his white waist-coat, and it looked a real treat on him, with a bunch of pinks in his buttonhole.

But Bronwen.

Everybody said how beautiful she was. She had her great-grandmother's dress on, so her mother said, and indeed even though it had been washed special, the lace was still looking a bit brownish, or so I thought and no wonder being that old.

There was my mother and Bronwen's crying down on the front, and my father and Bronwen's standing next to them, and then my older brothers, Ianto, Davy, and Owen.

I was down farther with my sisters and my other brother, standing with my aunts and uncles. The Chapel was packed so full there was no room to lift your arms, and opening a hymn book was out of the question. It is a good job they all knew the words of the hymns backwards.

The preacher gave a fine sermon. He used some big English words I had never heard before because our meetings were taken by the grown-ups in our language. But I remember the tunes of some of them and asked my father afterwards. I suppose I must have got the tunes wrong because although my father tried and said them over again, we never found out what they were and I am still in ignorance to this day.

But everybody there listened very close, some leaning forward holding their ears, and some leaning back with their eyes shut, and some just sitting down.

Whenever he said something extra, some of the men hummed to themselves and you could see all the older women's bonnets nodding like the wind passing over a field.

I hummed myself, once, when nobody else did, and of course it was in the wrong place, and my uncle gave me a push with his elbow that sent me flying in the aisle with a bump. I got up trying to wipe the dust off my new coat and the preacher stopped what he was saying to look down at me, and everybody turned round to look at me, and you could hear them clucking their tongues all over the Chapel. I wished I could have dropped through a crack, and indeed I often dream of it, and I can still feel how I felt, as though I was still small, and all those people were still alive.

It is very strange to think back like this, although come to think of it, there is no fence or hedge round Time that has gone. You can go back and have what you like if you remember it well enough.

I will never forget the party after the wedding when Ivor and Bronwen had gone up to the house to go away. They went in Dai Ellis' best trap with the white mare that used to take the Post.

In the big tent they had the food and in the small one the drink. There were tables for the grown-ups under the trees by the Chapel garden, but the children had theirs in their hands on the grass by the baptism tank.

The big tent was a picture inside with all the food laid out on tables running round the sides, and the women in their best dresses and bonnets, and flowers in jugs and buckets.

Bronwen's father had baked till all hours and you should have seen the stuff he brought over. There were pies so heavy that two men had to lift them, and the crust on top so pretty with patterns it was a shame to cut. The wedding cake was out under the trees, white and going up in three rounds, every bit of it made by Bronwen's father, with horse-shoes and little balls of silver spelling out Ivor and Bronwen's names and the date.

And, of course, everybody in the village and from all the farms, and the friends of Bronwen's family had brought something made special, because everybody knew everybody else would be looking to see what had been brought, so by the time it was all on the tables, it looked as though it could never all be eaten, and in any case, it would be a shame to start and spoil the show.

But when my mother clapped her hands at the crowd and told them to eat, you would be surprised how quick it went. Indeed if me and Cedric Griffiths had not found a hole in the back of the big tent we would have been empty. Not, mind you, that anybody rushed with their plates, but they were all so busy talking and eating, and the grown girls were full of small children to be fed, and the grown-ups were serving other grown-ups, and Cedric and me were the wrong size, too big to be fed by girls, and too small to be with the other boys, that we had to make the best of it, and indeed we did very well for ourselves under the long table.

The women were walking right by us, but all we could see was their boots and the bottom of their dresses, and the table cloth covered the rest. When we wanted more, we crawled out, and one would kneel while the other worked whatever came handy. Every time Cedric got up to get more he chose jelly or blancmange, but I took cakes or a pie.

"Go on, boy," Cedric whispered, "there is soft you are to eat old cake when you can have jelly with you."

I think perhaps he kept to that way of thinking all his life because he always did very well. Last time I heard, he was running a boarding house on the coast and doing splendid.

Still, we had to suffer for being pigs later on when they started the races for all of us. My brothers had been look-ing for me to go in the little boys' race and never mind how I shouted and struggled, I had to go in too. I always hated people in crowds, and it was that and the thought of being beaten in front of them all that made me kick and shout.

But in the end I started because Davy threatened to take off my trews in front of the girls and smack my bottom.

That was enough for me. Davy was never one to promise and not keep his word. So I went in the race with about a dozen other boys and I won and I was sick.

Davy thought I was dying and indeed I was so giddy I kept falling over, till Dr. Richards gave me a glass of cold water, and that did it. Then Davy and Ianto gave me a whole sixpence each and I won the prize too, and *my* father gave me a shilling for that. Mama called me in the tent and took all my money away for the box, and gave me three pennies to spend instead, and put a chair to the table for me to sit on for more jelly and cake.

In the evening after we had finished tea we all sat on the grass on horse cloths and sang hymns and songs, and we had prizes for the best. Indeed if I was not chosen again for the best voice among the small boys. There is pleased my father was. I will never forget the way he looked when Mr. Prosser, St. Bedwas, gave me the sweets.

Singing was in my father as sight is in the eye. Always after that he called me the family soloist. That night he held my hand tight all the way home, with my mother on his other side, and my sisters behind us.

There is strange how things come back if you start to think of one thing and become tangled up in memory. Because sometimes you think of a thing, and it reminds you of something else, but nearly always you forget why it should remind you, and you find you have forgotten the link between them.

Ianto was married after that to a girl in the village who was staying with relations. I never saw much of her because her father invited Ianto to go and work with him after they were married, and go he did, and got married up there. I was out of that picture because I had the mumps, but my mother and sisters went, and they were sorry for Ianto when they came back. He had got in with the wrong lot, my mother said, and we heard nothing from him after that for years.

Mama always worried after him but it was no use.

Davy was the brain of the family. He always wanted to go in for doctoring, but Dr. Richards said he was too old. Whenever there was an accident in the pit you would know Davy was about with the bandage box, and if anybody was hurt in the village Davy was always sent for. He never charged anybody only for what bandage and ointment he used, and he was very well thought of all over the district.

He began to get very moody when I was going to school, and soon I stopped asking him questions about sums because he would never answer. My father asked him after supper one night what was the matter.

Davy was a long time answering. Such a long time I was afraid my father would take his mind off him and think of sending me to bed. He was always strict that I should be in bed by eight at night.

"Dada," Davy said, and he was staring into his empty cup, "I am not a bit happy."

"I am sorry to hear that, my son," my father said.

"What is wrong here, Davy?" my mother asked.

"Everything," Davy said. "Everything. And yet nobody seems to notice. And if they do, nothing is done."

"Let me hear you," my father said, "and if it is something a man can do, you shall have it done."

"No, Dada," Davy said, "there is nothing you can do. It is something for all of us. It is this. Next week our wages are going to be cut. Why? Just as much coal is coming up, in fact, more than last year. Why should wages be cut? And then, look, the ironworks are closing and going over to Dawlais and they are calling for men for Middlesbrough. Are the men from the ironworks going to follow iron to Dawlais, or to Middlesbrough, or are they going to the pit for work?"

Davy was staring hard at my father, and his eyes were shadowed by his hair which was long and fell down over his forehead.

"Well," my father said, moving his pipe as he always did when he was worried, "wherever they will find work, I suppose."

"To the pit," said Davy, nodding, "and the pit is well supplied with men. The Owain boys have had to go over the mountain for work. So what chance have others, when their uncles and fathers have been here years? I will tell you what will happen, Dada," said Davy, and he got up to go to the mantelpiece and tap the box, "you will soon have this as empty as my pipe."

"Nonsense, my son," my father said, very surprised and looking at my mother. "Goodness gracious alive, that will never happen while there is coal."

"We will see, now," said Davy. "When those ironworkers gather round the pit for work, you will have some of them offering to work for less, and the manager will agree. You will see, now, and the older men and them with more pay will be put outside, too. And you will be one if you are not careful."

"There is silly you are, boy," my father said and laughing. "Come on, Beth," he said to my mother, "give us a good cup of tea, will you. And you," he said, catching sight of me, "off up to bed. Quick."

As Davy said, so it happened. The ironworkers started to work in the pit for not much more than some of the boys. Some of them even started pulling the trams in place of the ponies. A lot of the older and better-paid men got discharged without being told why, although it was put out that they were too old and could not work as well as they ought. But that was nonsense, because Dai Griffiths, one of them, was one of the best in the Valley and known for it.

My father had been working for some time on the surface as checker. When the coal came up, he put down how much coal was in the tram and who had worked it. On that figure, the men were paid. So he was a kind of leader, and indeed the men looked to him to settle most of the troubles that arose among them. And there were often plenty.

One night he came home from a meeting at the Three Bells and very glum he was. Davy was sitting at the table reading and I was doing a bit of drawing in the bed corner.

"Davy," my father said, "we are going to strike."

"All right, Dada," Davy said, with quiet. "Have you decided what you will do when you have had your discharge?"

"I will have no discharge," said my father, angrily. "That is what the fight is for. Proper wages, and no terms that are not agreeable to us all."

Davy looked up at the box and smiled. That only made my father angrier, although he kept it to himself.

"Why were you up here when you should have been at the meeting?" he asked Davy.

"Because I wanted to see what they would do, first," said Davy. "Now I know, I can do something. And the first is, you keep out of it, Dada, and let me do the talking."

"No," my father said, "I will not. They have asked me to put the case, and put it I will."

"Then," Davy said, "Gwilym and Owen and me will soon be keeping this house going. You will join Dai Griffiths and the rest of them."

"We will see about that," my father said.

And indeed Davy was right again.

My father and two other men went to see the manager

and came back quiet and cheerless. There was nothing to be done, they said, only strike work.

So strike work they did.

For five weeks the strike lasted, the first time, and the men were only back two days when they came out again because a dozen of them were discharged, my father among them.

The second time they were out for twenty-two weeks.

Pits were working all round the Valley, but nobody outside our village seemed to care. So on it went, right into winter. Then some men came down from Town with somebody from London, and my father went to see them by himself.

By that time people were feeling the pinch. Food was scarce and so was money, and if the women had not been good savers in better times, things would have gone very hard. As it was, savings were almost at an end, and my mother was dipping into our box to help women down the Hill who had big families still growing. Poor Mrs. Morris by the Chapel, who had fourteen, and not one older than twelve, had to go about begging food, and her husband was so ashamed he threw himself over the pit mouth.

My father came back worried but steady after speaking to the men. My mother asked him no questions.

"We have finished the strike, Beth," he said. "But our wages must come down. They are not getting the price for coal that they used to, so they cannot afford to pay the wages they did. We must be fair, too."

"Are you having your job back, Gwilym?" my mother asked.

"Yes, my girl," he said. But I thought he looked queer at my mother when he said it.

I found out why a couple of mornings later.

The men went back the morning after my father had spoken to the owners, and you should have seen the Hill as they went down.

It was early morning and cold, and the moon had not yet gone down. White frost was hard and thick on the roadway and roofs, and all the lit windows threw orange patches all the way down.

As the doors opened and the men came out, their wives and children followed them into the road and stood to watch them go. My father was one of the first, with Davy, and as soon as the men saw him they started to cheer, for they all thought he was the saviour of the village. But my father was not a vain man, and he disliked any show about him. So he waved them all quiet and started to sing.

As soon as they heard his voice, tenors and altos waited for their turn, then the baritones and basses, and then the women and children.

As soon as the singing started, all the doors opened all the way down the Hill, and men and women and children came out to fill the road.

I looked at the smooth blue sky and the glowing white roofs, the black road, choked with blacker figures of waving men passing down the Hill between groups of women with children clustered about their skirts, all of them flushed by flickering orange lamplight flooding out from open doorways, and heard the rich voices rising in many harmonies, borne upward upon the mists which flew from singing mouths, veiling cold-pinched faces, magnifying the brilliance of hoping eyes, and my heart went tight inside me.

And round about us the Valley echoed with the hymn, and lights came out in the farms up on the dark mountain, and down at the pit, the men were waving their lamps, hundreds of tiny sparks keeping time to the beat of the music.

Everybody was singing.

Peace there was again, see.

Chapter Three

I WENT TO SCHOOL with Mrs. Tom Jenkins in a little house far from the village. Tom had been burnt by molten iron at the Works and had done nothing for years only lie in a chair, and his wife had started a school to keep things going. She had two little girls of her own, and while she was teaching they used to sit on stools by the board, separate from the payers. Tom was always in pain, so lessons were often broken off when she went out to see if she could do anything for him.

We learnt sums and letters, some history and the names of towns and rivers and where they were. Mrs. Tom Jenkins had come from Caernarvon where her father had been a book seller, so, of course, she knew a lot.

Indeed I will give her what she is due, for she gave us

more than our fourpennyworth a week. That was when I was taught to think, but I was never aware of it until I started to work. The other boys and girls who were there with me have all done well, though I am not certain they would say the same for her.

We used to sit in her front room on stools and rest our slates on our knees. Mrs. Tom stood in front of a blackboard nailed on the wall and wrote with knobs of chalk.

First thing when we got in, she made us hang up our hats and coats tidy, and then walk into the front room and say good morning to her, and to the little girls. Then we turned about, and the boys set stools for the girls, and the girls got the slates and pencils for the boys.

When we were all ready, we stood to sing the morning hymn, and Mrs. Tom said a little prayer, asking a blessing on us all, and strength of mind and will to live and learn for the benefit of mankind.

I remember well trying to think about mankind. I used to try to build up something that would look like mankind because the word Man I knew, and Kind I knew. And I thought at last, that mankind was a very tall man with a beard who was very kind and always bending over people and being good and polite.

I told that to Mrs. Tom one evening when the others had gone and I was helping her to put Tom right for the night.

"That is a good picture of Jesus, Huw," she said.

"Is Jesus mankind, then?" I asked her, and very surprised I was.

"Well, indeed," she said, and she was folding Tom in a blanket, "He did suffer enough to be mankind, whatever."

"Well, what is mankind, then, Mrs. Jenkins?" I asked her, for I was sure to have an answer because I had puzzled long enough.

"Mankind is all of us," Mrs. Tom said, "you and me and Tom and everybody you can think of all over the world. That is mankind, Huw."

"Thank you, Mrs. Jenkins," I said, "but how is it you ask every morning for us to help mankind, then?"

"Because," she said, "I want you all to think not only of yourselves and your families but everybody else who is alive. We are all equal, and all of us need helping and there is nobody to help mankind except mankind."

"But why do we pray to God if there is only mankind to

help?" I asked, because my father was always saying that God was the only help a man could put his trust in, and what Mrs. Tom was saying was new to me.

"Only God will tell you that, Huw," she said, and she was looking at Tom. But Mrs. Tom never knew I heard what she said under her breath. "If there is a God," she said to herself.

She was looking at Tom just before she slipped his night-cap on. He had caught the iron over his head and shoulders. He was blind, of course, and his nose was burnt off, and his mouth was like a buttonhole with his teeth all black inside, and his head was naked and a purplish colour. He would have been about thirty, then, and my father said he had been a well-favoured man and the finest tenor in the Valley. Now he could only make funny noises in his throat, and I am not sure he knew Mrs. Tom or his little girls. So looking back I am not sure I can blame her for saying what she did.

That was when I started to think for myself, and perhaps that was what made me come down to this.

Not that I am not satisfied with what I have become, or that I am where I am. Only that if I had not started to think things for myself and find things for myself, I might have had a happier life judged by ordinary standards, and perhaps I might have been more respected.

Though neither happiness nor respect are worth anything, because unless both are coming from the truest motives, they are simply deceits. A successful man earns the respect of the world never mind what is the state of his mind, or his manner of earning. So what is the good of such respect, and how happy will such a man be in himself? And if he is what passes for happy, such a state is lower than the self-content of the meanest animal.

Yet, looking round this little room, such thinking is poor comfort indeed, and strangely empty of satisfaction, too. There must be some way to live your life in a decent manner, thinking and acting decently, and yet manage to make a good living.

My father was a great one for honest dealing, but he never had his reward down here, and neither did my mother. I am not bitter about anything, and I have no feeling left inside me to be scornful. I am only saying what is in my mind.

The first time I saw my father as a man, and not as a

man who was my father, was when I was coming home from school to my dinner the day the men went back to work after the strike.

We were all running through winter rain, cold and grey and stinging like needles, splashing in the ruts and puddles, with the hedges whispering aloud as the bare twigs whipped at the drops, and the ditches bubbling and frothing on either side, feeling our feet freezing as the water went over the tops of our boots, and our chests growing cold and sticky as the wet coats got wetter, when we came up the rise where the lane joined the colliery road. Just over the low hedge we could see the cage and power house, and nearer still the place where the checkers stood to rate the trams.

The checkers had their own little huts to stand in when it was raining or cold, and ever since I could remember there had always been three huts, one for each checker, and the one used by my father was the green one in the middle.

I stood still as the others raced on, looking at the gap between the other two huts. My father was standing in the rain, checking a tram into his book held under the fold of his sopping coat. He was standing in a puddle made by the drips that fell from his coat, and his hair was plastered down his face.

His hut had been taken away.

Whether my staring eyes made him look up or not, I do not know to this day, but when he saw me he moved his pencil from his mouth and put his finger up as though to say I was not to tell my mother, and then waved me to go on home.

That night I was in bed in this room when I woke up and heard my father talking to Davy, and my mother crying.

"You will get nothing without a fight," Davy was shouting. "Do you think I will allow my father to stand like a dog in the rain and not raise my hands to stop it?"

"Look after yourself," my father said. "You shall not make my case a plank for your politics. Leave me out of it. I can take care of myself."

"Yes, by God you can," Davy said, "and drown like a rat."

"Hold your tongue this minute," my father said. "You shall use no blasphemy in this house."

"But, Dada," Davy said, "what are you going to do? You will die of cold when it starts to snow. Let us all stand together and you will see how they will act, then. It is no use one pit coming out. It must be all the pits at once."

"If I freeze to death, no matter," my father said. "You shall not make me an excuse for more striking. I will not have people going without just because I am standing in the cold, and if I did, I would deserve a worse death than that."

"But if they find they can do things like that to the spokesman," Davy said, "what will they try and do to the men?"

"We will see," said my father. "I will have no more talk on it. Be silent, now, and go to your bed."

Gwilym was lying in the next bed and I could hear from his breath that he was awake and listening.

"Gwil," I whispered, "what does Davy want to do?"

"Shut your mouth, boy," Gwilym whispered. "Do you want Dada up here with the strap?"

"But what is it Davy wants?" I whispered, so low I am sure only a mouse and Gwilym could have heard.

"Fight against the bloody English," Gwilym whispered, and got up on his elbow.

A cold tickle went down the bones of my back, and the hair on my neck came up like a brush.

Gwilym was only fourteen then and just started work on the coal face, although he had been working the ponies for nearly a year. And here he was, the quietest of us all, swearing, and not only that, saying something that was so wicked it made my body ice.

Davy came up to bed then, and stopped us talking. He slept in my bed, so that I could see when he put the candle down and sat looking at it, that his eyes were open wide and staring black and his face was white and covered with sweat that winked in the light. I shut my eyes in fear and kept them shut a trembling long time, and then I must have gone to sleep.

Ivor and Bronwen had their own house further down the Hill, so Bronwen was often in with my mother, although my mother never went down there unless she was asked. On Saturday they came in to dinner with us, but nearly always on a Sunday they went over the mountain to see Bronwen's father and mother and go to the Zion there.

Ivor felt just as badly about my father as Davy did, but he held his tongue where Davy either would not or could not. He told my father that Davy would have himself known for a rebel and get himself put on the black list at the pit if he was not very careful, but my father said it was no use to talk. The boy had the blood in him and there it was.

"Then what is it he wants?" Ivor asked, with impatience. "He would never stand to talk two minutes together with me."

I could have told him the reason, for I heard Davy call him an old stick in the mud before that, and say that married men were useless in any cause because of their dependents.

"Davy wants socialism," my father said. "And he wants a union with everybody in it, all over the world I think he said."

"There is nonsense for you," Ivor said. "Now if he said the colliers, I would be with him."

"You can call it what you like, Ivor Morgan," my brother Gwilym said. "But this I will tell you. There is more sense in Davy's big toes than you have got all over you."

There is surprised my father was, and how angry was Ivor. My father was out of his chair for the strap in a moment, but Gwilym was flying from the house and running down the hill like the spirit of the wind before my father reached the nail, even.

"There is more Davy in him," my father said. "I can see trouble coming in this family before long. It seems to me there is a nest of hornets growing in the back bedroom here."

My father was looking absently at me. I was in the back bedroom with the others and I felt bound to speak up even though I knew it was wrong.

"I will be one, too, Dada," I said, "if it will have you out of the cold."

"Go from here, now," my father said, "before you will have a couple."

But his eyes were full of laugh, so I walked out of the house instead of running, and went down to Bronwen.

I had stopped being shy with her. She had a way of looking at you that had a smile in it, and yet she never properly smiled, so you never knew whether to smile back or keep a straight face. She started to call me The Old Man just after she had set up house, and whenever I went down to her she stopped whatever she was doing and gave me that look till I had sat in Ivor's big chair.

"And what is the matter with the old man this time?" she would say. And I would tell here what it was, if it was anything. Else I kept my peace. That afternoon I said nothing to her till she had made a cup of tea.

"Davy is going to fight the English," I said to her.

"Go on, boy," she said, and laughed.

"He is," I said, "I had it from Gwilym."

"Gwilym is too young to have sense," she said.

"Davy has, though," I said. "And he is the one."

"And what is the old man going to do?" Bronwen asked, and knelt down by me.

"I am going to fight with them," I said. "I will have them for making my Dada stand in the rain."

Bronwen put her arms round me so quickly she knocked over the tea, but she seemed to care nothing for the broken cup.

"Well said, Huw," she whispered. "Fight you, now. That is why there are men and women. Men to fight, women to help."

"Are you a rebel, Bron?" I asked her.

"If that is a rebel," she said, "indeed, yes."

"Good," I said, "now I am a rebel properly. What is Davy going to do, Bron? Nobody will tell me."

Bronwen started to collect the pieces of cup, and she was frowning as she bent.

"Look, Huw," she said, "you are too small to know about such things. You go and call Ivor for me."

But I asked her again, and I felt angry that she should know as a woman, and yet I was a boy and ignorant. It is funny the ideas a small boy will have.

"Well, old man," she said, "if you will have it, Davy is trying to make things better his own way. That is all I know, so let it rest now. Go and call Ivor for me, will you?"

Chapter Four

I ASKED MY FATHER about Davy.

"And what do you want to know for, my son?" my father asked me.

"All the other boys know, Dada," I said, "and I should know, too, so that I can help them."

"You mind your own business," my father said, "you have your sums to learn and your own work to do. Do that and do it properly and that is all. Mind what I say, now."

I am sorry in a way I disobeyed my father after that because it was always a worry to me, and I knew I would never meeet his eye if he caught me, to say nothing of the strap.

But the truth is I found out about Davy in the usual way a small boy finds out things he is denied to know by older people, and that is through other small boys.

Mervyn Ellis, son of Dai Ellis the Stable, was one of my best friends then, and was still till a week ago. To him I went next day coming from school, and told him there was some plot or other with my brother at the head. It sounded very noble and desperate, I must say, and I remember I could do nothing with my lower lip when I was telling him. It seemed to go stiff with me, and instead of natural talking, my mouth was going all shapes as though it was feeling proud of itself.

There is silly you feel when you find yourself unable to control even your own mouth.

"I know, boy, I know," Mervyn said. "There is a meeting on the mountain to-night."

"For who?" I asked.

"Davy and the men, of course," Mervyn said, "there is dull you are. Your own brother and you never knew that."

He told me, then, of all the other meetings that had been going on for months, and of the men who had come over from the other valleys round about. They were going to have a union, Mervyn said, although he had no notion what he meant. So we both said we would go up on the mountain that night and see what there was to be seen.

Then I knew why Gwilym was never in bed till late, always coming in just before Davy, not through the door, but climbing up the shed to get in this little window. I knew that because the cold draught often woke me up, though I said nothing. I would never split on Gwilym, because he was always in trouble, and if my father had known he was coming in so late through the window, there would have been ructions.

That night, after I had kissed Mama and Dada good night, I went up with the candle and got under the blanket with all my clothes on.

"Are you in bed, Huw?" my mother called up, after enough time.

"Yes, Mama," I said.

"Good boy," my mother said. "Candle."

I blew out the candle and lay there looking at the blue criss-crossed square where the window was. I was not exactly afraid now that the time had come, but my heart was beating so loud I was sure they would hear downstairs. It is strange how loud little sounds become when you are in the dark and doing something wrong.

When I got up the old bed creaked so much I could have given it a good kick for its trouble, but at last, and inch by inch, I was out of it, and even then the bedclothes breathed so loud it was like putting back some old man.

The floor, then.

Each plank had something to say, scolding and moaning when I put down a foot and picked it up, and the carpet, too, was stretching and grieving all the way to the chest of drawers by the window.

To push up that window was to suffer for years, it seemed to me. I held my breath and pulled all sorts of faces as I raised the little sash, ready at the slightest movement from downstairs to leap for the bedclothes. Bit by bit it went up, and the more it went, the colder blew the draught and the more shivery I got, and what between listening for noise downstairs and squeaks in the window, and sounds of somebody coming outside, I got a sort of squint in my ears, until at last I could easily have shouted downstairs that I was going out and I could have taken the strapping without a murmur in pure relief.

But at last the sash was up enough for me to climb through, and that was when the real trouble started. The tiles outside the window sloped down to the guttering and from there you had to be made of putty. First I got one leg out in the cold, resting on the frozen sill, then I had to pull up the rest of me to get the other leg through, and that is where the fight started between my chin and my knees. There was one time there, when I thought I would stick there all night unless my head would be squashed through the wall, and my foot outside the window kept slipping on the tiles and making a shocking noise, indeed.

It was my father's chair scraping on the stones downstairs that got me through. I heard it as I was trying to force my head through the space between my bent knee and the top of the window.

It frightened me so much that I must have gone smaller or something, and the next thing I knew I was through the window and slipping on my front down the cold tiles feet first toward the guttering and a five-foot drop.

I was not sure whether to start shouting then or wait until I landed on the ground. I remember thinking that if I shouted on the ground, and I was hurt, I would get nothing from my father until I was well, but if I shouted now he would run out and catch me and perhaps skin me alive. I was saved all that trouble by catching the toes of my boots in the gutter edge and that brought me to a stop.

Sliding down and gripping the edge, and swinging for a bit before I dropped down, was so easy that I was calling myself all sorts for being such a cry-baby less than a minute afterward. As I ran down toward Dai Ellis the Stable, I remembered Dada saying that too many people shout before they are hurt, and there is a fine contempt I was feeling for myself as I climbed through the hole in the fence.

So contemptuous I felt, indeed, that I was ready to brave anything just to show myself I was not the coward I thought I was.

But Dai Ellis happened then to open the stable door where he was sitting up with Bess, the black mare who was sick, and the very sight of him framed in the light stuck my feet to my boots, and nothing would move me.

Good for me that he went back in, or I would have had it for sure. But when he went in, I crept double round the back of the house to the pigsty where Mervyn was meeting me, and there I found him, nearly dead with fright. He would not let on, of course, that he was ready to give up and go back to bed, but I knew how he felt because I was the same.

So we both pretended we liked coming out like this, and what sport it was, and how we would swank with the other boys in the morning, and have the girls looking at us the way girls do, when a boy has done something special.

We went over the pigsty and climbed the stone wall that led to the river, crossing the stepping-stones very carefully because it was dark and the trees shut out the light, so that we could see the stones only because of the white whiskers the running stream put round them.

On the other side of the river we started to run up the path up the mountain-side through the trees, and run we did till we were almost dropping. Now we were out, we kept thinking of the witches that lived up in the caves, and although Mervyn said nothing to me, and I said nothing to Mervyn, I know he was thinking the same as me because I saw him looking round once or twice and then go on faster when he found me watching him.

Out of the trees and in the fields we felt better off because the moon was giving a bit of light, though moonlight is something I can do without at any time for comfort. Nothing is so creepy as that pale light splashing over everything that makes white look shining and everything else greyish blue and soft black. Even the grass goes grey, and a boy's face is like death indeed, with black shadows in the cheeks and under the eyes, and silver points in the eyes themselves.

We were so busy being frightened we almost forgot what we were up there for, until we saw the light of lamps shining on the leaves of a may tree growing on a hedge in front of us.

I pulled Mervyn's arm just in time to stop him running full-tilt through Jones the Chapel's field. We stopped dead and crawled to the hedge, lying there looking both ways to see if we had been seen, and while we were waiting there holding our breath we heard a lot of low voices over on the other side as though a crowd of men had all agreed about something.

Standing, we climbed up the stones and looked over the hedge. I for one nearly fell backwards with surprise.

There were crowds of men there, hundreds easily, all in their overcoats with caps pulled down, standing in ranks, listening to Davy.

He was standing on a piece of rock, and although I could hear nothing only very faint, I could tell by his hands how his voice would be sounding, and I knew what his face would be like without looking. It was knowing that that made me more afraid than being caught up there.

I gave Mervyn a jog and climbed down.

"Back, me," I said, "quick, too."

"Not yet, boy," Mervyn said, "I want to hear what they are going to do."

"Stay you, then," I said, "but I am going from by here now."

And I went, and before long Mervyn came running behind me. We went down the mountain double fast, never mind the moon or the witches, and crossed the river, and I left Mervyn by the sty to go through the lane to our back way. But when I got underneath our window I found there was no way for me to get in.

I had forgotten there was five feet of brick to be climbed before reaching the gutter.

Here was something to cry for, indeed.

Then I thought of the water butt. It was much bigger than me, and stood under the spout by the kitchen door. So I started to wheel it inch by inch nearest to the place under the guttering where I could climb up. Never have I heard such a noise as that old barrel made.

First it scratched its old rim on the cobbles, then it splashed and slopped its water. Then it pulled itself out of my grip because it was so heavy, and bumped down with a boom like a drum, and more splash and slop. Indeed I have never made more faces at anything, as though the act of making a face would excuse the noise to the listening quiet.

And under my breath I was telling it to hisht and for shame, and if I had known any swearing I would have had that in, too.

And then, when I had it under the place I wanted and I had got up on the edge of the rim, I slipped on the sticky moss, and fell inside in the water with such a noise that the hens woke up and screeched to make your eyes cross.

For minutes I must have stood there dribbling wet and up to my knees in water that froze my legs and feet through to the bones. The dark old barrel covered me right up, smelling of old earth and moss and everything that is bent and cracked. So when I found nobody was rising, I was at pains to be out of it sharp and lively, indeed.

I pulled myself up over the edge and balanced there to let the water drip off me and the wind blew so cold where I was wet it was like razors cutting at me. Up I got, and cocked up my leg to get over the gutter, with my teeth gnashing so much they nearly shook my head off. So cold I was that the slates felt quite warm as I lay on them to slide up, and nothing felt better than to catch hold of the sill and rest there to breathe and feel I was up at last.

Quietly I got my legs through, and carefully I went in a little bit at a time until I was all in and standing on the carpet.

Then, it was, that my father lit the candle.

"Where have you been, my son?" he said.

I was colder with fear than the wind or wet. My tongue was like a piece of steel in my mouth, and if you had seen my father's face you would have known why, too.

He was not tall or very broad, but tidy in size and always carried his head well back. His head looked to be the biggest part of him, broad across the front and back. His eyes were grey, and sometimes when he was laughing they were almost blue. He had a small nose, scarred by a coal fall across the bridge, and a good mouth. His moustache was long and almost the same colour as his hair, black and going white, but his eyebrows were jet, and stood out from his pale face, especially when he stood near a light or if you saw him in the daytime with his cap off.

In this light his eyes were almost white, shining at me like jewels, and so stern that I wanted to die.

"Where have you been?" he asked again, and shaded his eyes with his hand. He was still dressed, and sitting on my bed.

"Up the mountain, Dada," I said, though it is a mystery to me to this day how I got it out.

"Did I tell you about minding your own business?" he said.

"Yes, Dada," I said.

"Do you expect your mother to clean that mess you are in?" he asked me.

"No, Dada," I said.

"Go downstairs and clean yourself and be sharp about it," he said.

Off I went like a black-beetle, dripping all over the floor, expecting a clout that would stretch me senseless. But nothing happened.

The kitchen fire was banked all night, so I had no trouble drying my clothes. But blacking and polishing my boots was another matter. For minutes I stood there rubbing and brushing my boots, naked in front of the fire, knowing my father was still sitting upstairs, wondering what I was going to get from him, and what Mama would say in the morning, and if Gwilym would come in before I could give him a sign to wait on.

When I went upstairs again I carried my dry clothes and my polished boots to show my father. He looked at them all very carefully one by one, nodding.

"Look," he said, when he had finished, pointing to the puddles on the floor. "Look at the mess Mama will have with her in the morning. Go you and get a cloth."

Down I went again and up I came with a cloth and rubbed all the puddles dry, and very careful I was to look along the floor to see if I could find any more wet places, knowing all the time that those grey eyes were upon me, and on that account being so careful in my work, and so vigorous when I found some to do, that my father got impatient.

It is strange how you will do a job with more than ordinary care when you have a fault upon your conscience. It is almost as though you thought to make your industry a form of penitence.

"Come here, Huw," my father said at last.

I put down the cloth and stood in front of him, hanging my head.

"Why did you go up the mountain when I told you not?" my father asked, and to my surprise his voice was quite ordinary, and not angry a bit.

"I wanted to help Davy, Dada," I said.

"Help Davy?" my father said. "And how about your poor Mama? What would have happened to her if you had come to harm? Did you stop to think?"

"No, Dada," I said.

"Think in future," he said. "Now go to bed and sleep. And mind you, no more of this Davy nonsense out of you."

"No, Dada," I said.

My father lifted me into bed and put the clothes over me, and patted me on the head.

"You will be a man soon, my son," he said, "and you will find all the troubles you are wanting in plenty. Plenty, indeed, I am afraid you will have it more than us, now. So till then, be a good boy and think of your Mama. She is the one to help. Good night, my son. God watch over you."

"Good night, Dada," I said.

I was so glad he had gone before Gwilym came in through the window. I fell off to sleep at once then.

But thinking back now, I hear my father's voice as he

spoke then, so sad and soft, as though he had known and seen.

Chapter Five

IT WOULD TAKE a lot to upset my mother, but she was quiet and worried when I came back from school at dinner-time next day. Gwilym told me that my father had given Davy a talking to that morning, and Davy was off down the Hill to live with Mrs. Beynon, who had four lodgers already, all of them Davy's friends.

My mother never said a word about it, but it showed the first Saturday when Davy came up to put his money in the box and have his dinner. She was not crying, but the tears were rolling down her cheeks when he kissed her. Davy and my father acted as though nothing had happened and were talking quietly as they had always done. It was Owen who caused the trouble.

Owen was a quiet boy then. He had nothing to say to anybody, and of course everybody thought he was a fool. He would stay quiet for hours by himself, reading, or out in the tool-shed putting iron together. I was a nuisance to him because I stole his tools or lost the place in his books, so of course I was always due for a clip in the ear whenever he saw me.

Owen had the voice of my mother, deep and from the chest, and to hear him read in chapel was a shock, so good it sounded, echoing up in the gallery and under the rafters. My father had a notion to put him up as a preacher, but Owen was not yet old enough, and in any case he liked better to use tools than study, though even then he knew almost any part of the Bible by heart.

I forget what exactly Davy and my father were talking about. I think it was about coal raising and the way the seam ran down the Valley.

"They are all fools," Owen said.

Davy was so surprised that he put down his knife and fork.

"Hisht, Owen," my mother said, and looked at my father with wide eyes. None of us were allowed to speak unless my father spoke to us first.

My father chewed what was in his mouth as though he had not heard, but as soon as he had swallowed he turned to look at Owen as though he had never seen him before.

"And what," he said, "do you know about the subject?"

"I am very sorry I was rude, Dada," Owen said, but with no fear in his eyes or voice. "But the way they are working the coal now is not only stupid but criminal."

"As it happens, my son," my father said, "you are right. But who gave you permission to speak? And where did you have your knowledge?"

"I said without thinking, Dada," Owen said. "I must have been dreaming or something. I got my knowledge from Dai Griffiths."

"Good," my father said. "There is no man knows more than Dai. But learn manners, too. Speak when you are asked and not before."

"I will speak against anything I know to be wrong," said Owen.

"Not in this house," my father said. "And that is enough from you."

"In this house and outside," Owen said. "Wherever there is wrong I will speak against it."

"Leave the table," my father said.

"I will leave the house," said Owen.

"Gwilym," my mother said, reaching out a hand to my father. "Owen," she said, turning to him, "tell Dada you are sorry."

"I am not sorry," said Owen, "except to lose my dinner. I am going down to live with Davy."

"So am I," said Gwilym, putting his knife and fork down and pushing back his chair.

"If you two leave this house," said my father, "you will never come inside again."

"Good," said Gwilym, nearly crying.

"Oh, Gwilym," my mother said, staring at my father.

"We are together, Gwil," said Owen.

"Davy," said my mother, "tell them to say they are sorry to Dada. They are following your example."

"Yes, Mama," Davy said, and got up. "But they are men, working for their living. I cannot stop them."

"I will give you two," said my father, looking at Owen and Gwilym, "one more chance. Behave yourselves, and we will say no more."

"We have done nothing," said Owen, "and if table manners prevent the speaking of the truth, I will be a pig."

"So will I," said Gwilym.

"Boys," said Davy, "there is no need for this."

"There is, Davy," said Owen, and white passion was in his eyes. "I am going, whether you will have me or not."

"So am I," said Gwilym.

"Get your clothes and go," said my father, and started to eat again.

"Oh, Gwilym," my mother said, in a whisper.

My father did not answer, but went on chewing, though his body was trembling and there was water in his eyes.

Nobody moved for a time. Then Davy sighed, and bent to kiss the top of my mother's head, here on this blue cloth.

"Good-bye Mama," he said, and walked from the room.

"Good-bye Mama," Owen said, waiting for Gwilym.

"Good-bye, Mama," said Gwilym, and went out with Owen.

It was quiet in the kitchen when they had gone, and the sound of their footsteps had gone down the Hill with them. My mother was looking at my father all the time as if she was sure he would call them back.

But he went on eating his dinner, looking up through the kitchen window at the rock-face outside. I was trying to be as quiet as I could while I was having my dinner, but then my spoon grated on the plate and brought his eyes to me.

"Yes, my son," my father said, "I know you are there. It do seem I will have only Ivor and you, now then."

"Gwilym," my mother said, in her ordinary voice, "how long, now, will those boys be from home?"

"The only boys I have got, my girl," my father said, "are twenty-three years of age and six. That is Ivor and Huw. Those are the only two, and Ianto is away. I have no other sons, and there is nobody else entitled to call himself my son unless I own to him."

"Oh, Gwilym," my mother said, and started to cry. I had never before seen my mother cry really and properly as I had cried and had seen others cry.

I wish now I had not. There is supposed to be something noble about the tears of a mother, but it is a pity that real, well-meant tears cannot come without the sounds that go with them. The scrapings in the throat, the fullness of spittle, the heavy breaths and halting, gulping sighs, are not fitted to be the servants of heartfelt grief, so there is that about them making for laughter and contempt, especially in the mind of a child.

There is first of all surprise that a grown-up can cry properly, and then curiosity to see how they cry, and that causes a cold scrutiny in which all feeling is lost, even when it is realised that this is your own mother who is crying.

You are intent upon the details.

The shaking hands, swollen blue veins, smeared cheeks, hair coming loose under the stress of an almost rhythmic sobbing, of points of light flicking from brimming lashes, and you are amazed at the growing wetness of the handkerchief and the never-ending flow of big tears.

This is your mother, you think.

This poor, huddled woman over there, is your mother, who has told you so many times not to cry. After that, her red face and swollen, wet eyes, so miserable and helpless, come as a shock to make you laugh, and although you know it is wrong, you feel you must laugh outright, or go under the table.

And when that is past, you will want to cry because your mother is still crying to herself, and cannot find comfort.

It will seem shame to me, now, but my mother never meant the same to me after that. I could always hear her crying and see her face, though when I grew up, of course, I learnt better. But there it is.

My father took no notice. I know now how he saw the matter. He was the father and head over all the house, and what came in and went out. His authority had been defied and he had taken the course he saw to be most fitting. For that reason he was clear in his conscience, and he said nothing to my mother for crying, because he knew tears to be a woman's last refuge. She can go no further, especially if she is a good woman. And I will swear with my blood that my mother was good.

My sisters were crying with my mother. Ceridwen was looking from the plates to my mother and then to my younger sister who was standing by the fire waiting for the kettle to boil. Angharad was about ten, then, and Ceridwen five years older. I was sure Angharad would say something from the look on her face. If you have never seen the look in the eyes of a cat when you have made a noise to frighten it out of sleep you will not know what was alive in the eyes of Angharad.

She was as tall as my mother, then, and very fair with grey eyes lighter than a snow sky, and so big and clear you would think it not possible. So when they were full of her spirit, and she looked straight at you, you would feel yourself going small inside yourself.

"Mama," Angharad said, loud and clear and in the voice of my mother. "I am going down with the boys to look after them."

My mother stopped crying, and turned so quickly she made my father jump.

"Angharad," my mother said, and indeed her voice made me all cold, "close your mouth this moment."

"Mama," Angharad said, "I am going down with the boys."

"This moment," my mother said, and stood up. "Outside in the wash-house and get your work finished. Not another sound. If I will hear another word, you shall have a smacking, my lady. Go you, now."

My father pushed back his chair and looked at me.

"Come on, my son," he said, "we will go up on the mountain and find peace. Beth," he said to my mother, "I will leave Angharad to you. But I hope she knows how far she can go. I have still got a strap. Come, my son."

I got down from the table very thankful, and ran to get my cap and my father's stick. I loved walking with my father. I have often wondered whether the trouble in our family could have happened if my father had gone walking with the other boys as he did with me. If I had only known my father in the house, perhaps I could have spoken to him as the others had done, but knowing him as he was up on the mountains, I was never able to speak to him other than with respect and with love.

He never once as far as I remember talked to me as though I were a child. I was always a man when I was with him, so no wonder Bron called me The Old Man. Everything I ever learnt as a small boy came from my father, and I never found anything he ever told me to be wrong or worthless.

But perhaps the things that he held to be good and right to do, were not the good and right things for our time, or if they were, then perhaps he carried them out with too much force or with too straight a tongue and through that, put men against him.

That afternoon we walked for miles along the river, first, and then up the mountain.

Our village, then, was one of the loveliest you could see. I will say it was lovely, because it was so green and fresh and clean, with wind from off the fields and dews from the mountain. The river was not very wide, only about twenty feet, but so clear you would see every inch of rock through the bubbling water, and so full of fish that nobody thought of using a rod. My father taught me to tickle trout up on the flat rock by Mrs. Tom Jenkins'.

Hour after hour we have sat there, dropping stones to frighten little ones away, and then watching a big one come up and making plans to have him.

First you would have to roll back your sleeve sometimes up to your muscle, and put your arm right in the water, holding your hand open and steady. Of course, the river would be so cold sometimes, it would almost make you shout to have it in, but no matter, if you wanted a fish you would have to suffer.

Then the old fish would come along very soft and quiet, and you would almost feel inside you that he was thinking to himself, watching your hand, and knowing that something was the matter and not sure what. Of course, you would not move a fraction, even your eyes, while all this was going on, because a good and sensible trout will swim back out of reach and stay there to laugh at you. Indeed, that is true, for I have seen them do it.

Well, then, if he was so silly, he would come up to see your fingers and nose round them, and rub himself against them. Then it would be your turn. Quietly, you would bend your fingers to smooth him under his stomach and tickle his ribs. Sometimes he would flash away and you would lose him, but oftener he would stay on. Then you would work your fingers along him until your little finger was inside his gill.

That was enough.

Give him a jerk and pull out your arm, and there he would be, flapping on the rock.

And there is good fresh trout is for supper.

My mother used to put them on a hot stone over the fire, wrapped in breadcrumbs, butter, parsley and lemon rind, all bound about with the fresh green leaves of leeks. If there is better food in heaven, I am in a hurry to be there, if I will not be thought wicked for saying so.

But there I am again, see.

The quiet troubling of the river, and the clean, washed stones, and the green all about, and the trees trying to drown their shadows, and the mountain going up and up behind, there is beautiful it was.

When birds were nesting we often went out to find the nests and look in at the eggs, though we never took any, mind. My father would never allow me to collect them, and he would stop the other boys, too. I think because of that, our Valley was never quiet of birds. There is strange you will never notice birds till they are gone.

We caught two trout that afternoon and I put them in leaves in my cap to carry them on up the mountain. There used to be a scent that the wind pushed in front of it in those days, which must have come from all the wild flowers and the sweet grasses that grew up there then. This scent was strong that afternoon, and my father often stopped to breathe in, for he had told me time and time again that trouble will not stop in a man whose lungs are filled with fresh air. He always said that God sent the water to wash our bodies and air to wash our minds. So you would often see us two stop and breathe in and out, and go on walking up the mountain, perhaps pointing at a small bush we had seen coming up last spring, or looking to see if anybody had been at the primrose bed up by Davies the Woodyard's field.

We had gone a little way when I started to feel cold inside me, for we were walking across the mountain toward the field where I had seen Davy talking to the men. It was a Saturday and the men would be off, so I thought they were bound to be up here.

"Dada," I said, "could we walk into the other valley?"

"No, indeed, my son," my father said, "I am only going to the top. I have got some writing for the Chapel to do. Gracious, what would we do over there?"

"See Ivor and Bron," I said, "it will be a nice surprise, Dada."

"Yes," my father said. "If I find myself over by there this afternoon I will have the surprise indeed. To the top, and then home, us."

I was trying to think of something to keep my father from that field, even to rolling down the mountain. I would have done that, but the hedges would have stopped me.

Sure enough, as we climbed the hedge by Meredith the Shop's field, there we could see the heads of a big crowd of men two fields away higher up. We were getting higher here, and the wind was blowing away from us, so that we could hear nothing of their voices.

My father stopped at once.

"Is this where you came?" he asked me.

"Yes, Dada," I said.

"Oh," he said, looking down at me. "So this is why you wanted to go to the other valley, eh? I will give you credit, my son."

The look-outs must have seen my father because one of them came running over, jumping the hedge as though it was only a foot high.

"Mr. Morgan," he shouted, "Davy wants you to come over if you will be so kind."

"What does Davy want with me?" my father asked back.

"The men are over from all the other valleys," Mog said, walking up, "and a lot of places. There are big things going on, sir."

"Big things, indeed," my father said, "and empty as drums. Not even fit to put a cap on. Where is Davy?"

"Over by there, Mr. Morgan," Mog pointed. "He is going to address the meeting in a minute."

"There is lucky the meeting is," my father said. "Very well, Mog, I will go. Take care of Huw for me, will you?"

I knew it was no good to say anything, so I stood by Mog as my father went through the other gate into the pasture land where the men were crowded.

But when he had gone, I told Mog I wanted to go to the back, so he told me to run over to a pile of stones behind some blackberry bushes, and be sure to come back to him in case my father would have his ears for supper.

Good. So off I went, but as soon as I was behind those blackberries and out of sight, I ran off again through the sheep-gap and into the crowd of men, working my way through carefully up toward the front. As soon as I could see my father through a little space in the men, I stopped where I was.

There was a lot of talking in whispers going on round about me, as though they had all decided on something serious. Up in front, on a sloping slab of rock, Davy, Dai Griffiths, and a lot of men I had never seen before, were all talking to my father. He was listening to them with his hands folded in front and his eyes shut, so I knew they were talking for the wind to make fun with, and it did make me laugh indeed.

One by one they set on him, and one by one they gave up. At last Dai came forward to the edge of the rock and held up his hands.

Everyone became still.

Only the wind moved the ferns above us, saying shish to everything except itself.

"Boys," Dai shouted, "before you make up your minds properly to do what we think is right and best, it is certain you should have a word from Gwilym Morgan. Fair play, now."

The men moved about and a deep murmur started, which became a big cheer as my father stepped out and stood on the edge, looking all round, and down at the village, and up at the sky. I knew he was praying, and the others must have known, for there was a low rustle and then every cap was off, and every head was bent.

"Boys," my father said, "if you were clear in your conscience about what you want to do, you would not be up here out of the way, but down in the village for everybody to be listening. Wait. I am here by some happening which I will call the Will of God. I did not want to come, but now I am here I will give you what has been in my mind these months. You are right in what you want, but you are wrong in your ways of getting it. Force is no good to you until you have tried reason. And reason wants patience. And if patience wants a tight belt, then tight belt it should have. You cannot ask the help of God with hate in your hearts, and without that help you will get nothing. It is no use to say you will all go together in a Union if you have no notion what that Union is to do. Get better wages? You will have better wages or as good as can be got without a Union. The owners are not all savages, but they will not give you whatever you want just because there are a lot of you and you use threats. Reason and civilised dealing are your best weapons. And if your cause is just, and your consciences are clear, God is always with you. And no man will go far without Him."

But the men were becoming restless, and I could hear shouts from all round, though I was so low in the crowd I could hear nothing of the words. I saw my father try to go on, but then a man standing behind me took me by the shoulders and pulled me round.

"You are Huw Morgan," he said, bending down to me, "the youngest of them. Can you hear your old man?"

"My father is not an old man," I said, "and if he heard you, you would have it."

"Oh," said another man, laughing, "the old man is in him for sure. Morgan, him, indeed."

Before I could run, the man who had me had picked me up and was holding me above his head.

"Morgan," he shouted, "here is one who will go without when you tighten your belt. And there are five of mine."

A roar cut my father's voice in half. All round me I could see men shouting before I was put down and forgotten. As quick as I could, I wound in and out of the crowd until I reached the sheep-gap and looked back.

My father was talking to Dai Griffiths up on the rock, and Davy was trying to get the crowd to settle down again. I saw my father shake his head and start to walk down the rock, so I ran back to Mog.

"Deuce," he said, "I did think you had taken lodgings, boy. Here is your father, now."

One look at my father was enough for me, and Mog was going to say something, but he stopped and began whistling under his breath instead.

My father was so white there were blue patches under his eyes, and the whites of his eyes were pink, so that his eyes scalded you to look at them.

And yet he was smiling.

"Come on, my son," he said. "Thank you, Mog."

"You are welcome, sir," said Mog, and pulled off his cap.

Nothing was said until we got to the top of the mountain, though all the way up the men were plain to be heard, and if we had looked back we could have seen them every step of the way. Over hedges and through gates, across fields and pasture, climbing rock outcrop, brushing through gorse and bramble, every second I tried to keep my eyes on my father, watching for some change in him, but even after all that climbing, he had not altered.

He sat up on the rock at the top of the mountain facing into the other valley, and leaned back on his elbow.

"Come and sit over here, my son," he called, for I had gone off a little way to leave him be. "Not afraid of your father, are you?"

"No, Dada," I said, "but I thought you would want to think."

"I have finished thinking, Huw," my father said. "My sort of thinking has no place now. Awful, indeed it is."

We sat in quiet for a time, looking down into the valley. The wind blew up here as though he had wet his lips to bring them smaller to whistle with more pointed music, but his tune was cold, and before long I was shaking. My father stared down at the Valley, but I did not put my eyes on him for long because I was afraid of waking him.

I remember how cold was the green down there, and how like a patchwork counterpane with all the browns of the ploughing and the squares of the curving hedges. The farms were small as white matchboxes and sheep were little kittens. Indeed, if they kept still they would look like little rocks.

Only in our Valley was there a colliery to poke its skinny black fingers out of the bright green. Over in here was all peace and quiet content, and even the wind sounded happier to be working down there, coming up from our Valley with a joyful rush and pouring down here, passing us sharp and bitter cold, eager to lie along the warm fields and tease the manes of the horses browsing in the sun.

"Sad it is, Huw, my son," my father said, after a long while. "Sad, indeed. Here is everything beautiful by here, nothing out of place, all in order. And over with us nothing but ugliness and hate and foolishness."

"How is that, then, Dada?" I asked him.

"Bad thoughts and greediness, Huw," my father said. "Want all, take all, and give nothing. The world was made on a different notion. You will have everything from the ground if you will ask the right way. But you will have nothing if not. Those poor men down there are all after something they will never get. They will never get it because their way of asking is wrong. All things come from God, my son. All things are given by God, and to God you must look for what you will have. God gave us time to get His work done, and patience to support us while it is being done. There is your rod and staff. No matter what others may say to you, my son, look to God in your troubles. And I am afraid what is starting down by there, now this moment, is going to give you plenty of troubles in times to come."

My father spoke with his eyes in the sky, and I was glad he was looking so much better. He had a terrible temper indeed, but none of us ever saw it except me, and that only once and outside the house.

"Let us go home," he said. "Say nothing to Mama unless she asks. She has had enough for one day without more to weigh her down."

Back down the pasture we went, but not toward where the men were still standing. Perhaps it was through looking at the other valley so long that I got such a worrying shock when I looked again at ours.

All along the river, banks were showing scum from the colliery sump, and the buildings, all black and flat, were ugly to make a hurt in your chest. The two lines of cottages creeping up the mountainside like a couple of mournful stone snakes looked as though they might rise up and spit rocks grey as themselves. You would never think that warm fires and good food would come from them, so dead and unhappy they were looking.

Our valley was going black, and the slag heap had grown so much it was half-way along to our house. Young I was and small I was, but young or small I knew it was wrong, and I said so to my father.

"Yes, Huw," he said, and stopped to look. "I told them years ago to start underground, but nobody would listen. Now, there are more important things to think about. That is something that will have to be done when you are grown up. There will be plenty for you to do, indeed."

When we passed through the village nearly all the women were outside waiting to hear what the men were doing up on the mountain. My father took his cap off to wish the time of day down by the Chapel to old Mrs. Rhys the Mill, and he held it in his hand all the way up to the house, because all that way he was wished by everybody.

My mother was sitting alone when we came in, and she seemed to have got over her distress, but the house was quiet, with that sort of stillness that a cat will have when it is waiting to jump with its back in a curl.

My father looked at my mother and said nothing, knowing her, but he made a sign to me to be silent before he went to change his boots. I went to the cupboard to get my slate, and while I was rubbing it clean my father came in.

Then my mother moved, and my father faced her.

"Gwilym," she said, "Angharad has gone."

"Oh," my father said. "Where is she?"

"Down with the Beynons, I think," my mother said.

"Wait you," said my father. "I will have a word with her."

When he had gone, my mother asked me to fill the kettle and give the fire a couple of shovels of coal, and when I had done, she called me.

"Huw," she said, "how are you going to grow up, I wonder?"

"Well," I said, "however it is, I will never leave this house for one, unless you send me from here, Mama."

"I hope that will be the truth, Huw," my mother said, looking right through me. "If any more of my family go from me, I will be sorry I ever had babies."

"Well," I said, "why did you have them, Mama?"

"Gracious goodness me, boy," my mother laughed. "Go from here, now. Why, indeed. To keep my hands in water and my face to the fire, perhaps."

But that question started me asking questions about babies, and nobody seemed to know, and if they did, they kept it to themselves. There is strange that a man will act as though money was being lost to tell the truth in such a matter. But that came after.

You should have seen my mother when my father came back with Angharad. There is pleased she was, and so gentle to put her in the corner chair and take her coat from her. Angharad was quiet and still full of thought, but she was clear in her mind and it was certain she had not been forced to come back. My father went straight out to the back to wash, and came in to shut the door of the next room to do his writing. During that time nothing was said, but I had toasted four rounds of bread which my mother put on the end of the fork as piece after piece was browned.

There is good dripping toast is by the fire in the evening. Good jelly dripping and crusty, home-baked bread, with the mealy savour of ripe wheat roundly in your mouth and under your teeth, roasted sweet and crisp and deep brown, and covered with little pockets where the dripping will hide and melt and shine in the light, deep down inside, ready to run when your teeth bite in. Butter is good, too, mind. But I will have my butter with plain bread and butter, cut in the long slice, and I will say of its kind, there is nothing you will have better, especially if the butter is an hour out of the churn and spread tidy.

"Angharad," my mother said, "what did Dada say?"

"He said he was sorry if he had done anything wrong, Mama," Angharad said, "and to tell him why I wanted to leave him."

"Well?" my mother asked, and very surprised she was.

"I said I wanted to look after the boys because Mrs. Beynon is too fond of her bottle," said Angharad.

"Angharad," my mother said, holding up her hands. "What next then?"

"It is true, Mama," Angharad said, and tears coming to sparkle in the fire-light. "Did you see our Davy with a big hole in his stocking here to-day?"

"Yes, my girl," my mother said, "I did. And Gwilym is bringing them all up here to-night for me to mend."

"I brought them with me," said Angharad, "and I brought a couple of shirts, too. If you will want rags for the boots, Mama, go you and see the sheets on Davy's bed."

My mother was still and so quiet, with her plate on her knee and her eyes big and staring into the fire.

"Oh, God," she said, "I will have my boys from there to-night if I will leave this house myself."

She put her plate down on the fender and got up to go to the door of the next room.

"Give Huw his tea, Angharad," she said, in a high voice. Then she opened the door and went in.

It was quiet in the kitchen, so that we could hear my father talking low to my mother, and her saying back to to him, but the door was so thick we could hear nothing of the words.

"Did you go up the mountain, now just?" Angharad asked me.

"Yes," I said, "and Dada tried to tell the men, but they shouted at him."

"Were the boys up there?" she asked.

"All of them," I said, "but nobody was for Dada."

"Right too," said Angharad.

"Are you against Dada, too?" I asked her.

"Yes, indeed I am," Angharad said, "though not him, but what he is trying to make them do."

"What is that, then?" I asked her.

"Well, if it will have you any wiser," said Angharad, with impatience, "he is trying to make them pray for what they want instead of going together and making the old owners give them it."

"Why is Dada wrong, then?" I asked her, after I had thought about it.

"Be quiet, boy, and eat your toast," Angharad said. "You are making enough noise with your old teeth to have the house down."

"But why is Dada wrong?" I asked her.

"Because you will have nothing through prayer, boy," Angharad said. "I have had nothing yet, and nobody else has, either. Look at Mrs. Mostyn the Grove. Everybody did pray for her and yet she went with her baby as well."

My mother came out just then, and started to pour tea for my father.

"Angharad," she said, and taking the cup in the next room, "go down to Mrs. Beynon's and get the boys' things, will you? Tell her I will pay my owings on Monday morning myself."

"Yes, Mama," said Angharad, and ran out through the back, clapping her hands and singing.

When my mother came out she pointed to the wall bed.

"You will sleep down here in the future, Huw," she said, "and the boys shall have the back room to themselves. You are too small to be up there now they are all men, with them."

And from that day to last night I have never slept anywhere else, except for the time when I lived in Bron's.

When the boys came home that night I was in bed with the curtains drawn, so I could hear all that was said, though I was so sleepy I kept falling off and waking up with a jump.

They all came in together as though they had feared to come in one by one. There is funny it is to lie in the dark listening to people you know, talking and moving, making the little sounds you know, doing the little actions you know, all of it happening in the dark and yet so clear in your mind that you could laugh, and you ask yourself what is the need of people themselves when only their voices and little sounds are enough.

I could hear Davy throwing back his hair before he spoke, because his hair made a soft whish and his chair creaked. Gwilym I knew because his throat made a bumpy sound when he swallowed. Owen always rubbed his forehead and pulled his ear. I suppose there is no sound for that, yet I heard it and knew what he was doing.

But though I knew my father was there, I heard nothing

from him, although I knew his sounds well. Yet I knew he was there, and even though Davy and Owen had made no sounds at all, I would have known they were there. There is a sort of hot stillness which you can feel, and yet it is not hot, nor is it still, but it will have you on edge and make you hot if you think about it. This feeling I always had for my father, and it was in my brothers, too.

This feeling it was that made the wall bed like an oven to me, and started me sweating till the drops were running down my cheeks into my ears.

They had broth for supper, but I suppose I slept through that, though I was sure I could hear all they said in a sort of underneath manner, like the sheets underneath me, that I never felt unless I thought of them.

My father it was who woke me up properly, even though he spoke very quietly, as though Mama had made a sign to the bed that I was in there and sleeping. Several ways he had of clearing his throat, and well I knew them. He had one way for singing, one way for speaking in Chapel, one way for reading the Bible, and another for reading anything else, except a story book, and that was different again. But he had a special way of doing it when he had something to say that was serious.

That was how he woke me up.

"Davy," he said, "you are the eldest here, and to you I will talk."

"Yes, Dada," said Davy, and I knew his eyes would be watching my father in the shadow of his hair.

"I asked you to leave this house," my father said, "because I thought I was doing the best. I thought you were a bad influence on the other boys. But I found that the others were as bad as you, and even a baby like Huw was going out of the house at night. That is not the way a house should live, and I said so. I have that authority because I am your father."

"I will never question that, Dada," said Davy.

"Good," said my father. "It was hurting me to have to do it. I am proud of my family, and I am proud to think that you are prepared to make sacrifice for what you think is right. It is good to suffer in order that men should be better off, but take care that what you are doing is right and not half-right. My sense is against what you are doing. If you were right, you would not have had such a disgraceful meeting up there to-day. There would have been a different spirit. But that is not what I want to say. I would not have asked you in the house again if your mother had not begged me, and I only said I would because she told me you were living with pigs. I will have you make a sacrifice and I will have you suffer. It will do you good. But no man ever made himself more useful to himself or his fellow men by living in filth and dirt, and I am surprised that a son of mine would allow it."

"They were lodgings, Dada," said Davy, moving in his chair, "and we could get nowhere else. By the time we had finished work and collected the men, there was little time."

"Where there is little time," my father said, "there is little use. Leave it, now. I will have Mrs. Beynon spoken to. As for you, as I said, your mother told me about it, and I said I would have you back. But only on one condition."

There was quietness for a time.

That hot, still feeling grew and grew till I thought I would burst.

"What is that, Dada?" asked Davy.

"We are all to be lodgers here," said my father.

I could hear from the sounds that my brothers were all sitting up and staring at my father, and I could feel the pale straining.

"But, Dada," said Davy, "how are you a lodger?"

"Because I am staying here," said my father. "But I am not a father because I have no authority. No man shall say he is father of a house unless his word is to be obeyed. Mine is not, so I am not a father, but somebody paying for his keep. I am a lodger, and so are you and the boys, and your mother will look after you and me. That is all."

"Dada," Davy said, "I am sorry for this. I wish I could make you think as I do, only to understand."

"It is too late to-night even to wish, Davy," said my father. "Tomorrow is Sunday and early Chapel. Good night all."

"Good night, Dada," said Davy, and the other boys said with him, but quiet, as though they were so surprised they had lost their tongues.

"So now then, Davy," said my mother, after my father had gone up.

"Yes, Mama," said Davy, "I know."

"Good," said my mother, "and when you go up, throw that old shirt down. You, Owen and Gwilym, too."

"Yes, Mama," said the boys.

"And no words round the table," said my mother. "If I am the boarding-house keeper I will have things my way."

"O, Mama," Davy said, and I am sure he kissed her. "I am for early Chapel, too. Good night, Mama."

"Good night, Mama," said the boys.

"Good night," said my mother. "One more day in that sock, Davy, and you would be showing your legs. There is disgrace."

"You should see Owen's, Mama," said Gwilym. "One more step and you would see the back of his neck, indeed."

"Shut up, man," said Owen.

I am glad my mother was so happy going up to bed.

Chapter Six

AFTER THAT there was peace in the house for a time, though I was too small to have the whole picture. I only know what I saw and heard, and I have often wished I had seen and heard more than I did. But there is nothing worse than a small boy with a sharp nose and a loose tongue, and thank goodness I was never that.

The family sat down to meals just the same, but there was a different feeling in the room always. Even when Bronwen came in it was not quite what it had been. We all seemed afraid to say what was in our minds, I suppose for fear it might start trouble. So instead of the laughing and joking there had been, you would have thought there was a preacher at the table with us.

Davy was still going up on the mountain and the boys were going with him, and coming back with him, openly now, not through the window but in and out of the front door. At that time Davy was meeting men of other valleys and coming to an agreement about forming a union of them all, so that if one lot came out on a complaint, they would all come out and put the coalfield at a standstill.

Just as it happens now, so they were planning then. And after weeks of work, Davy got what he wanted. After that it spread like fire over all the valleys. All the younger men were in, but the older men like my father would have nothing to do with it.

. . . .

Davy argued with my father for hours, but he had to give up in the end. He knew he would have won most of the older men if my father had given way, and that is why he tried so hard.

"No, Davy," my father said one night. "Never will I put pen to it. I am a man and I will deal with my own problems my way. I want no help from anybody."

"But, Dada," Davy said, "you were spokesman at the last strike. What is the difference?"

"A great deal, Davy," said my father. "We knew what we all wanted and we were able to point to it. It affected all of us, and I happened to be chosen to speak."

"But that is all we want to do," said Davy. "We put our demands and back them up with unanimous support."

"That is the trouble," said my father. "You are a crowd of bits of boys all in the thing for what you will get. Demands, you call them. Well, I am against demands of any kind. You cannot reason with demand, and where there is no reason, there is no sense. As for your support, whatever you call it, some long word, what is the use of it?"

"Unanimous, Dada," said Davy. "It means altogether. And the use is to make the owners give us fair terms."

"Unanimous," said my father, saying it carefully. "Yes. It do sound what it is. A collection of dull monkeys who cannot think for themselves. And the people who speak for them will have tongues a yard long and nothing else inside their heads. All the space will be taken to coil up their tongues. I have met them."

"I shall be one of them, Dada," said Davy.

"I wonder," said my father. "At all events, I shall not. That is final."

"There will come a day, Dada," said Davy, "when you will have to."

"When that day comes, Davy," said my father, "I will think about it again."

. . . .

Ivor was with my father from the start. Nothing Davy would say could move him, and that caused trouble between them. Davy even stopped speaking to Bronwen because of it.

So indeed for a time we were a happy lot there, with my father acting like a lodger, and my brothers doing everything they could to make him be a father, and my mother trying all ways to keep them together.

The owners must have found out that my father was against the union idea, because as soon as old Mr. Rhys the Superintendent died, my father was offered his job, and, of course, he took it. Being superintendent made my father next to the manager, and put up his pay, and made him one of the most important men in the village.

But at the same time the men began to think he had gone in with the owners, and that talk hurt him more than his trouble with Davy. He hated to think that anybody would suspect him of being disloyal, especially to the men, but there was no way he could fight the talk because it was never said in the open.

He often spoke to my mother at night and I heard every word. My mother was always ready to try to make him happy again, but it was not from her that he wanted it. It was from the men, and there was no way of reaching them, because they never came to him now as they used to. He noticed the change from the moment his name was put on the board.

For the first few days the men passed him without greeting, except to touch their caps civil. But when it passed into two days and more and then a week, and still the men were not speaking to him except about matters of work, he began to know that he was distrusted. As though he was to blame for being made Superintendent.

Mama spoke to Davy about it, when she found that nobody would listen to Ivor.

"Davy," she said, "what is this about your father?"

"Well, Mama," said Davy, and he knew, of course, what my mother meant. "It is this. It is very strange Dada was chosen for Super when everybody knows he is my father."

"Why is it strange, boy?" my mother asked, with the knife half in and out of the pie.

"Because I am his son," said Davy, "and living in the same house. I am the union rebel to the owners, and Dada is known to be against me. Why did they choose him instead of Tom Davies or Rhys Howells? They are both senior, though they cannot do the job better, it is true. Dada was picked to slap my face and the boys who are with me."

"There is nonsense, boy," my mother said, and putting

the plates down with a noise. "You are like a lot of children with you. Dada has always done what was good and for the best. There is no better man in all the valleys. If you do grow up to be one like him, God will smile indeed. You tell those fools of men that your father is as much for them as he ever was. Wait you till he do have a chance."

"The men will wait till then, Mama, I am afraid," said Davy. "It is useless to talk to them now. And you had better warn Ivor that his life will be in danger if he do go about talking so silly as he have. He had better keep his mouth shut or he will have it closed for him."

"David Morgan," my mother said, "you can talk of your good brother in such a way? Indeed, I never thought to hear it. If anything do happen to Ivor while he is doing his duty by his father, I will curse you with my last breath."

"Mama, Mama," said Davy, and he got up to put his arms round my mother, but she wanted to push him away. "Saying nothing against Ivor I was, only warning. The men are ugly and they are in a mood to be dangerous."

"If Davy had not been strict with them," said Owen, "they would both have been put over the bridge days ago."

My mother was standing as though in sleep, and new lines coming into her face, and her eyes going wide with a feeling worse than worry.

"Is it like that with them?" she was whispering. "Oh, Davy, my little one, I thought it was only talk."

"No, Mama," said Davy, kissing her. "It is serious. The men will have what they are after this time, and if they thought anybody would stop them, they would have them, my father or not. There is a move to strike for a new Super to take Dada's place."

"Will you allow it?" my mother asked.

"Who am I against twenty thousand and over?" asked Davy.

"Twenty thousand?" my mother asked, and her eyes were lighting and shading while she tried to think how many it was.

"Twenty thousand, Mama," Davy said, and very sad he was, "and likely to be a hundred thousand before the month is out."

"Oh, Davy, my little one," my mother said, and she sat

down in the old chair by the fire. "Where will you end? What trouble will you cause?"

"There is no end, Mama," Davy said, staring down at her. "Only a beginning."

"In the beginning was the Word," said Owen, and deep was his voice to shake, "and the Word was with God, and the Word was God."

"We shall be late," said Davy, and looking at the clock. "Mama, nothing will happen to Dada or Ivor if I will have anything to do with it. That is all I can say."

He kissed her on the forehead and signed to the boys to be moving. When they had gone, my mother looked over at me.

"Huw," she said, "say nothing to Dada about this."

"No, Mama," I said.

"Come here," my mother said, and I went to her. "Do you know where the men are meeting at night?"

"Yes, Mama," I said. "Up by Jones the Chapel's field."

"Oh," she said. "Up by there, is it? Now look you, Huw. Your father is late shift to-night. You shall take me up there. And you will say nothing, do you hear?"

"Yes, Mama," I said, and my stomach was turning to see the look in her face.

"Good," she said. "Angharad and Ceridwen will be here in a moment. Not a single word, my boy."

. . . .

I had been in bed about three-quarters of an hour with the curtains drawn when my sisters went to bed. As soon as they had gone, I heard my mother opening the cupboard to bring out her cloak and bonnet, and the rustle as she brought them from the paper.

Then she pulled the curtains aside and looked down on me, hiding the light.

"Huw," she whispered, "are you sleeping?"

"No, Mama," I said.

"There is pity to bring you from the warm," my mother said, with tears. "Sleep you, my little one. I will find it by myself."

"No, indeed, Mama," I said. "You will be bound to fall in the river."

"Yes," she said, "I was thinking of that. I have been inside the house so long, indeed, I would lose my way from here to the Chapel."

"Let me dress, Mama," I said. "And I will have you there in a minute."

"Come you, then," she said, and holding up my trews. "There is your father in you, indeed."

"Good," I said, and Mama sat down to laugh.

When I had dressed we went through the back door and down the back alley behind Dai Ellis the Stable, and crossed the river by the little wooden bridge that was higher up than the stones.

The river was almost frozen and full right up to the top of the banks. We had nearly come through winter, but cold was still with us and snow was bound to come, and indeed that night I could smell it like rain only colder, and with a sour flavour that seemed to burn my nose right up between my eyes.

"Careful, now, Huw," my mother said, as we crossed the logs. "You are so small you could slip through. Give me your hand."

I put my hand in my mother's muff and up we went, with me under my mother's cloak and just my face showing to see the way.

There was no question in my mind why my mother was going. I cannot remember thinking about it. But I could feel her warmth all round me, and I could hear her speaking under her breath when the way was not too hard.

It was darker up this way because there were more trees, but the sky was so black there was no chance to see the tops, and we could see the path only because it was blacker than the grass at the sides. My boots struck the hardness like a hammer and often gave up little sparks, and I tried to make more till my mother gave me a pull.

"Boots cost," my mother said, with her breath like a veil about her face. "Lift your heels, boy. You are like a tinder, with you."

Higher up the mountain we had to stop many times while my mother took her breath, but always she went on. There was no hope to turn back once my mother had started. Even when the snow was dropping wet when we came out of the trees into the pasture she said nothing, though she held me tighter. We had not gone far when it was snowing so thick it was like trying to go through a rain of bits of paper, but I was sure of the way and I never stopped once.

"Are you sure, Huw?" my mother asked me, and let snow fall on me from her bonnet as she bent. "Is this where it is?"

"Yes, Mama," I said, and surprised to be questioned. "I would tell you if not."

"Oh, Gwilym," my mother said. "Go you, then, Huw."

Up and on we went, but my mother was tired and leaning on me, and I felt proud to be leading her and helping her like this. So you will know how I felt when we saw the fires the men had made only a little way above us, looking like big red blooms through hosts of blown, streaming, snow shadows that whispered as they fell and squeaked beneath our feet.

"There you are, Mama," I said, "there they are, look."

"Right you are," she said. "Go quietly, now."

We went round to the side of the two biggest fires and when we got nearer I saw that they were built on the rock, and more fires were burning in the field, and the men were standing round them.

Somebody was speaking, not Davy, from the front of the rock, but just as we got to the foot, he finished and went back.

"Quick," my mother said, "help me up here, now."

Indeed I have never been more surprised to this day. My mother was scrambling up the rock, with her cloak dragging in the snow. Up and up she went, and turned when she reached the top to look down at me.

I could hardly hear what she was saying because the men were still cheering the last speaker.

"Huw," she shouted, through her hands, "wait you by there."

"Right you, Mama," I shouted back, and I watched her going carefully across the front of the rock to where the last man had stood to speak.

The cheering fell when the men saw her standing there, but nobody could see properly who it was because of the snow and being blinded by the light and smoke of the fires. Some men down in the front saw it was a woman and started to shout to others, but they could see only the shape of her cloak. Her face was hidden in her muff to keep the snow from hurting.

I had run round the front of the rock to see what my

mother was going to do, when she took the muff away and started to speak. Some men had come from one of the fires on the rock to see who it was, but when she started to speak, they stopped where they were.

"I am Beth Morgan," my mother said, and her voice was as deep and strong as any man. "I have come up here to tell you what I do think of you all, because I have heard you are talking against my husband. Two things in this world I do hate. One is talking behind the back, and the other is lice. So you should know what I do think of you."

The only sounds when my mother stopped were the crackling of wood and the hushing of snow.

"You are a lot of cowards to talk against my husband," my mother said with a full voice. "He has done nothing against you and he never would and you know it well. He is Superintendent of the colliery now because every man will have his reward for working, and that is his. And for you to think he is with the owners because he has had his reward is not only nonsense but downright wickedness. How some of you can sit in the same Chapel with him I cannot tell. I would look for a flame of fire upon me, indeed. But there is one thing more I will say and that is this. If harm do come to my Gwilym, I will find out the men and I will kill them with my hands. And that I will swear by God Almighty. And there will be no Hell for me. Nobody will go to Hell for killing lice."

"Mama," Davy called from the back of the rock.

My mother turned round to look for Davy, but she could not see him at first.

"I am not your mother," she said, "when you are with these. You are lice with them. And if your father comes to harm, you shall be the first to go."

Davy came out of the darkness to go to my mother but she turned away and started to stumble down the rock. I ran round to help her find her footway, and Davy stood at the top watching in quiet. There was low talking from the men and not a sound else, and indeed if ever I heard the voice of shame, then it was, while my mother was crying as she felt her way down.

I only knew she was crying when we had gone a little way down and she took my hand from her muff to blow her nose.

"Mama," I said, "would you kill men?"

"Yes, Huw," she said, "I would."

"But Dada said the Bible says you shall not kill," I said.

"What is in the Bible and what is outside is different," my mother said. "But if they do touch your Dada I will keep my word. Be quiet now, and find the way down. Are you cold?"

"No, Mama," I said. "Except my feet, and they are like stones with me."

"Huw, my little one," my mother said, and stopped, "come here and I will carry you."

"No, Mama," I said, and I could have shouted. "You shall not. I can walk with the next. Come you, and I will show you."

"There is like an old mule you are, boy," my mother said. "Go you, then. And be careful. I can see nothing, indeed."

The snow was falling faster now, and we were still out in the pasture, so the wind and snow were both busy about us, and the darkness was thick. I knew my way only because of the slope of the ground, and the sound of the earth under my feet, hard in some places and soft in others, but I knew where it should end being hard and where it should start to be soft.

Down we went, with my mother leaning heavily upon my shoulder, and stopping often to have breath, and the wind beginning now to have the voice of a woman in grief. It was better, and we went faster when we came to the trees, but snow was piling as we reached the river level, blown down from the branches, so we had to pick up our feet and feel them sink again and not know if we were in deep till we touched ground.

Just before we got to the bridge, I fell in a mound right up to my shoulders and my mother fell in on top of me when she came to pull me out. I was lying face down, and I could feel her trying to get up, but the more she tried the farther I went down, face first, and I fought to have my breath. I must have lost my sense then, because when I woke up, I was on my mother's lap and she was sitting in the drift with her bonnet off and her hair all covered with snow, and looking down at me.

"Huw," she said.

"Yes, Mama," I said, and I wanted to cry but I stopped.

"Are you hurting?" she asked, in the same voice, as though she was sore in the throat.

"No, Mama," I said. "But there is cold."

"Come then," she said, and she tried to lift me, but she fell back.

I was able to stand up but I felt as I had when I won the race, all giddy and willing to fall over. But I was sure to stand up straight because my mother was wanting help, so I went to her and caught her hand.

"Come you, Mama," I said. "Up a dando."

"Up a dando?" my mother said. "Yes, indeed, and who was up a dando just now and frightening his Mama sick?"

"Not my fault it was, Mama," I said. "It was the old snow."

My mother took me to her and squashed me so tight I was nearly giddy again.

"Huw, my little one," she said. "Your mama thought the old snow was going to keep you, too. And it will be having us both if we will not go from here. Up a dando, now."

I found her bonnet while she was tying her cloak, and went on in front, but carefully this time until we reached the bridge.

But by the bridge we met the full wind and it carried snow with it so thick that nothing could be seen through it. I felt my way across the logs by holding on to the plank rail, and my mother holding me by the hand. Careful and slow we had to go, and all the time the wind was alive to push us in the ice.

But we found the other side and then we were lost, except to guess.

From where we were was not far to our house but we could see nothing except the blackness knitted with snow. From the bridge I was sure I knew which way to go but after we had been walking a few minutes my boots touched stones and I knew that one more step and we would be in the river.

"I am sorry, Mama," I said. "I am wrong here."

"Very well, my little one," my mother said, "you had a good try, indeed. Shall we turn round, now?"

"These stones are down nearly by the Chapel, Mama," I said, "so if we go across from by here, we will go straight in Morris the Butcher's."

"Go you, then, Huw," my mother said, "you are the man, here."

So hot I went when my mother said that, I was fit to shine in the sun. It gave me a new spirit indeed, and I struck out to where I thought Morris the Butcher's lay as though it was three o'clock on a spring afternoon.

But if I was strong and sure, my mother was not.

We had got about half-way across the rocks and gravel, and she was heavy on my shoulder and having her breath in pain with her, when she put her hands to her chest and fell down on her face flat, soundless, not moving.

Fright took me.

I looked at her, black in the snow, and snow going white upon her, and I was afraid. But I remembered she had called me a man, and I made tight my fists. What to do, I was asking myself. If I ran for my father, perhaps I would not find my mother again. If I stayed here with her, perhaps we would both not be found and then she would die of cold. Perhaps if I went, leaving her here, I would not reach my father.

And all the time I was thinking what to do, I was kneeling beside her, brushing and scraping the snow from her, hating each piece and handful as though it were living and able to understand, the white, quiet, cold, cruel snow.

Then I thought of the boys. They would all be coming down soon, and some would be coming over the bridge. If I could have my mother down by there I would be bound to meet somebody. As soon as I thought, I started.

But there is heavy my mother seemed to me. I tried and tried but her arms were loose and slipped through when I tried to lift her by the shoulders. And it seemed too rude to take hold of her by the leg as I would have done with a boy. So I tried and tried, and I cried in rage to be so weak and I wished the snow had been harder and with shape to throw myself upon it with my teeth.

At last I got my arms about my mother's waist and, kneeling in the snow, clasping her like that, I crawled backwards toward the bridge, pulling and dragging her as I went.

Hours it did seem, and no feeling or sense was in me, but I was crying to God to help me to save my mother, and I was helped for sure, or I cannot tell where I found the strength.

*   *   *   *   *   *   *   *   *   *   *   *   *

I knew I had reached the bridge when my shoulders came against the rail. I pulled my mother into the shelter of the post and tried to sit her against it but she was far off and her mouth was open and I had to keep closing it. Then I found I could not stand up. Strength had gone from my legs. So I had to crawl to find the middle of the bridge and scratch away the snow to feel the logs to be sure that I would be near when the boys crossed over, and then crawl back to my mother. She had slipped sideways and almost she was falling in the river. I pulled and pulled to have her back, but she was too heavy, and my arms were weak and there was nothing to be done with my fingers, they were so frozen.

And when I knew I would lose her in the river, I knew there was only one thing to be done.

I held her flat by lying on her and pressing her, while I rolled over her into the river. I knew it was not deep by there, only about up to my waist because that is where I had learnt to swim.

But now it was up to my chest and when I went in, so cold it was, it seemed to open its hands and grip, and so strong that I was without a good breath for minutes. I had my mother with my head in her middle, and my hands holding her chin and leg, so she could not slip, but I was afraid my legs would go from under me, for I was not standing but kneeling against the rocks, and the ice was cutting my chin.

My mother made no sound nor did she move, but I was too senseless to be afraid.

How long it was I cannot tell, but there was a weariness of time before I saw a light, a yellow lantern light swinging near me in the paining dark. I tried to shout but my voice was gone from my throat. Madness was in me to shout, to have that light nearer, to have my mother taken back to the house.

So my voice came, but the voice was not mine, for there is no voice that will make the sound I made. All the fury of living kind, fighting against useless pain, was in the cry that brought the lantern to us.

It was Davy, but I had only enough in my eyes to see his cold, blue face, lit with yellow light, and his eyes glistening big and staring, and his hand about the lantern to shield it. I remember falling among the ice when I felt him take my mother from me.

"Huw, Huw," I heard him crying. "O, Huw."

Chapter Seven

I WOKE UP in the bed downstairs in the kitchen, and saw the lamplight shining red on the wooden panels. There is funny to wake up and not know yourself to be You.

Although you are like yourself as you are ordinarily, still there is somehting missing, and you ask yourself where you are, and who you are, and why. There is a lot missing in your life when you have no notion who you are. You have only a picture in front of your eyes and nothing but emptiness behind them, not even the comfort of knowing your name. Indeed, it is that which makes you so afraid and you will start to shout to keep yourself company. Man is a coward in space, for he is by himself, and if you feel you are alone, with not even yourself, that is fright for you. I wonder where the real You goes to when you are strange like that.

I started to shout.

But I had nothing to shout with, and that made it worse. Try as I would, nothing would come.

You have never been frightened if you have never lost yourself and your voice.

That is real fright, and awful, too.

For there are in pure space, hearing, thinking, and seeing, but speechless and without knowledge, and you begin to cry and tears blind you, and you are frantic to wipe them away to be able to see, but still they come and you are lost in a fog of shining wet.

Then I heard Bronwen singing, quietly, just near to me.

Lightning quick I found myself, and blood rushed warm all over me and brought on such pain that I tried to twist. I was held tight in bandage. My face, arms, all my body and legs, all of me was a sausage of soft slippery bandage.

The smell of goose grease was sweet and fat about me, and I knew then why the bandage was slippery. I was bound up in goose grease to cure cold.

The memory of holding my mother came back to me, and now I found time to be afraid. I tried to look at Bronwen, but I could not move my head, and it was hurting all over. But Bronwen must have seen me strain to move and speak, for she left her chair quickly as though she had jumped.

She did smell always of thyme and lavender because she made little bags of it for the sheets, and I suppose she put a couple in with her own wash. So that smell was always with her, and lovelier than that you will never have.

She knelt by me, whispering, but I could not hear for the bandage. She wiped my eyes for me, and rose up to look down at me.

Beautiful, beautiful, was Bronwen, indeed.

"Huw," she said, as though she ought not to be speaking, "are you hurting with you?"

I made to nod, and her teeth went fast in her lip.

"O, Huw," she said, smiling so kind and crying soft, "little Huw, there is proud I am to have your name. Proud, indeed."

She bent to kiss me, quickly and so lightly, it was the touch of a warm moth, and ran then to call my father, who was upstairs here, sitting with my mother.

Dr. Richards came in first to make a fuss over me and feel my pulse and look at his watch with his eyebrows up, and then my father came to stand by his shoulder and look down at me, with his hands in his jacket pockets.

"He will do," Dr. Richards said. "But it is beyond me to say why, indeed. You are breeding horses in this family, Mr. Morgan. This boy should be in his coffin, for my part."

"Thank God he is not," my father said to him. He looked again at me and smiled. "Your mother is doing very well, my son, and so is your new sister. Thanks to you, of course. Your old father is very proud of you, Huw."

He bent down to kiss me and left the smell of him near me, of his pipe and himself. My silence seemed to make him afraid for me, but Dr. Richards pushed him out of the room and told him I was sleepy.

"Mrs. Ivor," Dr. Richards said to Bronwen when my father had gone, "let us undo the bandage now and see what has gone with him. I am afraid of a fracture."

Well, that is the last I remember, for as soon as Dr. Richards pulled back the clothes and put his hand on my leg, I had such a flash of hurt that I suppose I dropped off.

. . . .

Strange it is to think back like this and be a small boy again, and talk to people who have been gone these years.

I had fever in the bones of my legs for nearly five years after that. Five years of lying in the wall bed, and not able to get up, or go out, or move at all.

I have had plenty of time to think.

For months, at first, I was not quite balanced because of pain. Then it got better, and at last I was having no pain at all. But still I was not allowed to get up because of the fracture, which kept on having to be broken and set.

While I was only just living I took no notice of what went on, and indeed I remembered nothing very much about it.

I only know that it was Bronwen who nursed me night and day, until she had her baby, a little boy.

They called him Gareth.

The boys were often in to see me. They all had their meals in the parlour during the time I was bad, and sometimes in the evening they were allowed in for a minute, though I still could not speak to them because of a broken jaw.

But they were very kind to me, later on, and Davy and Owen took turns to read books, but they had to stop reading Mr. Boswell's *Life of Johnson* because it made me laugh, and laughing hurt too much.

There is a man was Dr. Johnson. Indeed I do wish we had a few of his kind living to-day. Mind, I have heard him called an old busybody and other things, too. But I have always noticed that those who said such things were the very ones whom Dr. Johnson would have had under the table with a look, never mind a word. I owe a big debt to Mr. Boswell, indeed. How happy he must have been to write about so great a man.

It was during that time that I found out about books. We had not many in the house, but what there were, were good, although a bit solid for me, mind. But my father, and Davy, and Ivor when he had time, were all at pains to explain when hard words came up, and so by easy stages I grew with them.

But we were in agonies there with Mr. Stuart Mill's *System of Logic*. It was so hard that we laughed no end at ourselves. But we got through to the end and all the better for it. There is another man with a head.

The Bible, of course, my father and Owen read before going to bed, and I knew it in the end as well as Owen.

It was then that I had thoughts about Christ, and I have never changed my mind. He did appear to me then as a

man, and as a man I still think of him. In that way, I have
had comfort. If he had been a God, or any more a son of
God than any of us, then it is unfair to ask us to do what
he did. But if he was a man who found out for himself
what there is that is hidden in life, then we all have a chance
to do the same. And with the help of God, we shall.

Indeed, I am going from this house to-night to try and
find out what is the matter with me and the people I know,
because there is something radically wrong with us all, to
be sure.

Davy used to say the same thing, and if ever a man had
cause to question his fellows, that man was Davy. I used
to write his letters for him when I got better, not that he
was unable to write his own, but because I had all day to
write in. So I got to know all about matters concerning
the Union and from the first I knew that things were wrong.

Mrs. Tom Jenkins used to come up after school with her
little girl, and give me the lessons for the day to follow,
and take away the work I had done during the day. There
is kind of her to come up all that way day after day, just
to earn fourpence a week and do her best for a sick boy.
And make no mistake, best it was. She got handwriting
primers for me, that my father paid for, so that I would
have a good hand when I was ready to leave my bed. And
I could write beautiful, too. I have never said so, but I
cannot put in words what came in me when I won a handwriting competition set by a paper in Town.

And you should have seen the look in my father's eyes
when he brought in the paper. They were all in the kitchen,
for it was reading time, and we were waiting for my father
because he was late, and a strange event with him.

But when he came in, breathing a little extra from the
Hill, he had the paper under his arm as he carried his
Bible, and we knew from the way he came in and sat down
in his chair that there was something serious to be said.
So we all sat quiet. We could hear my mother singing to
my new sister upstairs.

My father put on his glasses, and picked up the paper,
and looked all round at the boys, but he gave no look to me
at all. I thought I had done something wrong, and I was
bruising my brains trying to think what, when my father
cleared his throat, and then I knew it was nothing bad, but
good.

"Handwriting Competition," he read, and my heart

bumped almost to the roof of my mouth. "Boys under twelve years of age. First prize of Two Guineas is awarded to Master Huw Morgan, son of Mr. Gwilym Morgan, for an entry of great merit."

Well, everybody was dumb with it.

My father put the paper down and took off his glasses and started to tap them on the chair.

"And that boy," he said, "have been lying there for going on three years and no sound from him but laughing and no words but cheerful. I am afraid," he said, looking over at me, "I will have to stop by here to tell you what a good son you are, Huw, my little one, because if I went to you now, I would be acting very silly, I am afraid. Bless you, my son. You are a comfort, indeed."

Well, then, they all started. They read the few words in the paper over and over, as though to get more from it each time, or to see if anything was hidden that had been missed. Gwilym ran down to fetch Ivor and Bronwen, and of course that was the cap for the evening.

"There is clever you are, boy," Bronwen said, pretending to be fainting and smiling in her own way. "You are making me feel like Red Riding Hood in front of the old wolf. Have you got big, strong teeth with you?"

She put her finger-tip in my mouth. My jaw was better now, though a little weak, but I gave her finger a good nip and held on and she screamed.

"O, dammo," she said, "jaws he has got like an old mule, here. Right, you. I will have you for that. You shall eat your dinner tomorrow by yourself."

Davy came and sat down by me when Bronwen went to get supper ready with the girls, and he looked at me for a moment, saying nothing.

"You are a clever boy, Huw," he said, "and the first in the family to have your name in the paper. Good. Now then, let us turn this to good account. You shall have two-pence every time you write a letter for me. How does that suit you?"

"I would rather write for nothing for you, Davy," I said.

"No, no," he said. "You shall write for the Union. And the twopences shall pay for your school and for a holiday when you are better. Is it?"

"Yes," I said, for to be able to pay for myself was a good thought to me.

Bronwen gave me my supper that night as usual, but a

piece of pie instead of bread and milk. There is good it did taste, too.

"If you have trouble with the meat," she said, "tell me, and I will put the old man back on his old baby's food."

She knew I would chew all the more for that, and chew I did, resting back in the crook of her arm, with the smell of lavender and thyme about me, and her warmth near me, and her face made gold in the lamplight and laugh in her eyes. Perhaps it was wrong for a boy to feel in love with a woman ten years older than himself, but nobody ever knew, even Bronwen down to this day. So no harm was done, though she has been a sanctuary to me all through my life. And she would have been seventy-two next month.

So the years do go.

But I never knew I was in love, of course, until much later. There is a lot of nonsense talked about love, and most of all by people who have never known it, who have no spirit within them to inspire it in others. Talk of love in such mouths is a grossness, indeed.

I had my first taste of it when Owen met Marged Evans. Marged was daughter of one of my father's oldest friends, and she came to us because her mother thought she should learn how to run a house for a family. My mother was still too weak to do a day's work properly, so she stayed on in bed. My father's orders, and sensible, too.

Marged had quiet prettiness with dark blue eyes that would change colour when she laughed, and make you feel so pleased you would want to laugh more than you knew you should. For the first week she was so shy no one would have more than four words from her, and they were yes, please, and thank you. Bronwen tried all ways to have her talking, I tried, and so did my father. But no use. Marged would hold her head down, and if you tried to make fun, you would see tears and then you would be sorry. How is it that people who have shy strangers to stay never think that home sickness and many strange faces, habits, and voices, may put aches in the heart. You are so used to the house and people yourself, you never come to think that what is ordinary to you may be a desert of woeful newness to another.

She had been with us for four or five days, and she had just got to the stage where she could smile at you quickly and look away in case you spoke, when Owen became her champion.

Of course, lying there as I had been, I could have told anybody that Owen was in love with her, because I remembered how Ivor had been with Bronwen. And the signs are all the same with the same family.

My father was carving the chicken and he asked Marged what she would have, leg or wing?

"Anything, Mr. Morgan, please," said Marged, still shy, and with eight pairs of eyes upon her, and going red under them.

"A nice wing," said Bronwen.

"How about the parson's nose, then?" asked Davy.

"Marged is our guest," Owen said, and black thunder he was looking at Davy. "If there is any joking, perhaps you will have it out on me."

"What is the matter with John Willie, now?" asked Davy, knowing well. "There is a scowl, man. Take it off, quick. You will have a hole in the table-cloth."

"Never mind about the table-cloth," Owen said. "You leave Marged alone."

"Owen," said my father, "if there is any rebuking in this family, I will be the one to do it. Davy may have been forward in his remarks, and he knows that the part he spoke about is never left on a chicken in this house. But there was no wrong in it, and Marged was not offended. Were you, my girl?"

"No, Mr. Morgan," Marged said.

But only I saw the look she gave Owen, except Owen, of course.

And you should have seen it. I cannot blame poor Owen for falling in love. There was flame in that look, that made you feel as though you had put your eyes too near the fire.

It was a couple of days after that, at night, when I had proof I was right. My father and the boys and Bronwen had gone down to choir practice, leaving Marged in the house in case my mother called, and Owen was out in the back doing his inventions.

He was sure he would make a machine to cut coal so that colliers could have an easier time of it, and work less hours, with more pay because the machine would cut more coal to be sold. Every night he was hard at work in the back, hammering and filing, and running down to Howell the Blacksmith to melt and fashion pieces of iron for him, and calling to someone in the house to come and hold something while he hit it, and making a nuisance.

Well, to-night, Marged was doing her tapestry by the fire and I was in the wall bed as usual, with the curtains drawn in case I would sleep. I could see her well, and I was having games to count how many stitches with one colour, how many with another. But so fast she used the needle, my eyes got tired and I was just going to sleep when the door opened quietly and Owen came in, black and with a handful of iron.

"Oh," he said, and stood.

Marged smiled at her work and said nothing, but kept her back to him and made plain her face.

"I had no notion you would be here," said Owen. There is a liar he was.

No answer from Marged, but plenty of good stitching, indeed.

"Have you got any hot water, with you?" asked Owen, nailed to the floor. Nobody knew better than he that the cauldron was brimming with boiling water, as it always was. You could hear it.

Marged said nothing for a moment, then she put her needle in a part she was coming to, and looked up, though not at Owen.

"How much do you want?" she asked him.

"O," said Owen, as though he thought it was a miracle she could speak. "I would like a wash."

"I will fill a bucket," said Marged, and got up.

"No, no," said Owen, as though it was shocking to think she could touch a bucket.

"How will you have a wash, then?" asked Marged, still with her back to him. "In a cup?"

I had to stuff a corner of the blanket in my mouth to have quiet from myself.

"No, no," said Owen, and very serious. "I will get the bucket myself. There is no need for you to do things like that for me."

"Where is the bucket with you?" asked Marged, still not looking.

"Out by here in the wash-house," said Owen.

"Good," said Marged, and she sat down to stitch again.

But Owen made no move to the wash-house. He was watching Marged.

There is a look in his eyes of a man in love that will have you in fits unless you are in love yourself. If you are, you will feel something move inside you to be of help to him, to try and have him happy even if there is no chance for you.

This look was in the eyes of Owen. You will see a part of it in the eyes of sheep fastened to the board and waiting for the knife. The other part you will see only in the eyes of a good man who has put his heart into the hands of a girl. It is a light that is rarely of the earth, a radiance that is holy, a warming, happy agony that do shine from inside and turn what it touches to something of paradise.

Marged felt that look, because she straightened her shoulders and made to shiver.

"Are you going for the bucket," she asked him, and making a big swallow.

"O," said Owen, as though he had smashed a window. "Yes, indeed. Now, just."

He had no notion where to put his iron, so he put it outside the door while he went for the bucket. Of course, if one of us had only touched his iron, never mind leaving it outside, blood would have run in the gutters. That is love for you.

Back he came, then, and went forward step by step till he was at the side of her, but still she was stitching.

"Ermhh, mhh, mhh," said Owen, scraping like an old hen, "shall I have some, now?"

"Give it to me," said Marged, and down went the work again.

She stood up, trying not to look, but burning coals are not as hot as the eyes of men like Owen, and so, wanting to or not, Marged was forced to look up, slowly from the bucket, up his arm to his shoulder, and slowly again, so slowly, up his face.

To his eyes.

At first I could not see Marged in the face because her back was to the fire and the lamp was behind her. But I had no need to see, for I could feel. And I could see her hands tight fast in her apron.

"Marged," said Owen, for the first time.

"Yes," said Marged. I nearly fell through the bed so cold was her voice.

"I have got my bucket," said Owen, so silly I was sorry for him.

"Here is the water," said Marged, and waved behind her.

"Yes," said Owen, but no move.

"They will be home from choir in a minute," said

Marged, and I could see the shadow bless her throat as she swallowed again.

"I wish they would never come back," said Owen.

"There is wicked you are," said Marged, but not a bit stern.

"I am speaking the truth, Marged," said Owen. "There is beautiful you are."

"No," said Marged, between a sigh and a sob.

"Yes," said Owen.

"No," said Marged, not so certain.

"Behold," Owen said, from Solomon, "thou art fair. Thou hast dove's eyes."

"Dove's eyes are small," Marged said.

"Your's are so big they are all my world," said Owen.

"No," said Marged, high.

"Yes," Owen said, and put down the bucket. "I love you, Marged Evans."

"There is silly," said Marged, going cold again, "only five days you have known me."

"I knew from the moment," said Owen, and I believed him. "I have known you five thousand years. In jewels and gold."

"Jewels and gold?" said Marged. "Since when, now?"

"By the brook of Hebron," said Owen. "Oh, Marged."

Marged's hands flew up on wings to her throat so pretty was his voice with her name.

"I have no jewels or gold," she said, trying to be cold again. But even Owen knew now.

"You shall have them," he said, and meant it. "Wait you till I sell my inventions. You shall have everything to your heart's want. And no work about the house."

"No work about the house?" asked Marged.

"No," said Owen.

"What will I do all day, then?" asked Marged.

"You shall wait for me," said Owen. "When will you marry me?"

"I will have to ask Dada," said Marged.

"Make your own mind to answer," said Owen. "When?"

"You will wake Huw," Marged said, shaking.

"When?" asked Owen.

"You will make me cry," said Marged. "Leave it, now."

Owen looked at her, and Marged's hands dropped again. For minutes, it did seem, they looked at each other. They were still, hardly a breath, looking.

Almost before my eyes could see, Owen caught her by the shoulders and kissed her, so long I thought they were turned to salt.

"Marged," he said, and his voice was rough and sore with him. "O, Marged."

"Owen," she was whispering.

"I love you," he said.

"Me, too," she said.

"No," he said, as though astonished, unbelieving.

"Yes, indeed," she said, and you will never hear deeper truth. "When I saw you first."

"No," he said. "Like I did?"

"Yes," she said. "Like you did. And when you stood up for me about the chicken, I wanted to kiss you."

"Marged," he said, and holding her again. "There is beautiful you are."

"I wish I was," she said.

"Beyond compare," he said. "I will worship you all my life. You shall be happy every minute. I will stab myself for every tear."

"Owen," she said, "there is nice things you say."

He would have said more, I suppose, but then my mother tapped on the bedroom floor with her shoe. That was her sign that she wanted to speak to me. Every night, at this time, she spoke to me, but if I had gone to sleep, we would speak in the morning, so nothing was lost.

"Yes, Aunty Beth?" asked Marged, and making a sign to Owen.

"Is Huw sleeping?" my mother called down.

Owen turned toward the wall bed.

"Are you sleeping, boy?" he asked me, but so quiet that he would never have had me awake if I had been sleeping. Then I was in a pumpkin jelly, not knowing whether to say yes or no, because I wanted no black looks from either.

"Yes," I said, but dull, as though I had been sleeping. So are liars made.

"Mama wants to talk to you," said Owen.

"Yes, Mama," I called, and they stood looking, hand in hand.

"How are you to-night, my little one?" my mother called back.

"Extra, Mama," I said. "How are you?"

"Lovely, indeed," my mother said. "Is your leg paining now?"

"No, Mama, thank you," I said. "Dr. Richards is going to let me get up soon."

"I will be up on Saturday," my mother said, "so I will see you. Are you having plenty to eat with Bronwen?"

"Yes, Mama," I said.

"But Bronwen is not such a good cook as Mama, is she?" my mother asked me, and there was such longing in her voice that I pretended to cough to have time to rid my throat of the stone.

Without taking time, I saw the months of lying in bed and thinking of her house and children under the care of another woman all go screeching through my mother's mind. Bronwen was a cook above good cooks and it seemed unfair to say that my mother was better. But my mother was my mother and her voice was full of longing to know that she was missed by us, that she was not forgotten, that she was still Mama, to be wished for and welcomed. Even though a lie had to be said.

"No, indeed, Mama," I said. "I often think of apple and ginger fool, and plum pie, and meddlar trifle."

"All of them you shall have," my mother said, and the sureness in her voice would make you smile to yourself. "Wait you till I am from this old bed, and you shall see what those old pots shall cook. I am going mad here, thinking what I should be doing instead of lying down and nursing this fat old lump of a girl."

Lovely was my small sister, and Olwen was her name. She was often brought to play on my bed while Bronwen and Angharad were making my mother comfortable up-stairs, so we were great friends from when she was born.

"Make her say bubbles, Mama," I said, because she was good at bubbles, and if you pressed her cheeks they blew off and broke in colours.

"Go on, boy," my mother said, with laughing, "she is sleeping these hours. Go you to sleep, now."

"Yes, Mama," I said. "Good night, then."

"Good night, my little one," my mother said. "Tell Marged not to put more on the fire."

So it was, nearly every night. That night I remember well, for while we were speaking, Owen and Marged went hand in hand on tiptoe through to the back, and they were still there after my father came in with Ivor and Bronwen from the choir practice.

"Where is Marged?" asked Bronwen.

"In the back," I said.

Marged came in looking red, and trying to have her breath without a struggle, as though she had heard them come in, and run. I saw Bronwen look at her with that smile that was not a smile, and go to the cupboard for the plates.

"I wonder should Owen have a fire out there," Bronwen asked, and rattling plates.

"Yes, indeed," Marged said. "It is shocking cold there, still."

"O?" said Bronwen.

"He told me so," said Marged, but too quickly.

"Never mind, girl," Bronwen said, and gently. "There is no harm done to go in and find out for yourself. Is there?"

"I have never been," said Marged, looking at Bronwen with big eyes. "Not once."

"Never mind if you have," said Bronwen, smiling properly now. "No matter, girl. Put the baking stone on, will you? I will make milk cakes for supper."

When supper was ready and Owen was called in by Gwilym, you would never have thought there could have been any feeling between Marged and him. He seemed not to notice her, and he did not exist for her.

But I caught the looks they sent across the table while everybody was eating. Small, quick looks, with everything they were thinking crushed into them, with enough heat to cause blazing. They sat nearer to me than to the others, and since they thought I was asleep they were careless of the gap in the curtains and the eyes that looked from the shadow inside.

This it was that went so near to spoil my mother's coming down that Saturday.

My father had made all sorts of surprises for her. He had the choir coming up the Hill to sing outside the door, and the new preacher and the colliery manager and Dr. Richards to tea, and all my uncles and aunts, and all Bronwen's family, and I cannot say how many more, never mind all the village.

Four harpists were coming from other valleys, and fiddlers, and a piano was brought up from the Town, but I knew that afterwards it was going to Bronwen for a present from my father and mother for the first grandchild, Gareth.

Then Idris John started to paint the house from top to

bottom, inside and out, and furniture, all new and elegant beyond words, came from Town with the piano.

If you had seen my mother's face when she came in the house, you would have laughed first and then wanted to cry. She had been carried on the mattress down to Bronwen's a couple of days before, to be out of the house for Idris to paint the bedrooms. But she thought she was being taken away to have the wooden bedstead riveted, for it was old, and it creaked to make you hold your teeth, and she had sworn to have an axe up there and chop it up and throw it away through the back window for the fire, so sour she was with it. There is a fool an old bedstead can be, too.

I had seen everything from the wall bed until it became time to move me, and then Ivor carried me into the front room. There is beautiful all the new paper and paint looked. The new furniture was in the houses next door, piled up in their front rooms and passages waiting for Idris to finish and the girls to wash down.

When I was carried back next morning I knew the kitchen was ours only by the shape. It was so changed with Idris and his brush.

The ceiling was white, with paint on smooth boards, and the walls were pale blue and yellow with all the rough places and the cracks filled in.

My wall bed was so pretty in yellow it was a pleasure to go back in there and look up at the sun shining upon it as though he was glad to have something his own colour to land on and live with.

All that morning my sisters and Bronwen, and the women from the Hill, and my aunts as they came, all washed and polished and scrubbed to have the house tidy for my mother.

My father was in and out of the kitchen every minute, giving things a little push, or looking at half-made curtains, or frowning at piles of crockery on the floor, with his fingers itching with him, as though impatient to do everything himself, there and then, without waiting.

And when he looked round and found me watching him, he pulled his moustache as though he was ashamed of his feeling, and looked down at the floor and up at me and winked, then.

"Supervising I am, see, my son," he said, and pulled his

coat down at the back and walked out funny to make me laugh.

Well, it was all ready, at last.

Hundreds of people there were outside. The choir came up in a crowd and I could hear them singing as they walked up the Hill, beautiful indeed. Everybody joined in the hymn, the girls cooking out in the back, and Bronwen and Angharad and the others with me in the kitchen, and my aunts and uncles in the front room, and the women upstairs hanging the last curtains.

Everywhere was singing, all over the house was singing, and outside the house was alive with singing, and the very air was song.

My father brought the new preacher in to see me before my mother came from Bronwen's, and Mr. Nicholas, the colliery manager, and Dr. Richards stood in the doorway because the kitchen was full up with girls and women, all cooking or cutting bread and butter.

"This is Huw, Mr. Gruffydd," said my father. "Huw, this is the Reverend Mr. Merddyn Gruffydd, the new preacher. Bow your head, my son."

"Leave your head on the pillow," said the Reverend Mr. Gruffydd, and he was looking at me, and frowning. "Huw Morgan, never let that light go from your eyes. Never mind how long you are here. Do you want to go out with the other boys?"

"Yes indeed, Mr. Gruffydd," I said.

"Are you sure you will go from here one day?" asked Mr. Gruffydd, smiling now.

"Yes," I said. "I am, sir."

"Good," said Mr. Gruffydd. "And not a doubt about it, never mind what all the doctors have got to say."

Of course, that was a cut for Dr. Richards, in fun, mind, so everybody laughed except the doctor.

"The boy will be no better for those ideas, Mr. Gruffydd," Dr. Richards said. "Nature must take her course."

"Nature," said the Reverend Mr. Gruffydd, "is the hand-maiden of the Lord. I do remember that she was given orders on one or two occasions to hurry herself more than usual. What has been done before can also be done again, though perhaps not so quickly, indeed. Have you faith, Huw, my little one?"

"Yes, sir," I said, and I was on fire.

"Good," said the Reverend Mr. Gruffydd, "you shall see the first daffodil out upon the mountain. Will you?"

"Indeed I will sir," I said, and his hand was cool on my forehead.

"God bless you, little Huw," said the Reverend Mr. Gruffydd. "I will come to see you every day. Yes?"

"Yes, sir," I said.

"Thank you, sir," my father said, and strange he was looking, but the Reverend Mr. Gruffydd only shook his head and waved his hand and smiled at me before he went back in the other room.

The kitchen was quiet when he went. Bronwen was looking after him with her hands all flour with her and the other girls were nodding at one another and looking as though something serious had happened.

"What is wrong, Bron?" I asked her.

"Nothing, boy," said Bronwen, so I knew there was something. "There is a fine man he is. There is crowds there will be at Chapel, now then."

"Yes, indeed," said Mrs. Idris, and starting again on the potatoes. "He have had a revival wherever he have been to preach."

"Well, we can do with one here," said Bronwen, and back she went to her cakes.

All this time there had been singing outside, but not all of them together except for the choruses. But now, because my mother was coming, a shouting and cheering started that made the very pots on the table shake together.

Quick as quick Bronwen and the others finished all they were doing and ran to be from the kitchen when my mother came in.

There is a rush they made, with a rattle of bowls and a clashing cutlery, and all of them trying to wipe down the table at once, and leaving it for something else, and then finding everybody had left it half done, and all of them rushing back again to do it properly, and picking up bits of peel and rubbing flour off the tiles, and putting more coal on the fire, and bumping against one another and laughing, and the cheering growing louder outside, and their faces going straight with them again, and another rush to pat my bedclothes tidy and giving me smiles, and kisses from Bronwen and Angharad, and then they had gone, with a click of the latch and a tapping on the cobbles.

And there was left only the chickens on the spit, and the new furniture, and the cheering, and me.

. . . .

You will never know how silly is cheering until you lie on your back, and look up at sunlight stretching itself on a bed of yellow paint, and try to do a bit of cheering by yourself.

First you will make a noise in the same key in the back of your throat, but it will sound as though you had an old fish bone by there, so you will try louder.

Then you cannot make up your mind whether it should be Hurray or Hooray or Hurrah or just Ay, and carry the Ay on a few beats till you stop for your breath. If you will have Ay, then you try it louder and louder until you are screaming at the top of your voice, and in the middle of that comes a thought.

There is a fool you look, with your mouth wide open, and your throat hard with effort, and your good voice wasting in Ay. For the sake of making a noise.

So I stopped cheering and listened for somebody coming in, and presently I heard the front door open. Just then, I suppose because they had been told to watch for it, the choir started to sing.

There is lovely after that senseless noise. In dignity and harmony, in rich beauty rose their voices now employed in noble purpose. Glorious is the Voice of Man, and sweet is the music of the harp.

I looked round quickly at the doorway and found my mother watching me with diamonds in her eyes, and her hand to her mouth. Whether to laugh or cry, now.

"Huw," she said. "Huw, my little one."

No words would come from me, and I turned my head.

My mother came over to me and I heard her skirt sighing across the tiles, but when she bent over me and saw me pulling faces, she began to pull a few, and then we looked at each other and we started to laugh at the same time. There was nothing to cry about, see, so there was no sense in crying.

"Wait you," my mother said, and wiping my face, "there are some blackberry tarts coming up the Hill now in a minute. Wait you."

"Are you better, Mama?" I asked her.

"Better, boy?" my mother said, and laughing she was, now, with her. "Of course I am better. Do I look better?"

"Your hair is white with you," I said.

"The snow got into it," she said. "You had your old cap on."

But my mother was only joking, of course. Women are so brave.

"Are you ready to see the house, Beth?" my father asked. He was standing in the doorway, watching us.

"Yes, indeed I am," my mother said, and she got up. "There is beautiful, Gwilym."

She was looking about the kitchen, and then she looked quickly at me and ran, yes, ran, from there, and up the stairs.

My father and mother were up there a long time, enough time for the choir to go through four hymns and Comrades in Arms, and then I heard them coming down. Back they came to the kitchen again and they stood by the table.

"Well, Gwilym," my mother said, and looking at him.

"Well, Beth," said my father, and smiling.

"There is beautiful," said my mother.

"Glad I am you like it," my father said.

"What is left in the box, now?" my mother asked.

"Plenty," said my father.

"After the doctor and all this?" asked my mother.

"Plenty, plenty, and to spare," said my father, still smiling and giving a wink to me.

"There is kind you are, Gwil," my mother said, putting her hand on his arm. "There is a wife you have got, staying in bed all this time and leaving her family to strangers."

"Yes, indeed," my father said, pretending to be angry, "and bringing another little sister for Huw, too. Dear, dear, there is a wife."

"I wanted to get up, Gwil," said my mother.

"Sweetheart mine," said my father. I had never heard him call my mother that before. There is pretty it did sound. She did think so, too. There is a blush, indeed, and white hair.

"Sh," she said, and looked quickly at me, and saw me smiling, and blushed more, looking on the floor and curling her fingers in her chain.

"Shall we go out to Mr. Gruffydd now, Beth?" my father asked her, and frowned at me to say nothing.

"Yes," my mother said, "but there is to be no say from me, mind."

"You will have to have a couple of words with them, girl," my father said, and laughing. "They will be shouting if you try to run."

"But what will I say?" my mother said.

"You found something to say last time you spoke," my father said. "It should be easier, now, with friends."

"Right, you," said my mother, nodding as she did when there was nothing more to be done. "But if I will start shouting laughing in the middle, you shall have the blame. Then I did talk for good reason to a parcel of dull men. But now, there is no profit to talk."

"Only to say thanks, girl," said my father, urging her.

"I will say that with a good cup of tea," my mother said. "Have those girls got ready?"

"Yes, Mama," I said. "Out in the back they are waiting."

"Good," said my father, "and the rest are out in the front, waiting these months. Come you, Beth. Let me see a smile with you, then, girl."

No good to keep straight your face when my father looked at you like that. So my mother struggled with her mouth for a moment and then she started to laugh.

"Go on with you, boy," she said, and taking his arm from her waist and giving him a little push to the door, "I am coming back again, now just, my little one," she said to me, "blackberry tart for you this minute."

"Thank you, Mama," I said, "speak so that I will hear you."

"Gracious goodness," my mother laughed, "there is like your old Dada you are, boy."

Out they went, then, and such a shout to meet them as they opened the front door. A big voice called for silence, and I knew that the Reverend Mr. Gruffydd would not find it hard to be heard over in the next valley if he had notions to try.

"Beloved," he said, standing upon the window sill of the front room, "I give you greeting in the name of the Crucified."

"Amen," they said, and the deep sound of it slid down the Hill.

"Great is my joy," he said, "to be thus honoured upon the first day of my ministry among you, to be called to this house of sacrifice to welcome back a wife and mother, whose name shall for ever be borne upon a shield of shining gold through the Five Valleys and beyond."

He had to stop, for the crowd was big and shouting was loud.

"It is evident," he said, with laughing in his voice, "that your patience will not permit an oration. But I will have you in Chapel, indeed."

A big laugh from the crowd who knew they would have to be silent in the four walls of the Zion.

"Beth Morgan," he called, and his voice tolled about the Valley, "come into your house. O woman, O noble mother, enter thou in honour while we give thanks to Almighty God for His many mercies, for the gift of thy life, and for the sparing of thy gallant son."

Again the crowd were shouting, but a different note in the shout.

The kitchen went so quiet that I could hear the grease dropping from the chickens on the spit. Not a sound else was to be heard except the littler sounds of the new paint finding homes in the cracks, and the table getting comfortable on the new tiles, and the chair resting itself, and my breath coming slow and steady and making the bedclothes hiss.

"Friends," in my mother's voice, "there is nothing to say except thanks to Mr. Gruffydd. That I have come home, thanks to God I have said a thousand thousand times, and for somebody else inside here. No more to be said. Come you, now, and have to eat. There is plenty."

Shout, then, shout. Mouth on mouth, open and shouting, that soon will be filled with food. There is patient is the mouth.

In a moment the kitchen was full. All the girls ran round the back lane and through the back door, and processions came and went through the front, all taking out plates of bread and butter and pies and cakes and buckets and baths of hot water for the teapots, all getting in each other's way and laughing and pushing and pretending to be stuck in the doorway.

My mother came through the crowd with a big blackberry tart in one hand and my tea in the other, carrying them high and with care not to spill, keeping off the people with her elbows and eyes.

"Now then," she said, and put them into my hands, "wait you till I will have a cloth here."

"No matter, Mama," I said. "I have been waiting long for this, not the cloth."

"If your Dada will see you eating without a cloth," said my mother, "what will he say to me? You are bringing up your son fit for a sty. Wait you, now."

But before she had turned her back, I was into that tart.

O, blackberry tart, with berries as big as your thumb, purple and black, and thick with juice, and a crust to endear them that will go to cream in your mouth, and both passing down with such a taste that will make you close your eyes and wish you might live for ever in the wideness of that rich moment.

Angharad came over with the cloth while my mother was pouring tea in her place, and Bronwen came to spoon my cup for me. There was no talking to be done for now the house was packed solid with people to see the new furniture and paint, and make a noise, and some to look at me and smile.

I was thankful that Bronwen was sitting by my pillow for she hid most of them. But those who had made up their minds to see me, poked in their heads and patted my feet. Strange it was to see tears in their eyes and to feel their sympathy, and yet to be able to say nothing to them in thanks.

But the noise was beyond words, indeed.

Cups and saucers and plates and knives and forks and spoons and boots and shoes were clattering and scratching and shuffling, and women were talking and laughing in soprano and contralto, and men were shouting and joking in tenor and in basso, but it was all stirred up as though someone was bent on making a cake out of sound and would have a good mixing for a start.

Then it was that I heard Owen shouting out in the back. Almost then, everybody heard him, for a quiet fell, and people near the door were hushing others in the front who were still talking.

"I will take no orders from you," he was shouting, in anger.

"Let me find you near my daughter again," Marged's father shouted back, "and I will thrash you till the end of your life, you wastrel."

"Leave me go to smash in his head," Gwilym was shouting, as though hands were holding him.

"Close your head, Gwil," Davy said. "Mr. Evans," his

voice went on, "there is no need for language like that from you."

"I will be judge of that," said Mr. Evans, "and I will thank you to keep out of this matter."

"Give the old fool a good kick," shouted Gwilym. "Loose his teeth, the old devil."

"Shut up, man," Owen said.

"Be silent, Gwilym," said Davy. "You are making it worse. Mr. Evans, please to see my father before you say more."

"I will have my daughter from here, now," said Mr. Evans, in anger.

"I will run away from you," Marged said, and tears were in plenty.

"So now then for you," mocked Gwilym, "you old fool, you."

"Hisht, hisht, Gwilym," said my mother, pushing through the crowd from our side, "go from here, now, this moment."

The crowd in the kitchen made way as my father and the Reverend Mr. Gruffydd moved out of the front room toward the crowd outside the back door.

"Beth," my father called, "what is it?"

"Come you, Gwilym," my mother said, with relief, "there is an awful thing to happen indeed. I am ashamed of you, Owen. And as for you, young man, I shall never know why you were called after your father. Say you are sorry to Mr. Evans."

"No, Mama," said Gwilym, stubborn as a pig of iron.

"Wait you," said my father. "Now then, what is the trouble, Mr. Evans?"

"Your son was in this shed with my daughter," said Mr. Evans.

"Eh, dear, dear," said the crowd to one another.

"What were they doing?" asked my father.

"O," said Mr. Evans, as though he had no wish to air the matter. "He was holding her about the waist."

"I was kissing her," said Owen.

"O," said my father, as though that was the end of the matter. And I suppose he started to smile, and the crowd began to laugh.

In a moment the whole house was shaking in laughter. But presently it drained off, and people in front began hushing again.

"Glad I am," my father was saying, "that it has ended like this. I will be very happy to have Marged in the family."

"There are none better," said her father. "I am sorry, Gwilym, for causing this trouble. But I am strict about such things."

"Right, too," said my father. "Gwilym, say you are sorry."

"I am not sorry for saying what I did, as he was then," said Gwilym, "but if I said it as he is now, I would be very sorry indeed, Mr. Evans."

There was quiet for a moment.

"That is the best you will have from that quarter," my father said, and again everybody started to laugh.

"The tea is getting cold," Bronwen called. "Come you, now, quick."

Bronwen took my cup from me and pinched the crumbs of tart from beneath my chin.

"There is an old fool that Evans is," she whispered. "Her mother have known these weeks. Wait till she will have him home. Only pretending, he was."

As though Mrs. Evans had heard, her voice rose out in the back.

"Shame on you, Sion Evan Evans," she said, plain to be heard, and making all the talk fall away again. "Of course she will marry Owen Morgan, and thankful I am, too. Shame I do feel, dear Mrs. Morgan, that this old fool of a man should cause trouble on this day of all others."

"Let us go now," said my father, "and have a glass in health. Come, all of you."

Up went the talk again, and somebody started to sing.

"Owen will never forget that as long as he is living," Angharad said, bringing back my full cup. "If you had seen his face."

"I will have a talk with him," said Bronwen. "If he will listen."

But now everybody was singing and it was getting dark and the lamps were rising into yellow flowers and the women had work to do, while the men went down the Hill to drink healths and sing on their own.

Owen was not to be found that night.

· *Chapter Eight*

IT WAS MANY DAYS before Bronwen had chance to speak to Owen because now she was not in our house such a lot, for my mother was having her way about things, and she took care, now that she was downstairs, to see that they were done.

Bronwen used to come in at night when Ivor had finished supper, and sit with me to hear my lessons, ready for Mrs. Tom Jenkins in the morning, and then help Angharad with the food boxes for the men next day.

One night, my mother went down to a prayer-meeting with my father, the first she had been to since she was ill, so they were giving her a special meeting and everybody was going. All except Owen, who was hard at work on his invention.

He had been very quiet, lately. Several times he had missed his meals, and although my father had said not to worry, I knew that my mother was unhappy about him. But she always was if any of us ever missed having a meal, for it was a certain sign, she said, of sickness in us.

Not only my mother was unhappy, but Marged, too. I saw it clearly though she tried not to show it. Often she stood looking through the window toward the shed where Owen was working, and tears were in her eyes for so long that I would start to count the beats before they fell. Then she would shake, once, from head to foot, as though she were bitten through with cold, and turn to run out in the wash-house, with her hand to her mouth, and the door coming to shut quietly behind her.

When my mother had gone with my father, and the house was still, Bronwen came in through the back and took off her cloak as though she had work to do.

"Is Marged here?" she asked me.

"No, Bron," I said. "Gone with Mama and Dada and the others, she has."

"Good," she said, and opened the door. "Wait you. I am having a talk to Owen for a minute."

"Good," I said, and back to my books as she closed the door.

I was learning Euclid at the time. Even till now I have enjoyed his theorems. So simple they are, and so wise, and good for the training of the mind. I shall always remember the drawing I made of an isosceles triangle inside a circle, for it was while I was trying to thread lead in the compass that Marged threw open the door, and stood with the wind blowing her cloak against her, staring at me as though she could kill.

"Who is with Owen?" she was whispering, and not blinking.

"Bronwen is," I said.

"I will have a knife in her," she said, and pulled the buttons from her cloak as she threw it from her.

"Only talking they are," I said.

"Talking?" Marged said, in a high voice, as though we should be laughing. "For weeks he has treated me like a ghost. Only talking? Now I know."

"What, then?" I asked her, for I was so surprised at her, acting as she was, with her hair all ends against her face, and her eyes staring and froth at her mouth.

"Shut up," she said. "You will know this minute."

She turned round to face the shed and lifted her chest to have a deep breath.

"Owen," she shouted, "Bronwen Morgan. Come you out from by there."

She had no need to shout twice. The shed door opened before she had finished and Bronwen came running to her, catching her by the shoulders and pushing her in the kitchen.

Owen came in behind and closed the door, standing with his back to it, looking drawn knives at Marged, who was in the lamp shadow, pressed against the wall, facing Bronwen.

"There is silly you are, girl," Bronwen said, looking from Marged to Owen and across at me.

"Not silly I am, now," Marged said, as though the life had gone from her. "I have watched you these weeks looking at him."

"Hush, girl," Bronwen said. "You know well there was a better reason than the one you thought."

"Tell her," Owen said, as though he was throwing bones to a dog.

"Wait now, Owen," Bronwen said, "there is a child in the room."

"Not much misses him," Owen said. "Tell her why you came out there."

"I went to ask Owen why he was so cruel to you," Bronwen said to Marged.

"Tell her what I told you," Owen said, in the same voice, worse because it was so deep.

"Take her outside and tell her yourself," said Bronwen.

"Am I going to be treated like an old bit of rag between you?" Marged asked. "Pull you, now. Settle it."

"Tell her, Bron," said Owen.

"He said he is not in love with you after everybody had a hand in the courting," Bronwen said.

"After you had finished with him, he meant," said Marged.

"Shut up, and behave yourself," Owen said. "You are talking like the women at the pits."

"You made me," said Marged. "Owen, was it my fault my father called us in front of them all? It was you who wanted to kiss. I had the teapots to fill and I told you to stop but you only kissed me more."

"Take her outside, Owen," Bronwen said, looking at me.

"No use," Owen said. "My mind is hard."

"Harden not your hearts," I said, and had a mind to fly under the bedclothes, quick. But not one of them moved, so I stayed as I was.

The three of them looked at each other, Bronwen and Owen at Marged, and Marged at Owen.

"Owen," Bronwen pleaded.

But Owen was still.

The clock rocked away, seeming to get louder at every stroke, as though it were rowing Time toward us, until I was wondering why it was never heard at other, ordinary times. I suppose it is because when such things as this happen, the minds of men reach out for something ordinary to think about, to try and take the hurt out of the matter, using ordinary little sounds, perhaps the tick of the clock, as a buffer for their mental engines.

Marged put down her head and started to cry so hard that when she sobbed, her head bounced up and back to her breast. Her neck at the back was so white it was a lovely surprise.

Bronwen looked again at Owen, but Owen looked at the blue tiles that ran round by the table legs.

"Right," she said, as though that was the end of it for one night. "Come you, Marged, my girl. Let us have a cup of tea at my house."

Marged went without a word, and Owen came from the door as they passed out.

He stood looking at a cut on his hand for a minute.

"Huw," he said, without looking at me, "there is no need to tell you to keep this to yourself."

"No," I said, "but it was pity she should cry like that. There is white is her neck with her."

"Be quiet now," Owen said, and went to the fire.

I could still hear Bronwen talking to Marged out in the back.

"How did you come from Hebron, Owen?" I asked him.

"Where, boy?" Owen said.

"Hebron," I said, looking in my books, "where you met Marged. This is beautiful she must have looked in her jewels and gold."

"Hush, boy," Owen said.

"Long time you did wait, too," I said. "Five thousand years. I counted five thousand bricks outside here. That was long enough. Indeed, I had my eyes crossed, looking at them."

Owen was looking up at the ceiling.

"You can spend your time better than that," he said. "Better than a lot of us, too. Good night now."

"Good night," I said, watching him go to the door. "Tell Bron, I am waiting to do my lessons."

Out he went, quick, and the door shut to wave the house.

But Bronwen never came.

My mother sent Angharad down to fetch Marged when she came back from the meeting. But Marged had left hours before, when Morris the Butcher had come up to ask Bronwen to sit with his wife, who was waiting, then, for her third boy.

All night they searched for Marged, up on the mountain and down by the river, and at last, early in the morning, when the men were going to work, they found out from Ellis the Post that she had met some people going from the meeting the night before who were driving into the next valley, and she had gone with them.

There is angry were my father and mother.

But not so angry as when Mr. Evans came over that night.

I heard nothing of it because they met in Bronwen's house. But when they came home my father was so angry he would eat no supper. So nobody had any, and I had mine after the others had gone to bed.

So Gwilym married Marged.

They were the same age and Gwilym had always been in love with her, I suppose because Owen was, in the first place. Owen was away from home when the wedding happened, and only my mother and Angharad went. Bronwen was tied to the house because of Gareth at the time, and my father refused to meet Mr. Evans on any excuse at all.

Gwilym took Marged to live over in the new houses in the other valley, furnished with money out of the box. Our box.

Old Evans gave them nothing, not even a cup and saucer or a bit of fat for the pan. But when he died a couple of years after, he left over three hundred pounds to the Chapel. I never heard my father mention his name after the wedding. They had been friends, but something must have altered Evans, or else my father was having more sense.

Owen stayed away a long time after that. He was working on his patent models at the steel works, where they were giving him tools to make his invention. He went one night when I was asleep. So the house was nearly empty of boys, except Davy and me, and Davy was away so often that he was almost a stranger when he came home.

The Union was climbing. I knew, because I was writing his letters when he was home, and I often read his letters to his friends who could not read for themselves. He was trying at that time to join with the men on the Railways, but he had so many enemies among them, and so strong were the companies, that he was unable to make much progress, hard as he tried.

But I was making progress, with the help of the Reverend Mr. Gruffydd. Every day he called in to see me, sometimes for a minute in the early morning, or at night, and sometimes, but few and far, in the afternoons for an hour at a time. He was a hard-working man, with a conscience that would not allow him to rest idle. Day in and day out, he was over the mountain to see people and ask them why they were not at Chapel, or to sit with the sick, or to talk to old people who could not walk the miles across the gorse on a Sunday to come and pray.

From him I learnt our history. Caradog, Cadwaladr, Lud, Coel, Boadicea, all the princely, shining host passed into

my keeping and from me to little Gareth, who was old
enough now to understand all that was said to him. I saw
in his eyes the light that Mr. Gruffydd must often have seen
in mine.

"Men who are born to dig coal," Mr. Gruffydd said to
me, "need strength and courage. But they have no need of
spirit, any more than the mole or the blind worm. Keep
up your spirit, Huw, for that is the heritage of a thousand
generations of the great ones of the Earth. As your father
cleans his lamps to have good light, so keep clean your
spirit."

"And how shall it be kept clean, Mr. Gruffydd?" I asked
him.

"By prayer, my son," he said, "not mumbling, or shouting, or wallowing like a hog in religious sentiments. Prayer
is only another name for good, clean, direct thinking. When
you pray, think well what you are saying, and make your
thoughts into things that are solid. In that manner, your
prayer will have strength, and that strength shall become
part of you, mind, body and spirit. Do you still want to see
the first daffodil out up on the mountain, my son?"

"Indeed, I do, Mr. Gruffydd," I said.

"Pray, my son," he said, and left.

Christmas that year was quiet with us because Davy and
Owen were away, and Gwilym had taken Marged over to
see her parents. Angharad had gone to the farm where
Ceridwen was working to take our Christmas presents, and
Ivor took Bronwen and Gareth over the mountain to see
her father and mother.

So it was an empty house, until Mr. Gruffydd brought
some people up for a night of singing on Boxing Day. So
big was the harp in the kitchen that the harpist had to sit
in the doorway so that all might come to have warmth of
the fire. Besides my father and mother and me, there was
Mr. Gruffydd and the harpist, Miss Jenkins from over the
mountain, Mrs. Tom Jenkins and her two little girls, growing fast now, Morris the Butcher and his wife, Mr. Christmas Evans the Colliery, Dr. Richards and his wife and
daughter, Mr. Bowen ap Rhys, the cashier, Mr. Owen
Madog from the new railways, and a couple of people I
cannot remember, with their children, who were sucking
their oranges in a way that was making my mother to look
at them sideways and bite her lips.

People heard the singing, and, of course, everybody knew

Mr. Gruffydd was in our house, so very soon the front and back of the house was thick fast with people all standing and listening, and any of them who knew my father, even by sight, were trying the old trick of putting their heads in at the door to wish us all well, in the hopes of being asked to come in. But there was soon no room, and as for the air, indeed, you could have stood things on it without them falling down, and for me in the wall bed it was so hot as being in the oven with the geese.

But the fingers of Miss Jenkins on the strings of the harp took all feeling from us, excepting the joy of song and the desire to sing. Songs and part-songs, cantatas, arias and dance melodies, hymns and psalms, all followed as fast as one would stop. Now the men singing, now the women. My mother started cradle songs she had taught us years before, and taught the strangers, and the strangers sang their songs and taught us. Then Mr. Evans danced a couple of songs he had learnt from a gypsy, tapping. He had a voice like a little crake with him, and so funny it sounded against the basso of my father that I was bound to push my fist in my mouth not to be rude.

In between songs, plenty of home-brewed beer, and bottles, and wine for the women, or tea in abundance. And if the songs made them hungry, the table was heavy with every mortal thing that can be made by women who are anxious to please the stomachs of their guests, and their own vanity. Nothing pleased my mother more than to be told how good were her dishes. Perhaps vanity is not the right word, for it pleased her to know that she was a good cook and that people enjoyed what she made for them, for she spent hours in cooking and making new dishes, so she deserved the praise.

I had just finished a song when Elias the Shop pushed his way through the crush at the back door and stood pressed in with his face and one shoulder showing, looking at us all as through we were all ripe to be swept into the Pit, and he was ready with the broom.

"Gwilym Morgan," he shouted, above the clapping for me, "you should think shame to be acting like this on such a night. As for you, Mr. Gruffydd, your conduct is fit for a meeting of the deacons. I am surprised and deeply hurt to think that such a man has been teaching my children in Sunday School. Shame upon you. Upon all of you."

"Give Mr. Elias a pint of home-brewed, Beth," my father said, and put the pipe back in his mouth.

"If I will reach it," said my mother, "I will give him a good clout with the frying-pan."

"Shame on you," Elias said to my mother, "so soon delivered from the jaws of death to repay your Maker by fouling His holy day."

"Strike the note, Miss Jenkins, my dear," said my father, and everybody looked uncomfortable. "Let us have Comrades in Arms again."

"A moment, Mr. Morgan," said Mr. Gruffydd, looking at Elias. "What is your object in making this outburst, sir?"

"It does not concern you," Elias said, "till you will meet the deacons."

"There are eight deacons present," said my father. "Shall we have a session now, then?"

"Shame on you," Elias shouted, and struggling to come more to the front, but the crowd leaned against one another to hold him tighter. "Profaners of the holy days, what next will you do in your iniquity?"

"Well," said my father, "if it is all the same to you, I will have the leg of that goose if Beth will pass the plate."

Mr. Gruffydd got up while we were all laughing, and went as close to Mr. Elias as the crowd would allow, looking not at him, but into him. Fine eyes had Mr. Gruffydd, and bright, sharp points to them like the needles poking from my mother's apron front.

"Mr. Elias," he said, "I am very sorry if you have been hurt in your good conscience, by any conduct of mine, which you may have judged to be out of keeping with the time. But you must not forget that the Man Himself attended at Cana, and also provided the best wine. What do you find wrong in this meeting?"

Mr. Gruffydd's quiet voice, so filling in the close space, sent everybody so still and soundless that I could hear the water coming from the stream above the garden.

"If you do not know," Elias said, in a voice that told very plainly that he did not, "it is not my place to tell you. This is a holy day. That is enough."

"It is far from enough," said Mr. Gruffydd. "You have forced your way into this house and you have been abusive, and you have chosen to take your authority from the Bible. There are too many of your sort walking the earth. Now go, before I take you by the neck and throw you. I will have a word with you in Chapel, sir."

How could we have known, then, that what happened that night, so small, so foolish, would be the cause of misery to us all. Elias never forgot that night. But his revenge was the sweeter when he had chance to have it. Sweet it was, and greatly he relished it, and every morsel of it he took.

But even of him I can think of with sorrow, now at this moment.

Those times, those people, even Mr. and Mrs. Elias, their son and daughters and their shop, have gone. How can there be fury felt for things that are gone to dust.

Chapter Nine

HERE IN THIS QUIET HOUSE I sit thinking back the structure of my life, building again that which has fallen. It do seem to me that the life of man is merely a pattern scrawled on Time, with little thought, little care, and no sense of design. Why is it, I wonder, that people suffer, when there is so little need, when an effort of will and some hard work would bring them from their misery into peace and contentment.

The slag heap is moving again.

I can hear it whispering to itself, and as it whispers, the walls of this brave little house are girding themselves to withstand the assault. For months, more than I ever thought it would have the courage to withstand, that great mound has borne down upon these walls, this roof. And for those months the great bully has been beaten, for in my father's day men built well for they were craftsmen. Stout beams, honest blocks, good work, and love for the job, all that is in this house.

But the slag heap moves, pressing on, down and down, over and all round this house which was my father's and my mother's and now is mine. Soon, perhaps in an hour, the house will be buried, and the slag heap will stretch from the top of the mountain right down to the river in the Valley. Poor river, how beautiful you were, how gay your song, how clear your green waters, how you enjoyed your play among the sleepy rocks.

I shall always remember the day I saw you after I had been in bed so long.

That morning Mr. Gruffydd came to the house early and opened the door of the kitchen so that the sun shone in all round him. Big he looked, and full of happy purpose.

"Good morning, Mrs. Morgan," he said.

"Good morning, dear Mr. Gruffydd," said my mother, in surprise. "There is good to see you."

"I have come for Huw," he said, as though he was asking to take a loaf for old Mrs. Llywarch.

"Huw?" my mother asked, and looked over the table at me with her eyebrows almost touching this little blue cloth.

"Yes," said Mr. Gruffydd, "this is the morning he has been waiting for."

I looked at Mr. Gruffydd and knew. But my mother was still in fog with her.

"The daffodils are out, Mama," I said.

"Oh, Huw," my mother said, and put down the bread knife, and turned her head away.

"Where are your clothes, Huw?" he asked me, but quiet, and looking at my mother's back.

"Under my pillow, sir," I said.

"Your pillow?" he said.

"For these months," I said, "ready for to-day."

"Come you, then," he said, and smiling he was. "You shall bring back a posy fit for a queen for your brave mother, is it?"

"Indeed I will," I said, and back I pulled the pillow, and out came my clothes that I had made ready ever since I had put my mind to the matter.

Pain there was, and a helpless feeling in all my bones, but I was determined to have those clothes on. On they went, and no nonsense, though the stockings were big and the trews too short, but I had grown and got thin, so it was no use to grumble.

There is a sight I must have looked when I put my legs out and stood up. But neither Mr. Gruffydd nor my mother looked at me, so I was spared to blush and very thankful.

"Up on my back, Huw," Mr. Gruffydd said, and bent his knees so that I could put my arms about his neck. I shall never forget how shocked I was to find myself up on the shoulders of a minister. It seemed wrong to be so familiar. But there I was, and carried to the door.

"He will be back in two hours, Mrs. Morgan, my little one," said Mr. Gruffydd.

"God bless you," my mother said, and still not looking.

"Good-bye, our Mam," I said, with my legs falling about at the back. "Get ready the big pot for the daffodils. I will have an armful for you, and some for Bron."

Outside, then, and through the blessed curtains of air, spun with morning mist and sunshine, blown upon us by wind from the southeast and the draughts that played in the Valley.

"Are you right, Huw?" Mr. Gruffydd asked me. "Am I too quick?"

"No indeed, Mr. Gruffydd," I said. "Go, you."

"Right," he said. "Here is the road, and up by there are the daffodils. Tight, now."

For the first few minutes I was shutting my eyes to get used to the sunshine, so raw and pure and shining white. Then I got used to it and less tears came and I was able to see without screwing up my eyes and having to blink.

The first thing I saw was the slag heap.

Big it had grown, and long, and black, without life or sign, lying along the bottom of the Valley on both sides of the river. The green grass, and the reeds and the flowers, all had gone, crushed beneath it. And every minute the burden grew, as cage after cage screeched along the cables from the pit, bumped to a stop at the tipping pier, and emptied dusty loads on the ridged, black, dirty back.

On our side of the Valley the heap reached to the front garden walls of the bottom row of houses, and children from them were playing up and down the black slopes, screaming and shouting, laughing in fun. On the other side of the river the chimney-pots of the first row of houses could only just be seen above the sharp curving back of the far heap, and all the time I was watching, the cable screeched and the cages tipped. From the Britannia pit came a call on the hooter as the cages came up, as though to remind the Valley to be ready for more filth as the work went on and on, year in and year out.

"Is the pit allowed to do this to us, Mr. Gruffydd?" I asked him.

"Do what, my son?" Mr. Gruffydd asked.

"Put slag by here," I said.

"Nowhere else to put it, my son," he said. "Look up by

there at the top of the mountain, by the Glas Fryn. There are the daffodils, see."

And indeed, there they were, with their green leaves a darker sharpness in the grass about them, and the yellow blooms belling in the wind, up by the Glas Fryn and all along the Valley, as far as I could turn my head to see."

Gold may be found again, and men may know its madness again, but no one shall know how I felt to see the goldness of daffodils growing up there that morning. The Glas Fryn was the nearest place to our house where they grew. It was later that I pulled bulbs to grow in our garden, but the garden was so small and the earth so blind with dust from the slag that they gave up trying and died.

But that morning Mr. Gruffydd put me down among them all, close to them, where I could take them in my hands to breathe the cool breath of them and give thanks to God.

Below us, the river ran sweet as ever, happy in the sun, but as soon as it met the darkness between the sloping walls of slag it seemed to take fright and go spiritless, smooth, black, without movement. And on the other side it came forth grey, and began to hurry again, as though anxious to get away. But its banks were stained, and the reeds and grasses that dressed it were hanging, and black, and sickly, ashamed of their dirtiness, ready to die of shame, they seemed, and of sorrow for their dear friend, the river.

"Will the salmon come up this year, Mr. Gruffydd?" I asked him.

He was quiet a moment, feeling for his pipe.

"I am told," he said, "that no salmon have been seen these two years."

"And no trout either, then?" I said.

"I am afraid not, Huw," he said. "They cannot face that black stretch, there."

"Good," I said. "No one shall tell me again that fish have got no sense with them. Pity, I do think, that more of us are not thinkers like the fish."

"Collect your flowers, Huw," he said. "Two hours I said to your Mama. She will be waiting."

There is pity that we cannot dig all round the growing flowers and take earth and all with us. It is hurting to have to break the stems of blossoms and see them lose their rich white blood only for the pleasure of putting them in a pot of water. Still, I had promised, and there it was. So break them I did, an armful of them, and up on Mr. Gruffydd's back, and off home, down the mountain.

There is pleased were the people to see me, indeed. Every door was open, and as we passed, the women ran out to wave to me and wish me well.

Up at our house, my mother was waiting with Bronwen and Angharad in the doorway.

"Well," said my mother.

"Let me have him from you, Mr. Gruffydd," Angharad said, and put her arms about my waist, but I pushed her away.

"Go on with you, girl," I said, "I am walking now."

And walk I did, though a bit like an old spider with a drop too much in him. The wall was my friend till I came to my father's chair, and into that I fell.

"Good," said Mr. Gruffydd, and my mother was making noises under her breath.

"There is hungry I am," I said.

"Wait you," said my mother. "You shall have a breakfast like your father now this minute. Cup of tea for Mr. Gruffydd, Angharad. You are standing there fast to the floor, girl."

Bronwen came in with the daffodils in the pots and beautiful she looked with the gold shining into her face.

"Soon you shall take little Gareth for walks, is it, Huw?" she said, and pulling a blossom out here, and pushing another in by there.

"No," I said. "Soon I will be going to school and finishing and then down the pit with Dada."

"Why down the pit, Huw?" Mr. Gruffydd asked me. "Why not to school and college, then university and then a doctor or a lawyer?"

"Yes," said my mother. "Indeed that is beautiful. Dr. Huw Morgan, and your own house and a lovely horse and trap. With a good black suit and a shirt with starch. Oh, there is good, Huw, my little one. There is proud would I be."

"I will not be a doctor, Mama," I said. "Not six months ago and Dr. Richards said I would never put my feet on the floor. This morning I went up on the mountain. To-morrow I will go and the next morning and all the mornings to come. I will not be a doctor."

My mother gave Mr. Gruffydd his cup of tea, and started

to hit sparks out of the fire, so I knew she had plenty to say but holding it because of Mr. Gruffydd.

"Say what is in your mind, Mrs. Morgan," he said, and smiling he was.

"There is a pack of obstinate donkeys I have got for boys," my mother said, and angry, too, turning to me and throwing the poker wherever it went. "Like old mules, they are. If you say something that is good, no. If you say something that is bad, no. Whatever you say, no. They are the ones who know. If Dr. Richards is an old fool, does it mean that you cannot go to school and do better? Have sense, boy. You are not old enough to talk."

"Yes, Mama," I said, and the bacon smelt so good it was sending spit bubbling in my mouth.

"We shall see," said Mr. Gruffydd, and he stood to go. "On Sunday, he shall come to Chapel and sit in the choir. And he shall sing a solo. That will keep his mind awake till then."

"Oh, Mr. Gruffydd," my mother said, "there is pleased Gwilym will be. Thank you, indeed."

"And no more talk of doctors or lawyers," Mr. Gruffydd said. "There is more than enough talking done by them without us wasting our time with them. To-morrow morning, Huw."

"Yes, Mr. Gruffydd," I said, "and thank you."

"God bless you, my son," he said, and smiled at my mother and went.

Chapter Ten

WELL, I disgraced myself for ever that Sunday I sang the solo, and I have never been sorry.

Every night of that week, as soon as my father was back from the pit and bathed and a good supper inside him, he brought out the tuning-fork and practised with me. "Now Thank We All Our God," I sang, and before the first verse was over my father was in tears with the music of it. And indeed I sang it because I meant it, not because it was to be sung. Be without your legs for more than two years and then stand upright to walk the earth again, and you will find your heart bleeding thanks with every step you take.

On Sunday morning everybody was up early. When I

looked out of the window while my father was lighting the fire, I saw all the chimneys start rolling smoke almost together, as though all had risen early to have a good seat.

We had cold breakfast as usual, but my mother boiled me an egg in the water made hot for little Gareth's bath and excused her conscience by having a glass of cold water instead of her tea.

Down to the Chapel, then.

I went first with Angharad. Ceridwen, home for Sunday from the farm, with Gwilym, behind us, then Bronwen and Ivor, and then my father and mother.

And every door opening as we passed down, and men coming out in their best, and smiling and greeting, and the women in their best, some with the tall hats like my mother's, and some with bonnets, like Bronwen's and Angharad's.

On the way down we passed other families like ours, but ours was one of the smallest. But if all the boys had been home, it would have been another tale.

Mr. Gruffydd was waiting outside the Chapel, shaking hands with all who went inside. He lifted me up and gave my sticks to my father.

"Up in the choir, you," he said to me. "Are you in good voice with you?"

"Splendid," said my father. "The tuning-fork has been useless all the week."

"Good," said Mr. Gruffydd. "Something good for God this morning, then."

The Chapel was bigger than I had thought it, so used I was to our kitchen. White, and built solid, with a varnished wood gallery round the top, and a scrubbed floor you could have your meals from. At the other end from the door the pulpit rose high above the heads of the people, and below it a platform for the deacons and head men. To the right and left, four rows of seats, each raised higher than the one in front, for the choir, women on the left, men on the right. And a smell of best clothes, and polish, and inside old hymn books everywhere from top to bottom.

But I was put on the platform next to Dr. Richards, and there is shy and funny I did feel with all the people looking at me and smiling and whispering to one another. I thought it was my thin legs they were laughing at, and tried to put them round the chair legs, but I was so weak in my grip that I almost fell out and head first on the floor.

"Sit straight and put your feet flat," Dr. Richards whispered to me, "or you will split your head on the floor. Once more like that and I will tie you with my braces."

The hymn, then, and after that a prayer from Mr. Gruffydd. More hymns, and everybody singing strong and deep and marvellous on the beat, with the last two words of each verse falling upon us from the roof, and the pauses for breath filled in by the sounding glory of the tone just flown.

Then Mr. Gruffydd leaned over to look down at me, and I stood while Mrs. Tom Harries played the opening.

There is a fright you will have to stand up before lines of faces that have become wet and shaky through the nervous water in your eyes. Your mouth is dry, with sand on the tongue and in the throat, so that your breath comes hot and sore with you. Then it is time to sing and you have forgotten the words. Each one has grown a wheel and rolls away from you down into the pit of Forgot. You reach out for the welcome feel of words well remembered. If you could think of the first word, all the others will hurry to form behind it, and all will come threading through the needle eye in your mind, and you can put them to the tune and sing.

But the first word hides behind the bonnet of Mrs. Phillips the Glas Fryn, and although you are ready to go on your bended knees to have it safe in your mouth, that big feather hides it too well.

Three times Mrs. Tom Harries struck the notes; and then I opened my mouth to show them I was willing, and as though they had taken pity, back came the words and I threw my voice up to the back row of the gallery into the laps of the Prossers, who were bending double because the roof came down almost to the floor.

After Mr. Gruffydd gave his sermon, and then the collection, then another hymn and the blessing, and then we should have gone home.

But after the blessing, hardly anybody moved except young women and some of the unmarried elder women. My sisters and Bronwen went, and so did my mother, but all round me on the platform, deacons and those busy with Chapel business were putting chairs. Dr. Richards lifted me down to be ready for my father to help me outside, but before he could reach me, Mr. Parry the Colliery was on his feet and addressing the people, so I had to sit still and my father stayed where he was.

I thought it was the usual Chapel notices, but since they never trouble me, I spent a few minutes multiplying the number of the first hymn by the second and dividing by the third, an old game my brothers used to have with sixpence from my father for the quickest right answer, and fines for mistakes and slowness.

But then Mr. Parry turned his eyes so sternly and his voice was so sharp that the figures jerked from my head and I thought he was after me, but instead, I heard a girl crying behind me and then she passed by, and went up the steps to the platform.

A girl from the pits she was.

Tidy in her dress, not good, but very tidy, and a good little bonnet with her, and her poor face so red and risen with weeping that I could have gone to her straight to give her comfort.

"Adulteress," Mr. Parry shouted, and all the men, young as well as old, nodded and said "Ha" or "Hmm" and some of them shook their heads and wrinkled their eyes and foreheads as though a shocking hurt had been done to them.

The priests and the scribes and the pharisees were in session, and bitterly enjoying themselves.

"Your lusts have found you out," shouted Mr. Parry, and thump went his fist on the handrail, "and you have paid the price of all women like you. Your body was the trap of the Devil and you allowed temptation to visit you. Now you bring an illegitimate child into the world against the commandment of God. Thou shalt not commit adultery. Prayer is wasted on your sort and you are not fit to enter the House of God. You shall be cast forth into the outer darkness until you have learned your lesson. I am a jealous God, and the sins of the fathers shall be visited upon the children unto the third and fourth generation. Meillyn Lewis, do you admit your sin?"

Meillyn Lewis coughed terror into a sopping rag and made noises to say Yes, She Did.

"Do you wish to make peace with the Eternal Father?" Mr. Parry asked her.

Yes, Meillyn Lewis wished to make peace of any sort with anybody, even the Devil himself in a stink of sulphur, only to be out of that Chapel and running up the mountain away from those nodding heads and Ha's and Hmm's and the eyes of Mr. Parry and his voice.

"But before you make your peace you shall suffer punishment," Mr. Parry said, dropping his voice down into the flower-pots, for at that level it did sound like the Last Trump, and indeed Mr. Parry knew it.

"Oh, there is sorry I am." Meillyn Lewis bled into the rag. "Have pity. I will never do it again, God knows."

"Taking the Name of God in vain," Mr. Parry said, two tones up in surprise. "Be quiet, girl, and listen to your betters. You shall have nothing from the Father, and we are here to see to it."

That is when I disgraced myself.

I can think of nothing that caused me to jump up and shout back at Mr. Parry. All I had learned was against such a thing, especially in Chapel, and my mother would have died to think of it. But such anger took me in the throat that the very air before me went red with it and I could hear my good heart doing its work double strong inside me to pump blood and give strength.

"Thou hypocrite," I shouted up at him, and indeed surprised at my high voice. "First cast out the beam out of thine own eye and then shalt thou see clearly to cast out the mote out of thy brother's eye. But woe unto you, Scribes and Pharisees, hypocrites, for ye shut up the Kingdom of Heaven against men, for ye neither go in yourselves, neither suffer ye them that are entering to go in. Woe unto you, Scribes and Pharisees, hypocrites, for ye are like unto whited sepulchres, which indeed appear beautiful outward, but are within full of dead men's bones, and of all uncleanness. Even so ye also outwardly appear righteous unto men, but within ye are full of hypocrisy and iniquity. Ye serpents, ye generation of vipers, how can ye escape the damnation of Hell? Behold your house is left unto you desolate."

If you could see the face of Mr. Parry.

Then I was sorry.

Quickly, before Mr. Parry could close his mouth or shut his staring eyes, before Mr. Gruffydd moved, before I heard my father coming, I was sorry. For Mr. Parry was a good man, none better. He paid his men better than most, and gave plenty away to those who needed it, besides paying for the schooling of half the children in the Valley.

So like that, I was sorry, and my voice cracked in half and fell to pieces and the bits went to breath.

Then Mr. Parry shut his mouth with a sound you could hear, and Mr. Gruffydd came down from the pulpit very slowly, while the deacons and head men looked at each other and at Mr. Parry, and Mr. Parry stared at me, and my father ran up behind me and took me by the shoulder.

"You rascal," he said, "you rascal. You would dare do such a thing."

"Leave it now, Mr. Morgan," said Mr. Gruffydd, and very gently. "Take the boy home and let nothing be said. There is no need to bring him to Chapel to-night, and this afternoon, take him up on the mountain. Huw," he said to me, without feeling, "I will see you to-morrow morning."

"Yes, Mr. Gruffydd," I said.

"Come, you," said my father, and we went out in the pale, cool, sunny silence, but feeling the heat of the thoughts of those who sat so still. Not one head turned as we passed.

The people who had heard in the lobby looked at me and made a serious face at my father, and their lips moved to greet him but they said no words. It seemed that even speech was at an end, so great was my disgrace.

"Did I do wrong, Dada?" I asked my father, when we were a bit up the street.

"Wrong, my son?" he said, and stopped to look at me with surprise. "Wrong? For a bit of a boy to say such things to Mr. Parry? I am so ashamed I could dig a pit for myself and you, too."

"But they were cruel to Meillyn Lewis," I said.

"That is one thing," said my father, "and the business of Mr. Parry and the deacons. Not for you."

"But you are a deacon," I said, "and every bit as much as Mr. Parry. But you were not sitting in the big seat? And why not?"

"Shut your mouth, and home to your dinner, my son," said my father with weariness. "Eh, dear, what a nest of scorpions came from the back room there. Not one of you with thoughts for others. Always ready with the tongue. What will become of you is beyond me to tell."

Up the Hill we went in quiet, and although curtains moved in windows, and I knew faces were looking out from the shadows in the open doorways, nobody came out, and nobody was in the street. Even the birds kept away from me, it seemed, and the sun was hot to make the quiet quieter.

So we went into our house and my father went into the kitchen to talk with my mother, and closed the door.

Angharad looked at me with her top teeth fast in her bottom lip, and fearful light in her eyes, and with much wagging of the head.

"Wait you till Mama hears," she whispered.

"Who told you?" I asked her.

"Mrs. Prosser told Bron," Angharad said, "and I was there."

"What did Bron say?" I asked her.

"She sent me out of the house," Angharad said. "And why should she? I heard the worst, anyhow."

I sat down and felt a river of fright rushing through my stomach. I wondered what would be done to me. I had thoughts of the policeman coming from over the mountain to take me down to the jail. My father's voice was deep from the kitchen, then it was quiet.

My mother came in to get plates from the cupboard. There was more pink in her face than usual, and I thought for a moment she was too angry to speak. But in the middle of reaching to get a plate she looked round at me and a smile was on her mouth and tears were in her eyes. Her skirts made circles with hurry as she ran to me and knelt with her arms about me, almost lifting me from the chair.

"Good," she said. "Good, my little one. Your Mama is so glad, she could scream."

My father came in and stood to put his hands in his pockets, helpless as helpless.

"Well, Beth," he said, as though the air was going out of the world, "you are as bad as he is, girl."

"Yes, Gwilym Morgan," my mother said, up on her feet and going to the plates, "and you are as bad as that pack down by there."

"There is a nice thing to say," said my father. "No wonder. Now I know."

"What, now?" asked my mother, stopping by him, both looking at each other, and neither of them a bit angry.

"Why I have got such a tribe of sons," said my father. "It is you. That is the trouble. Beth Morgan is the cause."

My mother looked at him and he looked back at my mother. And Mama smiled.

"Go and scratch," she said, and went quickly to the Kitchen.

My father clucked his tongue and looked across at me, and the laugh in his eyes ran down the cuts in his cheeks and poured in his mouth.

"There is a family, we are," he said. "Come and wash, my son, and let us eat."

Chapter Eleven

WHEN we were almost on top of the mountain that Sunday afternoon my father stopped to fill his pipe while he was having back his breath and looked down into the Valley.

"You see, my son," he said, "you cannot say what you like. There are things to be done, and things not to be done. Things good and things bad. And the best judges are those who have lived longest, and thought most."

"Yes, Dada," I said.

"Yes," he said. "I am not liking the sound of that, at all. What you mean is no, Dada, is it?"

"Yes, Dada," I said.

"Say your mind, boy," my father said, with anger. "Always say your mind to me. How will I help you if you speak lies?"

"But, Dada," I said, "you called me a rascal when I said my mind this morning."

"Yes," said my father, "but that was another story. Then, you were speaking of things outside you. You had no business to speak this morning. If your legs were right with you, you would have gone home with your mother and Angharad."

"Then poor Meillyn Lewis would have had all that and worse," I said, "and nobody saying a word to help."

"Meillyn Lewis is a bad girl," said my father, and pulling on his pipe.

"Because she had a baby?" I asked him.

"Be quiet, now," said my father, "you are talking of things you know nothing about."

"Yes, I do, Dada," I said. "Meillyn Lewis went up on the mountain with young Chris Phillips, and now he lets her be spoken to in Chapel like that."

"How do you know?" my father said.

"How many times have they passed our window?" I

said. "And how many times have the women said there would be trouble before long if he saved his money, instead of buying a ring and the furniture."

"Well, indeed," my father said, "you are an old mother's meeting on your own. I will have you out of that kitchen in future. Your ears are like a donkey's with chat."

"This morning is the first time I have opened my mouth," I said.

"I have hopes it will be the last," said my father. "One more set-to like that and we will be thrown out of the Valley."

"Why, now?" I asked him.

"Because, my son," he said, and earnest indeed, "it is not fit and right for a boy like you to make remarks. We have never had trouble in the Valley because we have always been strict. Men have thought twice before doing a wrong. The same with women. If all the women like Meillyn Lewis were allowed to go their own way, what would happen to us?"

"What?" I asked.

"You would have a police station in the Valley, for a start," said my father, "there is a nice thing for you. As though we were all a lot of jail-birds waiting to be taken off. And what about our homes and your mother and your sisters? Would you like Angharad to have the same as Meillyn Lewis?"

"Oh, Dada," I said. "Not Angharad. She never goes up the mountain."

"Gracious God," said my father, and dropped his pipe. "There is a boy you are, man. I never meant to talk about Angharad. Only saying 'if,' I was. And if I caught her I would strangle her."

"Would you, Dada?" I asked him.

"Yes, indeed I would," he said, and he was meaning it. "Let all things be done in order, with right and decency. Those things are worth a man's life or two. Life without would be a hell, indeed. Meillyn Lewis was an example. I will swear that what happened this morning will make many a girl think twice before she makes a slut of herself."

"She is a slut," I said, "because she went up on the mountain with a man, instead of to her bed with her husband. Is it, Dada?"

My father was quiet for a little, with his back to me, looking down into the Valley.

Bright shone the sun, but brighter shone the Valley's green, for each blade of grass gave back the light and made the meadows full of golds and greens, and yellows and pinks and blues were poking from the hedges where the flowers were hard at work for the bees. May and almond were coming, and further down, early apple was doing splendid in four tidy rows behind Meirddyn Jones' farm. His herd of black cows were all down in the river up to their bellies in the cool quiet water, and their tails making white splashes as they dropped after slapping flies, and up nearer to us, sheep were busy with their noses at the sweet green. When the wind took breath you could hear the crunching of their jaws.

Beautiful was the Valley this afternoon, until you turned your head to the right. Then you saw the two slag heaps.

"Yes," my father said. "That is why she is a slut."

"Then what is Chris Phillips, then?" I asked.

"He did very wrong," said my father, but there was no body in his voice. "Mr. Gruffydd will have a word with him."

"But not in front of all the people," I said. "If Meillyn Lewis is a slut, Chris Phillips is a coward. And I know which of them is the worst."

"Tongue again," said my father. "Leave it, now. And say no more on the matter. You are not old enough and you have said too much as it is. More sums and books, and less tongue. Let us go back for a cup of tea."

Half the women on the Hill had been in to see my mother while we were out, so my mother said when we got back to the house. All of them had come to say how sorry they were, and they had all gone away with the same answer.

"Nothing to be sorry about, I told them," my mother said, while she was cutting bread and butter, with the knife flashing red in the firelight, and the kettle having a little whistle on the hob. "And nothing to be done."

"Was that all you said?" asked my father, looking up at the lamp.

"Well," said my mother, "I said that, and other things, of course."

"Good," said my father. "I will hear them later. But now, the matter is ended. He can go into Bron's to-night and do his lessons while we are at Chapel."

"I am going to no Chapel to-night," said my mother, and

put the dripping down flat on the table to make the cups jump.

"Are you starting, now then?" asked my father, but with no surprise. "Chapel, Beth, for both of us to-night. And no nonsense. Never mind about the people and what they say. It is the home of the Word of God. Chapel for us both to-night."

"Yes, Gwilym," said my mother.

. . . .

Next morning I was waiting for Mr. Gruffydd long before he came, for I wanted to know what he would say. I had slept nothing all night, making ghosts for myself, filling my mind with them and giving myself pale frights. And the ghosts had a different punishment for me, some of them shocking, indeed.

Foolish is the mind of man to make bogeys for itself and to live in terrors of fear for things which lack the substance of truth.

But Mr. Gruffydd called as though nothing had happened. Indeed, the only sign that something was wrong was made by my mother. She was shaking so much that she had to put down the pot, and Angharad poured Mr. Gruffydd's tea for him.

Up on the mountain we went higher than usual for I was stronger and using only one stick, now. So to the top we went, where we could see the Valleys all covered with pale blue mists, and with long rolling grey shapes and deeper blues where the mountains rose up to guard them.

Cold it was, and wonderful the song of the north-east wind.

"Now, Huw," said Mr. Gruffydd, "good lungfuls, now. Breathe deep, and count five slowly before you are full. Then count five full up. And then five to breathe out. Is it?"

"Yes, Mr. Gruffydd," I said.

"Good," he said.

So we breathed, both of us up on top of the mountain, while the mists went to purple and rose, and the sun burnt through and covered us both with warmth and came out across the Valley in such strength that we could not bear to look. So it may be, I think, when we meet God. But worse.

The wind was doing all sorts to Mr. Gruffydd's hair, and

his nose had grown a gem that glistened to fix your eyes, making you count how many before it would fall. But he took out his handkerchief for a good blow, and then I knew he was going to speak.

Big in the shoulder was Mr. Gruffydd, and in his black clothes a figure to make you afraid. But I never felt any fear of him, though I was always afraid of losing his goodwill, and having the sharp side of his tongue.

"Huw," he said, "let us sit by there, my son."

We went over to the rock that marked the top of the mountain, where everybody using the path stopped to have their breath, and thank the stars the road was downhill all the way after.

We sat in the sun, on a turf as soft as my mother's tablecloth and greener, with the wind kept away by the rock, and angry because of it. You could tell by its voice how angry.

"Huw," said Mr. Gruffydd. "I want to speak very seriously to you."

"Yes, Mr. Gruffydd," I said.

"Something happened yesterday in the House," he said, "which I still think I dreamt. A boy spoke in a matter of which he was ignorant. He raised his voice. He spoke without permission. He interrupted. He was offensive."

"Yes, Mr. Gruffydd," I said.

"Why?" he asked me, and looking over the Valley as though it was of no consequence.

"Because," I said, trying to make my voice small, "I was sorry for Meillyn Lewis. It came out of me. I was sorry after, sir."

"You did wrong, Huw," said Mr. Gruffydd, taking me by the chin and looking at me, "and you must make up your mind not to do such a thing again. Once is more than enough."

"Yes, sir," I said, but feeling like No, Sir.

"Make up your mind," said Mr. Gruffydd. "There is a right way and a wrong in everything. Your father was very worried about you. If you will do that in Chapel, what will you do outside? What will become of you?"

"They were cruel to her," I said, and the heat was in my throat again to think of it. "And all those men were groaning and nodding to make her hurt more. That was not the Word of God. Go thou, and sin no more, Jesus said."

"You know your Bible too well and life too little," said

Mr. Gruffydd. "Let there be moderation in all things, Saint Paul said, and a more sensible man never trod the earth."

"But why did you allow it, Mr. Gruffydd?" I asked him, and I was feeling injustice stiff in me.

"Because I am a pastor," said Mr. Gruffydd, with sadness in his voice. "But I will change their foolishness in my good time and without the help of Huw Morgan."

For a little time the wind snarled and tried to put cold fingers on us round the rock, but always the sun pushed him back.

Mr. Gruffydd looked far across the Valley above the tops of the mountains, and his eyes were blind with thought.

"You must realize, Huw," he said, speaking in his blindness, "that the men of the Valleys have built their houses and brought up their families without help from others, without a word from the Government. Their lives have been ordered from birth by the Bible. From it they took their instructions. They had no other guidance, and no other law. If it has produced hypocrites and pharisees, the fault is in the human race. We are not all angels. Our fathers upheld good conduct and rightful dealing by strictness, but it is in Man Adam to be slippery, and many are as slimy as the adder. The wonder is to me that the men of the Valley are as they are, and not barbarians all. I was sorry for Meillyn Lewis, too. But that session of the deacons was helpful as a preventative. It was cruel, but it is more cruel to allow misconduct to flourish without check."

"It is not right to do it before all those men," I said.

"It is not, Huw," said Mr. Gruffydd, "but we must act according to the times, and I am just as much a servant of the Chapel as of God. And the deacons are my masters. I must make alterations slowly. I must think, and then speak. I must consider what is to be done and then choose my time to do it. Not like Master Huw Morgan, or I would be out in the street to preach in the hedges. And no chance to make changes or to do good. Now, do you see?"

"Yes, Mr. Gruffydd," I said. "And I am sorrier, now, too."

"Well, now, Huw," said Mr. Gruffydd, smiling wide and showing good long teeth. "For that handsome apology I will tell you that I thought you were a brave boy, but misguided in your bravery. Never mind what you feel. Think.

Watch. Think again. And then one step at a time to put things right. As a mason puts one block at a time. To build solid and good. So with thought. Think. Build one thought at a time. Think solid. Then act. Is it?"

"Yes, Mr. Gruffydd," I said.

"Come, you," he said, up on his feet. "Home. I can smell your mother's good bacon from by here, indeed."

Chapter Twelve

THEN IANTO came home.

If there was a fuss made over the prodigal son I cannot think what he could have had more than Ianto.

Ellis the Post pulled up the white mare right outside the door while we were having breakfast, and called to my mother.

With all the boys away, my mother looked to Ellis as to an angel, with joy but also in fear, in case his letters brought bad news.

"A good fat one, by here, Mrs. Morgan, my little one, for you," Ellis said, laughing out loud. "And fourpence to pay for no stamp, too."

"Come you in, Mr. Ellis," said my mother, running for her purse. "Angharad, put the pan on and bacon, quick. A good cup of tea, Mr. Ellis, to warm you."

"Well, indeed, this will be the third breakfast I have had this morning," said Mr. Ellis. "There is good to have a belly to hold it."

"Hisht," said my mother, and gave him the money and snatched the letter to cut it open.

"From Ianto, indeed," she said, holding the letter to the window. "Wait, now. My dear Parents, I am sure you must have thought I was dead, but I have been in London."

My mother put a hand to her head and looked at us in shock.

"In London," she whispered. "London. All that way and not a word. There is brave." She looked again at the letter, and softly screamed: "Coming home he is. Coming home. Ianto is coming home. My Ianto is coming home to us. Oh, Ianto, my little one."

Ellis started to shout and hit the table with his knife and fork, and my mother danced round the table holding Angharad and jogging from side to side, with her eyes full.

"Wait, now," my mother said, and wiped her eyes. "Angharad, down to the pit and tell your Dada, and call in Bron's. Then back, straight, and we will settle the house."

If there is one thing that happened to the house when Angharad came back, settle is not the word. The house was in uproars all day with soap and water, and the next day Angharad and me whitewashed front and back.

Ianto was coming the next day, so the night before, everybody who knew him met at our house, and walked down with my father to the Chapel house to make up their minds what to do for the welcome.

Ellis had sent telegraph messages to Davy and Owen, and Gwilym he had told on his way over the mountain. Ceridwen had come home for a couple of days, Ivor and Angharad and me were home, so there was the family together all one again.

There is pleased was my father.

As soon as he got in the door when he came back from the meeting, with Mr. Gruffydd, he went on his knees in prayer to give thanks. The very skin of his face seemed to shine, and his moustache was like pure silver, with him.

"Oh, Father in Heaven," he said, with his knuckles on the edge of the table, "how you feel when your sons return to you, so I feel, now, in my little way. I give thanks to have seen this day. I give thanks that my boys and girls are in health. And, O God, I thank Thee for to-night and for to-morrow. Amen."

Then we all sat down to supper and after, Mr. Gruffydd and my father drew up the procession, starting with the band and ending with Twm Pugh's coal-cart to carry the bottles and casks.

Up early next morning, and my father home an hour before the night shift finished to go with Thomas the Carrier in the wain down to the railway station to meet Ianto and the boys, with Ivor.

No climb on the mountain for me that morning, indeed. Washing cups and saucers and plates and cutlery out in the back, me. All the women on the Hill were bringing their own, but for the people coming from over the mountain, we always borrowed china to have enough, and my mother would always have it washed before using. That was my job, and though I had no liking for it, I did it because of Ianto and the boys.

The hooter had just blown for noon at the pit when we heard the band down in the Valley, where the procession was meeting my father and Ianto and the boys.

Well, there is excitement.

My mother stopped putting butter on the bread and put down the knife to hold her chest.

"There they are," she said. "Ceridwen, help me with my dress. Angharad, finish the bread and butter. Bronwen, watch the pots."

Then everybody made haste to finish what they were doing so that when the band came up the Hill they would be outside watching.

When Ifan Owen came round the corner at the bottom by the railings with his big silver stick and the cord round it, and the brass blazed up and the drums thumped and boomed, indeed my heart nearly stopped to beat. The band was not very big, only ten all told, but they played all together, and all of them by ear, and all very good, too.

Up they came, and blowing to push down a house.

After them a procession of our friends from all round the valleys, and from the pit, of course, and from the farms. Four choirs were there, all from the mountain, and our choir, and then the football clubs in their jerseys, and the women in their tall hats and red petticoats, and then everybody from the Chapel, and all the other chapels, with the preachers all walking together, then the children's choir.

And behind them, on Thomas the Carrier's wain all dressed up with flowers and grasses and coloured cloth, my father was standing with his five good sons.

I was standing in our front room at the open window but so great was the crowd that once the band was passed I could see nothing, except the heads of my father and my brothers, and when they got down, nothing except hats.

So, knowing my brothers, I went through the kitchen and out in the back and met them coming down through the back lane, dodging the crowd, see.

Ianto was even bigger than Ivor. And in good clothes, too, from London. There is strange you can tell London in a man's suit. Why is London such a wonderful place that it will speak to you even in a piece of cloth?

"Well," he said, "there is a big boy you have grown, man. How old, now?"

"Twelve," I said, "and a birthday next week."

"Oh," he said, "like that, is it? Birthday next week, so put your hand in your pocket?"

"No, no," I said, "only telling you, I was. If you want to give me a present, good. And if not, good."

"I brought you a coming-home present from London," he said. "It is in my trunk. So if you have a chance, look inside the lid."

"There is one in my box for you, too, Huw," said Davy.

"And mine," said Owen.

"You will have mine on your birthday," said Ivor.

"And I will give you a sixpence now," said Gwilym, "and I will see about your birthday when it is your birthday."

"How are you liking married life, Gwil?" asked Ianto.

Gwilym's eyes went once to Owen and down on the mat.

"O, all right, you know," he said. "How is your wife?"

"Dead," said Ianto.

"Dead?" said Ivor. "We heard nothing of that."

"I chose to say nothing," said Ianto, and put me on my feet very kindly.

"O," said Ivor. "Very long ago?"

"Six months," said Ianto. "She and the baby. But say nothing to Mama. I will tell her to-morrow. And keep close by me or she will be asking questions. Quiet, now."

The singing and shouting outside was something to marvel at, and now a press of people were all round the house, shouting for Ianto, and all the women were coming in to get the food and make the tea.

The boys were dragged away by their friends and I was left standing in the corner to watch. But the room was so hot, and so many people were trying to get in and so many in already, that I climbed out through the window and went in the back shed out of the way.

There was a little loft up in the back, a quiet little place full of the smells of soap, and oil, and coal, and wood, and potatoes, and apples, and onions, where my mother put the blankets and linen when she had no use for them. A little window let you look right up to the top of the mountain if you lay flat on your back on the blankets. Here I looked at my school lessons and read during the day when my mother had friends in, or wanted the kitchen so that she and the girls could bathe.

So I was up there, in quiet, and resting, with the sound

of the crowd a long way off, when Marged came in quietly and shut the door.

I made no sound but turned my head to watch her going to the bench where Owen had worked while she had been in the house with us. Some of his tools were still in the racks, and the brace and bits and the vice were shining as though Owen had only just been in. I was at them every day with sandpaper.

Marged sat on Owen's little stool and put her hand on the vice and started to turn the screw, very slowly, as though she was thinking.

And I knew she was crying.

Even while I was wondering what to do, the door opened again and Owen was standing there looking at her. For a moment he stood with the door open wide and then, knowing that people were all over, he came in and shut it, and stood again, with his back to it, very still, and in his black suit almost hidden in the darkness.

"Marged," he said, in a whisper. "I saw you come in. I had to come."

"Owen," she said, and the words were riding on her tears, "I have starved for you."

"Marged," Owen said again, and went nearer. "Many and many a time I would cut my throat but I am a coward. My life is a curse to me. I loved you, Marged, my beautiful one, but I loved too much. I love you still."

"There is nothing to be done," Marged said. "I am married. That is the end."

Owen was kneeling by her. She was still holding the vice.

"Do you remember when you kissed me in here the first time?" she said, with smiles in her voice. "You pressed me against this old thing and my back was nearly cracked in pieces."

"Is Gwil good to you?" Owen said, with hunger.

"None better, not even you," said Marged. "And he is so like you sometimes it is like being married to you, indeed."

"Why were you crying just now?" Owen said.

"Because the old ache was back," said Marged. "I had it with me too long to forget it. Ache, ache, ache, for days and weeks and months. And only one voice, one kiss would have burnt it away. But it went on aching. Then it stopped."

Owen got up.

"Stopped?" he said, and his voice was higher than hers.

"Stopped," said Marged, solid as a house. "One night I was in torments and going mad and shouting, and poor Gwil going mad, too, trying to soothe. And I prayed for strength to forget you."

"And you did?" asked Owen, with a full throat.

"I will never forget Owen Morgan," said Marged, and got up to settle her cloak, and I saw her waist that a man's hand could span. "Owen, who kissed me, and said I was his before the times of the Pyramids. Never. I will love him with my soul till the day I die."

"And now?" said Owen.

"And now I am Mrs. Gwilym Morgan," said Marged, "and Owen Morgan has gone away and will never come back."

"But, Marged," said Owen, "here I am, girl, look."

"You?" Marged said, and looked up at Owen, full in the face and shook her head. "No, you are not Owen Morgan. There is no man like Owen Morgan. He went away. He will never come back. And he gave me away to his brother."

"Oh, Marged," said Owen, and turned his back.

"Yes," said Marged, "and I am living in that little house with him."

"Would you come away with me if it will make you happier?" said Owen.

"Nothing will make me happy," said Marged, "only Owen Morgan. And he will never come back."

"Have sense, Marged," said Owen, and turned quickly to catch her by the shoulders and look down into her face, as though to beg.

But he spoke to himself and his words went to powder, and his eyes went wide and then tight shut. His hands fell from her, and quickly, with a cry, he went to the door, and threw himself against it.

"Marged," he was sobbing. "Oh, Marged, my beautiful one. What did I do to you, devil from Hell that I am? What did I do?"

He went out and closed the door. Marged stood.

Then boots ran across the cobbles and Gwilym threw open the door and stood to hold his breath. He went quietly to Marged and put his arm about her shoulders.

"Come, my pretty one," he said, and indeed I had never heard him in that voice before. "We will get in the trap and go home, is it? And I will bathe your head and nurse you to sleep, is it? Come you, my little heart, and have rest."

And talking like that, Gwilym took Marged quietly outside and shut the door.

I was boiling with heat and dry for a cup of tea, so I climbed down and went into the house among the people. Most of them were out on the mountain, having their food in the open, with the women hiding under umbrellas afraid of the sun, and the air full of talk and laughing.

In the kitchen my mother was looking white, and Angharad was crying in the corner, with Bronwen standing beside her patting her shoulder. My father and the boys were in the front room with Mr. Gruffydd and the other preachers.

"Huw," said my mother, standing quickly and holding out her hands to keep me from the front room, "take what you want and go out on the mountain like a good boy."

"Yes, Mama," I said, and Bronwen came smiling to help me choose and pack.

"No use," my father said, in a voice above all the noise, that made my mother turn to hold her mouth. "No doctor can do her good, Mr. Gruffydd. We have spent much on them. The poor girl is mad, and I am worried from my life for my poor boy."

"Go you, now," said Bronwen, whispering to me, in a hurry, "and be tidy for a couple of hours, will you?"

So out I went, and down to the river to tickle a couple of trout, and eat and drink on a rock in the sun with the river all round me.

Tidy, indeed.

．．．．．．．．．．．．．．．．

That night we had supper all over the house The tables were not big enough for all to sit down at once. So we had to manage.

I was in the kitchen with my father and mother and my brothers and Mr. Gruffydd and a couple of other preachers, and Mr. Evans the Colliery, Dr. Richards, Mr. Parry, Mr. Owen Madog, and a number of the deacons and elders.

We were all with our elbows under the ribs of the next one, but there was plenty to eat and drink so nobody was troubling. Ianto was telling about London and what he had done up there. He was in the counting-house of Hopkin Jones, the draper, and then cleaning engines in the Great

Western sheds, and then clerk of works on a road-building job, and goodness knows what, he said.

"There is a jack of all trades for you," said one of the preachers. "Why not one job?"

"Because I was never in the right job," said Ianto. "So I went on looking till I found it."

"Did you?" asked the preacher.

"No," said Ianto. "We were treated like dirt. In the clerking jobs we were supposed to dress like princes on the money of a maggot. And in the rough jobs we got more pay, but the conditions of living were worse than the animals out at the back here. So I left one for the other and kept on looking."

"But you never found it?" asked the same preacher, who was one of those men who enjoy making an ill-natured joke of all that goes against his understanding.

"No," said Ianto. "I never found it. And never likely to."

"So," said the preacher, "you are going to be a rolling stone all your life? Not much credit to that, at all events."

"At all events," said Ianto, with the lights in his big grey eyes set stone-still at Danger, "I am going to have credit for not squatting on my bottom like you, talking a lot of rubbish three times every Sunday, and mouthfuls in the week. Thank God I am not a limpet on society."

Down went everybody's knife and fork, except mine and Davy's, and Owen's, and Ianto's. I had known what was coming so I was ready.

"I am not prepared," said Mr. Gruffydd, "to sit here while my colleague is insulted. His observations might have been put in a happier manner, it is true."

"His observations," said Ianto, "should never have been made. I would have punched his nose if he had been a man."

"Well, indeed," said the preacher, and very distressed, "I am sorry to cause such trouble. If I have said anything, I am deeply sorry."

"Good," said Ianto. "Now I am sorry. Have some more of my good mother's blackberry."

After that, it was like trying to talk through a net. Words seemed to stick in the air. Nobody seemed willing to look at anybody else. And when somebody laughed, you could tell how hard they were trying.

Mr. Gruffydd had been rolling little pieces of bread for minutes on end, looking straight at the butter. Many times my mother took up the butter to help people, but his eyes never moved. My father kept looking at him out of the side of his eyes, and trying to talk business with Mr. Parry.

Presently Mr. Gruffydd blinked his eyes as though coming from sleep and cleared his throat, and at once the room was still. Angharad, coming through from the wash-house with more plates, first stood still, and then at a sign under the table from my mother, quickly went out backwards.

"Ianto," said Mr. Gruffydd, "at any other time, and in any other house, I would not start this discussion. But this matter to-night requires airing. Why am I a limpet on society?"

"Because you are doing useless work," said Ianto, quick as that.

"Ianto," said my father, across the table, and angry, with my mother's hand on his arm. "Mr. Gruffydd healed Huw."

"Mr. Morgan," said Mr. Gruffydd, "Huw healed himself. Ianto," he said, "why is mine a useless work?"

"Because," Ianto said, with knife and fork idle, and his eyes on fire, "you make yourselves out to be shepherds of the flock and yet you allow your sheep to live in filth and poverty, and if you raise your voices, it is only to say it is the Will of God. Sheep, indeed. Man was made in the image of God. Is God a sheep? Because if He is, I understand why we are all so damned stupid."

"I cannot tolerate this," said the preacher who had not yet spoken, a little man with glasses, who sniffed when he spoke and had a little cough with him that he used all the time.

"True," said Mr. Gruffydd. "Perhaps, Ianto, you would come down to my lodgings to-morrow and talk there. I am interested in your views."

"But, Mr. Gruffydd," said the sniffing preacher, "your dignity surely will not allow you to talk with him."

"Go from the house," Ianto said, looking knives at him, "before I will throw you, and your dignity. I will be with you at eight to-morrow morning, Mr. Gruffydd."

"Good," said Mr. Gruffydd. "And God bless all in this house this night."

"Amen," we all said.

Chapter Thirteen

I WENT DOWN THE HILL with Ianto next morning before eight o'clock to start school again with Mrs. Tom Jenkins. A big morning it was for me. More than two years had gone by since I was last in the little front room, but nothing had changed, not even the curtains, though they had been washed, of course.

Eunice and Eiluned had grown nearly big enough to wear their mother's dresses without cutting, but they still went about the house in bare feet to save their shoes and stockings for going out. The blackboard was still cracked across at the top, and with all the lessons chalked on and rubbed off into the minds of the boys and girls since, greyer still than I remembered it, so that the alphabet, which Mrs. Tom always wrote at night for us to copy first thing in the morning, was barely to be seen.

Even the smell was the same, of frying bacon, baking bread, sage in a bunch, the herbs she burnt for Mr. Tom Jenkins' comfort, and chalk, old books, airing washing and mice. It was not the smell of our house, and I was always a stranger to it for it reminded me of the purple head of Mr. Tom Jenkins and his noises.

When Mrs. Tom came in we had prayers, and then a prayer for sending me back to school nothing worse except for thin legs, and then we sang "Let my life be all thanksgiving."

But when we started lessons I had a shock, for there was nothing Mrs. Tom could teach me. All the days I had been in bed I had either read books or listened to Bron or my father and brothers, and hour after hour I had talked with Mr. Gruffydd.

Mrs. Tom tried me with the names of the kings, starting from Canute, but I could go back hundreds of years and tell her of British kings who ruled before Rome became nasty with us. Oceans, seas, continents, islands, countries, rivers, towns, and industries, I knew all of them she asked me, and at last she put down the pointer.

"I had better see your father, Huw," she said. "You are wasting time coming here. Only your sums want a bit of help from me, and I can give you that every night after tea. Go to your dinner now, and stay home."

So back we all went up the Hill, and the boys and girls looking at me as though I knew everything.

Ianto was in the house when I got there and looking very straight. Owen was in the back doing a bit of filing and putting my mother's teeth in brine, and Angharad was peeling apples in the wash-house. When I got a wink from her I knew there was trouble to come, so I went in with Owen.

"O," he said. "You, is it?"

"Yes," I said. "Do you want help?"

"Give this bolt head a scrape," he said. "Can you?"

"Give me the file," I said.

While I filed, Owen was fitting together a lot of parts all new and shining and looking beautiful indeed, when they were fast and whole.

"What is this, Owen?" I asked him.

"An engine," he said, "to drive people instead of a horse and trap. But say nothing."

"No, no," I said. "Why is Ianto looking at the wall in by there?"

"To rest his eyes from the faces of fools," Owen said. "Why are you home so early?"

Then I told him what Mrs. Tom Jenkins had said, and he laughed.

"Right, you," he said. "You shall go to a proper school. It is time, too. No man ever learnt anything from a woman."

"Mrs. Tom has taught me a lot," I said.

"She passed information to you," Owen said. "Figures and names and facts. You have learnt nothing very much. But you have a splendid memory. It will help you when you start to learn."

When my mother called us in the house for dinner, I told her about Mrs. Tom. She was so surprised that she stopped with her spoon in the sprouts and a leaf sticking to the thumb on the plate.

"Eh," she said, with round eyes. "Another worry, now then. School for Huw. Where, then?"

"Technical school," said Davy.

"Boarding school," Owen said.

"All he will learn in that kind of place," Davy said, "is how to look down on his father and mother."

"His Dada shall say," my mother said. "Perhaps Mr. Gruffydd will say a word about it, too."

"Perhaps," Davy said, "this family will do something without the help of Mr. Gruffydd. Not yet, mind. But one day in the future."

"Eat your plateful," my mother said, pointing her fork at Davy. "If we have a friend, Mr. Gruffydd is his name. Not a word about him in this house from anybody."

"He is a good man," Ianto said, "but I wish he was out of the Chapel."

"Did you get a slicing this morning, then?" Davy asked him.

"No," Ianto said. "But I found out how much I have to learn."

"About what?" asked Owen.

"Men," said Ianto, "and the way we live, and treat each other."

"O," said Davy, "that should be interesting. What are Mr. Gruffydd's views?"

"The Sermon on the Mount," said Ianto. "Brought up to date, and given out with a fist on the end of each arm, and a good voice."

"When is he starting?" asked Davy. "I will be there to hear him."

"He started on me at eight o'clock this morning," Ianto said, "and there will be a meeting again on Saturday afternoon."

"Did he have you on the floor?" Davy said, and laughing, though not unkindly.

"Yes," said Ianto. "We disagreed on nothing, except method. I said to start now. He said to wait. The time is not yet."

"I have heard those words before, at any rate," Owen said. "When will it be time? Shall we know? Will it be given for a sign? Did you ask him?"

"No," said Ianto. "I listened. I have a good mind to join the Chapel."

"But, Ianto," my mother said, while we all looked at him, "you are in the Chapel now, boy. Since you were born."

"I mean as a minister, Mama," Ianto said, and put down his knife and fork, and excused himself, and left the house.

"Dear God," my mother whispered, with his boots still on the cobbles. "There is beautiful."

"It would be more beautiful if there were sense and purpose in what he wanted to do," Davy said, and put his knife and fork together, though his dinner was steaming.

"There is plenty to be done outside the pulpit," Owen said, and stopped eating, too.

"If Ianto thinks he can do more from the pulpit," my mother said, "he shall try, and I will help. We can do with a few more like Mr. Gruffydd."

"Mr. Gruyffdd. Mr. Gruffydd. Mr. Gruffydd," Davy said, and pushed back his chair to stand. "I am tired of his name. There are men in the Valley without food in their bellies or boots to their feet. There are children without houses and mothers without hope. What has Mr. Gruffydd to give them? The Sermon on the Mount? God's holy will?"

"For shame, David Morgan," my mother said. "Mr. Gruffydd has collected more for them than a dozen of you. Not another word, now. If you have left the table, go from here."

"I am sorry to leave your pudding, Mama," Owen said, and followed Davy out.

"I suppose I am to look to you for a few words, now?" my mother said to me.

"I will say them after I have had my dinner, Mama," I said.

"O?" said my mother. "Well, let me warn you. One word from you and you shall have a good couple round the ears. Now then."

"Mama," Angharad said, "Mrs. Beynon is having her baby in the old shed down by the ironworks."

"Which baby?" my mother asked.

"The new one she was going to have before they put her from the house," Angharad said, and put gravy over her potatoes.

"Eh," my mother said. "How do you know?"

"Tegwen told me now just," said Angharad eating fast. "I gave her a sheet for tearing and the two old red blankets."

My mother put down her knife and fork and looked at Angharad with her eyes in slits and her lips together and puffed up.

"Do you mean to sit there," she said, very slowly, "with that sheet in pieces and two good blankets gone from the house, without a word from me?"

"They had nothing, Mama," Angharad said, and no sign of fear. "The landlord's men put her from the house with nothing. Not a stick or stitch. And the new baby is coming to-day. Only straw she has to lie on. And the seven other children."

"Hisht, now," my mother said, "I know how many. I

will see to it. But no more sheets and blankets behind my back. I am mistress in this house."

"Yes, Mama," Angharad said, and we had a wink together.

"I suppose," my mother said, as though her mind were over the mountain, "nothing else went with the sheets and blankets? It would be too much to expect of Miss Angharad Morgan, of course?"

"Well, Mama," Angharad said, and so pretty your mouth would run, "there were some old pots and pans out in the back."

"Go on," Mama said. "Pots and pans."

"And some of the boys' old clothes," Angharad counted on her fingers, "and some of Dada's."

"And some of mine," said Mama, in a voice you could barely hear.

"Yes, Mama," said Angharad, "and some of mine. And my cloak."

"Your best cloak, of course," said Mama, in the same voice, and cold in the face.

"Yes, Mama," said Angharad. "I only wear it on Sundays and winter has gone. And they are cold down there with only old straw under them and holes in the roof."

"Just put your eyes round the house," said Mama, in her ordinary voice, "because I am sorry to say there are a few things of ours Mrs. Beynon has missed. But perhaps if we have a cart up here we can put it right. Is it?"

"O, Mama," Angharad said, and her eyes that were so big were bigger now with tears, "poor Tegwen Beynon only had on a dress. Nothing else. And no breakfast this morning. And her poor face so white with her."

"Angharad, my little one," my mother said, and went to put her arms about her, for she had pushed away her dinner and her face was flat upon the table. "Hisht, now. I was angry because I was not asked. Ask in future. Is it?"

"Yes, Mama," Angharad said, and reached out for my handkerchief. "What shall we do for the new baby?"

"Go you and ask Bron for some of little Gareth's baby clothes," my mother said. "I will have a basket of food now in a minute. Huw, go you up and down the Hill with a basket and ask for anything to eat they can spare."

"Yes, Mama," I said.

Well, if you could have seen the collection.

The clothes would have covered a shift in the pit. The

food was enough for the village. And by the time the furniture was all together, two houses would not have held it.

Well, there it was, and no lack of hands to take it down to the old shed at the ironworks, either.

I went down there first with the first basket of food, and indeed it was a poor place.

Mrs. Beynon was lying on one of our old red blankets and another one hanging over her to keep out the water coming in from the roof. Evan Beynon had broken a plank to make a fire, and an old bucket was heating water. Rusty iron wheels, and broken rods of iron were red among the growing grass and dandelions. Puddles were plenty and a rill ran right through to the river. Cold and damp, too.

The three youngest children were sleeping by Mrs. Beynon's feet, and two more little ones were playing shop with stones at the window. Tegwen and her smaller brother were putting straw in sacks to make beds for the night.

"Hulloa, Teg," I said, and stopped by the door, though there was no door.

"Hulloa, Huw," she said, and looked shame. "Putting straw in sacks, we are. The straw do go from under you if you turn in your sleep," she said, trying to make fun.

"Yes, yes," I said, as though I slept on straw every night of my life. "Here is a pie in by here."

"Good," she said. "Mama will be glad of the taste."

"And tea," I said.

"Tea?" said Tegwen. "O, God. Let me have it in the kettle, quick."

"How is Mrs. Beynon?" I asked her, for as far as I could see, she was in pain with her, and mumbling, with froth on her mouth, and red in the face, with sweat binding her hair.

"Mrs. Price will be down now just," Tegwen said, and blowing the fire. "Then she will be better."

"What has Mrs. Price got to do with it?" I asked her.

"Then the new baby will come, boy," Tegwen said, laughing. "That is why Angharad gave me the sheet."

"Does Mrs. Price bring the baby, then?" I asked her, and surprised I was, see.

Tegwen sat down laughing out loud, and then put a hand over her mouth and looked at her mother.

"There is dull you are, boy," she whispered, with lights in her eyes. "The new baby is with Mama, see. But Mrs.

Price do know how to have it from her. Bring cups, quick."

The only cups I could find I would not have drunk from, but Mrs. Beynon drank and drank though with no sign she knew where she was, or what it was she was drinking.

"Where is the new baby, then?" I asked Tegwen, for I could see no signs.

"Are you going to sit fat by there and say you know nothing about new babies?" Tegwen asked me, and looking as though she thought I was a fool.

"No," I said, "we have had new babies at our house and Bron's, but I thought Dr. Richards brought them in his bag."

"Who told you?" Tegwen asked.

"My mother and Bron," I said.

"Lies," Tegwen said.

"How do you know?" I said. "You are only twelve, so you can still do with a lesson or two."

"Lies," Tegwen said. "Wait, you, and you shall see."

"How, then?" I said.

"When Mrs. Price comes, she will send us from here," Tegwen said, "so we will go round the back and look through that hole up by there."

I looked up where she was pointing and saw a piece of wood hanging down from rot. There was darkness at the back.

"Right, you," I said.

Then everybody started to come in with the collections, and all the women were saying O and Eh and clicking their tongues, and taking off their coats to tidy the place, and chop grass, and move iron. Then the men started coming in and knotting ropes to put up canvas over the bad places, and boards over the open window and doorways. Indeed, in a couple of minutes it looked so good I could have lived in there myself.

Mr. Beynon came in and looked for a moment and went outside to cry, and then Mrs. Price came in with a bundle and an elegant bag with patterns on it, made from carpet.

"Now then," she said, with her foot barely inside the door. "Let us be having a couple of you outside, please. All the children, this minute, for a start."

"Come you," Tegwen whispered to me, and off we went, out in the yard, up the steps of the works and inside where the bats were thick in the roof, and flying like angry whispers.

We went close to the hole and looked in.

Mrs. Price had put the smallest children in the bedstead at the side, and the other woman with her was pulling their clothes off. Mrs. Beynon was crying, not quietly, but out loud, like a boy who had fallen and hurt his knee. She was kicking at the clothes and her face was swollen, with veins.

"Poor Mama," Tegwen said, below a breath, "she always has this for a new baby."

It was in my mind to ask why, but it was no business of mine. There was something ugly and cruel in it that I could feel but not describe. Mrs. Beynon was a big, fat woman, always very cheerful, but to see her like that was like being in a dream. I found myself getting hot and having trouble to breathe.

There was a strange smell coming up to us, too. I have often smelt it about the house where a baby has just come. It is a deep smell, an early smell, with the secrets of blood and milk in it, with tenderness and terror.

Mrs. Price went to the fire and brought back the bucket to the bedside. Mrs. Penry had finished the children and had come to stand at Mrs. Beynon's head. Mrs. Price pulled off the blankets as Mrs. Beynon started to scream, and Mrs. Penry was guiding her hands to the wooden rail above the head of the bed. The children awoke and began crying, but nobody took notice of them. Mrs. Beynon's legs were like white stalks, and they made little kicks, and her toes curled in, and her heels dug in the bed. Her mouth was open with shouting and her eyes wide, and wild, and terrible to see upside down as she was to me. Mrs. Price and Mrs. Penry were doing something to her, but what I was not sure, for I could see only their backs beneath there, and the bats were all round us, pulled from sleep by the crying and wailing and sobbing and shrieks, and flying at us as though we were something to do with it.

"There," Tegwen said, in my ear, pulling my arm to be closer to the hole. "There you are, see. The new baby."

But I looked only enough to see a redness in the deepening light, and stained cloths in Mrs. Price's wringing hands above the bucket and Mrs. Beynon's toes set at peace. And I turned away in shame and sickness for I felt I had been where only fools do tread.

"Let me go from here," I said.

"Wait, you," Tegwen said. "There is plenty more to be seen."

"I am going from here this minute," I said, and went on hands and knees to the doorway.

"Do you believe now?" Tegwen said, with laugh in her voice.

"Yes," I said, sick, and looking down the dark steps.

"Tell nobody, mind," Tegwen said. "Else there will be trouble, sure."

"Well, good-bye, now," I said, and went through the yard smart as I could. Savage glad I was to be in the air and feel it freezing me. I felt I deserved more than freezing. I felt I should throw myself over a pit mouth or go under the wheels of a hay wain or get tangled up in the cables of the big winding wheel, so low I did feel.

But instead I went inside Bron's, and sat down in the usual chair. Bron was ironing, and sprinkling water on the stiff white clothes, and spitting on the iron and hitting the table hard to rub a clean shine into the plain parts, and smooth frills in the embroideries.

"Well," she said, "and how is the old man to-night?"

"I have just seen a new baby come to Mrs. Beynon," I said.

Bronwen went on ironing as though she had heard nothing, but her face was flushed, and her eyes were wrinkling as though the heat of the iron was too much.

"How did that happen?" she asked, but quietly and still looking at the washing.

"I was looking through a plank," I said.

"And now you are satisfied?" Bronwen said, and looked up at me.

"Is it true, Bron?" I asked her, and hoping she would say no.

"If you saw what you saw," Bronwen said, "then it must be true."

"Will I get in trouble for knowing it?" I asked her.

"The only trouble you will have is thinking about it and having it on your conscience," Bronwen said. "People who go where they are not wanted will always have trouble. So will those who poke their noses."

"Are you angry with me, Bron?" I asked her.

"Not angry," Bron said. "Only surprised. I thought you were growing up to be a gentleman. But gentlemen never poke their noses. And if they do by accident, they keep it to themselves."

"I wish I had shut my mouth, now," I said. "But I had to say something to somebody. There is terrible it is, Bron."

"Hisht, now," she said. "Have to eat. Are you hungry?"

"Yes," I said.

"Right, you," she said. "Lay the table. I am just going to Mama's for my meat dish."

But I knew she had gone to our house to tell my mother.

There is a funny feeling you will have in you when you know trouble is being made and waiting for you, in a little time to come. It is as though you had an open window below there, and all the fears putting their hands in carelessly, not to hurt, but to make discomfort.

"Mama wants to see you," Bronwen said, when she came back, and without the meat dish.

"You told on me," I said.

"Yes," Bronwen said, "your Mama should know. You came to me but you should have gone to her, first."

"I never thought you would have me in trouble, Bron," I said. "I would never tell on you."

"Go on with you, boy," Bronwen said, half a smile and half a frown. "Nobody has told on you. There is too much weight on that brain of yours and there is nothing I can do to lighten it. Your mother is the one. Have something, and then go home, is it?"

"No," I said. "If there is to be trouble, let me have it now."

So out I went without saying good night, and walked straight in our house and found my mother by herself in the kitchen, darning socks.

"Well," she said, busy, careful to pull a thread,

"Yes, Mama," I said.

The light was in her grey eyes when she looked up at me above the shining needle. There was nothing there to frighten me, yet I was trembling. Nothing to be heard in the house but the clock, and sometimes the resting fire.

"I hear you have been somewhere," my mother said,

"Yes, Mama," I said.

"And you saw something," my mother said.

"Yes, Mama," I said.

"Why?" my mother asked, with ice.

There are some questions that cannot be answered at all, so I looked at her slippers, and hours went by me.

"Do you feel well?" my mother asked me, with a little tremble in her voice that made me feel worse.

"Yes, Mama," I said.

"Dada will have to speak to you," my mother said. "Go to bed, now."

"Yes, Mama," I said, and she held her cheek for me to kiss, and I went to my bed in the back room, thankful to be in the cold darkness. I cannot tell how long I had been asleep when I woke up and found my father looking down at me with the lamp.

"I am sorry I woke you, my son," he said. "I hear you had a bit of trouble to-night?"

"Yes, Dada," I said. "Will I take off my shirt?"

"Stay where you are, boy," my father said, with a smile well on the way. "Not strapping you, I am. Only talking. Are you awake and clear?"

"Yes, Dada," I said.

"Right, then," my father said. "Listen to me. Forget all you saw. Leave it. Take your mind from it. It has nothing to do with you. But use it for experience. Now you know what hurt it brings to women when men come into the world. Remember, and make it up to your Mama and to all women."

"Yes, Dada," I said.

"And another thing let it do," my father said. "There is no room for pride in any man. There is no room for un-kindness. There is no room for wit at the expense of others. All men are born the same, and equal. As you saw to-day, so come the Captains and the Kings and the Tinkers and the Tailors. Let the memory direct your dealings with men and women. And be sure to take good care of Mama. Is it?"

"Yes, Dada," I said.

"God bless you, my son," he said. "Sleep in peace."

I did, indeed.

Chapter Fourteen

THE AFFAIR of the white turkeys will always be clear in my mind because it was the start of the wickedness of old Elias the Shop against us as a family, and it happened when Mr. Gruffydd began the revival.

We kept good hens out in the back. Brown, and white, and some good layers that were black from my father's

sister's. There is happy are hens. All day they peck for
sweet bits in the ground, twice they come for corn, and in
the mornings they shout the roof off to have you to come
and see their eggs. And no trouble to anybody. I do like a
little hen, indeed. A minder of her own business, always,
and very dainty in her walk and ways.

Every year toward June, we had young turkeys from my
mother's brother, and these we made fat for Christmas.
But instead of the usual turkeys this year, Uncle Maldwyn
sent a new kind, white, and lovely fans in their tails, with
pale yellow legs, and bright red combs. White turkeys we
had never seen.

All the village came up to see them and for a few hours
the back was like a fair, and for days farmers used to come
up to see the White Ladies, they were calling them. After
a little, of course, we took no notice of anyone in the
back, and anybody could come up, and just take his time
to look in, and go his way again.

That is how they went one night, without a sign or a
sound.

The hens at any other time would have screeched to have
your teeth out, but so many people had been to see the
turkeys, that I suppose they thought it was usual, and made
it no matter.

Angharad found out, for she always went for the eggs
for breakfast.

She came in running, with her face red, and her eyes
wide, and stood holding the door while my father looked
up from strapping his trews.

"Dada," she said, "the turkeys have gone."

"Gone, girl?" my father said. "Where, then?"

"The door is broken," Angharad said; "and there are
feathers on the ground."

"O," said my father. "Well, let us have breakfast, first.
Then we shall see."

"Will I go for the police?" Davy asked.

"Police?" my father said. "Why should we invite police?
I will be my own police while I have health and strength."

At breakfast we were all quiet, for there was a look in
my father's face we all knew well. Indeed, I would rather
have seen a hundred police than that look.

So we were all taking a good breath when Ivor called for
him to go on the morning shift. It was getting light outside,
so I went out with my brothers to see what could be seen.

There was nothing, only the broken door of the hutch and a couple of white turkey feathers. We stood about the hutch with our hands in our pockets, looking up at the mountain, watching the pheasants.

"Who could have taken them?" Davy said. "Nobody on the Hill, for sure. The best thing is for us to go to every farm in the Valley."

While the boys were away on their long walk, I went down the Hill feeling like a man who has sold his business, for all I had to do was nod to the boys and girls who were on their way to school, and look for things to take my time till dinner.

I went in Tossall's for some toffee, and sat on the bridge to watch Ellis come in with the Post. The river was running very slowly and I could see small trout down by the rocks, so I went down the bank to see if I could reach to tickle a few. Tossall's back garden was on one side, with Dr. Richards' next to it, and on the other side of the river was the public house, Three Bells, and next to that Elias the Shop.

I saw the men carrying the slops from the Three Bell, but Old Elias carried his own buckets, from his back door to the corner of the little lane on the river bank, and went back in, closing the door with a lot of noise because it was old and the bottom scraped on the ground.

This, I thought, was strange, because the men were always saying that Old Elias would never touch the buckets and they always had trouble to fetch them. I wondered why he should bring them out himself this morning, and I heard the men making a joke about it, too.

The fish were half dead when I got closer, and I was sorry enough for them to leave them to die in peace, if peace was to be found in that dirty water, among those stained rocks. So I went up over the bridge again and down the other bank by the side of the Three Bells, walking along till I reached the little lane that led to Old Elias' back door.

On the ground, in the middle of the lane, was a little white feather that might have come from a hen. But the feathers of hens and turkeys are not the same, to those who know hens and turkeys.

This little feather belonged to a white turkey, from underneath his fantail.

The wall of the yard was too high for me to climb, and

my legs were too weak to do it if it had been lower, so I went back to the road, and down to the shop of Old Elias. I had a penny.

The shop was big, with a square window each side, and a double door between that opened with a clashing of bells. The windows were packed full of men's and boys' suits, and boots, and underclothes, and soap, and tea, and pinafores, and women's dresses, and hats, and red cabbage, and ham, and picks and shovels, and grain and chicken food, and cards of combs and boot-laces, with crinkly paper all round the frames, faded and torn, now, with years of hanging there.

In I went with the bells rattling overhead, and bringing Old Elias from behind the counter. He was tall, thin, and bent forward, with a beard all round his face, but no moustache, and hair watered down so that it was darker than the beard. His eyes were not blue or grey, but pale, and they would look to the side of you when he spoke.

He had on a coat that was polished like a grate down the front, and narrow trousers strapped upon his boots. One boot had a little round patch sewn very tidy where the big toenail had rubbed through the cap. Pink and blue were his hands, and the nails long and dug down deep with his pocket-knife, so that they looked like thick, squared claws, with a blackness along the tops.

"Well," he said, looking right past me.

"A pennyworth of liquorice, Mr. Elias, please," I said.

"I saw you chewing down by the bridge, now just," he said. "Did you have toffee from Tossall?"

"Yes," I said.

"And now you are going to put your teeth in liquorice?" he said, still looking past me.

"Yes," I said.

"I will see your father, first," he said. "All this fuss about you is going to your head. Twopence in a morning for sweets is iniquity. Go from the shop this moment."

"Will I have a pennyworth of liquorice first, Mr. Elias?" I asked him.

"No," he said, and making a lot of it, with a frown, and a deep voice, and a fist on the counter. "Go from here, rascal that you are."

"Thank you, Mr. Elias," I said, and out I went.

Up the Hill I ran and into our house to my mother. The

smell of thyme was gentle in the house, for she was stuffing a piece of lamb.

"Mama," I said, "I know where our turkeys are."

"O," she said. "Where, then?"

"In Old Elias the Shop's back," I said.

"Go on with you," she said, "there is silly you are, boy." So out came the feather from my pocket.

"I found this in his back lane," I said, "and it came from under the tail of one of them, Mama."

"The wind blew it," she said, looking at the feather.

"There was a bit of turkey's mess on his boot," I said.

"How do you know?" said my mother.

"I went in the shop," I said.

"What for?" my mother asked.

"Liquorice," I said.

"Where did you have the money?" my mother asked, back at the lamb.

"From Ianto," I said.

"Did you have the liquorice?" my mother asked, picking sage.

"No," I said. "Old Elias said it was iniquity."

"Right, too," said my mother. "Put it in the box."

So I climbed on the chair, and put the penny in the box, feeling very flat.

"We will put the feather in the vase for your Dada," said my mother. "Now go you to the back and put tidy that old mess Owen has made with his tools and wheels. I will tell Ianto how to use his pennies, too. Go you, now. Since when has Old Elias started to save for others, I wonder?"

My brothers came back one by one, nothing gained from their walking round the Valley. I said nothing. I was out in the back with Owen when my father was bathing, and then Mama called us to supper.

"We are going to have a walk afterwards, Huw," my father said to me, with the look on his face and in his voice.

"Yes, Dada," I said.

"Shall we come, too, Dada?" Davy asked him.

"Yes, my son," said my father, "as many as you please."

"Where are we going?" asked Ianto.

"Elias the Shop," said my father, in such a way that we all stopped talking. Nobody spoke again until we were at the foot of the Hill.

"What are you going to see the old——" Davy stopped

himself in time and made a face at Ianto, "Old Elias about, Dada?"

"My turkeys," said my father.

"Turkeys?" Ianto said. "What has he got to do with them?"

"We shall see," said my father. "Ianto and Davy round the back by the river in case there will be a leak through the back door. Owen, go you to the door round the side. Huw, with me to the front."

Two oil lamps and a couple of candles lit the shop and gave Old Elias a new colour to his face. He seemed not surprised, but shaking glad to see my father, though of course he never looked once at him straight.

"O, Mr. Morgan," he said, looking beautiful between me and my father, "the little matter of the penny this morning, is it? I do hope Master Huw have told truth, now. He was down by the bridge there, so happy as a squirrel swinging his poor little legs, and indeed my heart was melt with pity. Toffee he had with him, and I thought, good, he is having some of the sweets of life. Then a moment later, he put his little head in the door and he asks me for a penny stick of liquorice. Well, well, well, I said, Huw, my little one, you had toffee now just. Liquorice on the top? Sick you will be, my son. And your Mama will be angry for you to spend twopence in a day on sweets. Go you, now."

All this came out like sour milk from a tipped jug, quick, and with splashing. His eyes were shining with a smile not a smile, and his mouth open to show small brown teeth spaced apart, pointed, and wet between them. Still he looked between us, but pointing at me.

"I have come about my turkeys," my father said.

Old Elias took a step back and the smile that was not a smile went from his face as water goes into the earth, gently.

"Your turkeys, Mr. Morgan?" he said, with his voice going high and cracking.

"My turkeys," my father said. "This feather was found in your back lane. There is turkey's mess still dried on your boot, by there."

Fair play, I can say that I did see Old Elias look straight at something for once in his life, and that was at his boot heel. Then he put the foot from sight behind the counter.

"Hens," he said, looking above us, now.

"Then you will allow me to see your back yard, Mr. Elias," said my father.

Old Elias slipped into the opening of the counter, and still looking up, pointed up.

"Nobody is to go by there," he said, as a man says his prayers in Chapel, "only except me."

"Make way," said my father. "Huw, stay here."

"Yes, Dada," I said.

"I will have the English law on you," said Old Elias, in a woman's high voice, with tears in his eyes.

"To hell with the English law," said my father, and took Old Elias by the front of his coat, and threw him into the apple barrel, and went through the back.

Old Elias kicked and struggled to be out, but he was stuck fast. He could not speak, his temper was so great and the effort he made to have his voice made his movements weak. The barrel was at an angle, resting on blocks, but with a bit of kicking and rolling from side to side, it slipped slowly, then faster, and Old Elias, with his bottom stuck fast in the mouth, turned over and over again as it fell off its supports and rolled down the shop, with the apples rumbling inside, and some falling out over his shoulders and between his legs, while he cried like a wounded hare, and fell out down by the biscuit cask, sitting up untidy, with his fists clenched and beating his chest.

There is strange that you will detest a man in one moment, and then the next you will feel so sorry, you will go to him to help him, and ready to kiss him quiet.

So I felt for Old Elias, then.

But I had no chance to put my feelings in practice, for in a moment he was on his feet and making for the back, picking up an axe handle on his way. I skipped behind some bales of cloth until he had gone, and then went to the door to shout for Davy and Ianto. I heard them shout back, then I ran to see where my father was.

Through the back passage, full of boxes and sacks, into the back room, full of boxes and sacks and paper and bits of old furniture, and through the little glass-house full of boxes and sacks and broken flower-pots, out to the yard, and there was Old Elias holding his nose, and blood coming out between his fingers, and the axe handle in two pieces on the floor, and my father with a turkey back to front under each arm with his hands about their legs.

With the evening going to night, and a good blue sky,

and candle light coming through the little side window to
shine on them, the turkeys looked very white against my
father's black suit. But if his face was shadowed, I will
swear I could see flame from my father's eyes. For moments he looked at Old Elias, and no words came.

And Old Elias was too full to speak. To be found out in
theft, and a deacon well respected, and to be rolled with
his bottom in an apple barrel, and then a good hit on the
nose, is enough to dry the words in any man. A lovely
smell of candied peel and currants and sultanas and spice
and mint, and earth from the greenhouse there was, there,
too.

My brothers came running through the shop with enough
noise to be heard in the next world, and came to stop still
by me.

"Well, Mr. Elias," my father said, "this is your last night
in this Valley."

Old Elias took his hands from his nose and beat them together and bloody drops flew about him.

"There will be a reckoning," he said, with thickness.
"There will be a reckoning. I took them from you for a
punishment. Your heart was swollen with pride in owning
them. You were coming to be a son of Satan. You would
have had them back in proper season. Now there will be
a reckoning."

"The reckoning is paid on my side," said my father, "but
to-night is the last time you will open this shop. For if you
open your doors to-morrow, I will burn it about you."

"O," said Old Elias, moving from one foot to the other,
eyes shut and fists making little circles up by his shoulders.
"O. O. O."

"Come, my sons," said my father, "another eyeful of him
and I will be sick of my food for weeks to come."

"I was going to my shop over the mountain," Old Elias
screamed, in a whisper to hurt the throat, turning quickly
as my father moved. His face came in the light. Still his
eyes, open wide, and wet with red rage, looked between
us all, nose shiny in its new size, and his mouth spilling
spit and bloody bubbles. "Over there I was going, or to
my shop in the next valley, or the other in the valley beyond that, or the other in Town. I have got shops. I have
got shops. Shops. I was going to the next valley. I was
leaving this den of thieves, and robbers, and murderers. I
was going over the mountain."

"Go you," said my father, a bit surprised at Old Elias, for such raging, and so quiet I have never seen in any man. Near to madness, it was, and discomforting. Rage can be a cleanser, but this one would make the most righteous feel in the wrong to be the cause of it, so inhuman and so unclean.

"And I will do as I promised," Old Elias whispered in a scream, when we went through the back. "I will have the English law on you."

"Well," said my father, "you have had a bit of Welsh law to-night, for a change. I will be glad to see what will English law do in return. And remember. Closed doors to-morrow."

We heard him hitting his fists against the thick back door as we went out through the shop and crying in the back of his throat.

"Eh, dear," my father sighed, when we were outside and walking up the Hill, "there is terrible, indeed. He could have had the old turkeys if he had asked."

"Let me carry one, Dada," Ianto said.

"No," my father said. "All the people on the Hill shall see me with them. Then if there is trouble, it will come to me and not to you. Him and his English law.

All the way up the Hill people looked and wished my father good night, but nobody asked questions. It was enough for them to know that the turkeys were home again. They could find out where they had been later.

Mr. Gruffydd was in the house when we got in, so that was more shock to us. My father went round the back to hutch the turkeys, so he came in after, to a silence.

"Good evening, Mr. Gruffydd," he said, and went to the mantel for his pipe.

"Good evening to you, Mr. Morgan," Mr. Gruffydd said. "I hear you have had trouble with Mr. Elias?"

"Bad news has good legs," said my father.

"It is all over the Valley," Mr. Gruffydd said.

"The trouble is finished," my father said.

"He stole your turkeys?" Mr. Gruffydd said, and watched the smoke from my father's pipe.

"The turkeys are in the hutch outside," my father said. "Is there anything to be done for you, Mr. Gruffydd?"

Mr. Gruffydd was quiet for a moment or two and then he started to laugh. It started in the depths of his chest and slowly rose until he was shouting laughing. Well, of course, when we had finished to be surprised, we started to smile first, then our cheeks went fat with laughter trying to get out, and then we laughed, too. We were in stitches. Nobody knew why. Mr. Gruffydd kept trying to say, but laughter would catch up with him, and off he would go again.

Then Ianto, with tears, would point to his nose, then at my father and make a weak little punch, and that would start us all off again. Laughter is foolish to think about, but good to have.

"Mr. Gruffydd," my mother said, "have to eat."

"Thank you," said Mr. Gruffydd. "Indeed I will. To-morrow night, I shall be speaking on the Chapel field down by the river, Mr. Morgan. I hope I shall see you beside me?"

"Well," my father said, and very pleased and surprised, too, "thank you, Mr. Gruffydd. I will be glad, indeed. What is the subject, sir?"

"The bringing of men closer to the spirit of God," said Mr. Gruffydd.

"I punched a man's nose to-night," said my father.

"I know a few more that would be the better for it," said Mr. Gruffydd. "And if things are not better very soon, I will go out of my way to deal a few in person, too."

"Good," said my father. "I will be with you to-morrow night, sir. Eat, now. Eat plenty."

. . . .

The Chapel field was where Mr. Gruffydd baptized those who were ready. Along the river it was, outside the village, and in that day a little paradise, with the river so clear and broadly green, and silver about the rocks, and willows bending to wash, and reeds in plenty for the frogs, and fish for the herons, and quiet for the ducks and little water-hens.

Everybody went that way on Saturday for Mr. Gruffydd's meeting. There was a crowd in front of us, and a crowd behind. Up the mountain side we went and turned down for the gate leading to the field. There was a big crowd outside, and their voice came up like the low note of the north wind. When we got to them we saw why. There was a notice nailed on a board, and it said that the landlord had left the district and withheld permission, hitherto given, for meetings of any description.

The landlord had signed his name Abishai Elias.

The crowd wanted to go in, never mind the notice, but

Mr. Gruffydd refused to set foot beyond the gateway. So we all walked a little farther up the mountain, and there Mr. Gruffydd found a place to stand where we could all see him, and spoke until the sun went, and evening put a coldness upon us. But if we were chilled outside, we were well warmed within from the heat of his discourse, and we walked home fast as well, to have the blood full pitch in us.

He wanted to start his fight that evening down at the baptizing place, he said, because it seemed a fitting meeting place for crusaders. Wickedness was creeping into the Valley without halt or check. Thieves there were, and vagabonds, and drunkards by the score, and even bad women.

"Before you are much older," he shouted, and his voice was running in a ring all round the Valley, "you will have policemen here to stay. A magistrate next. Then perhaps even a jail. And the counterparts of those things are hunger and want, and misery and idleness. The night is coming. Watch and pray."

"Amen," said the people, soft and deep.

"How shall we fight?" Mr. Gruffydd asked us. "How? It is simple. Men lose their birthrights for a mess of pottage only if they stop using the gifts given them by God for their betterment. By prayer. That is the first and greatest gift. Use the gift of prayer. Ask for strength of mind, and a clear vision. Then sense. Use your sense. Not all of us are born for greatness, but all of us have sense. Make use of it. Think. Think long and well. By prayer and good thought you will conquer all enemies. And your greatest enemy now is coal. You must become stronger than coal. Coal is lifeless, but to subtle men it lives in the form of gold. To you it is so many trams at so much a ton. To others it is so many shiploads, so many credit notes, so many loans, investments, interests. Your enemy is usury. And the usurer takes no heed of men, or their lives, or their dependants' lives. Behold, the night is coming. Prepare, for the time is at hand."

He went through the history of the Valley and spoke to them of the steady fall in wages, and their willingness to work for less and less, while others who had nothing to do with coal, but handled only paper, or owned the land above the workings, took more and more.

"You must fight," he said. "Fight. Fight now."

"Tell us what to do," men were shouting. "Show us a way."

"Elect men to Parliament," Mr. Gruffydd told them. "Gain for yourselves representation. Then form a society among yourselves. Elect a body of officers to tabulate your wrongs and give them authority to approach the chief men in the coal trade and in the Government. Do all things with order."

"Mr. Gruffydd," shouted Mr. Rhys, a check-weighman with my father, "are you coming outside your position in life? Your business is spiritual."

"My business," shouted Mr. Gruffydd, in a voice that made us jump, "is anything that comes between men and the spirit of God."

"Amen," said the crowd.

"Let it not be forgotten," said Mr. Gruffydd, in the same voice and waving the people quiet, "that the Lord Jesus drove the money-changers from the Temple, not only because they profaned that holy place, but also because they were corrupting the people, who were too simple to see how they were being cheated, and by degrees, poisoned, till they were in their own way corrupt as their masters."

"Now then for you," said Ianto to Davy, and Bronwen gave my hand a squeeze. "There is how to talk to them. Sense."

There was more talk then, and shouting, but Mr. Gruffydd said the women would be cold if the meeting went longer, so after a prayer and a good hymn we went back home singing.

Even Ivor and my father were ready to work with the boys, and that had never happened before. Indeed, when Gwilym came over after tea, he was so surprised he stood looking in at the door.

"Come on, my son," my father said. "Sit you by here, now. You can take the message to the men on your side."

"What is this, then?" Gwilym asked, looking all round us, Ianto, Davy, and Owen with pen and ink, my father with a board and chalk, and Ivor with a ruler. Angharad and my mother were in Bron's, fitting a dress on Ceridwen.

Owen told him, while my father wrote a notice of a meeting to be held at the Three Bells a couple of nights later. Ianto, Davy, and Owen were writing notices to be sent to every colliery in the district, for the men to turn out in force. Then we all took copies of the notice to take to the pits we had chosen, and my father took Mr. Boswell's *Life of Dr. Johnson* from the shelf and read a couple of chapters aloud, and passed it round for us to read in turn.

There is good were those nights, indeed.

Chapter Fifteen

HAPPY we were then, for we had a good house, and good food, and good work. There was nothing to do outside at night, except chapel, or choir, or penny-readings, sometimes. But even so, we always found plenty to do until bedtime, for if we were not studying or reading, then we were making something out in the back, or over the mountain singing somewhere. I can remember no time when there was not plenty to be done.

I wonder what has happened in fifty years to change it all. I can remember nothing, except death, to account for it. Gaslight, when it came, made people want to read less, for comfort perhaps, and electric light sent them to bed earlier because it was dearer. But when did people stop being friends with their mothers and fathers, and itching to be out of the house, and going mad for other things to do, I cannot think. It is like an asthma, that comes on a man quickly. He has no notion how he had it, but there it is, and nothing to cure it.

Dear little house that I have lived in, there is happiness you have seen, even before I was born. In you is my life, and all the people I have loved are a part of you, so to go out of you, and leave you, is to leave myself.

That great black bully who presses upon you with such hurt will soon cover you. Your windows will break, and your doors, and slag will fill your rooms. Your roof may fall, and this room and the others may become filled with slag. But you will stand upright inside, with the slag behind, above, and beyond you, but you will never fall. You shall be buried, but you will never fall.

Ceridwen stood in that doorway by there, with her new dress tight about her shoulders, and her face laughing among her long hair hanging down, bending forward to do up the fastenings at the back, and struggling to reach.

"Come you, Huw," she said, pretending to be halfway to crying, "do these old things up for me. Tight it is, see."

How soft, warm, pale, the skin, and touched with the light, not flashing, not even shining, but as though polished soft, and then breathed on with half of half a breath.

"Ceridwen," my mother was shouting, downstairs, "you will be late, girl."

"O, dammo," Ceridwen said, and struggled again. "Hurry up, boy. There is slow."

"Keep still, then," I said to her for when she moved, all I had done up came loose again. "Like an old eel in the pocket you are."

"Right, you," she said. "So an eel I am, is it? No present from Town for you, now."

"Right," I said, and stopped working. "No present, no dress done up. So now for you."

"O, Huw, my little one," she said, all eyes and soft voice, and laugh tears, "nasty you are to your sister. You will have me late and then no Town and no bottom drawer, and Dada will be angry and Blethyn will marry someone else. Come you, now, is it?"

"Will I have a present from Town, then?" I said.

"O, God, boy," Ceridwen said, making claws at me, "nine old presents you have said. But put me in this old dress before I will jump from that window."

And the dress was done up, and downstairs we went, to see her go off with my mother and father with Thomas the Carrier to catch the train to Town.

"Another one off," Davy said, when we were waving to them down the Hill.

"When is it your turn?" Owen asked him.

"Yes," Ianto said, "while there is still something left in the box."

"O," Davy said, "plenty of time."

"Bring her home, man," Ianto said. "Are you afraid one of us will take her?"

"One of you?" Davy said, and pushed back his hat to laugh. "Just for that, I will have her home here on Saturday."

"By damn," Ianto shouted, "I knew well he had a girl, see. There is an old devil, keeping quiet. Roll him down the bank, boys."

But Davy had too long a start and they had no chance. That was the first I knew of Davy having a girl.

But it was no wonder when we saw her.

Ceridwen came home with my father and mother on Saturday afternoon, full of parcels, and talk of Town, and the railway, and the sea, but everybody was talking so much, all at the same time, nobody had a good listen, ex-

cept me to a lot of old noise and words piled up on one another.

Blethyn Llywarch was a good size and fair looking, with
a broken nose from fighting and black hair in a mop that
got in his eyes when he was excited. He was shy at first,
and blushing when he was near Ceridwen, but she was cool
as a stream up the mountain, pushing his tie, and patting
his handkerchief and putting the flaps straight on his pockets, but his hair was too high for her to reach.

My father was trying to make him sit back in his chair
instead of having a bit of himself on the edge, and my
mother got a him a cup of tea and took the spoon away
after he had dropped it twice and splashed his good trews.
Everybody trying to think of something to say, not to be
rude, and our faces with smiles so tight as to be stitched.

In came Davy and Ethelwyn on top of it.

Well.

Wyn we called her from the start, see. Nothing else to
be done with a girl like that. Brown eyes she had, big, with
eyelashes that touched her brows, and a smile in her voice,
and looking to Davy as to a brother of God.

There is a big family we were that night. My father and
mother, Ivor and Bronwen, Ianto, Davy and Wyn, Owen,
Gwilym, Ceridwen and Blethyn, Angharad and me, and
little Olwen upstairs and sleeping these hours, and Mr.
Gruffydd, and old Mrs. Rowlands the Villa, who was
managing his lodgings for him, Mr. Evans from the colliery
and more who called and went. I did so much washing up
that night, because Ceridwen was out in the back with
Blethyn, I never wanted to see another old pot while I lived.

"Good God," Angharad said, with impatience and a
stamp on the wet stone, "are they using six plates for
every bit of devil-ridden food they are stuffing in their old
bellies, out by there?"

"Down on the floor I will put them," Gwilym said, for
the sink was crowded. "Nearly finished they have, now.
Have heart, girl."

"Heart?" Angharad said, and nearly crying in temper.
"Fifty pairs of hands, a new sink and dry feet is what I
want, not heart. Tell them in by there to take their old
snouts from the trough before I will come in and push
the rest down their gullets with the poker."

Wash and wipe, wash and wipe, plates and dishes and
knives and forks and spoons and basins and cups. More

kettles to boil for more hot water. More steam, more soda, more wash and wipe, more wet on the floor. Wash and wipe. Dear, dear, there is glad I was that night that I was born a boy. A man will never know a woman until he knows her work. Wash and wipe, hot water and soda, kettles and saucepans, heat and steam, and always the water.

At last we finished, and Angharad threw the last wet dish-cloth over the line.

"Let us go out up the mountain, Huw," she said, and there is surprised I was.

"What for?" I asked her. "Let us go in by there now, and listen to the talk."

"Talk," she said, and her eyes were dull with contempt. "I have had enough for one day. Come on up the mountain where we shall be quiet. Talk? I would be looking at their old mouths and thinking how many platefuls that one took in it. Come, you."

So up the mountain we went, and sat on the branch of a big oak that the storm had pulled off. There is beautiful to watch a mountain sleeping, and other mountains in the other valleys rising up like bits of blue velvet to make you feel you could cut a piece and wear it for a coat, to dance in above the fat clouds.

We had been there only a minute or two and then somebody came up toward us, a man, and whistling as though he expected to meet somebody. Right, too, for Angharad got up quickly and ran headlong down to meet him.

Young Iestyn Evans, son of Christmas Evans the Colliery, it was with her. He had just left Oxford University and a proper swell, and starting with his father. There is surprised I was.

"Iestyn," Angharad said, "this is Huw."

"Hulloa, Huw," Iestyn said, in an English manner. "It is very kind of you to bring your sister to meet me."

"I knew nothing about you or I should have stayed at home," I said. "And if my father knew Angharad was meeting you, he would strangle her."

"For shame, Huw Morgan," Angharad said, but still on Iestyn's arm, "only meeting for a moment, I am."

"The moment has gone these minutes," I said, "come you home."

"Wait," Iestyn said, "and I will come with you."

"If you do," I said, "my father will know about this meeting. Better for you to call after Chapel to-morrow."

"How old is this Daniel?" Iestyn asked Angharad.

"Fourteen, I think he is," Angharad said. "Not old enough to give orders. Come. Let us go to the top of the mountain."

"I am going home this minute," I said.

"Wait," said Iestyn.

"I am too young to give orders, perhaps," I said, "but too old to take orders from you."

"There is a mean old thing you are," Angharad said, and almost crying, this time properly. "Only a minute."

"Home, me," I said, and started down the mountain.

"Huw," she called. "Wait. I am coming."

So I waited, and I heard them kiss, and then Angharad caught up with me and home we went.

"What is the matter with you?" she asked me, and there is a temper for you. "I could kill you. Five minutes would have been no harm."

"That is what Meillyn Lewis might have said," I told her.

"Huw," she said, with her face white and her eyes black and her hair blowing about her, and her cloak like a witch's in coils with the wind, "you would say that to me?"

"I would rather say it now than after," I said. "Why does he want to see you up the mountain? Why not come home?"

"I hate you," she said, and wrapped her cloak round her so that she was a black pillar, with a white face and her eyes with glitter and shine to make you afraid.

"See if he asks Dada after Chapel to-morrow," I said. "Then you shall start."

But she was running down the path, and I was too unsteady to catch up with her, so when I got in the house, she was making tea for them all as though nothing had been amiss.

They were all talking about the Unions when I got in, and Mr. Evans looking very black indeed.

"I pay my men well," he said. "The best wages in all the valleys they have from me and always have."

"But your colliery is only a small one," Mr. Gruffydd said, "and the rest of them think differently from you. And they pay differently, too. That is the evil. You manage your own colliery. But others are managed by paid servants with the owners interested only in the profits. Rich, lazy lordlings and greedy shareholders are our enemies."

"And middle-men," said Davy.

"Keir Hardie says the mines should belong to the people," said Ianto. "Like the Post Office."

"Hyndman says the land should all belong to the people," Davy said, "and I am with him."

"Marx has always said so," Owen said.

"I am not in favour of anything put up by a lot of old foreigners," my father said. "Owain Glyndwr said all there is to be said for this country hundreds of years ago. Wales for the Welsh. More of him and less of Mr. Marx, please."

"The peoples of all countries should own their countries," said Mr. Gruffydd. "This world was created for Mankind, not for some of mankind."

"It is a good job some of us have done something with what land we have got, whatever," Mr. Evans said, still sour. "Enterprise is in the individual, not in the mob."

"Then let enterprising individuals pay rental to the mob," said Mr. Gruffydd, "and the mob will be that much better off. It is money that enables men to come from the mob by education, and the purchase of books, and schools. When the mob is properly schooled, it will be a less a mob and more of a body of respectable, self-disciplined, and self-creative citizens."

"We have come off the Unions now, properly," said Mr. Evans.

"The Unions are only part of a whole," Mr. Gruffydd said. "Let the Unions become engines for the working people to right their wrongs. Not benefit societies, or burial clubs. Let the Unions become civilian regiments to fight in the cause of people."

"We are trying to join the Social Democratic Federation, now," Davy said.

"Have you got members in this Valley for a Union, yet?" Mr. Gruffydd asked him, and looking at his pipe.

"Only a few," Davy said, and went a bit red in the lamplight.

"Have a strong Union of your own first," said Mr. Gruffydd, "then you can join fine sounds and names."

"The sliding scales are stopping us," Owen said. "They are not even wanting to join the Miners' Federation because of it."

"They are fools," Mr. Gruffydd said. "Tell them so and tell them why."

"You do it," Ianto said. "I had a try last week."

"I have other work to do," Mr. Gruffydd said, and got

up. "You do it, and when you have done it, you will find that my work has met yours, like forks in a road. Then we shall help one another."

"That meeting last week showed," my father said, and helped Mr. Gruffydd with his coat. "With the sliding scale the men know they have got something to work for and take home. The women are behind them and that is their strength."

"If more coal is sold at a cheaper price," Mr. Gruffydd said, "wages will go down. The cheaper the selling price, the less the wages, and the more the selling price, the more the wages. That is sliding scale, and it's working, is it? Now think, knowing your enemies, what could be done by using a little guile. Has coal gone up? No. And not likely to till your sliding scale is thrown aside and a fair living standard adopted as a basis for a working wage. Not only by the miner but every other working man in the country. Good night to you, Mr. Morgan, and good night, boys."

When they had all been seen off down the Hill, the boys came back very quiet indeed and stood about the fire.

"Well, Dada," Ivor said, "what shall we do? I kept my mouth shut by there, but I wanted to tell old Evans, the old hypocrite."

"Is this our Ivor?" Owen said, looking at him and pretending to be fainting. "Never."

"Who put the pepper into you?" Davy said.

"Nobody, man," Ivor said. "Do you think I have been living and working here with my eyes fast shut? Old Evans only pays a few pence more because he knows the men would work at an easier pit if not. A fine one to talk."

"How about having a crusade on our own?" Davy said. "We can take a valley each. After work."

"After whose work?" Ivor asked him. "You and Ianto and Owen are gentlemen of ease."

"We are starting work in the colliery on Monday," Davy said. "We went down this afternoon. We will pay our way, Dada."

"There was no need for that, boys," my father said. "This is your home and there is no question of paying."

"And live off the box?" Owen said. "No, indeed. I can do my work after I have been to the pit."

"What about the crusade?" Davy said.

"To-morrow is Sunday," said my father. "We will speak

more on Monday. Quiet to bed, now, or you will wake
Mama. Then you will have another crusade."

There is good it was to walk to Chapel on a Sunday
morning when the sun was shining, everybody in Sunday
clothes and polished boots.

All the people on the Hill started about the same time,
and you would hear nothing for a long time but Good-
Mornings and How-Are-You-This-Mornings all the way
down to the road at the bottom, all the men taking off their
hats, and the women nodding their bonnets and the boys
touching their caps and the girls dropping a knee.

Our family started with me and little Olwen, walking
now, with her little hand in mine and very important with
Owen and Angharad behind, then Davy and Ceridwen,
then Ianto with little Gareth, and Ivor and Bron behind,
with my father and mother last. The Tribe of Morgan my
father called us, but there were lots of other families as
big, and many bigger, that we met on the way, and knew
well, of course.

We used to walk quietly for a bit till we were out of the
houses of the village, and then my father or mother started
a hymn softly, and the girls caught up with their parts,
Angharad and Bron in contralto, Ceridwen in soprano, and
then the boys all came in, and you heard the echo running
to catch up, all over the Valley.

Beautiful were the days that are gone, and O, for them
to be back. The mountain was green, and proud with a
good covering of oak and ash, and washing his feet in a
streaming river clear as the eyes of God. The winds came
down with the scents of the grass and wild flowers, putting
a sweetness to our noses, and taking away so that nobody
could tell what beauty had been stolen, only that the winds
were old robbers who took something from each grass and
flower and gave it back again, and gave a little to each of
us, and took it away again.

And as we all climbed the mountain side to the Chapel,
there was Mr. Gruffydd, big and strong with the blackness
of his beard gone gold in the sun, waiting for us, and
everyone starting to sing the same hymn, from those nearest the Chapel to those down at the bottom of the mountain, and to listen, you might think the mountain himself
was in song with him.

The Chapel always smelt the same, of wax, for the woodwork in the gallery and the big seat and pews and pulpit,

of soap and water for the stones, of paint a bit, and of hymn books, and camphor from the best suits and dresses, and of people, and of smoke from the wood in the stove.

But when you were near Bron, there was only lavender. My mother always made rose water from the wild roses of the mountain, and though it was a lovely smell, it kept close to her. The girls used it, too, and little Olwen was drowned in it. But Bron was lavender, and three away from her, you could tell Bron. It was faint, so faint as a baby's breath, yet there.

We had two pews, one behind the other, and my place was just in front of Bron's in the back, so I was always with lavender, and thankful. I could never have a liking for old camphor, and just in front of me was old Mrs. John, who must have bathed and cooked food in it, so strong it was with her.

My father went up to sit in the big seat with the other deacons, and then one of them would choose a hymn, while Mr. Gruffydd was coming in with the last of the people.

Sing, then. Sing, indeed, with shoulders back, and head up so that song might go to the roof and beyond to the sky. Mass on mass of tone, with a hard edge, and rich with quality, every single note a carpet of colour woven from basso profundo, and basso, and baritone, and alto, and tenor, and soprano, and alto and mezzo, and contralto, singing and singing, until life and all things living are become a song.

O, Voice of Man, organ of most lovely might.

When Mr. Gruffydd started his sermon, he always put a few sheets of paper on the ledge by the Bible, but never once was he seen to use them. He started to speak as though he were talking to a family, quietly, in a voice not loud, not soft. But presently you would hear a note coming into it and your hair would go cold at the back. It would drop down and down, until you could hear what he said only from the shapes of his mouth, but then he would throw a rock of sound into the quiet and bring your blood splashing up inside you, and keep it boiling for minutes while the royal thunder of his voice proclaimed again the Kingdom of God, and the Principality of Christ the Man.

That is how we came from Chapel every Sunday re-armed and re-armoured against the world, re-strengthened, and full of fight. As we came, so we went back home, but now some of the elders would stop to talk outside the Chapel, especially those living far apart, with the mountain between their homes, and the children would go to talk together, too. So there might be a crowd of people outside the Chapel, all talking, with laughing going on, with black bowler hats and top-hats nodding and bonnets with feathers bobbing, and the crowded black clothes and white linen very plain against the green of the mountain and the grey of the Chapel.

Back home, we had time to eat dinner in our house or Bron's, and then off to Sunday School at the Chapel again, Angharad, Ceridwen, Owen, Davy, Ianto, and me. Going to Sunday School was not so serious as going to Chapel, so we could join the other boys and girls on the way, and pick flowers, or nuts and berries for our favourites to eat on the sly in school. I had no favourite, then, neither was I the favourite with anybody. That came later. But we always had a few sweets in the pocket. Sunday School was very flat, indeed, without a sweet or two when teacher was looking in the book.

Who was outside the Chapel when we got there, but Iestyn Evans, very smart, with a buttonhole. That was wrong, for a start, on a Sunday, but I thought it looked very good, indeed, and I have worn many a hundred since. There is good to have a little flower so near to you, good colour and good smell, too.

"Hulloa, Angharad," he said, the fool, with Owen and Davy and Ianto right behind her.

"Who are you talking to?" Ianto said, and stopped, white in the face and pale in the eye, quiet, with a small shake in his voice. Murder, to anybody with sense.

"Angharad," Iestyn said. "Your sister, perhaps?"

I was looking at the face of Angharad, but from the side of my eye I saw Davy's fist flash in the sun and heard the fat click of it meeting Iestyn's jaw. When I looked he was falling backwards, flat, out.

"You devil," Angharad screamed, and went to claw, but Owen and Davy took her by the arms and dragged her inside the lobby and shut the door on her.

"There is a swine for you," Ianto said.

"What shall we do with him?" Davy said. "Throw him in the river?"

"London tricks," Ianto said, looking at his knuckles. "He

must be taught. Leave him there for everybody to see."

"If Dada hears about this," Owen said, "he will have it out of Angharad."

"Say nothing," Ianto said. "She knows what will happen if there is more of it."

We went through the quiet, big-eyed crowd and Owen opened the door, Angharad was crying under the notice board, and Ceridwen trying to hush.

"I will not allow my sister to be treated like a pit-woman," Ianto said to Angharad, but so quietly that only a few could hear. "Next time, if there is a next time, I will kill him. If he wants to speak to you, let him ask permission. We have a home and he knows well where it is. Now go in to Sunday School."

The text for the lesson that afternoon was "Love ye one another," and when it was read, everybody was looking at Ianto over their books, but only when he was not looking up. Mrs. Talfan must have chosen it on purpose, because when she read it, she stopped and looked straight at Ianto, and then to each of us about him. But we all looked up at her as though there was nothing behind it, so her score was nothing.

After Sunday School we always had a play on the mountain, the boys chasing the girls, or the other way about, or Red Indians among the boys only if there were no grown-up people near us. But that afternoon we went straight home.

And there was Mr. Evans and Iestyn, with my father and mother and Iestyn pale, with a swelling round his chin.

"Did you hit Iestyn Evans?" my father said to Ianto.

"Yes, Dada," Ianto said, and put his hands behind him.

"Outside the Chapel, on such a day?" my father said.

"That was where he was," Ianto said. "Buttonhole and all."

"I will have you in Court, young man," Mr. Evans said, and went to get up, but Iestyn stopped him.

"Doubtless you had a reason," he said to Ianto, but speaking as though Ianto were four foot the shorter.

"Doubtless," Ianto said. "And doubtless I will break your back if I will have another reason."

"Ianto," my father said, "why did you hit him?"

"Let him tell you, Dada," Ianto said.

"I spoke to your daughter, Angharad," Iestyn said.

"O?" said my father, "and how do you come to speak to my daughter?"

"Well," said Iestyn, and there is surprised was his father, "I have seen her several times."

"Did seeing her give you the right to speak to her?" my father asked him.

"This is a civilized community," Iestyn said. "We are not brute beasts."

"That is because there are men here who use their fists," my father said. "If you had spoken to her in my hearing, you would have had worse."

"Gwilym," my mother said, and looking with her teeth in her lip at Mr. Evans' face.

"Hisht, girl," said my father. "There is too much of this slack talking done."

"I was coming here with Angharad after Sunday School," Iestyn said.

"There is kind," said my father. "We are honoured, indeed."

"Look here, now, Gwilym," Old Evans said. "I knew nothing of the girl. I only knew there had been a fight. I will have back what I said of your son, for if a man spoke to Iestyn's sister, there would be murder done again. I will shake hands with you, Ianto, my son."

"Thank you, Mr. Evans," Ianto said.

"Now, where is the girl?" said Old Evans. "Let us see the bone these two dogs have lost hair over."

"She is upstairs," said my mother, "and she will be down tomorrow morning, not before."

"There it is," said Old Evans, and got up to go. "No malice anywhere, is it?"

"None," said my father.

"I will call to ask your permission to-morrow evening, Mr. Morgan," Iestyn said.

"Good," my father said. "I will wait for you."

Mr. Evans gave my father a wink and a little punch as he went, and Iestyn shook hands with Ianto, but an unhappy little shake, like boxers touching hands.

"Iestyn Evans and Angharad," my mother said, and looking in the fire to dream. "Too young."

"How old were you when we were married?" my father said, with his hand over his mouth not to laugh.

"Much older, boy," my mother said.

"Go on with you, girl," said my father. "You were younger still than Angharad. A good cup of tea now, quick. Nobody is too young to be married. That is a law. Where is the tea with you, girl?"

After that, there was nowhere in the house to go without coming in to black looks from Angharad and Iestyn, or Ceridwen and Blethyn, and sometimes Davy and Wyn when he brought her over to us, instead of staying at her house over the mountain.

So I spent a lot of time with Owen in the back, trying to make his engine go. There is a noise the old thing made. But it did go at last, and that was a night of nights, indeed.

It was a long way from our house to Gwilym's and with little Olwen, and the meals for my father and the boys on different shifts, my mother had plenty to do all day and little strength left for walking, though she went over sometimes twice a week.

Extra tired one afternoon, she asked me to take them the basket, so off I went, down the Hill, and round into the flat of the Valley, along the path by the river.

I have never liked that road since.

That way, I had to pass the two heaps of slag that had grown and grown till they looked half as big as the mountain. Even grass was growing in some places, as though to take pity on us and cover the ugliness of them. The river running between was drying up, so sick it was of the struggle to keep clean, and small blame to it.

Farther on, past the last of the cottages, green grass grew again, and happy it was to see a flower growing after all the brute sadness, though the river was still running black and the plants and reeds dead and dying on both banks.

Up the mountain it was better, and on the top it was good to look back and see all the filth hidden behind trees and blackberry bushes, even though I knew it was still there.

Gwilym's house was the end one in a row on the other side of the mountain from us, a tidy little house, but open to the weather, and the winds had choir practice whenever they could on every side of it. There was washing hanging when I got there, so I felt it and found it dry, and gathered it in to take inside with me.

The house was in uproars. Gwilym's bath water was still in front of the fire, dirty from last night. Pots were on the table for at least three meals. The floor was brittle with coal dust from Gwil's boots and clothes, and furniture was everywhere except the right place.

So I set to work and emptied the bath, and put on water for Gwil's fresh bath, washed the floor, washed the pots, lit the fires, peeled potatoes and pulled a cabbage from the garden, and went next door to have a bit of meat for Gwil's supper.

The woman next door was very civil, and gave me a shoulder of lamb, with a lesson in cooking, as though I had watched my mother and Bron for more than two years for nothing. She asked no questions and I told her nothing, though I knew she was losing years keeping it back.

When the lamb was in the oven, I went upstairs to see if I could do something to the beds. Just the same upstairs as down, so I made the double bed, and I was just putting the windows up when I heard a noise in the second room. It was going from evening to night and not a lamp alight in the house, and I have never been a great one for noises in darkness.

I waited a bit, and I heard it again. A little laugh, it was, not very loud, but clear.

Now lamps were going yellow down in the Valley, and the sky was smoking blue, with the trees black in it, and the wind singing flat, and going loud, and then dropping away.

There is funny to have your feet fast to the floor in fear. You can see and hear and think so well that it will hurt. But you cannot move. There is a force outside yourself which makes you stand still, and it will take a grinding of teeth and tears to the eyes to turn against it.

One step at a time I went to the door of the second room on the little landing, though how I got there I will never know. There is a spirit greater than you, always within reach of you, but he only comes to take charge when your own spirit is lost, and cries out in his own tongue, which you cannot know but only feel, and it is in feeling that you will have orders. Yet not even in feeling, for I felt nothing, only surprise that I was going forward. I heard no voice, I felt no hand, yet I was at the door, knocking, and wondering how I had come by there, and then I opened it to look in.

Marged was sitting over in the corner by the window, and looking at me with the light from outside touching the wet of her eyes and mouth.

The room was just like our back, with the same sort of bench and vice, all the tools in racks, with a hay-cutter on the side, and sacks of potatoes and seed piled along the wall, and onions and hams and leeks hanging up. Even beams had been nailed up, the same number and the same colour as ours, though there was no need of them, only to make the room more exactly like our back.

Marged stayed still, just looking, with her hands in her lap and her feet flat on the floor, going back into the darkness with every moment, and the wind blowing tin trumpets round the house.

"Owen," she said, from the black corner, and laughed again. "You have come then?"

"No, Marged," I said, and indeed I sounded very loud even to me. "Huw, this is, see. I have put Gwil's bath for him, and a bit of lamb to cook. Now I will go back."

"No," she said, and moved. "You shall never go from me again. I have waited too long."

"But, Marged," I said, "it is dark, girl, and a long way to go over the mountain."

"You shall stay," she said, and stood, and I saw her black shape against the window, reaching over to the tool rack. "I will have you with me. I will have you in pieces and hang you on hooks, is it?"

I saw the light on a tool, white in her hand.

"Come you," she was whispering. "Long I have waited in this old place in the cold and now I shall be warm. Come and kiss me, Owen, come and kiss. Kiss your Marged. Never leave me again, is it?"

And in between her words were whisperings, and noises. I waited till she was so near that I could feel the warmth of her fingers on my face, and then quickly I pulled the door shut. Kick and scream from her, then, and digging at the door with the tool. Down the stairs I went, and ran to have my cap from the kitchen, and off through the back door and up the mountain.

But when I looked back in the darkness, I could see the pale mark of her apron running up the path after me, so quietly that the breathing of the trees was louder. I stopped dead, with my legs like bars screwed to the ground, and then she screamed, and that seemed to have them free, and I turned and ran.

I ran through bushes, and round rocks, and through bushes and over rocks, and through grass and ploughed land, through briars and over hedges, I ran and I ran and the breath gone before taken, until my legs were dragging along the ground and my mouth wide to the sky, the air red about me and sickness inside me. Up on the top of the mountain I fell flat, face down to the cold short grass, with sheep at peace near me, looking up as I ran, but going back to crop as I fell.

And in a little while the sheep looked up again, but this time they ran down the other side, and Marged came up over the edge, slowly, holding her chest with both hands, and I could hear her breathing, like a tearing of sacks, and walking as though she had drunk too much. She went to the rock and leaned against it, and hit her head against it and the wind brought the sound to me, with her crying, and hit, hit, hit, with her head against the rock.

Trembling I was, but with tiredness, when I went to her, and pulled her away. She was bent from the waist and hitting herself by ducking her head into the rock, but as I pulled her she fell and I beside her.

"Owen," she was saying, "Owen."

"Hisht, you," I said to her. "Sleep, is it? Sleep, now. Owen will come in a minute, yes?"

"If he will come, yes," she said, and indeed, she slept, not good sleep, but as one dead.

In the Valley it was pitch black, with only a light from the farm. The moon was on us, but not yet high enough to see over the mountain. I knew well we would perish of cold if we were there much longer, so I covered Marged as far as I could, and then made a start to light a fire with twigs. In a few minutes I had a fire roaring by the rock and giving good heat, too, so I pulled Marged where she would have warmth, and started back to Gwil's for help.

Half-way down in the darkness of trees I heard her screaming again, but it only made me travel faster, and farther down by the first lot of rocks I saw Gwilym with some men carrying lanterns, all beating the briars, and some of them pushing the lamps under the hedges. I shouted until I was almost into them, but the wind was out of me, and Gwilym dropped his lantern to run and meet me when the other men shouted.

He and most of them started up the mountain ahead, with me on the shoulders of a big collier who was straight from the pit, no bath, black, and smelling of coal and strong tobacco. We were at the top almost as soon as the others, because I knew the way, and Gwil and his men came up on the wrong side of the rock, and had to run all the way round to where the fire was burning.

Up over the edge and out on the flat we ran, and across to the fire. The two men who were there first started to shout and ran into showers of sparks, beating with their caps and jumping back again. Gwil came round and stopped, staring, and then screamed, and ran to go in the flames, but the other men held him away, and they fought with him to hold him down.

More men were all round the fire trying to stamp it out and getting in my way. Then they stood clear of the heat as we came closer, and I could see.

Marged was lying in the fire, and burning, with smoke.

I slipped from the collier's shoulders and looked away, up at the sky, and down in the dark of the Valley. Behind me the shouts, and Gwil crying, and a bubbling among the snapping of burning wood, and boots stamping the ground, and the wind humming to the fire.

I walked away, in no hurry, but just walking, down the path and home, thinking nothing and seeing little. I went in round the back, in the quiet, and saw the light where Owen was working, and went in to him. His face was wet with sweat, but his eyes were bright with smiles as he looked up at me, and back to the engine.

"Come on, boy," he said, "missing the best of it, you are, man. Give me the number three, now, quick."

I gave him the tool from its place in the rack and thought of poor Marged and started to cry, but Owen was too busy on the engine to notice.

"Now, then," he said, "you prime her, and I will start her. Huw, my little one, you are helping to make history. Hold on, now."

He put the crank handle in, and I stood above the funnel, with the tin of spirit ready to pour in.

"Right, you," he said.

In I poured the spirit, and tears dropped with it, but Owen was winding and winding, with the engine waking up at every turn. And now it fired, and fired again, and Owen turned no longer but pulled the handle clear, and looked as though to make it run by his will. Quick as quick the firing came until it was in a storm of firing, shaking the place under my feet, making me clench my jaws.

The engine was going. After years, it was going.

Owen looked and looked and then threw the crank to the roof and started to dance with his knees bent high, shouting, but barely to be heard.

The door slammed back and my father came in with his eyes wide, going from Owen to the engine, and my mother and Bron behind with some of the people next door, all surprised and some of them afraid, speechless in the noise. My father looked at me, smiling, but I was crying and nothing would stop me.

I could see Marged so plain in the fire.

My mother ran across to me, pushing Owen and telling him to stop the engine, and my father lifted me over the heat of it, and carried me into the kitchen. But my mother took me from him and held me in her lap by the fire, and I felt her strength about me and her kiss upon my forehead, and her voice with love.

"There, my little one," she was saying, "too far for you with that big basket. Your Dada was coming to look for you, now just. And there you were in that old place making all that noise, and your Mama worried in case you were lost on the mountain."

"Mama," I said, with tears nothing would stop, "Marged is burning."

My mother looked up at my father and his eyes changed.

"What is that you are saying, my son?" he said, and came to kneel by me.

"Marged is burning," I said, "and they have got Gwil on the ground, crying."

"O, God," my mother said, "go you, Gwil, quickly. Owen, go for the boys to follow Dada. Angharad, go you for the doctor."

Then I had broth, and went to sleep.

For weeks our house was quiet. Owen and Gwil went away, nobody knew where, and my mother was worried pale for them. The doctor came and wrote down what I told him of that night, and that was the last I heard of it. Marged was never spoken of in the house after that, but I often thought of her.

School for me came up one night, when my father had come back in the house after looking at Owen's engine, still in the back, but kept clean and shining by me.

"If you were able to go to Town every day," he said to me, "you would go to school to-morrow morning. Wasting your time on a machine like that."

"Where is the boy to go?" my mother said. "Weeks, now, I have been asking, but no notice."

"He shall go over the mountain to the National School," my father said, "till the one is built here. Not very far for him and much better than hanging about the house."

"National School?" my mother said. "No son of mine is going to a National School. There is a thing to say."

"Then where is the boy going?" my father asked her. "The others could walk and look after themselves, and no trouble."

"Are you going to blame him for his weakness?" my mother said, "because if you are, you had better say it to me, first."

"Go on, girl," my father said. "Not that, I meant. If he is not going over the mountain, where is he going?"

"Has he got to go to school?" my mother said.

"Well, Beth," my father said, and standing up as though strangers were in the house, "how will he make a way for himself without good schooling?"

"There is something about the National School I will never like," my mother said, "but if that is all there is, very well. National School."

So next morning Bron took me over the mountain to the National School. The way we went was not one we took often, and in all my life before I had only been in that valley twice, for it was where the iron works were, with even more dirt over there than on our side.

The town over there was getting bigger every day, and rows upon rows of houses were building, and plenty were being lived in without a road or even a good path to them. Public houses were on every corner, almost, and most of them full even so early as we were, but there were some tidy little chapels in building and built, so somebody was awake over there. Bron liked the look of the shops, and so did I, for they were bigger, and more in them than the little couple we had, so we had a walk round before we went to find the school.

Chapter Sixteen

GOING IN TO A NEW SCHOOL is a lot worse than drawing teeth, I am sure. That morning I would have given anything to grow wings and be a dragon fly, or anything without a tongue and hands. But Bron was with me so I could do nothing only follow behind, past the yellow-rick, long, low, big-narrow-windowed school building to the doors, and go in to the dark with her. Inside it smelt of chalk.

Mr. Motshill was English, a tall man, thin in the leg, high of collar, and with long fair whiskers on both sides of his face, and a bald head, and no moustache.

He came out of his room as we went in.

"Are you looking for someone?" he asked her, in English, and as though his throat had a cord about it pulled tight.

"Yes," Bron said, "this is my brother-in-law. His parents want him to join the school here."

Then Mr. Motshill asked questions. Who was my father, and what did he do, how much could he afford, and things like that. Bron answered civil with a face like a white cloud, but I knew that if she had caught my eye we would have shouted laughing like fools, and that would have settled school.

"Well, Master Morgan," Mr. Motshill said to me, with a big lump of my cheek between his fingers and thumb, and bending over me so that I could smell the snuff on him, "shall we take you?"

"Yes, sir," I said.

"Very well," he said. "To-morrow morning, with copies of references, fees, and fees to cover books, and bring pencils and pens with you. You will be examined as to the present state of your education, and remanded for a class. Fourteen eighteens?"

His face flew down at me and his voice blew in my ears. His eyes were big near mine and his glasses made them smaller. A lot of little red paths in them, too.

There was no sense in a question like that, for we had played figures ever since I could remember, and the tables I had known almost from the time I could walk.

So I told him, and he stood up, but slowly.

"Yes," he said, as though he had made a discovery, "yes. But say it in English, you understand. You are to instruct his parents," he said to Bron, "that he must on no account be allowed to speak that jargon in or out of school. English, please, at all times. Good morning."

And off he went, leaving Bron and me in the hall. From down at the far room, children were chanting arithmetic tables in a sing-song. I could tell where they were from the sound and length of it. Bron looked down the hall at Mr. Motshill going round the corner, and turned about sharp, walking out and slamming the doors in a stamping temper.

"What is the matter, Bron?" I asked her.

"You heard what he said, boy," Bron said, "to speak in English. What will your Dada say? You shall never go to that school. You shall see."

"More trouble in the house, now then," I said.

"What trouble, boy?" Bron asked me, in the middle of the street, and people looking at her because she was lovely.

"Mama and Dada," I said. "Dada will say no school, and Mama will say you and your old National School, and I will still be about the house all day. But if nothing is said about speaking English, I can go to school and nobody wiser, and Mama and Dada in peace, see."

Bron looked down at me with her hands on her hips, then looking at her shoe, and then at me.

"Right you, old man," Bron said, and gave me a kiss. "School, then. But if you let that old slug by there make you speak English when you want to speak Welsh, tell me. That is all. Just tell me."

"What will you do?" I said, to see her face.

"Do?" Bron said, and her mouth came together and her eyes went to slits. "I will put him upside down on his old desk and hit the flap on his old head."

"Good," I said, and we were laughing, to think of his thin legs waving, "let us have toffee, is it?"

So up the mountain we went back home with our faces swollen with toffee we used to have, called stickjaw, and laughing loud at nothing very much because the sun was shining and we were happy.

The rest of the day I was going up and down for references, one from Mr. Evans the Colliery, one from Dr. Richards, one from Mr. Silas Owen, solicitor, and one from Mr. Gruffydd.

"Well, Huw," Mr. Gruffydd said, "to school at last, then?"

"Yes, Mr. Gruffydd," I said.

"Good," he said, "and learn. Learn anything. Here is a pencil-box for you. It was mine and my father's, and his father's. Go you, now, because I am busy. But come you to-morrow night and tell me about the first day, is it?"

"Yes, Mr. Gruffydd," I said, and took the letter home, with the pencil-box in front of me. There is a beautiful box it was, too.

About eighteen inches long, and three wide, with a top

that slid off, and a piece cut out for your thumb to press it through the groove. On the top tray, three lovely red pencils, new, and without the marks of teeth, with sharp points, and two pens green, with brass holders for nibs, and at the end a little pit for a piece of rubber. The top tray was fast on a pivot, and you pushed it round to come to the second tray, with five more lovely pencils, three yellows, and a red and a blue. Under that one, another then, with dividers, a compass, a ruler, a box for nibs and drawing-pins, a couple of ivory angles, a drawing pen, and crayons. And all so good you wished it had more trays again underneath. Nothing so pretty as good pencils, and I do think the feel of a long pencil in your fingers is as good to the taste as something to eat.

That night Mrs. Tom Jenkins came up to give me a polish in sums, written and mental. My father and mother, Ivor and Bron, and Davy were all round the table listening, and everybody quiet, pretending not to look.

We were doing very well, up to the kind of sum when a bath is filling at the rate of so many gallons and two holes are letting the water out, and please to say how long will it take to fill the bath, when my mother put down the socks she was darning and clicked her tongue in impatience.

"What is the matter?" my father asked her.

"That old National School," my mother said. "There is silly the sums are with them. Filling up an old bath with holes in it, indeed. Who would be such a fool?"

"A sum it is, girl," my father said. "A sum. A problem for the mind. Nothing to do with the National School, either."

"Filling the boy with old nonsense," Mama said.

"Not nonsense, Beth," my father said, to soothe, quietly, "a sum, it is. The water pours in and takes so long. It pours out and takes so long. How long to fill? That is all."

"But who would pour water in an old bath with holes?" my mother said. "Who would think to do it, but a lunatic?"

"Well, devil fly off," my father said, and put down his book to look at the ceiling. "It is to see if the boy can calculate, girl. Figures, nothing else. How many gallons and how long."

"In a bath full of holes," Mama said, and rolled the sock in a ball and threw it in the basket, and it fell out, and she threw it back in twice as hard. "If he went to school in trews full of holes, we should hear about it. But an old bath can be so full with holes as a sieve and nobody taking notice."

"Look you," my father said to Mrs. Jenkins, "no more baths. Have you got something else?"

"Decimals, Mr. Morgan," said Mrs. Tom, "but he is strong in those."

"Decimals," said my father, "and peace in my house, for the love of God."

"Hisht," Mama said.

Decimals, then. And the look on my mother's face when the decimal point started his travels up and down the line was something to see.

In bed that night I heard my mother come upstairs and speak to Angharad, and then my father came up with the lamp, and left their door open a bit to hear the clock.

"Gwil," my mother said, "who is in charge of this decimal point?"

"Who?" my father said, and flap went his braces on the cupboard door.

"Decimal point," my mother said, "this thing Huw has got downstairs."

"More of this again, now," my father said, and laugh strong in his voice. "Look, Beth, my little one, leave it, now. Or else it will be morning and us fit for Bedlam, both."

"But what is it?" my mother said. "Why is a small boy allowed to know and I am such a fool?"

"Beth, Beth, Beth," my father said, "bless your sweet face, there are things for boys and things for girls. Decimal point makes fractions out of a whole. Instead of saying one and a half, you say one point five. Because five is half of ten, a one and a nought. The one is a whole one and nought is nothing. Now you are wiser."

Minutes went, and only the sound of clothes coming off and somebody late walking up the hill outside.

"But whose is it?" my mother said, as though a gate had been loosed. "Does it belong to somebody?"

"Well, Beth," my father said, "there is silly. Why should it belong to somebody? It is a decimal point, a dot on the paper. How can an ink dot belong to somebody?"

"Then who knows what is to be done with it?" my mother asked. "Multiply by ten, move the point, add a nought."

"No, girl," Dada said, "not add a nought. That is division. Multiplying, move the point down. Dividing, move the point up."

"Go on with you," Mama said, "it can stop where it is. I would like to know who found it out, anyhow."

"The French, I think," my father said, "and leave it now, will you?"

"Well, no wonder," my mother said, and glad to blame someone, see. "Those old Frenchies, is it? If I had known that, the book would never have come inside the house."

"O, Beth," said Dada, "there is an old beauty you are. Go now, before I will push you on the floor."

"Frenchie, indeed," my mother said, "and decimal points, move up and down. Like monkeys. With Frenchies and old baths full of holes, what will come to the boy?"

"A scholarship," said my father, "that is what I would like."

"Scholarship? Well, I hope so, indeed," my mother said, for the sound of the word was like the name of an anthem. "What the world is coming to, I cannot tell you."

"Sleep, now then," my father said, "not for you to worry about the world, is it? Think of the old Queen with a Jubilee of worry to think about, and be thankful."

"I wonder does she know about this decimal point?" my mother said.

"Oh, hell open and crack," said my father, and out went the lamp. "The poor old lady is asleep these hours. Let us follow. Good night, now."

"Go and scratch," said Mama.

I started off to school at a quarter to seven next morning with my pencil-box and books in a bag on my back, and a tin box full of food to swing in my hand. Up the mountain with a little rain to wet my face, but most of the wind held back by the trees until I got to the top, and then it could have blown me all the way down again.

The town looked even worse than it had, with big grey clouds hanging down between the tops of the mountains, and a mist dragging across the roof-tops, and yellow smoke from the furnaces thick over there. The school I could see easily, with three long roofs of slate among all the houses, and a few trees near it. And the river running grey with dirt, and the rocks in it black.

The streets were quiet, only a few traps and wains out, and a milk wagon going to the station with all the churns grumbling together as they bumped on the cobbles.

School, then.

A few boys were playing in the yard when I got there, but I waited until they had run down to the other end before I went in the door. The same smell of chalk, that I hate to this day, and quiet. So I went all round the hall to look at the pictures, some painted, but most of them drawn and painted by scholars, and very good, too, and the roll of honour with names in gold.

The door opened, and I learned how Mr. Motshill opened doors, by kicking first with the toe, and then pushing with the shoulder, a double bump, one loud, one softer, because he saw little.

"Well," he said, when he saw me, "what is it?"

"I have come to join school," I said.

"Speak English," he said. "What is it you want?"

"To join school," I said, in English.

"Much better," said Mr. Motshill. "You were here yesterday, were you not?"

"Yes," I said, "and here are my references."

"Sit there until I send for you," he said, and I sat.

The bell was rung outside for some minutes, and teachers began to come in, shaking rain from their coats and hats, and nodding to one another, not speaking because of the bell, five men, two women, and both the women old and thin, in black. The boys and girls came in by two and two, and lined up with their backs to me, but plenty turned to have a look at me, some of the boys to pull faces, and a couple to laugh and dig the one next to them to turn round to me and laugh too.

Mr. Motshill came from his room to stand on the platform where one of the women was sitting by the piano. He stood looking at them for a moment, very solemn, and then put his hand to his face, with some of his fingers round his jaw, and his first finger upright between his eyebrows.

"Let us pray," he said, in that voice of his, but on a higher note like tragic poetry. "Our Father," he started, and the children all said the prayer with him, most of them making their own time, and Mr. Motshill raising his voice at the start of each line to over-ride them and have them with him. But no use. They were well in front at the end, and some had opened their eyes before he was at Glory be.

He opened his eyes and looked up, pious and with feeling.

"Let us lift our voices in a hymn," he said, and turned to nod his head to Miss Cash, shutting his eyes on the downward bend, and opening them coming up, all slow, and as though he was hurting with goodness. Miss Cash nodded too, at the piano, and lifted her hands to play, with her fingers stretched and the little ones a bit crooked, and touched a couple of bass chords, with two notes sour, and one missed.

"O," sang Mr. Motshill, in a couple of keys, and then sliding to find the note, "Ah. Take your note, Ah."

"Ah," sang the boys and girls, with mouths like buttonholes, no tone, no depth, and no heart.

"Rock of ages cleft for me," sang Mr. Motshill and Miss Cash played any notes near her fingers, and pulled a face for every note wrong, while the boys and girls rambled at will.

"To your classrooms," said Mr. Motshill, "dismiss."

Some lines turned one way, some another, and all tramping hard on the floor and glad to make noise, the classes marched out. Mr. Motshill stood until the last were almost gone, and then got down to go to his room. But half-way there he seemed to remember me, and turned.

"Come along, come along," he said. "You will be given a paper by Mr. Tyser, and then we shall know exactly what to do with you."

Big bump, little bump, through another door, and into a classroom. Mr. Tyser always looked tired. A good little man, no harm in him, but at wits' end in dealing with noisy fools of boys.

"Mr. Tyser," said Mr. Motshill, "this is Morgan. I have already had to check him for using Welsh. Give him the senior paper and see what he can do with it."

"Yes, sir," said Mr. Tyser. "Come along, Morgan. Sit here."

I sat and quickly got up to pull a bent pen-nib out of myself. The boys behind were looking blank at the blackboard, with their arms folded, pictures, indeed.

"Did you put this here?" I asked one of them.

Red as summer roses Mervyn Phillips looked at me, and James Herriot looked, too.

"Did you speak, Morgan?" Mr. Tyser asked, with surprise.

"Yes," I said.

"Kindly use the English tongue in future," said Mr. Tyser, "or there will be trouble."

"I will see you in the playground," Mervyn Phillips whispered to me. "I will punch your head from your shoulders."

"Right, you," I said.

Mr. Tyser gave me the papers, one arithmetic, one grammar and composition, one religion, and a history and geography, and I took out my pencils and books, and made a lovely show on top of the desk.

If they had put silk ribbons about those papers they could have done me no greater favour, for I waltzed through, and it was good indeed to see the pleasure in Mr. Tyser's face when he looked through them.

"You write a beautiful hand, Morgan," he said. "Who has been teaching you before this?"

"Mrs. Tom Jenkins," I said, and everybody had a little laugh into their hands, that sort of laugh that makes you want to take burning iron and put in their eyes. "And my brothers and my sisters-in-law."

"It is a great pity," Mr. Tyser said, "that Mrs. Tom Jenkins was not invited to direct the education of some of these young ladies and gentlemen. What did Mrs. Jenkins do if you were lazy and rude, Morgan?"

"The strap," I said, "and no dinner, and a note home."

"Come with me," he said, and I went.

Outside he put his hand on my shoulder and looked down at me.

"You are not a cripple, are you, Morgan?" he asked, and very kind.

"No," I said. "Thin about the legs, I am, but not a cripple."

"I am very glad," he said. "Come along."

Down to Mr. Motshill's room, knock at the door, and Mr. Motshill saying to come, and inside to a bare room, with grey light coming in on a table piled with papers and books, books on shelves and on the floor, and a couple of scratched leather chairs with bow legs, and a picture of the Queen as a young woman, very pretty, with a small crown and lace. And Mr. Motshill just come from sleep and tasting his mouth, and finding it little to his liking.

"Mr. Motshill," Mr. Tyser said, but so different, as though he were afraid for his life, in a little bit of a voice, and not looking up at all, "I am afraid Morgan is too advanced for Standard Four. Standard Six is the lowest possible standard, sir, if you will permit me to say so."

"Show me the papers," said Mr. Motshill, and reached across to snatch them away, looking at them with flicks of the eyes from side to side, and turning over the pages in haste so that they were torn at the top.

"New brooms sweep clean," he said to me. "Standard Six, then. Take him to Mr. Jonas."

"Thank you, sir," Mr. Tyser said, and we went out.

"Shall I get my pencil-box and books?" I asked him.

"Get them by all means," Mr. Tyser said, as different again, "and when you come out, knock on the next door but one, there."

I went in to Standard Four room and across to my desk, looking at nobody, but they were looking at me in that quiet that seems to stretch, when you know something has happened to concern you.

There was my desk, shifted a bit, and the two boys who had been sitting on the end gone now to sit in the desk in front, and the sun looking his brightest through the window and alive on the desk top to show me why.

My pencil-box was in three pieces. The pencils were all cut, and dirty with grit from rolling on the floor. Ink was on my books, and wet in the grooves of the box. Drawing pen, ruler, nibs, pens, all broken or chipped, and dirty.

I know well the feeling of murder.

It is hot, too hot to keep inside, and it rises to the head, and burns as it goes, making the throat dry, so that breath comes in jerks and with a low noise. Trembling takes you, and the eyes fill, but not with tears, and a cloud comes before your sight, and in the darkness there is a torment to take flesh in the fingers and tear until the blood spurts, or to take a knife and plunge until the point blunts, or to take a weapon and smash until strength has gone, to pound, to stab, to strangle, to pulp, to kill, kill, kill. O, I know well the feeling.

But soon comes a calm, and though you tremble still, there is no more room inside for more feeling. You live as one dead, and for no good reason you want to cry.

And as I looked at my little box, I tried hard to hold the tears, I prayed to hold the tears, but the dear little box with scratches on the patterned lid and ink and grit all over it, and all its riches in ruins, one by one I saw them bleeding their own blood with unjust wounds, and I cried for them.

There is a terrible feeling when your head is in your arms and your knees sharp on the floor, and sob, sob, sob, and laughing going on all round you. You call yourself names, you are so shamed that you feel sight should be taken from you, yet there you kneel, and the more names you call yourself, the more shame you feel, the worse becomes the sobbing, until you are not sure whether your tears are in sorrow at what has happened to you, or rage at yourself for being such a fool.

And then the tears stop. Not a drop more would come if knives were put in you.

So I picked up the broken trays and tried to fit them together. There was no harm in that little box. A hundred years before, a craftsman in wood had put love into his job for all men to see in that little pattern of grained woods on the lid and round the sides. There was no need for him to spend those hours, for the box was made, but that pattern was his kiss of love, and I could see his hands passing over its smoothness, feeling its weight, having joy from the look and feel of it, and slow to let it pass into the hands of a buyer. I could see Mr. Gruffydd's grandfather having it, and passing it to his son, and then Mr. Gruffydd himself, and I knew how they had felt for it, for so I felt myself.

Solomon never felt for his storehouse as I felt for that little box, and three men before me. To have pens, and pencils, and the tools of writing all your own, to see them and feel them in your fingers ready to do anything you tell them, to have them in a little house fit for them as good friends of yours, such is sweet pleasure, indeed, and never ending. For you open gently and take what you want, and careful in closing again, and you look at it before you start your work, and all the time a happy fullness inside you that sometimes will make you put out your hand to touch it as though to bless, so good you feel with it. God bless the craftsmen who give their fellow men such feelings even out of pieces of wood.

I dried the ink on the books and inside the box, knowing well what my mother would say to my handkerchief, but careless, and put them back in my bag and went to the door. Still they were laughing, but not in comfort, for they feared I was going to tell. Hard it is to suffer through stupid people. They make you feel sorry for them, and if your sorrow is as great as your hurt, you will allow them to go

free of punishment, for their eyes are the eyes of dogs that
have done wrong and know it, and are afraid.

"I will fight you all one by one," I said, "but nobody will
be told about this."

"Go now," Mervyn Phillips said, "before I will empty
red ink on you."

"No matter," I said, "I will fight you all, and you first."

Outside I went, and Mr. Tyser was standing in the door
of Standard Six, talking to Mr. Elijah Jonas-Sessions, but
Mr. Jonas for short in school, and him I saw with my heart
falling inside me.

Sandy coming to ginger was Mr. Jonas, and small and
pale in the eyes, with that look in them to warn you he had
the tongue of a mountain adder, to be careful in what you
said, or he would twist every word of it for you.

"What a long time you took, Morgan," Mr. Tyser said.

"Perhaps he is used to taking his time," said Mr. Jonas,
and smiling with his lips going back over his teeth to look
as though he had nothing in his mouth but tongue. He
spoke English with pain, making his words to sound more
English than the English. Pity it is that a beautiful
language should be at the mercy of such. Dr. Samuel
Johnson would have had a word to say to him, and I told
him so, but that was later.

"Have you been crying, Morgan?" Mr. Tyser asked me.

"Yes," I said, "but no matter."

"What a dirty little sweep it is," Mr. Jonas said, still
smiling, and pulling from my pocket my handkerchief
all ink and dust.

"It was clean when I came from the house this morning,"
I said, and pulled it from him. "The dirt is from that room
in by there."

"You will address me as sir," said Mr. Jonas with no
smile, "or I will put a stick about you. Inside and sit down,
on the instant."

And as I passed he made a slap at my head but I ducked
and went to my place in the fourth row where a boy had
moved up for me.

Mr. Jonas closed the door and came to stand in front of
me.

"We have with us an intellectual giant," he said, still
looking at me and smiling as the boys and girls smiled with
him, "so we must all bend the knee. We shall now presume
to test his knowledge in algebra, and on the result we shall

know whether we may live in the same room with him, or petition the Commons for a special building."

Plenty of the boys and some of the girls made no sign they had heard, but most of them tried to laugh more than the joke was worth to try and keep on the credit side of that tongue.

Four quadratic equations he gave me, but Mr. Gruffydd and Davy had drilled me too well. They were simple to me. But Mr. Jonas never lost his smile.

"A model scholar," he said, and looking closely at the book. "But your books are in a dreadful state, and your hands are filthy. If you are thinking of becoming a scholar at this school you will have to adopt a more civilized way of living. You must tell your mother that if you arrive in such a state to-morrow morning you will be sent home. Your dirty coal mining ways are not wanted here."

From that moment I was the enemy of Mr. Elijah Jonas-Sessions. There was nothing he could teach me, for my mind was against him, and all he taught. I answered him nothing, but I looked.

"Insolence will gain you nothing," he said, and threw the book down to bend the corners. "Pay attention to what I say, and write 'civilization is the highest aim of human kind' one hundred times before you leave to-day."

And while he taught the others algebra, I sat.

For nearly a year, I sat.

His voice passed over me like the voice of the wind at a school-treat, there, but never noticed.

I sat.

There was a break at eleven o'clock, and we all went out to the playground to eat what we had brought with us. As soon as I came from the door, Mervyn Phillips pulled me by the arm.

"Fight me, will you?" he said, and the others all round us. "Come you, then."

He was a head above me, and big, the son of a coal merchant in the town, used to lifting sacks, and strong because of it.

But it was not a fight we had, for there were too many boys about us and no room. It was like a bad scrum, with the hookers missing. I had two good punches at him, and he had one at me on the side of the head, but then the weight of them pulled me down and there was nothing I could do in the press but guard my head from their boots.

What would have happened I cannot tell, but I felt it all stop and the boys easing and standing away, and when I stood up against the wall, Mr. Motshill was looking at me from a side window.

"Which boy started on you, Morgan?" he said. "I will make an example of him. There shall be no ruffians in this school."

"I said I would fight them," I said.

"Oh," he said, "Mr. Jonas told me you were inclined to the rougher style of living. Understand me, then. If I catch you fighting anywhere near the boundaries of this school, I shall thrash you and expel you. As for you others," he said to the boys, "kindly remember that you attend here to qualify for responsible positions in life. You are the self-respecting citizens of the future. Remember it, and revise your conduct accordingly."

It was a good job for me that Ellis the Post was in the Square when I came from school, outside the hotel where my mother had told me to wait for him, or I would have been rolled in the mud. He cracked his whip above them, and snapped the lash in rings on the ground while I climbed up on the driver's seat, not another breath in me.

"These town boys are like little rats," said Ellis, coming up and taking the reins, "never one to one, but always a hundred and more to one. Why did they chase you?"

"New boy," I said.

"We will see about it," Ellis said. "They would have killed you, man."

"Say nothing," I said, "or my mother will be worried and more trouble, then."

"Right," he said, "but I will wait for you every night by there, is it?"

So every night, except for a few times, I went with Ellis the Post round the long way home, on the road that ran round the mountain and followed the river. Lovely it was to sit behind Mari the mare, and breathe the smells of the mountain, and greet people in the road, and wave to people in the houses, sometimes stopping to give them a letter or a parcel, or a bit of news, for of course Ellis knew all that went on in and out of the Valley.

When I got home that night I went in Bron's first, to wash my face and hands, but nothing would take the bruises from cheeks and eyes, and a cut lip is a cut lip. Bron was out and so was Ivor so I was spared to tell a second tale.

When I came in my mother put her hands to her face and looked at me with a scream in her eyes, but nothing came from her mouth.

"What have you done, boy?" Angharad said, looking closer and trying to feel. "Are you hurting?"

"I fell on the mountain," I said. "No hurt, only stiff."

"Go to the doctor with him," my mother said. "Fighting, not mountain, him. Wait till his father sees him."

"Shall I have tea first?" I asked her. "Not hurt I am, only touched."

"National School," said my mother. "Wait till I see your father, only just you wait."

"I only want a poultice, Mama," I said, "but I would like a cup of tea first."

"A cup of tea you shall have, my little one," my mother said, and took my hot face in her hands, with her thumbs over my eyes, cool, and making plain the heat of blood under my skin. "How many fists made these marks? Your brothers were always in fights, but not one of them had a face like this. Go down to Bowen and ask him for a piece of steak with the blood in it, Angharad."

Then Bron came in and screamed, and ran to put her arms about me.

"Huw, my little one," she said, and crying, "who was it? Tell me and I will strangle him. I will go down now and strangle him."

"Wait till his father comes in," my mother said, and nearly crying, too, "I will tell him. National Schools."

And down went the poker with a noise to send the cat from the house, belly to floor and the white tip of his tail like a shooting star.

There is good a cup of tea is when you are feeling low. Thin, and plenty of milk, and brown sugar in the crystal, in a big cup so that when your mouth is used to the heat you can drink instead of sipping. Every part of you inside you that seems to have gone to sleep comes lively again. A good friend of mine is a cup of tea, indeed.

When Angharad came back with the steak, Bron put it on and tied it in place with a cloth, and I went out in the back to give Owen's engine a clean. So I was from the house when my father came back, but not so far that I missed my mother's voice. Then the back door opened.

"Huw," my father said, "come you here, my son."

He was black from the colliery, so Angharad took off the cloth and he held the lamp to see my face.

"One good black eye and half another," he said, and wanting to touch but keeping his hands away. "A couple of fair ones on his cheeks, but no cuts except his lip. Good. But when I have bathed I will look at your nose. Go now, and finish what you are doing."

Then Davy and Ivor came out to see, and then Ianto, but none of them said anything, only asking if I hurt. But I had sixpence from all of them, and a couple of sweets from Angharad, so I was well off.

In I went after my father had finished his supper, and he looked at my nose and tried to feel if it was broken, but there was nothing wrong except swelling.

"Hot water every half-hour," said my father, "and hot and cold one after another. In a couple of days there will be nothing there."

"That National School will be far from there if I will have a bit of gunpowder," my mother said.

"Hisht, girl," my father said, "the boy will have worse than that before he will lie in his piece of ground. Are you willing to go back there to-morrow, my son?"

"Yes, Dada," I said.

"Good," he said. "Now, look you here, Huw, my son. You are growing to be a man. It is a man's place to take punishment and give back more than he takes if there is a head on him. But sometimes he will have to take a hiding in the first ten rounds to give a bigger hiding in the next ten. But if you must have a hiding, make up your mind to a hiding. Have your hiding and learn from it. It is one thing to have a hiding, but quite another to be beaten. Never be beaten, boy. A hiding, yes, but never beaten. Come for more. Come always for more. And come for more until you are giving the hiding. Is it?"

"Yes, Dada," I said.

"Come you, then," my father said, and got up, and went to the box, and brought it to the table. "From to-night you shall have a penny for every mark on your face, a shilling for a black eye, sixpence for a nose bleed, two shillings for a broken nose, and a penny for every mark on your knuckles or on your fore-arms and body. Your money-box is richer this night by three shillings and sixpence. Now come you out in the back."

"Gwilym," my mother said, with tears on the move,

"leave him, now. He has had enough for one day. Another fight and he will be dead."

"So long as he shall die with his blood in front of him," my father said, "I will lift my head. A boy shall learn to fight, or let him put skirts about his knees. This boy has never been taught to fight, but he shall have his first lesson to-night. We will see if the National Schools can beat a Morgan."

Out in the back, my father took off his coat and rolled his sleeves while Ianto and Davy pulled the engine away and Ivor cleared the floor.

"Now," said my father, "a good straight left is the bully's downfall. That is lesson one from the book. Like this."

My father stood straight, head and eyes turned to the left, with his left foot pointing the way he was looking in line with his half-bent left arm, and the thumb closed over the fingers of the fist, back of his hand down, and held nearly on a level with his chin, but always just below and between his eyes, with his right foot pointing right, and his right arm bent across his chest with the fist not touching, but almost over the heart.

"Now," he said, and up and down on tip-toe, and moving his arms in a spar, "stand like this, easy, ready and loose all over. Let me see it with you."

So I was taught to fight.

That night I learnt how to stand, to give, and to slip, a punch.

"The best fighter is that one who will slip under a punch and give two in return," said my father. "When you can do that, you shall say you have started boxing. Too many call themselves boxers who are not even entitled to call themselves fighters. Look you, now."

He showed me by hitting at Ivor, and having one on the chin and one in the chest, and both so quick it puzzled the eye to see. Then Ivor and Davy showed a left, a left slipped, and a right cross.

"That is to teach a lesson," my father said. "When a man makes you take off your coat, make up your mind to teach him a lesson. A right cross, properly given, is a good lesson and very often the end of a fight. Every time he comes in, the left to teach him. When he goes back from the left, give him a couple more by following up. Then bring the right to the space between the breast bones to bring his head down, and as it comes down, your left to steady him, and your good right to his chin. And on with your coat, then, and off home."

Angharad put her head in the window and Davy pretended to punch, and she shouted because her head was fast in the small space and her hair falling about her, making it worse.

"Mr. Gruffydd is in the house," she shouted, and the boys trying to pull her head out. "Will you crack my skull, David Morgan?"

"Too hard," Davy said. "Only a girl would put her old head in such a little place. Is there a door or are you blind?"

"I was looking through the window, fool," Angharad said. "Would I see anything through a door?"

"Your nose will have you in the toils, young woman," my father said. "Break the window and take it from her pin money."

"O, Dada," Angharad said, trying to look through her hair, and trying hard to cry, but laughing instead, "there is nasty you are to me. These old boys can do what they like but we shall have nothing only hard words and take it from her pin money. Huw has had more for his punches than I have had for six weeks. I wish I had been born an old boy. I would have punches all day, indeed."

"Leave her there," my father said, "and let her think over what she has said."

So poor Angharad was left with her head in the window, trying to cry, but laughing instead, and Davy pinched her bottom as he passed, but he got such a kick that he was limping all night with him.

"Well, Huw," said Mr. Gruffydd, "some trouble with the Philistines, then?"

"Yes, sir," I said.

"How did this pencil-box come home like this?" Mr. Gruffydd asked me. " I asked you to take care of it."

"From the way he came home," my father said, "I wonder he had sense to bring it with him."

"Let Huw answer, Mr. Morgan," said Mr. Gruffydd. "Property must not be broken like this without some action taken to stop it happening twice. Huw had it in his care. He was not to blame. Who was?"

"Those who left their marks on him," said my father.

"I was out of the room when it was done, Mr. Gruffydd," I said, "but I said I would fight all of them, and I will. So they shall have their payment for it, whoever they were."

"Kennel-sweepings," said Mr. Gruffydd, "and only ken-nel-sweepings could smash a little box like this. I am in a mind to cut myself a handful of twigs and go down there to-morrow and take the skin off their backs."

"Good," said my mother, "and burn the old place up."

"Hisht, girl," said my father. "Better to let Huw fight his own way, Mr. Gruffydd. I am just as able to go down there, and God help them if I did. But it is Huw's fight. Not ours."

"It is our fight, Mr. Morgan," Mr. Gruffydd said, and putting the box on the table. "Huw can teach them he is better with his fists, but he will never teach them the sanctity of property. The vandal is taught physical fear by superior violence, but he cannot be taught to think."

"Will twigs do any better?" asked my father, and pulling on his pipe not to smile.

"Far better than fists," said Mr. Gruffydd, and starting to laugh, "for fists are between man and man. But twigs and reason are the universal law, good for all men. Fists will teach you to fight better if you have heart and head, and your fists will teach other men to let you have your share of the road in peace. But twigs and a talk will teach you to think and live better. And that is why I am in a mind to go down there to-morrow morning."

"I am going to mend the box, Mr. Gruffydd," I said. "There will be no signs when I have done with it. Like new, indeed."

"Come you, then," said Mr. Gruffydd. "It makes me sick in the heart to see it like this."

Outside in the back we went, with lamps, and poor Angharad still with her head stuck in the window.

"Who is this?" Mr. Gruffydd asked, with the lamp high to see.

"Angharad," I said.

Mr. Gruffydd smoothed the hair from her eyes and she looked up at him, with the light of the lamp throwing gold upon her.

I knew she was laughing, but she looked as though she were crying, with golden tears unsteady in her eyes, and her eyes gone lovely blue to call for pity, big, and round, like a little girl wanting to be carried, and turning down her mouth, only a little not to be ugly, and a tremble in the chin, and with hair almost the colour of a new penny about her face and hanging down three feet, with stray ones shining like the strings of a harp across her eyes and down her cheeks.

Mr. Gruffydd looked at her and I saw his face move, but how it moved there is no saying. He put down the lamp and took the bar above her neck in one hand.

"Say if I hurt," he said, but Angharad shook her head.

He put his feet flat after making little moves to find the right hold, and then with one pull he tore the bar and the top of the frame clean out of its place, nails, screws, and all.

"Now then," he said to me, not looking at Angharad, "you mend the box and I will mend the window."

"Yes, sir," I said.

"Thank you, Mr. Gruffydd," Angharad said, looking in where the window had been, and feeling her neck. "There is strong you are."

"Good," said Mr. Gruffydd, "I will have the pincers after you, Huw, my son."

Sandpaper took the ink stains from the bare white wood on the inside of the box, and made it white as a sheet again, but only with hard rubbing and patience at the corners. A new screw for the pivot, and a splice for the second tray, and my box was together again, but still chipped on the outside and scratched on the lid. That was another job altogether. Small pieces of wood, so small they were hard to see, I put in all the chips, and the scratches I filled in with splinters of the same colour as the woods in the pattern. Indeed, when I had finished there was nothing to show that the little box had come to harm. But I knew, and Mr. Gruffydd knew, and so did his father and grandfather, for there were little marks all over it that had never been there, and should never have been there, the marks of little wounds that would never heal. For wood is jealous of its age, and quick to make a new-comer feel its place.

Mr. Gruffydd had been watching, for quite a long time, but I knew nothing of it until I had finished and put the box in a clean place to look at it, and then looked at him and found him sitting on the bench and smiling.

"You are a carpenter, Huw," he said.

"Thank you, sir," I said. "Did you finish the window?"

"Well, indeed," he said, "do you think I would let a boy beat me? Look by there."

A fine job of the window Mr. Gruffydd had made, every

bit as good as Clydach Howell the millwright could have done, with joins you could see only if you knew where to look, and the nails and screws gone to nowhere but still there.

"There is a carpenter you are, too, Mr. Gruffydd," I said, and meant.

"You shall say that when I have made the furniture for my new house," Mr. Gruffydd said.

"Shall I help you, sir?" I asked him, for always I had wanted to make good furniture for the house.

"No one if not you, my son," he said. "Is your face hurting now?"

"I had forgotten," I said, and indeed I had.

Then Angharad called me to open the door, and came in with tea, and laver bread, and butter and milk cheese, and lettuce and cresses.

"Mama said to eat while you are working," she said, "but if you have finished please to come to the house. And if you will have beer instead of tea, there is plenty, and Dada says it is cold from the jar and good enough to drink to the Queen in."

"I will drink to the Queen," said Mr. Gruffydd, "and in the house. Give me the tray."

Mr. Gruffydd lifted the load from Angharad, and she stood to put some plates in place that had slipped, and touched a cup to bring the handle to its proper place, and put a spoon here, and a fork there, and the salt pot over between the milk-jug and teapot, and all the time Mr. Gruffydd looked down at her head, because he knew, and I knew, there was no need for any of it.

"Now then," she said, and looked up at Mr. Gruffydd, smiling.

She was going to say more but she stopped and her smile went, and she looked, and a dullness passed across her eyes, not a dullness of darkness, but a dullness of light, and all the time Mr. Gruffydd looked down at her straight, and then she blinked and pretended it was the lamp and put her hand to her eyes and turned away.

"There is strong that old lamp is," she said. "Go you, Huw. It is late, boy."

In the house I went, and Mr. Gruffydd behind, and my father coming to take the tray from him.

"What next?" he said, in surprise. "They will have you scrubbing a floor in a minute, wait you."

"Many a floor I have scrubbed, too," said Mr. Gruffydd. "Did I hear we were going to drink the health of the Queen."

"Poured and waiting," said my father. "Tea is good in its place, but a good swallow of beer is good, too. This my wife made, see, and you will never taste better in your life. Huw, a cup full."

"Up high, then," said Mr. Gruffydd. "I give you Her Britannic Majesty, our Royal mother, and may her crown rest lightly. Gentlemen, Victoria."

"Victoria," said we all, and the beer went down beautiful, indeed.

"Now, supper," said my mother, coming from the fire with the pan, "and eat plenty. Huw, bed."

"Yes, Mama," I said, and gave good night to them all. Angharad came upstairs to put the last of the hot and cold water poultice on my face, and when she had finished, she put a little handful of sweets on the chair by the bed.

"For school," she said.

"Thank you," I said.

"Has Mr. Gruffydd ever said anything to you about me?" she asked me, but quickly, as though she had thought long before saying it, and anxious not to think she had said it, or even thought it.

"No," I said. "Nothing. About what, then?"

"No matter," she said, quickly again, and looking down at me but not seeing me, for there was a smile in her eyes and heat in her face and her breath was quick but quiet. "If he does, will you tell me, boy?"

"Yes," I said.

"Good," she said. "Good night, now."

I saw her face as she bent to blow out the candle with her mouth in the shape of a kiss, still the smile in the eyes, but now as a mother will look at her child that cries in the arms of another woman, softer, and with more of want.

Not one of the boys had a word to say to me on the second day at school, though they looked at me with their hands over their mouths not to laugh. I was a picture, indeed, yellow and blue with bruises, and swollen about the eyes and nose. But no matter, I made sure of the boys who laughed, and added them to the list of boys I had made sure to have at the end of my fists.

Mr. Motshill stopped me after prayers and the hymn and asked me where I had the injury.

"Fighting," I said.

"You see what fighting brings you," he said. "Far better to behave yourself. Am I to expect a visit from your parents?"

"No," I said. "My father said it was my fight."

"Oh," he said, and took off his glasses to give them a polish, and winked his eyes over my head. "If you feel unwell during the day, go over to Mrs. Motshill at the school house and lie down."

"Thank you, sir," I said.

"Remember this, Morgan," he said, and put his hand on my shoulder, "I am here to help you. I want you to win a scholarship to Oxford University. You have it within your power. But your fists will only hinder you. Be warned, and work hard."

Why is it that kindness, even from a harsh man, brings tears to the eyes, I wonder. But there it is. When I went in Standard Six room, Mr. Jonas saw me trying to wipe my eyes and on went the smile, and down went my heart inside me again.

"Well, upon my soul," he said, in his English that was too English, "it is crying."

He came to stand near me, and look me up and down.

"Evidently its mother took my message to heart," he said. "Let me see your nose-rag."

I took out my handkerchief.

"Surprise on surprise," he said, while I looked at him. "Perhaps that hammering will teach you that your ways are not ours. There is no wonder that civilized men look down upon Welshmen as savages. I shudder to think of your kind growing up. However, I shall endeavour to do my utmost with you, helped by a stick. Remember that. And keep your eyes off me, you insolent little blackguard."

Then he started to teach history, and I sat.

I think he took a hatred for me because he felt that I distrusted him, and it hurt to think that a boy would not have him at his value of himself, for he liked to think he was much bigger than he was, so his self pride troubled him, and made him vicious.

But his greatest trouble was his Welsh blood, so ashamed he was of it, and so hard he tried to cover it.

Nothing that was of Wales or the Welsh was any good or had any goodness in his eyes. For him, even in his teachings, the science of history had a gap between the Acts of the Apostles and the Domesday Book. That Norman bastard, who skinned the snout on the good sands of the south, who sired an English aristocracy, was godfather to Mr. Elijah Jonas-Sessions.

If he remembered Rome, it was only as a place where Nero burnt Christians. He tried to forget that his fathers laboured with the sword through centuries to keep Roman feet off their roads, and he was willing to forget that Rome broke its back, and Vikings, Danes, and Goths broke their hearts, only trying to keep his fathers from fighting for what was their own, and if his fathers failed it was not because their fighting spirit had gone from them, but because the flower of them had fallen in battle, and their women could not bear males enough to fill the ranks.

Of such, Mr. Elijah Jonas-Sessions was ashamed.

And the day we had it out I remember well, for it was the day of my first fight, just after Dilys Pritchard died.

Chapter Seventeen

"I AM THE RESURRECTION and the Life," said Mr. Gruffydd in his voice that was the voice of a man, noble of depth and beauty.

"Amen," said we all.

Out on the mountain we were, with the cold winds of night about us, and the flames of torches to light us, listening to Mr. Gruffydd before we went through the village to clear dross and uselessness from the Valley.

That day a little girl had been savaged on the mountain, and when I came from school the people were out in the street on the Hill, and down in the village the shops were shut, and the Chapel bell was ringing. While I was having my tea, my father came in, for the colliery had closed early for the men to be home and start the search for the swine in the form of man.

"She is dead," my father said, and quiet in the voice, "but we will have him if we have to move the mountain."

"Go you," said my mother, in tears. "Poor, pretty little thing she was."

I went with the men to trim the torches and carry the oil with other boys. My father and my brothers were there in amongst the crowd of two or three hundred, and all of them quiet and not speaking. Mr. Gruffydd had them on the side of the mountain ready to go down into the village just after dark, after the men had just had time to bathe and eat. He told them that the time had come when their women were no longer safe to go their ways in peace.

"Beasts live among you," he shouted, "working with you shoulder to shoulder, who will kill your children and go their ways unpunished. They will make of your community a morass of corruption. Will you laugh if I talk to you of the Evil One? Will you smile if I mention the name of Satan? Then let me show you the body of a child, torn by murderous claws. Perhaps I shall see your heads flung back in guffaws. This little soul met her death not at the hands of a man, but at the talons of a beast. A beast. And beasts of that sort are the sons of Satan. Such beasts you shall exorcise, as He did with the Gadarene swine. Are we decided? Are we in one mind?"

"Yes," said the crowd.

"Then, come," Mr. Gruffydd said, "let us cleanse ourselves."

Down from the rock and out in front of the crowd, striking up a hymn as he went, down toward the village Mr. Gruffydd led us. The boots of the men beat time upon the ground, and their voices flung the anthem before them, and the blaze of torches lit their bearded faces and struck sparks from their eyes.

Into the village we went and everything quiet, doors shut, no lights, no people, and no sound but the march of men and the voice of justice.

Around each public house, and all round the three rows of houses where the half-breed Welsh, Irish, and English were living, the men took a stand, almost elbow to elbow, so that none could go in or out. Then Mr. Gruffydd and twenty men went into the first public house and warned the landlord to serve no spirits for a week, and to serve beer only to gangers in charge of five or more men, none to any woman. Then to the second and to the third. It was a bad night for the public houses, for nobody was in them, and indeed the landlords were not to blame. They were good men in themselves, but they had to make a living, too.

But they had to suffer, and they suffered with silence. They knew it would only take a match to put them in the street with nothing, and the flames of their property to warm them.

Up to the rows of houses where the dross of the collieries lives. These people did the jobs that colliers would never do, and they were allowed to live and breed because the owners would not spend money on plant when their services were to be had so much the cheaper. For a pittance, they carried slag and muck, they acted as scavengers, and as they worked, so they lived. Even their children were put to work at eight and nine years of age so that more money could come into the house. They lived, most of them, only to drink. Their houses were bestial sties, where even beasts would rebel if put there to live, for beasts have clean ways with them and they will show their disgust quick enough, but these people were long past such good feeling. They were a living disgust.

Up to those three rows of hovels went Mr. Gruffydd, and knocked upon the first door, but no answer.

The mountain went up black into the night on all sides of us, and the knocking flew about in an echo trying to find a place of rest. The torches made a ragged ring about the houses, and below each torch, that streamed flame like the blown hair of a running fury, men's faces were pale, and shadowy pink, and their eyes deep holes, until they moved to show the flash of whites. Shadows of men leapt up the sides of the mountain, or were flung against the walls of the houses, whichever way the torch flames blew, and breath was grey about them, for the night was going to frost, and the slates of the roofs were showing something of silver, and finger-tips were happy only deep in the pocket.

Again and again Mr. Gruffydd knocked, and at last a window, only big enough to let out a head, and the only window in all the house, opened and let out a head.

"Who is it?" in a woman's voice, and thin with fright.

"The Vigilants," Mr. Gruffydd said, and his voice rolled into the night and about the mountain, and the torches moved as the men quickened all about, and their voices breathed a deep note.

"Not us, not us," the woman screamed, "nothing to do with us."

"Open your door," said Mr. Gruffydd, "no harm shall come to the innocent. Open, and now."

Back went the head, and in a moment the door was opened, and Mr. Gruffydd went inside with my father and Rhys Howells, and a couple of moments later they came out pushing three men before them.

"Get you over there," Rhys Howells said to them, and pointed to the place where an old shaft had been sunk and closed up again. Into the hole they went, and men moved up to guard them.

Into house after house Mr. Gruffydd went, and now with no more trouble, for doors were opening before he had to knock. All the men were brought out, and the women told to keep inside with the children.

When the last was under guard, Mr. Gruffydd came to take his place upon the rock, with all of us about him in a ring.

"Now," he said, "let the men be brought one by one for questioning."

With them all it was the same. First, their names, their jobs, their wages, and which shift they were on that day. For if they were on the day shift they could not have been on the mountain to meet the little girl. It was the night-shifters, and the work-shys we were after. One by one they came and went, all of them quiet and in fear, and some Irish, some Scotch, some English, and some inter-breed Welsh.

So we came to Idris Atkinson.

Tall, and thin beyond his length, white in the face, and with sick spots, long in the hair and restless with his hands, with nails chewed to make you turn your eyes from him.

"Day or night shift?" Mr. Gruffydd asked him.

"Day," he said, and looking from side to side without moving his head.

"Which level?" asked Mr. Gruffydd.

"No business of yours," he said, to the ground.

"Which level?" asked Mr. Gruffydd, in the same voice, quiet and without edge.

"Third," he shouted, after a wait.

"Third was closed to-day," Rhys Howells said, and folded his arms, rocking on his heels, looking up at the mountain. Then he stood still, and his eyes went to Mr. Gruffydd.

Quiet, except for the whisper of the torches, and the tiny sounds that come from many men who wait with breath held tight.

Swine looked about him with his mouth open, and his nostrils wide, and his eyes gone red with fear, and his voice gone from him in the silence, with his blunt and twisted hands restless about his clothes that were polished stiff with grease and coal-dust, and fell about him, and showed his thinness through gapes at elbow and knee.

"Go down to his house," said Mr. Gruffydd, "and bring the women here. Look well for his clothes and his cap."

"Nothing there," whispered swine. "Nobody in the house. Not me. I never done it."

But men were on their way down at a run.

Quiet again, and nobody looking at swine crying on his knees, and looking round toward the house. Then a shout from down there, and men running back to us, and all talking and taking big breaths to ease themselves.

Evan Thomas, and Sion Prosser had an armful of clothes each.

Evan put a flannel shirt, black with dirt and dried hard with blood, on the rock in front of Mr. Gruffydd. All the other clothes, a coat, and a waistcoat, and a pair of trews, had blood on them, and on the cap it was yet damp.

"Did you have an injury to-day?" Mr. Gruffydd asked him.

"No," said swine, standing now, and shaking. "A pony it was."

"No pony was blooded to-day or yesterday," said Llewelyn John, the ostler, from the back of the crowd.

"Days and days ago, it was," said swine, in a woman's voice.

"But the blood is fresh," said Mr. Gruffydd, "and it smells. And you wore these clothes to-day. Open your clothes to show your chest."

"No," said swine, and put his hands about him, and fell to his knees.

"In her finger nails were pieces of flesh," said Mr. Gruffydd, with quiet. "So her spirit left its mark. Open your clothes."

"No," screamed swine.

Rhys Howells and Tom Davies went to him and took a piece of the coat on his back each, and pulled it in halves from him. And as he screamed they tore away the rags which covered him under the coat.

Deep scratches covered his chest like thick ruled pencil lines, and when they pulled away his trews, blood was on him, and all the time he screamed. Naked, he clawed at the ground and the screams tired his throat, and he sobbed, and spittle fell from his mouth.

"Where is the father?" asked Mr. Gruffydd, looking down at swine.

"I am here," said Cynlais Pritchard, and stood forward with his three sons, looking up at Mr. Gruffydd.

"Your daughter has gone from you," said Mr. Gruffydd. "Instead to see her grow to womanhood and have joy in your grandchildren, you walk behind her to-morrow because a beast put his claws upon her as she walked the mountain. Your daughter was not of an age to be forward, and small blame we can put to her, for she left a message to you in the body of the beast itself."

Silence, and Cynlais Pritchard trying to hold his tears with eyes shut blind, and fists digging into his thighs.

"To hand her murderer over to the police will give him an extra day to live, which your daughter was denied," said Mr. Gruffydd. "He shall be fed and housed until the day he meets the rope, but your daughter will lie beneath the dead wreaths long before then, and the rope gives a good death, quick and clean, without blood, without pain, without torture of the soul and body. Is justice done, then, with a rope about the neck of a man, and his victim, a child of seven years, torn and twisted, long in her grave?"

"No," said the crowd.

"Shall we burn him?" asked Mr. Gruffydd. "But if we do, he will die a death of honour, for martyrs died in the flame. What then?"

"Give him to me," said Cynlais Pritchard.

"Is that your common decision?" Mr. Gruffydd asked the crowd.

"Yes," they all shouted back.

"Take him," said Mr. Gruffydd, "and as we do with him, so shall we do with the next, if next there is. And remember, if you bury him, however deep, you pollute innocent ground. Burden not the earth with such."

One son took a torch, and the others helped their father to take swine from there, and we all knew without the telling that they would have him up where they had found the girl in her blood, and on that spot he would suffer.

So we stood, and the light got smaller as they climbed, and the screams passed, and presently they were over a shoulder of the hill and out of sight.

"Let us pray," said Mr. Gruffydd. "Lord God, we are weak men. If we have done wrong to-night, so be it. I will face Thy wrath at the Bar, and I will answer that we did right. Unto each his just reward. In Christ's Holy Name, Amen."

"Amen," said the crowd, and when Mr. Gruffydd got down, they started for home in quiet, saying nothing, watching for the light of the torch to appear above them on the mountain.

The spark appeared, and with it a deep note from the crowd, but nobody stood. It went slowly to the right until it came to the briars beside the path that went up to the farm. There they had found the girl.

It stopped, and went out, and the mountain was black.

The houses of the Hill hid us from it as we went up, but when we went round the back to go in, a strong light was burning, as though they had fired the grass up there, and in the smoothness of the flame I thought I saw the movements of men. But I thought of Marged, too, and went in fear to bed.

A policeman with a silver spike in his helmet, and a silver chain hanging on it, came to the Valley next day, but nobody knew what he wanted, and nobody could be found to answer his questions, so he went off again.

All the morning, I watched Clydach Howell, in his wheelwright's shop, making the little coffin from the white heart of an old oak, and learnt a lot from him in the matter of putting joins instead of nails and screws, and nails and screws where they are not to be seen. I helped to quilt silk for the lining and tap studs in the shape of flowers all round the edge to keep it in place. So good was the job when it was done, I felt it a shame to put it in the ground.

But I let Clydach take it to the house.

I have never been one for a funeral.

Cynlais and his wife and sons, and their married daughters, and their husbands, and families were all down in the house when I took Mr. Gruffydd's books down to him. All the people in front of the house were in their best, ready to walk in the funeral procession up to the graveyard over the mountain. As they waited they spoke of the night before, and many looked up at the black patch among the browns and greens of the mountain side.

Inside the house no other sound but the long indrawn breathing and choking dolour of women long in tears, and weeping with eyes that are puffed to red soreness, and throats thick with hours of wailing. The children were in the kitchen, sitting stiff in their best, the men were in the front, and the women were all upstairs sitting about the body in its coffin.

Mr. Gruffydd was in the front with the men.

"Thank you, my son," he said, when I gave him the books, and speaking as though he had been quiet for a long time. "Go you in the kitchen and bring the children up, will you?"

So out in the kitchen I went, and tried to make the small ones stop their tears, but they could hear their mothers crying, and so cried with them. Then the women came downstairs, and the coffin was brought down, and Mr. Pritchard came in to me and gave me a sign with the thumb to bring the children from the house.

When we got outside, the people had formed up two by two, stretching all the way down the street. Some, friends of the family, were walking behind the coffin, but most went on before. The hymn rose up in majesty, and white handkerchiefs were alive in the long untidy lines of black as the procession slowly went through the village and up for all in the Valley were in the procession, excepting only those who were bed-ridden and those who looked after them, and the men who were tending fires down at the colliery.

Up and up, slowly we went, one hymn going into another, all singing, and the echo getting less and less as we neared the top and came free of trees. Then we stopped for the bearers of the coffin to have a rest, and handkerchiefs went, not to the eyes, but to foreheads and the backs of necks, and coats came off and cloaks were folded, and boots that were pinching were eased off. The everyday things, those little jewels that stud the action of living, were making themselves known. A blister on the heel, sweat about the neckband, a wrinkle in the stocking, were coming to mean more than the feelings brought forth by that which filled the little white coffin.

Then up with the coffin again, and on, with another hymn to light the way, up and up, walking behind the lift and fall, lift and fall, of the little white coffin and the bowler hats about it, and the lines of black that now were breaking into threes and fours, with spaces coming wider, as men went to help women, and the slope got more and more. Now the leaders were going over the edge up there and passing from sight, then the carriers were up there, dark against the deep blue of the sky, with the sun dancing upon the brass ornaments and making the whiteness sing.

Over the other side, then, and faster because we were going down, though not too fast, but easier and with more of relief, down to the field, that had been made into a graveyard. Everybody made a big ring about the hole where they were going to bury the coffin, but Mr. Pritchard and his family went to stand close by where the carriers had put it to rest on the mound of gravel.

Handkerchiefs were busy again among the lines of black as Mr. Gruffydd started to read, and all about and around his voice were the sounds of weeping, and the voices of many men calling out to affirm the truth of his words.

Mrs. Pritchard had to be held down by her husband and sons when Mr. Gruffydd signed to the men to put the coffin down the hole, and she screamed herself red as all the people came near to pass by and look at it down there at the bottom. Women were fainting and men carrying them to the sides to slap the backs of their hands and fan them, and the children with me were crying and crying with none to take notice of them except me, and I could do nothing for them, or say anything, for I was never easy with small children.

At last the people had stopped coming and Mr. Gruffydd gathered a handful of earth to throw in. Then Mr. Pritchard let Mrs. Pritchard go to the edge and throw in some flowers and earth, and would have thrown herself in but she was held tight and pulled back. All the Pritchard women were shouting crying with their men holding them, and their children holding their skirts and wild with crying, except one little boy by me who had cried himself out, and stood with his hands in his pockets and his mouth turned down, with nothing in his eyes but tiredness.

Men came from behind me with shovels and threw in the hard earth, and it rattled and bumped on the wood, and with that sound, Mrs. Pritchard went forward, white in the face, and her husband lifted her like a baby and carried her away.

I could hear nothing of Mr. Gruffydd's prayer for his voice was low, and the sounds of weeping covered it. Then a hymn, uncertain in time and tone, and the burial was over.

We went home faster than we had come and not so tidily, with people going up the shortest way, not in lines now, but in families, and with friends. I was slower at first for the children wanted to play as soon as we were outside, but when they started to shout they were hushed by men who turned round with frowns and fists. So we found our own way up and over, and we were long in front of the first when we got back to the Pritchard house.

As soon as the first women got there they took off their coats and cloaks and rolled their sleeves to get out plates and boil water for the tea. More and more came, and then Mrs. Pritchard, who looked better, but still quick to cry if the wrong word was said or the wrong look given. As soon as she came in the food was set out and the tables were laid, and the setting and laying seemed to take her out of herself, for she worked with the best, and the first to notice what wanted doing, or had not been done properly, and no sign of tears then.

The men were all smoking out in the street in front, but when they were called in they tapped their pipes against the walls and sat where Mrs. Pritchard pointed to put them. Four houses had opened their doors for the funeral tea, and in every house rooms were full of people eating and drinking, but in quiet, not like a birthday, with the food all coming from the back of Mrs. Pritchard's, and carried by the girls and some of the boys to us, and to those outside who could not have places in.

I had mine in the corner of Mrs. Pritchard's front room, with two small Pritchard boys, near to the table where Mr. Gruffydd and Mr. Pritchard and the chief people were having theirs. Nobody spoke for a long time, but they were busy with the knife and fork and women were in and out with the tea, never stopping.

"Sad," Mr. Evans the Colliery said, "Sad."

He was leaning back, done, with a stick at his teeth, looking through the window.

"Yes, indeed it is," Rhys Howells said. "But a beautiful funeral, indeed. Clydach Howell made a lovely job of that coffin. Nothing so pretty I have seen in my days."

"Thank you, Rhys," said Clydach, and going a bit red, so pleased he was, "I will be glad to do it for you, one day, man."

"I will see you safe in for one," Rhys said. "And no danger. And that will be years, I hope."

"If I will go as that little one did to-day," Clydach said, "I will go to-morrow. Beautiful, it was indeed."

And everybody nodded, and Mr. Pritchard smiled a bit

about the table as though happier to think so.

"I wish she could have seen it," he said. "Do you think she saw it, Mr. Gruffydd? Is she in heaven yet, or is she waiting for her turn to come?"

"In heaven," said Mr. Gruffydd, and looking at his plate, "there is no waiting for children. Come unto me, said the Lord, and suffer the little children to come unto me. He said nothing about waiting."

"Glad I am," said Mr. Pritchard, and tears coming. "But why she had to go there is no telling. She was happy enough here with us. She used to bring down my box to the colliery every dinner time so happy as a bird in the sky, and always at the top here to meet me, early shift. Why, I wonder?"

"Who can read the mind of the Lord?" Mr. Owen the Mill said.

"Why is it, Mr. Gruffydd?" Mr. Pritchard asked, and trembling in the voice, and the other men clearing their throats, and going to their cups for tea to drink, not to look at him.

"I cannot tell you, Mr. Pritchard, my little one," Mr. Gruffydd said, and his voice deep and full of sorrow, and bringing the room to quiet. "No man can tell you. I could say she was taken as a punishment, or as a visitation. But what have you done? Or your good wife? And if you were to be punished, why your little girl and not you? No, Mr. Pritchard. I cannot answer you, for nothing I could say would be the truth. The truth is beyond us, and is not in us. We go forward in faith. That is all."

"Yes," said Mr. Pritchard. "I suppose so, indeed. But it is very hard."

"Nobody can tell why the Son of Man had to go," Mr. Gruffydd said. "He was Prince of Light. He could have ruled the world. But He was crucified, and when men would have fought for Him, He told them to put up their swords. He allowed a rabble to crucify Him. Why did He die in that way when He could have chosen any? To save us, we know. But why did He die in only that way? It was ordained? Then dare we say that Dilys was ordained to die as she did?"

"But why not me?" Mr. Pritchard said. "I have had my life. Not good, but I have done my best. I was ready to go in her place."

"I have no answer for you, Mr. Pritchard, my little

one," Mr. Gruffydd said, and putting out a hand to touch Mr. Pritchard's arm. "She was taken, and all argument is useless. We can only have faith in God, and resolve that the things which made her death possible shall be swept away, and now."

"Hear that, all," Mr. Evans said. "What can be done to that end, Mr. Gruffydd? Say, and I will do all I can."

"First," said Mr. Gruffydd, "let me call a meeting for to-morrow night. Now, and in this house, is not the time or the place. But this you shall make clear in your minds. That little soul has not gone from us for nothing. She shall be heard of for long to come."

"Amen," said all the men.

"Thank you, Mr. Gruffydd," said Mr. Pritchard, "that is a comfort to me, indeed. But not much."

Quiet came, then, and my father winked me from the house and I went home to my lessons.

Though I did no work in school I did plenty at night, and Mrs. Tom Jenkins or Davy or Ianto were always ready to help. Ianto and Davy had plenty of work of their own now, for the Union was growing day by day and Ellis the Post was outside our house morning and night with big bundles of Post for them, but they would always stop to give me help, and in return I wrote letters for them.

Davy was working in our front, with Wyn to fold the letters as he finished, and Angharad to stick them down, and Ianto was painting a big sign for a meeting when I went in.

"How was the funeral?" Davy asked me.

"Very good," I said.

"Was Jones Pentre Bach there?" he asked.

"Yes," I said.

"I thought so," Davy said. "Nobody could be buried without him at the funeral. Not one funeral missed in twenty years, him. A graveyard haunter. Such people make me sick."

"Well, Davy," Wyn said, in surprise, "the old man is only showing his respect for the dead, boy."

"Respect?" Davy said, with heat and contempt equal. "It is not respect to go crawling after every coffin you can find. Worshippers of death and the rites of burial. Human crows. They stink in the nostrils."

"The only part of the funeral they have got any interest

in is the tea," Ianto said. "Tears out and tea in, and thus the *status quo.*"

"You are too lazy to walk over the mountain," Wyn said, and angry. "That is your excuse. Laziness."

"I will walk to Town and back before I will go in any graveyard," Ianto said. "Not laziness, sense. Graveyards, indeed. If there is one place more ugly or sour to the taste than a graveyard, I hope my senses will never be burdened to see it."

"What will you have, then?" Angharad asked. "Will you have the poor little girl put in the cess?"

"Let a flame have her," said Davy. "Dust to dust. And the quicker and cleaner, the better. Quiet, now, and let us work."

"Huw," Ianto said, "get a hammer and nails from the back. We are going to have this up before dark."

Ianto carried the sign and I the tool box, down to the village and outside the Three Bells where there was an old stump of a tree, and to that we nailed the notice. It asked for all men interested in their own, and in the welfare of their dependants, to meet in Jones the Chapel's field at six o'clock the next night, and to come in force, to reach a decision against the operation of the sliding scale as a basis of the weekly wages, and to convene a committee to present that decision to the owners.

A crowd of men gathered round us as we finished the nailing, and those who could read, read out for those who could not. A lot of them coming from the funeral stopped too, and Isaac Wynn, a deacon, looked at the notice and clicked his tongue.

"When are you Morgan boys going to mind your own business?" he said to Ianto, and without good feeling. "You are always pulling the men this way and that. What right have you got to stand and speak to us? Let us see you more at Chapel and less at Jones the Chapel's field. You will have a lot more respect from a lot of people."

"If I can have more wages, I will have less respect and gladly," Ianto said. "Children eat from wages. No use to give them respect. And as for our noses, they will go where we think. I will speak to you of a wrong as long as you will stand to listen. That is my right. And if you think I am wrong, stand to speak against me. That is your right, and I will never question it. As for Chapel, it is good in its place, but it is not a place I like because there are too many of your sort in it. That is why I like Jones the Chapel's field better. Good night to you."

"Retribution shall come to you," Isaac Wynn called out after us.

"Good," said Ianto, "so long as it will come with more wages."

"Go on back to London," Isaac Wynn shouted. "Leave your silly notions with them up there."

"I will tell that to the owners," Ianto shouted back, "for that is where your proper wages are spent. If you are content to see what should be going into your pocket falling into the pockets of landlords, and bankers, and Jews, and on the backs of whores, I am not. And I will stay here to say so."

"How do whores get our money?" I asked Ianto, as we went back.

"I am sorry I had to use the word in front of you," Ianto said, "but I was angry with that old fool. You are too young for such things. You will learn in time to come."

So back we went home, and me with that empty feeling, that heating, empty feeling that rouses anger in you, when you want to know something which only a few words would give to you, and you are denied to have them.

Up at the house Davy was talking to a couple of men in the back, a couple not generally looked up to, and a surprise to find near our house, for Dai Bando and Cyfartha Lewis were prizefighters, rough but gentle men.

"Come you, Huw," Davy said, and put his arm about my shoulder. "You know Huw, Dai."

"Yes, indeed," said Dai, and smiled to show one tooth to the side of his mouth. He was not much taller than me, but broad as six, and long in the arm. His face was covered with little punch cuts, all dyed blue with coal dust, and his eyes were almost closed by skin which had been cut and healed time and time again. But his eyes were bright as a blackbird's. They said he had fought more than a thousand fights, and a Marquis had asked him to go to Oxford to teach the students to fight, with the knuckles, of course, but he had got drunk in London and put a couple of police in hospital, and landed in jail. So not many had a word for him.

Cyfartha Lewis was younger, taller, but tidy in the chest and big in the shoulder, well known to be champion in his weight at the pit head. Instead of going to Chapel he and

Dai were off to Town on Saturdays to fight at night, and they used to come back home in time for the morning shift on Monday. But it was certain that whatever they did on Sunday, going to Chapel was not one.

"Dai is going to give you lessons in the art of boxing, Huw," Davy said. "I asked him to come up and see if he could do something with you."

"Strip off, boy," Dai said, in his high little voice, and making a little move with his hands, that were bumpy and in funny shapes with him, and always half closed to show the big thumb joints.

So I took off my shirt to the waist, and Dai looked and pinched, as my mother did with a chicken for the pot.

"More in the shoulder, more in the back, more in the forearm," said Dai, with a look I thought was disgust. "And his legs want two more pairs like them before they will be going on to be enough, eh, Cyfartha? Hit me by here, boy."

He put out his chin and poked it with his short finger, but I had a fear to give him a good one.

"Go on, boy," he said, "hit to kill."

"Go on," Cyfartha said, and smiling. "A sovereign if you will have him on the floor."

So I hit, but his head was nowhere near my fist, and I never saw Dai move.

"Nothing to buy a stamp for," said Dai, "but he uses his shoulders, and he stands well, eh, Cyfartha?"

"I have seen many a one worse," Cyfartha said. "His legs are his trouble. He will never ride a punch with them. And one good clout and they will put him to bed."

"Look you, now, Dai," Davy said. "The boy's legs have stopped him going to a good school. But you shall teach him enough to fight his way through the school he is in now, legs or not. Yes or no?"

"Yes," said Dai, and meant it. "I was up there the night his mother came. God, there is a shocking night it was, too, eh, Cyfartha?"

"Yes, indeed," Cyfartha said, "and we built a fire on the rock all night and slid down the mountain to the pit next morning. Say nothing to me of that night, indeed. Twenty pound solid it cost me to have my hands right, with the frost."

"What time in the morning?" Davy asked, and impatient.

"Half-past four at the top here," Dai said, "and five

o'clock up the top of the mountain. An hour up there to six, half an hour down, to half-past, and breakfast then, to seven. Eh, Cyfartha?"

"Yes," said Cyfartha. "And nothing only water before he comes up."

"Good," said Davy, well satisfied. "You will have lessons from champions, Huw. Now in to your lessons from books."

So I went from Dai Bando and Cyfartha Lewis, in to Pericles and John Stuart Mill.

That first morning Davy came in to give me a shake and hold down the loose board while I crossed the landing in quiet at quarter-past four in pitch black, and cold to make your teeth chop, no wash because the bucket would rattle in the well to wake the Hill, and only enough in the house for breakfast first thing, then off outside the house into a wind with ice in it, bringing tears to the eyes, and a pain, like the grip of a clothes-peg, to the nose. Dai and Cyfartha came from the lee of the last house, both of them black lumps, and only their bootfalls to tell which was them and which not.

"That you, Huw Morgan?" Dai said, and shouting in the wind, but only a whisper coming.

"Yes," I shouted back. "Good morning."

"To hell," Dai said, and spat. "Come, you."

We went up the mountain together, but I saw in surprise that Cyfartha was following with a dozen or more from the sound, but Dai put his fingers down my neck and swore when I stopped to see. Up we went, quicker than I had ever gone before, but being late for school a couple of times had given me practice in running up, so I was not far behind Dai at the top and hardly a breath out of place.

"Off with your shirt," Dai said, and pulling his off, and all the others pulling the clothes from them. So off came mine, and I thought I would freeze, sure, for the wind was high and calling low and strong enough to push you over flat. It was still dark, but above the other valley it was just starting to show grey, black everywhere else, and nothing but black down in the valleys except where Merddyn Jones was getting up, with a little yellow light, and the light in the winding house down at the colliery.

In the coming of the morning Dai Bando was a man to fear.

His skin was pinkish with cold, and with muscle to make

you doubt your sight. His arm muscles were bigger than my thigh, and over the top of his trews, six squares, each as big as my two fists together, stood out so that you could have rattled a stick over them. His shoulders had great fat fingers of muscle leading down to the tops of his arms like opening a fan, and behind his shoulders, bunches of muscle lay about the blades, with two great cords going down on each side of his backbone.

I will never forget Dai Bando in that grey light, with night all about him and cold pricking his skin to little pimples as his shirt came from him and he pulled at his trews.

Cyfartha was not much less than Dai, and the boys and men with them were all the same. Only I was skin and bone.

"Come on, boys," Dai said, and slapping himself hard, "get the blood going with you."

For minutes we all danced about there slapping the cold out of us, and hopping and jumping about like mad flies, until the light was coming apple green and orange, with lines of gold, and we could see each other, and the trees taking shape and colours of deep green.

"Down on the back," Dai ordered, and down flat we went, on the short grass that was smooth as moss, covered with the crystals of frozen dew and sparkling lovely, but so cold it was like red-hot to the back.

"Kick the legs above your heads and back and fore with the arms," said Dai, and that we did.

"Sit up and lie back, no hands," Dai shouted, and up and down we went, until never mind the cold, we were sweating, and hot as hot.

"Now pair off, and straight left one, guard the other," Dai said. "Huw Morgan, over here."

Over I went, and while Cyfartha and the other boys paired off, Dai put up his fists, and I put up mine, and we did straight lefts, and slipping them, and riding them, and ducking, with the punches to counter, and those to score. Then Dai made me come in close and hit him on those muscles of his in the belly with half-arm blows to strengthen my punching muscles at the back, until I was ready to drop.

"Good," he said, and smiling he was, "there is plenty in you, indeed. Run to school and put fat and muscle on your legs. But run, not walk. Strong legs you want, nothing else. I will give you the rest."

"Thank you, Dai," I said, and so pleased I could have jumped across the Valley. "When shall I fight, now?"

"To-day," Dai said. "Fight all the time. You will only learn in a fight how much you have got to learn. When you know that, you can come and ask and I will show you. But fight."

"Good," I said, "I will fight to-day."

"Same time to-morrow," Dai said. "Put on your shirt, and run down the mountain home. And fight, is it?"

"Yes," I said. "To-day, indeed."

When I got in, my mother had my breakfast ready and when I had washed I sat to it, but she sat beside me and smoothed my hair.

"Did you go out on the mountain this morning, Huw, my little one?" she asked me.

"Yes, Mama," I said.

"To learn to fight, is it?" she asked me, as though she was hoping I would say no.

"Yes, Mama," I said.

"There," she said, and sat back, hopeless. "I knew it when I heard you go from the house. Right, you. But if you come back with bruises again, not a word shall you have from me. Nothing. Break your old nose and see what I will do. Nothing. Not a word, not a look."

"But I must learn, Mama," I said, "or I shall have them and nothing to stop them coming, and nothing to give back."

"I am not listening to you," she said, and over at the fire, now, with her hand over her eyes. "Breaking your Mama's heart every time you do go from the house. Remember what I say. Not a word, not a look."

"Yes, Mama," I said, and finished my tea, and picked up my bag and can, and off.

Chapter Eighteen

I HAD SETTLED DOWN at school by then, so I never had that fear to go in. An awful feeling it is, to look at a door, and find every feeling inside you telling you to run away. But the run over the mountain cured it more than anything else, for I got into the other valley with a head of steam on that would have carried me solid through brick walls.

I was knowing other boys, too, enough to have a kick and a run with the ball with them, but they were boys not on my list. The listed I kept away from, and even when they called after me I took no notice. But those calls went on the list against them. I remembered Motshill's warning about fighting, too, so I had kept my eyes open for a bit of ground away from the school which would hold us safe from the policemen and the masters, and give us room for a fight, however many there were to see us. A lovely little place I found by the hotel, and next to the drapery shop, where the buildings formed three sides of a square, and only one little window high up. That place I kept in my mind.

Lessons went on just the same that morning, Mr. Jonas taking no notice of me, and me just sitting, and then came playtime.

Out in the yard we went, and straight to Mervyn Phillips I went.

"I will fight you after school," I said, "at the back of Spackman the Draper. Is it?"

"Right, you," he said, and with his bread and butter half in and half out of his mouth, and surprise in his eyes. "I will murder you."

"Good," I said. "At the back of Spackman the Draper."

"Never mind to go to Spackman's," Mervyn Phillips said, and put his eating back in the box, "come you, now."

"Remember what Mr. Motshill said," I said.

"Coward," Mervyn Phillips said. "Excuses you are making, is it?"

All the boys were pressing about us, and Mervyn Phillips took off his coat. So I took off mine, and a boy on the list tried to tear it from me, but I gave him a little clip with the butt of my hand that made him feel silly for minutes. It is strange how one little action like that, of determination bringing hurt, will put a crowd quiet. The boys stopped to press about me, and made a ring instead, and a couple of the boys not on my list came to me and took away my coat and can, and another made a knee in my corner. Off came our shirts and the boys laughed to see the difference between us, but their laughing only made me colder to have Mervyn Phillips on the floor.

"Right, you," said Mervyn Phillips, and stood out, fists up and squaring well. A head and a bit taller than me, he

was, and well set to be a good big man. His face and neck
were a strong red colour, and going into rich white at the
throat and below, and his fists were black on the end of
fair-haired forearms, not from lack of soap and water, but
from coal dust grimed into the flesh.

I went round him a bit to see where his fists worked, and
he tried a left, but it went short and I put one into his chest
that made him take his breath. His eyes were deep blue
and clear, and wide, now, with watching me. I saw them
change colour as he started to come in at me, and I weaved
from left to right, watching the black fists from the corners
of my eyes come past my ears with whispers of wind, and
straightened my left to have him fair upon the nose, with
my shoulder behind it and my right swinging back for the
cross. But he knew his danger and quickly his right was up
to block me. Over came his left and caught me beside the
head and down I went flat on my back, with the feet of
the crowd over me and their faces going round and round.

"Corners," shouted the seconds, and mine came across
to give me a hand back to Mat Powell's knee. I was steady
on my feet, but inside my head was like the winding
house when the wheel is turning to bring up the cages, and
there is a shaking and a low hum of the engine at pressure.

"Are you right, Morgan?" Mat Powell asked me, and
his hair falling across his eyes and him blowing it away,
"keep away from him, man. A couple more lefts like that
and you will be good for the cats."

Time again, and in we went with a push from the
seconds, pulling up before we went full-tilt into each other.
Careful again, I worked round him, knowing the holes in
his guard and his habit of hitching his trews with his
elbows. But while a man is hitching his trews, his fists are
idle. So I got him moving faster to have them falling the
quicker, and sure enough, there they slipped, and down
went his elbows to hitch them up.

In I went, with my father's face near to him and his
words in a whispered shout loud in my ears, and Dai Bando
standing behind me with his hands working my arms as
they had that morning. A good long left hard on the base
of the nose, from the shoulder, with feet planted firm, a
pace forward as his head went back with drips of blood flying away from my fist, one, two, three, more short ones,
more poke than punch, to have him off his balance, then a
pace forward to be nearer to him, and right, half-arm, with

my swung body full behind it, to the spot between his breast bones, and my fist meeting flesh with a hard, clean sound, and going in as to a hole, a big grunt as he doubled forward, and now I swung on my heels to catch his chin with a left as his head came forward, and brought my right to the side of his jaw with all the strength of my muscles, and down he went full length, and down I went, too, backwards, from the force of hitting him.

And there he was, getting up to his knees with his hand holding his jaw and blood shining wet on his face, and there I was, on my feet again and waiting, and Mr. Jonas came round the corner.

"The bell has gone," he said to the crowd. "Are you deaf?"

Then he saw me over the boys' heads.

And he smiled.

"Dear, dear me," he said, coming closer, very slowly, with his hands behind him, and putting his feet with deliberate steps, "so our coal-mining friend has been indulging his favourite passion again?"

He came to stand over me, but I took no notice, and put on my shirt, and a couple of boys helped Mervyn Phillips into his. All the other boys had gone away quietly, but I could hear them running blind as soon as they were out of Mr. Jonas' sight. I wished I was with them.

"I should report you to Mr. Motshill, of course," he said. "But I shall punish you myself. You are in Standard Six and I am responsible for your conduct. You were warned, so you cannot complain. Go to my desk and get my stick, and wait till I come."

I turned from him and went into the school, with Mat Powell beside me. The day was a bit grey, not very cold, and a spitting of rain in the east wind, nothing to cheer. I have never hated anything without life so much as I hated the yellow bricks of that low schoolhouse.

"Stuff my coat down your trews," Mat said, "or he will have you in blood."

"No matter," I said. "There will be no change in it for him."

Inside the classroom we went, Mat to his seat in the long desk, me to take the stick from the hook and stand by the book cupboard. The class was more than forty in number, more than half of them boys and the rest girls. I had never had much interest to look at the girls, for they were always quiet, and I never troubled to tell one from another, for they were only girls. But facing them I had more chance to see them, and a dull lot they were, except two.

Ceinwen Phillips sat near her brother. Both of them were the same height and the same shape of face, but Ceinwen was shorter and finer in the nose, with a mouth always a little open to show good teeth and fat and square in the bottom lip. A good big eye she had with her, blue like her brother's, but with plenty of woman in it, and long curling hair to her waist the same colour as new hay.

She looked murder at me when her brother came in, and kept looking, straight and without a blink, while she felt for her handkerchief in her belt to give him to wipe off the blood. Past face after face I looked, along the long desks, past my empty place and more faces, some on the list and some not, to Mat Powell who was looking bright at me as though to cheer, past more faces to Shani Hughes, who sat at the end of the row nearest to me. In something of blue was Shani, a blue that you will see in the fire sometimes, a pale, but not watery blue, with depth in it, and plenty of sky.

Shani had hair the colour of September leaves, that shone, and a red ribbon coming up behind her ears with a bow on top. She was small, and gentle in her voice and movements, dark in the eye, and with a little line of a mouth, and sideways, looking like those queens on coins from Greece. In her eyes I found pity, and dark sadness.

From Shani back to Ceinwen I looked, and found murder in her still, and back to Shani. And I made my mind strong whatever Mr. Jonas might do to me, to keep shut my mouth.

He came in behind me, quietly, and without a look at him, I knew he was smiling, and the quiet grew hot as he came to stand behind me. He took the stick from my hand, but I still looked at the picture of the Duke of Wellington on the back wall.

"Mervyn Phillips," Mr. Jonas said, hitting the stick against his leg, "please be so good as to come to the front, and make a back."

Mervyn Phillips came out, not looking at me, and blushing with the stains still on his face, and stood to one side, bending down. Ceinwen Phillips was smiling now, and she nudged the girl beside her. Smiles there were all round the class, but not good smiles, only moves of the mouth, as though they were thankful not to be in my place. I felt that dragging inside me, deep down, not of fear, but of expectance, waiting for the next to happen and not sure when, but hoping it to be soon, when you find your hands wet and the skin of your face pricking with heat.

"Please to bend across his back," said Mr. Jonas, still behind me, still sweet, but sudden, to make me jump.

Across his back I climbed and locked my hands about his neck. The stick swished twice as though Mr. Jonas were getting his length. The sound screwed itself inside my brain and my will flew to my back that was naked with wonderment, and tender with nerves alive for a hurt.

The stick swished again, and I saw the swift shadow on the floor and heard in anguish the flat squash of it falling across me, and the sharp, shocking burning of its work. Swish again, and the shadow, and the grunt of Mr. Jonas, and the movement of Mervyn Phillips' throat under my hands, and his sway forward, and the spread of his feet to be firmer and again the sharp wounding. And again and again and again without pause, as clocks work, and the sound changing as the strokes fell upon me and worked upward, and down again, until my back was a long hurt that seemed to be in flames, and a blindness in my eyes, and thunder filling my head, and the strokes coming to be only a hard, dull laying on, mattering nothing, and hurting no more than snowflakes.

And the stick broke. The top flew over me and bounced where I could see it.

"Now then," said Mr. Jonas, in falsetto, and breathless, "fight again. Was just a taste. Back to your place. No more nonsense. Teach you manners."

I looked at him as I slipped from Mervyn Phillips' back, and found him pale, wet about the forehead, with a blueness about the mouth, and a shifting of muscles pulling one side of his face, and a pinkness in his eyes, and a trembling in the hands that he tried to have quiet by linking his fingers. His eyes stared hard at me, moving over my face, but I kept my eyes on his. His tongue put wet about his mouth, and his breath pulled him up short as though reins had been jerked, and then I turned away from him and got my legs to bring me to my seat. On my way I saw Ceinwen Phillips' handkerchief, with the blood of her brother on it, ripped in strips on the desk before her, and her face hidden and her shoulders trembling.

"Now," said Mr. Jonas, still in falsetto, but breaking more to his own voice, and forgetting his painful English, "we will have geography. Turn to your atlas and find India, be so good."

And while he taught geography, I sat.

Many times that day I wished I was on my back with the ice on the grass cold against me. I was on fire, and in no haste to move even an arm. Dinner-time came, but I sat on, wanting nothing except to drink, but unwilling to move even for that. And I was saved to do it, for Shani came in a few minutes before the bell to settle her books, and found me.

"O," she said, with the back of her hand quickly to her mouth, and her eyes going big, "are you here still?"

"Yes," I said.

"And no dinner?" she asked me.

"No," I said.

"Will I get it for you?" she said, and came closer with a look round at the door. "You can eat quick, see."

"Only a drink I want," I said.

"Drink, is it?" she said. "Wait you."

She went running from the room, quick but quiet, from toe to toe, with a rush of skirts, blue, with yellow braid in three lines all round the bottom and some in lovers' knots on the front, with her hair moving as a feather blown from the bed when a blanket shakes, gentle, and curving, and up and down. Back again, more careful, carrying a flower-pot with water running down and off her hands, and shining splashes dark on her dress.

"Drink now," she said, and warmth in her eyes, "and put the pot under the desk for a drink again. Are you hurting with you?"

"Yes," I said. "Sore it is."

"They said you had pieces of carpet down your back," she said, "and that is why you had a straight face."

"Feel if there is carpet," I said.

She came closer, and I smelt cloves and cinnamon about her as she put her hand to touch my back. Only a touch it was, but so heavy and sharp it felt, that she might have had hot iron in her hands.

"There is sorry I am," she said, and her mouth making shapes and tears coming to fill her eyes, that were brown and deep and big. "No carpet."

"It is nothing," I said. "No matter."

"Will you tell your mother?" she asked me.

"No, no," I said.

"Do you like birds' eggs?" she asked me, and a smile trying to come.

"Yes," I said, "I have got plenty."

"No," she said, and a smile, properly, now.

"Yes," I said. "Have you got a nightingale?"

"No," she said, and sat, with her eyebrows high, and still a smile, "have you? I was going to give you a robin's."

"Why?" I asked her.

"Because you are hurting," she said, and the smile was gone.

"I will have the robin's if you will have the nightingale," I said.

"Indeed I will," she said, and here comes the smile again, bigger than before. "I do love a nightingale. So pretty in song. Have you got nightingales over with you?"

"Millions," I said. "And pheasants, and partridges, and hawk, and kestrel, and chaffinches."

"We have got thousands of them," she said, "but I would like to see a hawk nesting and I would like to hear a nightingale. They used to sing to us, but not since the new ironworks opened. They burnt all the trees."

The bell went and so did her smile, and up she got, and off.

"After school," she said, and her hand was white in a wave at the door.

Long was the afternoon, and infinite my thanks to be up and going home at last. Out in the playground the air hit me as with a blow, and I had to lean against the wall to have strength. Then on, down the street, tired with ache, and ready to lie down anywhere.

Mervyn Phillips ran up beside me with Ceinwen coming on my other side.

"I am sorry you had all the stick, Huw Morgan," he said, "but his knife is sharp for you, and there it is. Will I carry your books?"

"Thank you," I said, "but no matter."

"Shall we shake hands, then?" Mervyn asked me, and a bit shy, a bit red with it, and having a push from Ceinwen.

"Right," I said, and we shook hands in shyness.

"Huw Morgan," Ceinwen said, and bright red, her, and not with running, and her eyes blue as blue, and big, and with shine, "I will kiss you."

And she did, and I felt her mouth on my cheek, warmer than my face, and her breath hotter and heavy with her life, and her hands hurting when she pulled me close. Then she went running, with her hair in lines behind her, across the road in front of a gig, and the driver turned to swear at her and she poked her tongue.

"See you to-morrow, Huw," Mervyn said, and he ran to throw a stone at the driver of the gig.

I was down at the Square and walking slowly when Shani caught me up, but I knew from her step who she was, though she had to come in front of me to talk for I was past turning.

"How will you go home?" she asked me. "Will I ask Dada to let me take the trap?"

"No," I said, "I am going with Ellis the Post, now just."

"There is glad I am," she said, and a shadow in her eyes, and putting her hands together in front with relief. "I am afraid you will drop every minute."

"Drop?" I said, and anger spurted up inside me. "The day I drop will be the day I die. Hurting, I am, only a bit. I will have the nightingale egg for you to-morrow."

"And you shall have the robin," she said, in a little voice. "Good-bye now."

"Good-bye," I said, and went to climb up beside Ellis, and O, there is sweet relief, for the cushion was soft, and the blanket behind was kind to my back.

Up at home I went into a quiet house, and pulled off my clothes. Nobody was in, so I was able to look at my back in the glass. It was striped with wide swollen marks that cast shadows, so bumpy they were. Then I heard Ianto whistling, coming from the pit, and made haste to dress, but he was in before I could get my shirt on.

"Hulloa," he said, and threw his can at me to catch, but I dropped it. "There is a mark-down you would have, man. The ball would be down the other end before you would have your eyes open."

He stopped still, with his eyes staring pink-rimmed in his face black with dust, and made to lift my shirt.

"What is that, boy?" he said, and whispering.

"School," I said.

"Did you have that in school?" he said, and looking again. "He have cut you to the bone, man."

"Say nothing," I said, and on with my shirt. "You know what Mama will say."

"I know well what I will say to him who did that," Ianto said. "Wait you till I have bathed."

I took my tea from the oven, and then Bron came in to take clothes off the line for Ianto and some for Ivor.

"How is the old man?" she said, and pulled my cheek.

"Good," I said.

"Good," she said, and picked up my can. "Did you like the apple pie I made for you?"

Then she felt the weight, and looked at me between a smile and a frown.

"Are you carrying stones in this, then?" she asked me, and took the staple from the catch to open it.

"Well, goodness gracious, boy," she said, in wonder. "Not a bite you have had from it. Where is the use in cooking special for you, and tramping it home again?"

"Leave him alone, Bron," Ianto shouted from outside, with the bucket going down hard on the stones. "Look at his back."

"No," I said, and ran from the house and up the mountain, with Bron calling after me.

Right up the top I went, and glad to sit down in the cold wind.

Pain is a good cleanser of the mind and therefore of the sight. Matters which seem to mean the world, in health, are found to be of no import when pain is hard upon you.

That evening while the cold froze the pain, while I saw again the faces of Mr. Jonas, and fought again with Mervyn Phillips, and saw Ianto's face, and tried to find rest for my boiling mind, I fell upon a loud dream that had no start and no end, and I saw the Valley outside its skin and bone of grass and trees, with clearness and with immortal truth. As ants do burrow, I saw men working, far below me, to bring money to their houses. I saw fewer men paying out that money, and keeping most for themselves. I saw the riches of the earth crumble before picks and taken away by the shovel. It came to me that presently, as with all other things, those riches would have an end. The money would not be paid, for there would be none for master or man. The pick and shovel would rust. The collieries would be left to flood-water and rats. The men would go. The houses would empty. The Chapel would be dark. The grass would try to cover all, out of pity.

And I was afraid.

I looked up in the darkening sky and saw the big winding wheel chopping the light with its spokes as it slowed down, and swung to stop. I heard the clatter of the last lamps and the rattle of the last brass checks as the men handed them in, and their boots heavy in the dust going farther and farther from my hearing, and the voice of a myriad rats, having happiness in the black waters of the empty pit, rose up to sweep aside all other sounds, and terror found me.

I awoke too stiff to move, in darkness, and still held tight by fear, so tight that I dare not move my eyes. Little at a time I had my legs at work, and as the sounds of night came more and more to comfort me, I sat.

The wind was sharp about his business and whistling a little tune to let his friends on the mountain know he was up and about to clean house, and no nonsense with loose leaves or dead twigs, for he would have them, and quick. The more he whistled, the more the trees tried to hush him, and the bigger the tree, the bigger the hush, and beating at him with their arms to stop him tickling them, but no use, for he was in one side and out the other, and nothing they could do only wave at him, and hush more.

The sky was full of thin light from the stars, and down below me the village was a long criss-cross of small yellow lights, one bright one outside the Chapel, two outside the Three Bells, and a couple of small ones up on the other side of the mountain in the farmhouse, all else dark, with the dark, clear softness that tells of coming rain. The mountain on the other side had turned over to sleep and his black hipbone curved up and fell away to thigh in the darkness, and farther over, the other mountains slept too, with shadows in the colour of lavender going to deep blue.

The wind held up above his head the sound of the choir from the Chapel for me to hear, and gave it back, but in those few notes I heard the rich, male voice of the men of the Valley, golden, brave, and clean, with heart, and with loftiness of spirit, and I knew that their voice was my voice, for I was part of them as they were of me, and the Valley was part of us and we were part of the Valley, not one more than the other, never one without the other. Of me was the Valley and the Valley was of me, and every blade of grass, and every stone, and every leaf of every tree, and every knob of coal or drop of water, or stick or branch or flower or grain of pollen, or creature living, or dust in ground, all were of me as my blood, my bones, or the notions from my mind.

My Valley, O my Valley, within me, I will live in you, eternally. Let Death or worse strike this mind and blindness eat these eyes if thought or sight forget you. Valley of the Shadow of Death, now, for some, but not for me, for part of me is the memory of you in your greens and browns, with everything of life happy in your deeps and shades, when you gave sweet scents to us, and sent forth spices for the pot, and flowers, and birds sang out of pleasure to be with you.

．．．．．．．．．．．．．

It was my dream, and the vision, that carried me to Mr. Gruffydd that night, for I wanted to know if they were right or wrong. I felt them to be right, but I wanted them to be wrong. As I went down, the nightingales were singing near the blackberry bushes by the Glas Fryn field, and I thought of Shani Hughes.

When I got in the village I found nobody about, not even a cat, but there was a voice coming from the Chapel, stopping now and again for people to shout, and I remembered the big meeting called for that night by Mr. Gruffydd. I went closer and tried the door at the back, but it was locked, so round to the front I went, and found the porch crowded with people pressed close together, listening, with their faces pale in the light of the oil lamps, and on each face an openness, a peace, a smile of hope, as though great news had come for each one and they were having joy of it.

Through the open doors I saw the packed rows of people, and down the aisles all were kneeling, with even the big seat crowded with kneelers. Mr. Gruffydd's eyes were closed and his fists were tight upon The Book.

"Beloved God," he prayed, "give light. The darkness is in men's minds, and in that darkness is Satan, ever ready, ever watchful, quick to find a way to harm, a deed to hurt, a thought to damage. Give light, O God."

"Amen," said the people.

"The evil that is in Man comes of sluggish minds," prayed Mr. Gruffydd, "for sluggards cannot think, and will not. Rouse them with fire, O God. Send upon us thy flames that we may be burnt of dead thoughts, even as we burn dead grass. Send flames, O Lord God, to make us see."

"Alleluia," said the people, with one voice.

"All things are expedient, but all things edifieth not," prayed Mr. Gruffydd, "but there are things needful which we lack, and which would edify. These things we know, and pray for, Lord God, the same things that Thy dearly beloved Son asked for, and died for. And of those, our daily bread, that others, blind in sight and soul, would take from us. Let them be brought from their blindness, Lord God. Let them see."

"Alleluia," said the people.

"As once the Voice sang in Darkness when the Earth was born," prayed Mr. Gruffydd, "so let again another voice sing through the darkness in men's minds and let it say Let There Be Light, and Lord let there be light. For the lighted mind of man can bring to fruition all good things for himself and for his kind, if he choose. But too many skulk behind the golden bars of the mansion of Mammon, and are filled and replete, and forget their brethren, and deny them, and allow them to walk in hungry idleness, and their women to die of want, and their children to perish even before they are born. Lighten our darkness, Lord God. Let there be light."

"Alleluia," said the people.

"Come unto me, all ye that are weary and heavy laden," sang Mr. Gruffydd.

"Hosanna, hosanna," sang the people.

"Come, let us sing unto the Lord," sang Mr. Gruffydd. The people in the porch were going to their knees in tears, and as the congregation started to sing, they lifted their voices with them.

"Huw," said Bronwen's voice, and I turned, and saw her, watching me, with the hood of her cloak over her head, and the cloak close about her, with her hands outside and held toward me. She was smiling the old smile, with her eyes closed up and showing only diamonds of light, and her mouth wide, but soft, and showing the tips of her teeth.

"Come, you," she said. "We have looked all night."

"I went to sleep on the mountain," I said, and she put her arms about me, and lavender was warm next to me, and the gentle soft of her firm bosom pressed against me, and the touch of her mouth on my forehead.

"You will have your death with cold," she said, and a shake in her voice. "Your Mama is in Chapel, but dragged there, and only because I said I would look for you."

"What is going on in there, Bron?" I asked her, under her cloak, with her arm about me, and hurting my back, but a good hurt and one to forget, as we went up the Hill.

"It is the Revival, boy," Bron said, and tears shining on the very tips of her eyes, long shining tears, shining in the shine of the stars, and her eyes sad, and her voice going from her.

"Why, Bron?" I asked her, and a bit frightened, because she was different.

"The men in the Three Valleys came out to-night," she said, "and our colliery will come out to-morrow, I suppose. Come, you. There is brandy broth for you."

Into the house I went, misgiving myself because of the news, and still a bit frightened of the Revival, but happy to wash for a bowl of brandy broth, indeed.

O, Brandy Broth is the King of Broth and royal in the rooms of the mouth. A good chicken and a noble piece of ham, with a little shoulder of lamb, small to have the least of grease, and then a paste of the roes of trout with cream, a bit of butter, and the yolk of egg, whipped tight and poured in when the chicken, proud with a stuffing of sage and thyme, has been elbowing the lamb and the ham in the earthenware pot until all three are tender as the heart of a mother. In with the carrots and turnips and the goodness of marrow bones, and in with a mixing of milk and potatoes. Now watch the clock and every fifteen minutes pour in a noggin of brandy, and with the first a pint of home-brewed ale. Two noggins in, and with the third, throw in the chopped bottoms of leeks, but save the green leaves until ten minutes from the time you sit to eat, for then you shall find them still a lovely green.

Drink down the liquor and raise your eyes to give praise for a mouth and a belly, and then start upon the chicken.

Bron left me to myself and went down to meet Ivor, so I went to bed, full, happy, and caring nothing for all the hurt of all the Englished Welshmen that ever festered upon a proud land.

Chapter Nineteen

UP ON THE MOUNTAIN next morning Dai Bando saw my back and dropped his hands, and his eyes that were always half closed went to nothing in a frown.

"What is this, boy?" he said, in his high little voice.

"School," I said.

"Have your brothers seen it?" he asked, and put his fingers to his mouth to whistle at Cyfartha.

"Ianto did," I said, "but there is nothing to be done because of my mother."

"Well, I will go to my death," said Cyfartha.

"Who is he?" Dai asked me, and looking at me sideways, with his head on one side.

"Mr. Jonas," I said. "Mr. Jonas in school, and Mr. Jonas-Sessions out."

"Mr. Jonas-Sessions," Dai said, and rubbing his knuckles together. "Have we got business to do over in there, Cyfartha?"

"There is the match for Thursday," Cyfartha said.

"So if we do go over there," Dai said, and staring hard at him, "we are only going over by there to fix the match for Thursday, eh Cyfartha?"

"No other reason I can think of, Dai, my little one," Cyfartha said, and very sober. "Unless you are thinking of paying a call social."

"There are worse ways of spending five minutes," Dai said. "Plenty, indeed. Mr. Jonas-Sessions, is it? Eh, Cyfartha?"

"A good man with a stick, Dai," said Cyfartha. "I wonder what would he do with a box of eggs?"

"Social, me, to-day," said Dai, "in my best breeches and bowler bloody hat. Eh, Cyfartha?"

"Me, too," said Cyfartha.

"Go you home, boy," said Dai, and very kind, "and come in three mornings from now. Is it?"

"Thank you, Dai," I said.

"And if you do see a couple in their best doing it big to-day," Dai said, "it is none of your business. Eh, Cyfartha?"

"Eyes open," Cyfartha said. "Mouth shut."

So off I went home, and into trouble.

"Huw," my father said, "off with your shirt."

"It is nothing, Dada," I said, for my mother was watching cold.

"Do you dare to answer me?" my father shouted, in black rage. "Off with your shirt."

Off it had to come and quick, indeed.

My mother went to stand by my father to put her hands about his shoulders. I stood for a moment with the heat of the fire on my side. There was quiet, but I could feel my mother's eyes.

"Why did you have that, my son?" my father asked me.

"I was fighting, Dada," I said, and back in my shirt.

"Did you win?" my father asked, and patting my mother's hand to stop the shake.

"Yes, Dada," I said.

"So you had your marks on your back, then, this time, my son," my father said.

"Yes, Dada," I said.

"Good," said my father. "Five shillings in the box for you."

"But Gwilym," my mother said, and ready to burst with anger and surprise. "Will you let him be beaten like that? Will you let a brute of a man treat your son like that and let him free?"

"If I will go down there to him, Beth," my father said, "I will have the bones hot from his body."

"Let me go, Dada," Ivor said. "Bron have cried all night."

"Nobody shall go, if not me," my father said. "The boy was beaten for fighting. I told him to fight and I tell him to fight again, even for such a beating. If it is against the laws of the school, then a beating he must have. But go on fighting, my son. Is it hurting with you?"

"Not much, now, Dada," I said.

"Good," he said. "Five shillings in the box, Mama, and he shall go with the boys and me to see Ireland playing us, is it?"

I went to school that morning three feet from the ground with joy, and the nightingale egg making a hard lump in the corner of my cap.

There was a different spirit among the boys, so different that I could have laughed in their faces. Instead of the whispered jokes and laughing that I had had ever since going there, now they looked at me with a look almost of appeal, as though anxious to show friendship. A couple of those on the list even smiled at me and said a good morning.

There is silly are people. You must suffer, or cause others to suffer, before you will have respect of one kind or the other from them. I was having both kinds that morning, and not liking it, either. I will not stand to be looked at by anybody, especially when the looking is done with wrong thinking.

And a man is a man, suffering or not, and entitled to just as much respect as he is, as he might be after suffering, or with the sufferings of others on his conscience. So I passed them all by, and went to look for Shani Hughes.

Not a word or a look from Mr. Jonas after he had just put his eyes on me for a moment when we went in to prayers. All through the day I sat, and sometimes Shani turned to smile at me, and sometimes Ceinwen looked round.

But there was a look there that made me draw back from giving her a good smile. Her eyes were bright blue, with the white nearly all round and very white, and yet, for all their brightness and white, there appeared in them not a darkness, but an inner fogginess, as though she saw me, not as me, but as part of her thoughts.

I was ready to run from that look, indeed.

We had been back from dinner about half an hour when there was a knock in the middle of religious instruction and please would Mr. Jonas kindly step into Mr. Motshill's room, from a little girl from Standard Three, who just put the top of her head round the door like a little mouse, and ran. Mr. Jonas gave his catechism to our monitor and went out.

As soon as he was gone Ceinwen came to sit by me. I took no notice for a little while, but then she slid an ivory ruler toward me, with calibrations on it, a lovely piece of craft and a delight to hold, with its age golden in it.

"That is for the one I broke," she said. "I was always sorry about your box."

"Where did you have it?" I asked her.

"From my father," she said. "I asked him first. Have it. I have put my name on the back with a pin."

"Thank you," I said. "But perhaps your father will want it."

"No, no," she said. "I told him I wanted it for you. Will you give me a nightingale's egg, now?"

"Who told you?" I asked her.

"Shani Hughes," she said. "She has got it in a little box with a piece of glass, and I want one. O, Huw. Give me a nightingale's little egg, is it? I would do anything for you, back. I kissed you, see."

"You shall have an egg," I said, "and I will make the little box. But not because you kissed me. Not one for one. Only because treat one, treat the other."

I looked down at Shani and found her looking at me straight, but darkly and for some reason I was sorry for her, and I wanted to go to her to put my arm about her and shield her, though from what it would be hard to say.

Then shouting came from the hall, and got louder, Mr. Motshill's voice, and Mr. Jonas', and furniture being broken, somebody screaming, heavy steps running in the hall and more shouts and screams, and all the girls in school started screaming, but nobody knew why. Everybody in class ran out of their desks to the door, but then the door burst open and Mr. Jonas ran in, with Dai Bando and Mr. Motshill, three of the masters behind, and Cyfartha Lewis just leading Mr. Tyser, who stood in the doorway clapping hands with one side of his collar loose.

Mr. Jonas was torn and in pieces, collarless, with a piece of his tie hanging like a rag, his coat ripped, his trousers torn all the way down, and his face white, and watery in the eyes, and purple in the cheeks from flat-handers that Dai gave him whenever his head came up, slap, slap, one, two, almost as quick as you can count, not with the knuckles, but with the palm.

Mr. Motshill was trying to stop Dai hitting, but Dai was taking no notice, not a bit, and Mr. Motshill was dancing with anger and shouting, and hitting Dai's broad back with his fists, but nothing could be heard in the screaming of the girls. Cyfartha put one of the masters on the floor with a hook, and the other two dropped their hands and stood watching Dai. As soon as he was sure there was no danger of the other masters joining in, Dai off with his belt and gripped Mr. Jonas about the neck and bent him over his knee, and with his foot on the step of the desk platform. The way that belt slashed and cracked, and the way Mr. Jonas shouted was a marvel, although he could barely be heard, for the screaming from the girls when Dai took him by the neck could not have been bettered beyond the bounds of purgatory.

Dai was finished and Mr. Jonas crying limp, then he winked to Cyfartha, and they gripped him, shoulders and feet, and swung him right through the open trap of the coal locker and shut the lid.

Dai took papers and tobacco from his bowler hat and rolled a cigarette, and with Mr. Motshill and the others watching them, helpless, Cyfartha lit a fusee for him, and he puffed blue clouds while the screaming went down and down like the end notes of the hooter. Dai wiped his forehead with a pull down of his sleeve, and put his bowler hat on straight, and turned to look all round the class. Although he saw me, nothing was in his eye, and I will swear nothing was in mine.

"You bully," Mr. Motshill was shouting. "You cowardly brute. You dare come in here to this school and assault a master. You shall be dealt with by the law. If I were younger you would carry my mark with you."

"I am paying a call," Dai said, soft, and almost as though he was saying he was sorry. "I had thought to have him up on the mountain, and not in here. I asked him to come, see? Eh, Cyfartha?"

"Invited he was," Cyfartha said, "and not polite to say no, either."

"He ran from me," Dai said, "so I had to run after him. I came a long way to find him, but I was willing to go through hell to China to have him. And I had him in by here. So what is the odds? Eh, Cyfartha?"

"Yes, yes," Cyfartha said. "Nice and comfortable, he is, now, see? Nothing more he could want in the world. So home for a pint, is it, Dai, my little one?"

"A good pint," said Dai, "would do me a blessing of good, indeed to God. A dusty old place you have got in here, sir, dusty indeed. Dry on the throat, and useless for a song, eh, Cyfartha?"

"A frog would have it hard to get a note," said Cyfartha.

"Good afternoon to you, sir," said Dai, and touching his bowler hat very civil to Mr. Motshill. "And good afternoon, everybody else, and to hell with him in by there."

And out they went and their boots knocking on the board floor, and the door outside bump, bump, bump behind them. Not until the last swing did Mr. Motshill move, and then he sat tiredly on the edge of the desk.

"Be good enough to bring Mr. Jonas to light," he said, almost in a sigh.

Two masters pulled open the lid, and Mr. Jonas came to light with his hair in a mop and his face streaked with coal, with the swellings of Dai's finger marks purple on his cheeks, eyes cold with rage, and shivering all over when they helped him from the room, wordless but with little sounds that might have been laughable, but made feelings of pity. It is strange how you shall hate a man, and yet pity him from the depths.

Chapter Twenty

GOING HOME that night with Shani, we found the streets and the square full of people, men and women, the men black from work, the women dressed for the house and bareheaded, all talking in groups and looking serious.

"What is wrong here, Ellis?" I asked him, while he was putting Mari in the shafts.

"On strike," Ellis said, and in sorrow, and with anxiousness. "I expect ours will be out by the time we are home. Your father and Ianto and Davy and a couple more have gone over to see the owners. God knows what will happen, indeed."

All along the road round the mountain by the river men came running from their houses to have the news from Ellis, who never stopped, but shouted as he slapped the reins on Mari's back, and at his words the men seemed to go dead, and the women were still, or wrung their hands or held their babies tighter.

Round in our village the people were out in the street, and all up the Hill they were out, not talking much for there was nothing to talk about, but waiting for the men to come back. I jumped off as the people crowded about Ellis, and I heard the low murmur as his words were passed back.

In our home my mother was peeling apples, and Angharad was chopping the peel for jam. Bron was ironing, and Olwen was playing with Gareth in front of the fire.

"Well," said my mother.

"The men are out in Three Valleys, Mama," I said.

Nobody stopped working, but Bron was crying as I passed her, but so quietly you would never know. All that night I was cleaning Owen's engine, for I had learned to take it to pieces and fit it all back again, and

I was taking the grease off my hands when I heard my father's step in the back, and he came in quietly, cap and coat on, and sat down, looking at the candles, wordlessly and with grief, with his moustache like silver.

He cleared his throat as though pain had been his only meal for hours.

"Huw," he said, and still looking at the candles.

"Yes, Dada," I said, and went to him with my hands dripping with grease.

"I am shamed to go in and face your Mama," he said, and still not looking at me.

"Why?" I said.

"O, boy, boy," he said, and if he had had the tears they would surely have come then. "How you and your sons will live, I cannot tell. Come you here, my son."

I went closer, and he put his arms about me, and rested his whiskery cheek against mine.

"I could see you all day to-day," he said, "while they were talking and arguing. You and your sons. What is to happen to you I cannot tell. The ground is cut from under our feet. Nothing to be done. Nothing."

His voice was close to my ear, and heavy with sorrow.

"It is your mother and the other women who will suffer," he said. "They will have the burden. I am shamed to go in and tell her."

"She is waiting for you, Dada," I said.

He was quiet for a little, and then he put me from him, and got up.

"God bless her," he said, "she always has. Stay you in here for a bit, Huw, my little one."

"Yes, Dada," I said, "there is grease on your coat."

"No matter," he said, and went into the house.

Ianto came in just after he had gone, white and brilliant in the eyes, as a man will look after a fight only half finished.

"Has Dada gone in?" he asked me.

"Yes," I said.

"Good," he said. "I thought we would never get him home."

"Why, then?" I asked him.

"Never mind, boy," he said, with impatience. "How was he?"

"In pain," I said.

Ianto hit his fists softly on the bench.

"Yes," he said, "we are all in pain. And we will stop there, too."

"Are we coming out?" I asked him.

"We are out, now," said Ianto, "since half-past three we have been out."

"Will we win, Ianto?" I asked him.

"As much chance of that as flies in a beer-trap," Ianto said. "No chance. No hopes. Good night, now."

He went out and listened at the kitchen window for a moment and then went down to Bron's. There seemed nothing that I could do so I climbed up the shed and went through the window to bed.

Next morning I was allowed only two slices of bread, with butter on only one, and no jam. For school, I had a pie and bread and cheese with lettuce, but no tea.

"It will have to be water, Huw, my little one," my mother said. "Your Dada cannot tell when the strike will end, so we must start to have the least of less."

It was strange to go out in the street and find the men out there, on chairs, or sitting on window sills, or just standing in the gutters. There was a feeling of fright in it, too, for the street was always empty at other times. The wind was full of the low rising and falling of their voices, but nobody talking loudly, or laughing.

I looked back at the top of the mountain and saw the Hill, and the street down in the village full with specks of people, and even in the farms, men and women were out in their gardens, standing at the walls, looking down into the Valley, as though they were expecting to see tongues of fire.

That was July, and a hot month, when the grass went brown and the river dried, and the rocks so hot that they would almost burn your feet as you crossed them. Meeting after meeting the men held on the mountain side, and it was strange to see them every day going browner and browner with the sun, and it was then I saw how pale they had always been, even my father and brothers, with lack of it.

Nothing was said, not a word, at home about the strike. It was never allowed to come past the door. Food got less. Tea we had without sugar and milk, and then no sugar, and after, no tea. Meat came less and less. Bread was spare, thick in the slice, and presently, butter only on Sunday.

August, September.

Still the men held meetings, not only in our Valley, but in the others. My brothers and my father were always tramping over the mountain to meetings. The men wanted more wages. The owners said they were getting less for the coal so wages had to drop. No one would give an inch.

Women were going thin, and children were not so ready to play. Men were fighting among themselves for nothing, for they were idle, penniless, and eating little, and their tempers were just under their skins.

At school, nothing was happening, only Mr. Jonas was teaching and I was sitting. We had nothing to do with one another. Not a word he said to me about his meeting with Dai Bando, and Dai heard nothing more, either. Some of the boys and girls stopped coming to school because their shoes were gone and their parents afraid to buy more in case the money was wanted for food. Some stopped coming because they were only eating once a day.

I only noticed it in Shani one morning when she stood next to Edith Moss, of Moss the Butcher's near the school. Edith was a lump of a girl with big red cheeks and black hair, straight, who said she drank blood hot from the carcass when her father slaughtered. Next to her, Shani was a dove to a raven, so small, and thin, and so white in the face.

Her father was in the collieries, too, in the manager's office, but out as well, of course. One dinner-time she stayed in class to sew. I went out with my can to the playground, but it was raining, so I went to sit in the cloakroom, and I saw Shani looking through the classroom window. I tapped on the glass and smiled at her, but instead of smiling back, she looked as though she wanted to cry, and jumped down from my sight.

Then she came outside and pretended she was going to have a drink, but when she saw me looking she came closer.

"Just going to have a drink, I was," she said.

"Good," I said, and ready to eat my bread and cheese. "Will I get it for you?"

"No, no," she said, but making no move.

It is a fact that if you are hungry and you see somebody eating something you would like to have your teeth in too, spit will flood to your mouth and you will swallow to make a noise. That noise Shani made as I watched her. Then I saw her eyes, and they were on my can.

"Why no home for dinner to-day?" I asked her.

"Oh," she said, and going to do something to her hair, "too much trouble to go all that way for old dinner."

"Will you have a bit of this?" I asked her.

"And take from you?" she said. "No, indeed. You have got longer to come."

"No matter," I said. "There is plenty, look. Have to eat, girl."

I held out bread and cheese, crusty bread, and yellow farm cheese, with cress and lettuce from the garden.

She looked at it, and swallowed again, with her hands behind her.

"Come on, girl," I said. "There is slow you are."

So she took them, and bit into them, and bit and bit and bit, until her little mouth was sure to burst, and her eyes had tears, and as she chewed she sobbed. Your throat goes dry and you cannot have your food in peace when somebody is hungry and shows it. So Shani had dinner for two of us that day, and in the afternoon she fell to the floor during history, and Mr. Jonas carried her outside, and she went home with another girl.

I told my mother when I got home but she said nothing, only clicked her tongue and looked tired. There were many in the village just the same. Next morning I went to school with my can packed tight, and more in a brown paper parcel hanging on my coat button. Not a word from my mother, only a little smile.

So Shani and me sat together to have dinner every day in my mother's smile. I never saw her mother or father, and never went home with her, and though I asked her, she never came over in our Valley because they had sold their trap and it was too far for her. And after we had been having dinner for a couple of weeks she stopped coming. It was said that her father had gone to find work in the north, at Middlesbrough.

I will always remember her in something of blue and three lines of yellow braid, and a little bow on top of her hair and her face so pale and looking from the side like the face of the queens on coins of ancient Greece.

July, August, September.

October.

All down the Hill, and along the walls in the village

street, a long black mark could be seen where men's shoulders had leaned to rub grease. Up and down in a dim, wavy line, but always at the height of the shoulder. Some of the women had taken a bucket of hot water to scrub it off, but soon it was back, and the line was un-broken again.

The public houses closed except for two days a week, when the farmers came through to sell at the market. The three shops gave credit for a bit, and then closed up. Friendly Societies paid out all they had, then those few shillings stopped. The men in the Union with Ianto and Davy had benefit for weeks and weeks, but then that stopped, too.

Women like my mother, who had sons earning, and had saved and kept a good house were putting money and food together each week for the babies of women who had just married, or for women with only a husband earn-ing and many children. But as the weeks and months passed by, more and more women had to stop giving, and needed help themselves.

Mr. Gruffydd went time and time again to the Town and came back with food, money, and clothes for the people down in the hovels. But the people of the Hill would never have any of it. He was thinner, and his clothes were loose on him, and my mother said he would have starved if people had not asked him to eat with them, for he was paid by the Chapel, and the money was all gone in food for the hungry ones.

From all the men in idleness he got together a choir, and made Ivor second conductor to him. All over the valleys they walked, singing for funds, and presently men from the other valleys were coming over the mountain in dozens and scores to join them.

One night I heard a choir of a thousand voices singing in the darkness, and I thought I heard the voice of God.

Then children began to die.

The processions over the mountain were long at first, and sometimes two and three a day. Then they grew shorter, and the hymns fewer, for the people had no strength.

July, August, September, October.

November.

The cold was on us and the snow was thick in the very

first week. People were burning wood, and some of the men went down to the colliery to get coal and were stopped by the watchmen, but they took no notice and loaded up. Next morning, police came by brake, and went to live in the lamp house. Two men who were caught were taken over the mountain and had six months in jail. So those who had no money for coal went up on the mountain for wood, and since all the people in other valleys were looking for wood, there was soon no wood to be had, except standing trees. But they were green and not to be lit by anything but a fire.

More and more children were dying, and now women were dying, and men. No more were coffins built by Clydach. A sheet had to do, and did.

Two, three, and four families went into one house to eat and have warmth together. Windows were boarded to keep out cold. Even Mr. Gruffydd had trouble to keep the men from a riot, and going down to the colliery and killing the police.

One morning in the third week, Ellis the Post stopped Mari outside our house and gave my father a letter.

"Come you in, Ellis," said my mother. "Breakfast is ready."

"No, indeed, Mrs. Morgan, my little one," Ellis said, and pale about the nose with cold. "I will have it when I get home, see."

"You shall have breakfast now," said my mother, "or never come inside this house again."

"Yes, Mrs. Morgan," said Ellis, and off with his cap, and sitting next to me. "But no tea, and no bacon, if you will excuse me."

"Tea you shall have, and bacon, and potatoes," said my mother and ready to fly at him. "And please to have what you are given."

"Yes, Mrs. Morgan," said Ellis, and hang-dog, with his eyes looking at her upwards and sideways.

"If there shall come a time when you leave this house without a proper something to eat," said my mother, "look for me on the floor."

"Beth," my father said, and passing the letter to Ianto, "the boys and me will go into Town to-day."

My mother looked at him straight, with her fork in the potatoes and one foot on the fender.

"Well?" she said.

"The owners," my father said, with more colour in his face then I had seen for weeks.

"We shall have to give in," Davy said, sipping hot water.

"They have promised a minimum wage," my father said. "That is a straw, at all events."

"And we are the drowners," said Ianto, looking at the letter still.

My father raised his fists and hit the table to make the crockery jump.

"No matter," he shouted, with flames in his eyes. "Let us drown, then. But by God Almighty, I will have food in those children's little bellies before the night is out."

"Good, Gwilym," my mother said. "Go you Angharad, go to Mr. Gruffydd and ask him to breakfast."

"O, Mama," Angharad said, and jumped from the stool, and flew from the house.

We had a lovely breakfast that morning, indeed.

Bacon sliced thick, and potatoes, and toast with butter, and strawberry jelly, and tea, with sugar and milk, too. There is good it is to have good food with taste after a long time without.

"Where have you been hiding all this, Beth, my little one?" my father said, eating the breakfast of two and a pleasure to watch.

"You mind your affairs," my mother said, and blushing red and beautiful, indeed, "and I will please attend to mine. Have I been living all this time and nothing to show?"

"Beth, my sweet love," my father said, "you were made and the mould was hit with a hammer."

"Go from here," said Mama, tears and laugh together, "before I will give you a good hit with one, too."

The people were crowding round our house, for they knew that Ellis must have brought a letter, and now they began to shout, and their shouting roused everyone, and presently people were running from their houses to fill the street.

"Shall we have a ride to the station, Ellis?" my father said.

"If I will ride on the back of old Mari, you shall, Mr. Morgan," Ellis said, and meant.

My mother went to the box and counted out the money for each, and kissed them, and out they went. As soon as the people saw them in their best, they knew they were off on business, and because of my father's face, they knew they would have good from it.

So they cheered with tears, and my father was crying when Ellis whipped up Mari, and went off down the Hill, with the people running after, all the way down and out of the village.

No school for me that day, but plenty to do, for I made copies of the letter with Ivor and we took them over the mountain for the checkweighmen of other collieries to read out to their men, and asked them over to meet my father coming back next night.

The news the strike was ended came through the telegraph about five o'clock that night, only a few words in pencil, but indeed, people could not have gone crazier if the writing had appeared again upon the wall.

Up and down the street they ran, shouting and dancing with everybody else, and women looking out of windows and waving, and children playing ring of roses.

When it was dark, about seven o'clock, a big waggon came round the mountain road, and stopped in the middle of the street. People had gone in their houses, for it was cold and starting to snow.

When the driver started to shout they came out one by one, but when he handed out hampers full of groceries, they came running to kill themselves, and he had to ask a couple of the men to make everybody take their turn or he would have been crushed underfoot.

Some said it was a London paper that had asked readers for gifts, and some said it was Old Evans, trying to make peace with the men, and others said it was Mr. Gruffydd again. But Mr. Gruffydd knew nothing about it, and we only found out who it was when my father and the boys came back next night.

Now that was a procession for you.

They came back by train to the end of the line, and then with Thomas the Carrier from there to home. To-night, the men took big torches with them through the snow right to the top of the mountain, where it was so cold that the brass was frozen and the band had to sing instead, and met Thomas as the horses came over the brow. Then they took out the horses and put in pairs of pit ponies from the colliery my father worked in, with all the hauliers dressed up in colours, and lit the torches, and got in lines back and front, and started off for home.

There is pretty to see all those little lights wagging down the mountain and to hear their voice coming nearer and nearer. Hundreds on hundreds were in the procession, more hundreds running to meet them, and hundreds more, with all the women, waiting in the village. So big was the crowd and so much the noise that my poor father could say nothing much himself, for he was tired, but never happier in his life.

"Back to work, boys," he shouted, and the people were cheering to burst the ears. "We will have less, but we have fixed a limit to the less. It has been signed, and it will be made law. Back to work."

"When?" the men were shouting. "When, when?"

"To-morrow," my father shouted back.

"To-morrow," shouted the crowd, and the band struck up for everybody to link arms down the street. The Three Bells opened up to hand out the last of the beer, and then more dancing, until Davy Pryse, who played the big brass horn, had a red ring big as half a crown round his mouth and looking very sore with him, and ice from his breath round the brim of his hat and on his mittens and muffler.

Only the cold, and the torches going out and no more to be had, and nothing much to eat and drink sent the people home.

"For all that has happened, Heavenly Father," my father said when he came in, and went to his knees with my mother beside him, "for the mercies, and the guidance to-day, I do give thanks from my heart. Yesterday I gave thanks, and to-day, thanks again, and to-morrow I will give thanks again, from the heart. In the Name of Jesus the Son."

"Amen," said we all.

"Gwilym," my mother said. "Bed, you."

"Will I have a bit to eat first, then?" my father said. "Starving we are."

"Wash and bed," said my mother, as though from far away. "You have always starved in this house. I know you have had a long way to come, but, of course, there is nothing in the house for you."

"Well, Beth," my father said, trying to find his way into her good books again, "not that I meant, only saying, I was, girl."

"Have you got a nose?" my mother asked, cold still.

"If not screwed off by that old ice on the mountain,"

my father said, and holding the tip with his finger and thumb.

My mother looked at him while we laughed. Her face was straight and her eyes cold, to let him see how insulted she was that he should think to come home and find nothing for his comfort. But Mama could never keep straight her face when Dada was funny, and now you could see the smile coming to her eyes and then she put her hand to his face.

"Oh, Gwil, my little one," she said, "there is tired you are looking. Wash, and to bed, and when you are warm, I will bring what there is."

"What, then?" my father asked, and trying to put his arm round her, but she pretended she was still cross, and pushed him away, but not hard.

"Hot water, boy," she said, and impatient.

"I will wash in that," said my father. "With soap. Is that all I am to have? Hot old water?"

"Smell, boy, smell," my mother said, right out of patience.

My father had a sniff, but he was too cold.

"If I was going to have what I can smell," he said, "there is no need for a pot to be washed in the house."

"O, dammo," my mother said, and took him by the shoulders to put him in his chair to undo his boots. "Hot water you are having, with an old chicken from the farm, and a bit of old beef and lamb, and old rubbish with it. What, now?"

"Beth," my father said, "I will give thanks till I die that I married you. Brandy broth, I will bet you. Let me go to bed."

"I have got a good mind to pour it down the drain," my mother said.

"Bring a bowl of it upstairs," said my father, "and a spoon, and you shall pour it to your heart's content. Is the bed warm?"

My mother smacked his foot, so angry she pretended to be.

"No, boy," she shouted. "Have I got the sense to warm your old bed? Angharad and Bronwen and me have been running up and down stairs all night with blocks of ice, melt one, put the other. Now then, for you."

"Good," said my father, and winking at us, "I do love a good block of ice in bed, indeed."

"Hisht," said my mother, and turned on us. "You are standing there grinning like a lot of monkeys in the circus. Are you washed?"

"Yes, Mama," we said.

"Come to the table," said Mama. "And no more nonsense from you or your father. Gwilym?"

"Yes, my sweet love?" said my father, straight in the face, with gems in his eyes.

"Bed," said my mother.

"Yes, Beth," said my father, and went to the door, and turned round. "Will I have a block of ice, Mrs. Morgan?" he said, in a little boy's voice.

And he flew up the stairs with my mother behind him with the shovel, and us laughing the paint from the ceiling.

Chapter Twenty-One

I WENT FROM THE HOUSE next morning before the men went to work, for with the snow it took longer to get to school, and I had missed two days, so I had to be early.

Wide, white, and beautiful was the Valley from the mountain-top, so clean and smooth and crisp, and my boot-marks going like little shadows all the way down. Even the slag was covered in snow, and only the pithead gear and winding wheel stuck out black, down there. All the village, except in a couple of places where the snow had fallen off the roofs, was inches under snow, and I could see all the marks Ellis and Mari had made going right along the street. The river was frozen, and grey in places, where the ice showed through the snow, but birds were still busy about it, though what for I could never tell.

School was cold as cold, and we kept all our clothes on inside and out, but even so we were cold, and we had clapping for minutes on end during the day to have our hands warm enough to hold the pens.

Mr. Motshill sent for me in the afternoon, and I went in his study and found him in his greatcoat before the little fire.

"Morgan," he said, with a cold in his head, "I have been looking through your homework and comparing it with your school books. There is a difference which I shall merely hint at if I allude to it as startling. Why?"

His eyes were kind, and his nose was red, and even his side-whiskers looked cold and flat to his head.

"Answer me, Morgan," he said, still very kind. "To look in your school books is to find a dolt, and worse, a lazy dolt. I find that three of your brothers had brilliant records in local schools. What is the matter with yours? Or should I say, half of yours? For your homework is the work of quite another fellow. Why?"

There are some times in your life when you are asked a question and you know the answer well, but you cannot find the words to fit. They do sound so dull and silly, you feel shame.

"I had great hope of entering you for a University College Scholarship, Morgan," said Mr. Motshill, and still, for all the trying of his patience, kind in the eyes and voice. "There is nothing I would like better than to see your name in gold out on a special board in the hall. Think how proud your school-fellows would be, and what an example you would be to future scholars here. Think, too, of your father and mother. I am sure they would be most pleased?"

"Yes, sir," I said, glad to have the words to agree.

"Then let us start from that point," said Mr. Motshill, and put a hand on my shoulder. "Why is your school work so immeasurably inferior to the work you do at home? Are you unhappy here?"

"I would like to learn with Mr. Tyser, sir," I said.

"Oh," said Mr. Motshill, and a smile, yet not a smile, just behind his glasses that made his eyes small. "I thought so. Yes, I feared so. Thank you, Morgan. You Welshmen are a funny crew. Back to your classroom, please."

"Yes, sir," I said.

"Remember this, Morgan," said Mr. Motshill, when I got as far as the door, "the man who goes to the top is the man who has something to say and says it when circumstances warrant. Men who keep silent under duress are moral cowards. You understand me?"

"Yes, sir," I said.

"Take it to heart," he said.

Back I went to the classroom, certain sure to work with the best for Mr. Motshill and no matter about Mr. Jonas or anybody else. I went to my desk with my teeth tight shut in firmness. I looked through my writing books and I was filled with bitterness to see the rubbish I had written, and the untidiness, and blots, and scratchings, and the geometry that was a disgrace to man and beast, and no need for any of it.

I had a feeling that something was wrong in the air about me, and though I still looked through the book, my mind was not in it, but outside. Mr. Jonas had stopped talking. He was not in front of the class. Then I felt his smile just behind me. His hand came over my shoulder to take the book away, and as he turned the pages I heard him laughing to himself.

"Come outside, Master Morgan," he said. "I shall have the pleasure to introduce an emeritus professor."

"I shall sit here," I said.

He took me by the ear and pulled me to my feet.

Ceinwen turned and I saw the animals leaping in her eyes. Her mouth stretched and her hands went to grip the front of her dress, and with a nod of the head she told me to fight.

But that was in my mind long before, for I was cold with rage that he should put his hands on me. I was waiting till we got to the front of the class where there was room. Out we went, and I pushing him, and as soon as we reached the space I hit from the waist and caught him in the wind and tore my knuckles on his chain.

Down he went to shake the school, with the blackboard falling and chalk flying. Then the girls started to scream again.

"Run, Huw," Ceinwen was shouting, "run, boy."

But Mr. Jonas was getting up, and as he came his fingers flew at me. I waited till he was on his feet. There is a feeling that comes to you when you long to see blood, and it was strong inside me, now. Not for nothing I had been going up the mountain with Dai and Cyfartha.

A left to the chin, and O, the joy to feel your fist bounce solidly on flesh you hate, and the look of startled pain in hated eyes, a right to the wind, and a left and right to the head put him down again, just as Mr. Motshill came through the door. Strange how in one minute you will be hot to fight and certain of the justness of your wrong, and the next, sick, and ready to fall in the dust with shame.

So I felt as Mr. Motshill came in, and stood looking.

"Morgan," he said, in a voice with a knotted lash, "your hat, and your books, and go home immediately. Do not attend any more this week. I shall see you on Monday next. Mr. Jonas, my study, be so good."

So off I went, and Ceinwen laughing at the ceiling with her hands together.

How to go home and tell my mother I had been sent from school for hitting a master was a problem to me. The more I thought of it the worse looked my part of it. I ran in snowdrifts, and went down the mountain the hardest way to take longer and have more difficulty, as though that might be a bit of salve for sore conscience, but instead of better I felt worse nearer home.

I went in Bron's, but she was busy upstairs, and though she called down, I went out without answering. I was afraid then that my mother would come out and find me, and I threw my books through the window of our back and ran down to Mr. Gruffydd. He was moving from old Mrs. Rowlands for she was going to live with her daughter, and he was having the little house by the Chapel, a dear little house with big windows, and a door with little pillars and a sea-shell porch outside.

I went in the front door to the darkness of the passage and picked my way across boxes, and planks of wood, and paint-pots, to the door of his study, and stopped there. Mr. Gruffydd was in shirt sleeves and very hot, even though it was cold outside and ice was on the windows. A teapot from our house was on a table, and our plates with bread and meat and green stuff beside it. And beside it again, Angharad, standing against a tallboy, with her arms on the top shelf, and facing it, with her head leaning on her arms, looking sideways at Mr. Gruffydd, with her hair hanging down across her cloak. Mr. Gruffydd had been making too much noise dragging a box to hear me come in, and before I could say anything he looked at Angharad and took out a handkerchief to wipe his head.

"I have thought and thought," he said, "but still it seems wrong."

"Not wrong," said Angharad, but not angry, only gently impatient. "I am not tied to Iestyn. Only a friend he is."

"But courting you for months," Mr. Gruffydd said. "Your mother is always saying how happy she is to know you will have plenty all your days."

"Not plenty I want," Angharad said, and there was my mother in her so plain I could have laughed. "There is more than plenty to be had."

"Still it seems wrong for your sake," Mr. Gruffydd said, with weariness.

"Care a little more for your own business," said Angharad, "and less for my sake. If I wanted him I could have him. I would rather have you."

"Angharad," said Mr. Gruffydd, "you are shameless."

"Good," said Angharad, "but only to shame the devil with the truth."

"No," said Mr. Gruffydd, "I am sure it is wrong."

"You are afraid what people will say," Angharad said, standing now, and collecting the pots. "Afraid of people's tongues."

"Nothing of the kind," said Mr. Gruffydd. "I am afraid that you will go threadbare all your life. That you and me will have to depend upon the charity of others for most of our good meals, and on my living for enough to exist. Do you think I want to see the white come into your hair twenty years before its time? Shall we see our children growing up in the cast-off clothing of others? Shall we thank God for parenthood in a house full of bits, and presents that had outlived their use to the givers? No, Angharad. I am a man. I can bear with such a life for the sake of my work. But I think I would start to kill if I saw it having an effect on you."

"Why?" Angharad said, going to him, and beautiful in the eyes, with her fingers spread wide but held soft, to look helpless.

"Because there is no need for it," Mr. Gruffydd said, and very sad. "Poverty is not a virtue, any more than poverty of the spirit. Life is good, and full of goodness. Let them be enjoyed by all men."

"But why would you kill if you saw an effect in me?" asked Angharad.

"Because," said Mr. Gruffydd, and looking for words, and looking everywhere except down at Angharad, "well, only because. Let me go to work now, again."

And he turned from her to pull the cords of a box and drag it away from her. She looked at her hands for a moment and I saw the frown and hopeless shake of her head, and while she turned her back to put the pots in the basket I tiptoed down the passage and went up to Bron's.

"Bron," I said, "I have been sent from school for hitting old Jonas."

"Did you hit hard, boy?" Bron said, and wiping the flour from her hands.

"Yes," I said, "him and the blackboard."

"Only once?" Bron asked, and coming near.

"Five times in all," I said. "And twice he was on the floor."

"Five kisses you shall have," Bron said, and caught hold of me and put five smacks of kisses all over my face. "Now go in and tell Mama."

"I am afraid," I said.

"Afraid, boy?" Bron said, high up. "Your Mama has done everything to him except put onions and grill with cheese. Go you, and come back for fresh strawberry tart."

"Right," I said, "but I am still afraid."

So out I went in the back, and walked along, kicking the ice from the cobbles and taking as long about it as I could. When you are afraid, there seems to be a centre in the mind that requires time before it gives the orders for you to go, and it will have you doing the most senseless things for minutes on end before your courage comes to you and takes you to do the thing you fear. It took me minutes to reach our back door, and more minutes while I went to extremes in cleaning my boots, and when I looked up, there was my mother looking at me and smiling through the back window.

"Come you," she said, and her voice dull behind the window, and down went the curtain.

In I went and stood. It is another strange thing that if you have something on your conscience and you expect punishment you will stand in the most uncomfortable way, as though that, too, would help you out of your trouble.

"Well?" said my mother.

"I have been sent from school, Mama," I said, in no voice at all.

"Bron told me," my mother said. "I have wanted somebody to take those book-shelves down to Mr. Gruffydd these weeks. Go you."

"But I had Mr. Jonas on the floor, Mama," I said, to know whether I was in or out.

"Did you give him a good kick?" Mama asked me, and tapping her thimble on the stone in the sock.

"No, Mama," I said.

"I should have been there," Mama said. "Shelves, Mr. Gruffydd."

I could have carried fifty shelves on my little fingers, so good I did feel.

But Mr. Gruffydd had other notions about it.

"You hit your master?" he said, when I told him, and every hair in his beard seemed to rise. "Think shame to yourself, Huw Morgan. Never have I heard such a shameful thing. Hit your master? A mere boy lifting his hand against a man set over him in authority?"

"I lost my temper," I said.

"You lost your temper," Mr. Gruffydd said, with enough contempt to cover the slag. "You lost your temper, did you? Temper, indeed. Well, well. So when we are put upon, or made to feel our places, we must lose our tempers and hit, eh? Did you ever hear of Jesus Christ? Did He lose His temper?"

"With the money-changers," I said.

"Because they desecrated a holy place," said Mr. Gruffydd, "but never against the law or constituted authority. Not even when they were going to kill Him. But Master Morgan must lose his temper and hit his teacher to the floor. Oh, yes. Did Master Morgan ever hear of Socrates?"

"Yes, sir," I said.

"Then kindly read the argument concerning the laws of the land between himself, that shining great one, and Crito," said Mr. Gruffydd, and pointed to the book. "Master Plato shall instruct you."

I went to Plato and found the place.

"Two thousand and more years ago that was written," said Mr. Gruffydd, "and shame to us that with all our fine educational schemes we still find a young bully putting his silly fists into the face of one set in authority over him. Go on, you. We shall find you on the gallows tree yet."

"I am sorry, sir," I said, and feeling I had a grievance sore as a wound in the chest.

"Sorry?" Mr. Gruffydd said. "Eh, dear, dear. He has the grace to be sorry. But he must spill blood first, to satisfy his precious temper, and he must feel sorry. Did you think, first? No. But Socrates was a man, made in the image of God, and noble because of it. Even did he take his own life rather than offend the laws of the state, or gainsay the word of those placed in authority over him. Did Master Morgan? Go from me, boy. I am ashamed down to my very shadow."

Slink from the little house I did, and up the hill, and slunk round our back, and in, to sit in the darkness on the covered engine, and see Mr. Gruffydd again, and hear his voice, and with every word to writhe.

And when I had had enough of that, I climbed the shed and through the window to bed, for there are times when bed is the only place on earth where peace is to be had, and that was one of them.

"The fault is on both sides," my father said, next morning. "But I might have done just the same, so I will say nothing. We will see what is said when you go back there on Monday."

"Mr. Motshill said he wanted to put me in the examination for university," I said.

"Your brothers could have had it," my father said, "but the stubborn mules would go to work instead. You win the first examination, my son, and you shall have ten sovereigns. We will see what next after that. Is it?"

"Yes, Dada," I said.

"Eat," said my mother. "Eat plenty, and grow brains, now."

That week went past me as though carried on the shoulders by a couple of slugs. I cleaned the fowl houses and put in pieces of wood where the foxes had been nosing, and did as much to the garden as I could, and whitewashed the front of the house, and Bron's, and cleaned the old engine till it shone gold and silver and I was sick of the sight of it. Only for Monday to come, and make a fresh start.

Angharad came to me toward the end of the week and said Mr. Gruffydd wanted some help at the little house. I was off down there at a run, and when I went in he smiled as he had used to, and held out his hand.

"Come, Huw," he said.

"Thank you, sir," I said, and that was all.

"I am going to start my furniture, Huw," he said. "Here are the drawings."

Well, indeed, the drawings would have made you almost cry with pleasure. Lines that started at the top and finished at the floor in a long, elegant curve, no bumps or knobs or silly bits, and roundnesses and squarenesses, with simplicity, but with craft, for it was plain that a knowing eye had observed that just proportion, which not merely balances design but gives to it that dignity which announces, as with a sound of trumpets, that the craftsman has set his hand and raised his monument.

"There is beautiful," I said.

"Good," he said. "Bring in the wood, and we will measure off."

The saw had not rasped an inch in the wood when Isaac Wynn came to knock on the front and run in straight from the pit.

"Mr. Evans slipped beneath a tram on the low level," he said, and reaching for breath. "Can you come, Mr. Gruffydd?"

Mr. Gruffydd was out of the house and running long before Isaac Wynn had started, but he left hat and overcoat, so I picked them up, and a muffler, and off after him. I might have saved myself trouble, for when I got to the pit they had brought Old Evans up and put him in the winding-house, so I gave the things to the lamp-man, and came back, and while I was coming back I heard the hymn.

All the way down the street, as far as the sound would reach, men were taking off their caps, and standing still. Women came from their doors and quietly called in their children, and stood. The village was full of people standing still while the hymn rose sternly from the pithead and the wind sighed miserably.

Old Evans had passed away among his own men, in the winding-house that he had helped to build, whose wheel had turned night and day through the years to enrich him, and now, at the last, had turned once more to carry him up to die.

I went back to cutting wood till Mr. Gruffydd came in, and when he did, I was sorry to see his face. He looked ill, and near to dead in the eyes.

"Home, Huw," he said, and sat on the plank. "Ask your good mother to excuse me from dinner to-day."

"Yes, sir," I said. "Will I come after dinner to finish?"

"No," he said. "Leave me to be by myself. I will tell you when."

So out I went, again, and home.

My mother said nothing when I told her, but she gave a look at Angharad who had been crying on the stool by the fire and clicked her tongue, and went to cut the bread as though she hated it.

Old Evans had a funeral that looked to be never ending. Not only did people walk over the mountain behind and before, but almost every foot of the way up was lined with people from all the other valleys. Every colliery, every railway yard, every ironworks, every customer and agent, every chapel, every society and choir and football team came over in strength.

Never had I seen so many people, and long, long, sad lines of red faces, shining with soap and redder and shinier because of the snow. And black, black, black, everyone, from top to toe, except about the collar in the men and to the nose in the women, where all was spotless white. Hymn on hymn for miles, with all the legs moving, sometimes together, sometimes ragged. And when the hymn stopped for a moment you heard the tramp and squeak of best boots, and the muttering of women's skirts going up, and up, and up, never stopping, and the snow giving a marvellous polish to the hundreds of top-hats.

Angharad was with my mother and father, just behind Iestyn, and his two uncles from London, who sold the output, and Mr. Gruffydd, and four other preachers.

I was with Bronwen, watching from half-way up the Hill, and glad to be out of it.

"Come you," said Bron, when it was not half gone by, "back to the house and a good cup of tea, us."

So we ran up all the way, but I had the kettle on before she was near the house.

"Poor Angharad," Bron said. "Though why poor, there is no telling. Two good men and make a choice. Not much poor in that."

"Do you think she will have Mr. Gruffydd?" I asked her.

"If Mr. Gruffydd will have her," Bron said. "His trouble is conscience. She is going on for eighteen. He is near to forty. And a poor man to the end of his days."

"Is he poor?" I asked her, and surprised, too.

"Twenty-five pounds a year," Bron said. "Your mother has had that from your father in ten days many a time not very long ago."

"Ten shillings a week?" I asked her, and surprised now outside words. "For Mr. Gruffydd? Only ten old shillings a week?"

"If they remember to pay," Bron said. "Your Dada has been on to them now for weeks, but they only say the strike has swallowed all and let Mr. Gruffydd wait. He will wait till the shoes do rot on his feet, and not a word will he say."

"How can we help him, Bron?" I asked her.

"By keeping our mouths shut, boy," she said. "Mr.

Gruffydd will be talking for himself when he wants. Not for us, him."

"So Iestyn will have Angharad, then?" I said.

"I hope," Bron said. "Marry a preacher and you marry the Chapel. Not for a hundred gold sovereigns a week, me. Iestyn is a rich man, now, so poor Mr. Gruffydd shall have it all the harder. There is sorry I am."

When Angharad came from the funeral she went straight to bed, and next day my mother sent her with Ceridwen up to the farm to be out of the way. Mr. Gruffydd came nowhere near our house for days, and whenever I went down there to help with the furniture, the little house was always closed. But we knew he was at his work, for Ellis saw him going up to the farms on the mountain, and he had big meetings every night of the week in Chapel.

Iestyn had gone to London with his uncles. Every morning Ellis came with a fat letter for Angharad that Bron took up to her, and not one morning except Sunday was missed all the time he was away. He must have spent his days in front of black-edged paper.

Back to school I went on the Monday and very anxious I felt every step of the way. Ceinwen met me down by the ironworks, and pretended she was only going that way for thread for her mother, but though we passed Meredith the Haberdasher she made no move to go in, even though I reminded her. We said nothing very much till we got to the gate and then she hung back because boys and girls were crowded about it.

"Huw," she said, "will you take me to hear the nightingales one night?"

"Nightingales?" I said. "It is winter, girl."

"Well, when nightingales are ready, then," she said.

"Right," I said, "in three months, perhaps more, you shall come."

"Right, you," she said. "A promise, mind."

"A promise," I said.

I went through the crowd and they made way very civil, smiling and wishing me good morning, until I was surprised to find myself swelling up as though I had become someone of importance, but I squeezed it from me with one look at the study door. I had another look at the boards on the wall while I waited for Mr. Motshill, and tried to imagine a board with only my name on it, in gold, there between the picture of the last headmaster and the board with the boys who had gained other awards. I made certain I would have it there if I had to bleed from the brains.

"Well, Morgan," said Mr. Motshill, behind me.

"Good morning, sir," I said, and going hot.

"I hope it is a good morning, Morgan," he said, but cool, and wiping his glasses, not looking at me. "Are you sorry for what you did?"

"Yes, sir," I said.

"Are you prepared to work harder than you have been doing?" he asked me, and putting on his glasses, looking up at the window to see if they were clear.

"Yes, sir," I said.

"Then go to your classroom," said Mr. Motshill. "I shall expect to be confounded with pleasure when I open your books on Friday next. Nothing less than confounded, understand."

"Yes, sir," I said, and went in the class, glad to be alone to crush the tears that were coming to my eyes. It is strange how kindness will bring tears, and so silly.

Well, there is a surprise I had when the class came in.

Instead of Mr. Jonas, there was Mr. Tyser.

So glad I was to see him that I stared, and felt the surprise hardening my face, and he smiled to see me, but then pretended not to notice and went to his books.

O, and then came to me a grim, grim feeling, when the blood inside my body froze and yet was boiling, and I shook, and my breath was stopped, while I resolved to repay a thousandfold the kindness of Mr. Motshill. Nothing would be too much, everything too little.

Work.

Out in the playground at dinner-time I had another surprise, but it made me feel sick, and angry, and then pleased, but not comfortable.

Mr. Jonas was in charge of the infants' class, the one just before they came to Standard One, with boys and girls of seven and eight. I saw him come from the infants' door and walk away with his hands in his pockets. There was a look about his back that made me feel sorry for him, for one shoulder hung down lower than the other so that his coat had a big crease at the back, and his heels dragged, and his hands were not right in the pockets, but just on the top, with his cuffs pushed up and his wrists red, as though he cared nothing if they were in or out, cold or hot.

I thought of the smile, and of the little children. I thought pity for them, and shuddered with gratitude to be free of it myself.

Chapter Twenty-Two

THE GLASS IN THE KITCHEN window-panes has fallen in at last. I am glad now that I took so many out and gave them away for it was good glass, made in a day when men did the rolling by hand. A lovely roundness they had to them, looking from the side as though they were rising from the pane as a pastry crust will rise from the edges of the dish, and a pleasure to clean, so clearly and bright they shone. Many and many a time I saw my mother clean them inside. She could reach up to the third line on tip-toe, for the fourth and fifth she used the stool, and for the sixth, she put paper on the sill and climbed on it from the stool to reach. Then she got down and looked at it from the side to see if she had left any marks, and if she had not, she folded the paper to put in the cupboard, gave the stool a good polish, and put it back by the fire, and then to the glass in the cupboard, for window-day was glass-and-china-day, and every pot, piece of glass, and window-pane shone at the end of it.

The next to go will be the doors downstairs or the panes up here. The next movement, the next downward slip of that heap outside there is bound to cover the house. It may take the roof off. Poor little house, I hear you groaning, and I feel your pain, with all these hundreds of tons bearing down upon you. Almost I can see your little face crooked with pain and looking at me to help you. But I am helpless. It would take me ten generations to move it from you with a shovel, and not even a shovel I have got to my name, now. All I have got are the clothes on me, and those couple of shirts and socks that I will take with me in the little blue cloth. I used to have such plenty, too. Good tweed from the cloth mill, and old Hwfa Williams to cut it and sew it cross-legs on the floor in his little shop.

The first time I went in there was with my father to have my measures taken so that he would know how much tweed to buy from the mill. Two and a half yards.

Down we went to the mill and inside the yard, and through the low doorway into the weaving-room. There is a lovely smell with tweed. Good it is, and honest, of the earth and of humankind, and a pleasure to wear, and always a friend to you.

I had a brown tweed, the colour of a ploughed field in the pebbly soil, when leaf has been put down about three months before, and grass is just poking through, barely to be seen, but there. That, and a grey, the colour of spring rain, and almost as soft to the touch. My father bought a bolt of it for my mother and sisters, and black for himself and my brothers, and we watched a piece come from the loom in green, and that my father took for Olwen and Gareth to have little cloaks.

We went from there like journeymen loaded for a trip to the Indies, and by the time we got to Hwfa Williams I was ready to drop, so heavy was my share.

"Long trews or short, Mr. Morgan?" Hwfa asked my father, and his eyes smiling and shining at me like little blue shoe-buttons. "Shall he be a man or stay a boy?"

"O, Dada," I said, "long, is it?"

My father looked at me, and turned to look through the window that was covered with pictures of elegant gentlemen with narrow waists and trews tight at the ankles, with capes, and canes with tassels. I was aching all over and shouting at him in my mind for him to say yes.

And Hwfa rubbed his thimble along his bottom lip, and his blue shoe-buttons went first to me and then to my father.

"Very well, Huw, my little one," my father said, and I could have swung on the beams, "long trews. You are grown, now, of course."

"Four button front, do up the top," said Hwfa, and coming very practical. "Front pocket trews, collar to waistcoat. Flaps to top waistcoat pockets?"

And the shoe-buttons went again to my father, and my father looked at me.

"Yes, Dada, please," I said.

"Yes," said my father, and looking through the window again.

"Fitting for Master Huw Morgan, Thursday next, five of the evening," said Hwfa, all business now, and speaking to old Twm, who kept the writings and the patterns, and put braid on coats and sewed buttonholes.

"Right, you," said old Twm, with needles sticking from the side of his mouth and all over his waistcoat. "And Nan Mardy coming in at half-past the hour for a three-quarter coat and a rain-cloak with black braid and pockets both sides."

"Never mind to talk of Nan Mardy, man," Hwfa said, "Master Huw Morgan, I said."

"Well, only saying I was," Old Twm said, with impatience, "in case."

"In case, in case," Hwfa said, and the shoe-buttons flying everywhere. "What, in case, for the dear love of God, you old fool, you?"

"In case he do have his trews about his boot-tops and the shirt tails above his chin, man," old Twm shouted, out of temper.

"O, to hell with you," Hwfa shouted back. "Mind your own shirt tails and let everybody else mind his and devil fly off with old Nan. A good look at a shirt tail would put life in her."

"Come you," said my father. "Mr. Williams, please to guard your tongue while this boy is near you."

"The boy will learn quick enough," Hwfa said. "Five on the evening of Thursday, and to hell with Nan Mardy and this old fool by here, is it?"

"Good afternoon, now," said my father, and I pulled the door the harder to have more noise from the bell. Hwfa was still shouting and old Twm was swearing back at him when we were two houses away, and my father looked at me and smiled.

"Why will a good look at a shirt tail put life in Nan Mardy, Dada?" I asked him.

"Mind your business," said my father, "then Nan shall mind hers, and we shall all be happy."

Again I had that feeling in me of helpless heat at being denied to know a matter which only a few words would explain. I made my mind firm to know about it, and tried to think of someone who would tell me without laughing at me. Tegwen Beynon I thought of, and Ceinwen Phillips, for I felt they knew much more about the things that the grown-ups wanted to keep to themselves than I did. But there was a look that I remembered in their eyes, and it came to me that Tegwen and Ceinwen had the same look, a heated fogginess within, that clouded their eyes, yet left them clear. Then I thought of Bron, and I knew with warmth that I had the right answer.

Ceridwen and Blethyn were going to marry as soon as their house in the next Valley was ready, in two weeks' time. For that, and Angharad's marriage to Iestyn, I was having the new suits.

Ceridwen and Blethyn made no fuss about their match, for they were happy, they knew they were going to be married, their house was going up brick by brick in front of their eyes, their furniture was bought, and Ceridwen's bottom drawer was full, so there was no need for fuss.

And if ever a girl had less fuss in her I would like to put eyes on her. As for Blethyn, well, nobody lived within a yard of her. She was his eyes, his heart, and his soul, and it was funny and yet sad to see his eyes upon her going with her wherever she went. And if she passed him, she tickled the back of his head with her fingers, and sometimes pulled the lobe of his ear, but gently not to hurt, and he looked up at her, then, with a smile that would go to the heart as a spear.

But Angharad and Iestyn.

"Mr. and Mrs. Kiss and Scratch," my mother said of them. "Kiss one moment, scratch the next. Arms round now, fists up then. I will chase them from the house with a dishcloth if there is more of it."

Indeed, my mother had cause to complain, too.

As soon as Iestyn was back from London, up to the house he came in a new dark blue gig with red lining round the wheels, and a polished brass rail with a long brass holder for a hickory and ivory coach whip, lovely, indeed, with a white lash that came round in a beautiful curve at the top, and then curled round the handle, and a little bay mare, polished like a piece of furniture, with a short barrel and a neck that came round like the top of a letter S, with knots in her mane and four white socks. And her little shoes shining like silver with her.

I could have cried to watch, so pretty she was, and so proud of her red leather bridle, and the sun strong upon her.

Iestyn, in a grey bowler hat and black-and-white check suit, with a white stock and pearl pin, and brown boots. There is a swell for you. A light flew to my mother's eyes and flew out again to make you wonder if you saw it or not, when she saw him. He took off the bowler hat and gave her a bow with his good morning, and she nodded, looking at him straight, and went to the kitchen. Iestyn stood with the bowler going round and round in his hands, not knowing whether to go in or stay out. Then Ianto gave him a wink and a nod, and he smiled as though he had caught a finger in the door, and went in as to a lion's den.

Out he came again in a minute, and gave us all a wink of discomfort, and climbed up on the seat, put the rug about his knees, and drove up the Hill toward the farm.

When we went in my mother was still having her temper out of the clothes in the washtub. Up comes a shirt of my father's frothed with soap, and quickly she screws it round and round, slap against the board, then, and rub, rub, rub till it was a wonder there was shirt or board, and a bit of her hair falling from under this little blue cloth, and hanging down across her face, and soapy from her impatient hand trying to push it away.

"Did you see him?" my mother asked us, with her hands in the froth, and looking at us, and trying to blow away the hair with her eyes going up at it.

"Yes," said Ianto. "There is a lovely little mare."

"Mare?" my mother said, and slap, slap, slap with the shirt, and froth flying. "Him, I mean."

"Well, if he can afford to dress like that," Ianto said, "he has got the money. Leave him, now."

"Money or not," my mother said, "let him dress in satin and diamonds. It is no matter to me a bit. But let him wait to dress like that till he can wear them with comfort. He was in pain with him to have them on his back. Wait till Miss Angharad sees him. She will pull the hairs from his head."

Next day Angharad came home just after I came from school. There seemed nothing wrong with her, for she looked just the same, and she laughed, and just as ready to wipe up after supper. Yet there was something wrong that I could only feel. It was as though an extra light had gone out inside her. Iestyn was there for supper, and he took her for a walk after, but although they were smiling at one another, they were not a bit like Ceridwen and Blethyn. I never felt for Iestyn that pity I felt for Blethyn. He never once made me sad as Blethyn did, or made me laugh. Iestyn was fierce to kiss her when he thought they were unseen, and Angharad was ready enough to be kissed. But she never once looked as I had seen Ceridwen look, with that happiness that is not of the earth, when the world could tumble to blue ruin and it would be no matter.

Then Ianto came in with *The Times* one night, and showed my mother and father a piece on the left of the front page with ink marks round it.

"From who is it?" my mother asked him.

"Well," said Ianto, "Ellis just gave it to me."

"By post?" my father said, and putting on his glasses to read.

"Yes," said Ianto, and smiling with a lot up his sleeve. "Who from, Mama? Guess, now then."

"Well, from who?" my mother said, and frowning.

"Owen," said my father.

My mother's hands fell to her lap and she looked about the kitchen as though the house was going from her. Ianto put his arms about her, and she held on to him.

"Goodness gracious me," my father said to the paper, "Evans, Morgan. A marriage has been arranged between Iestyn Dylan Evans, son of the late Mr. and Mrs. Christmas Dylan Evans, of Tyn-y-Coed. . . ."

He stopped and looked at my mother with his mouth tight shut.

"Read, boy, read," my mother said, in wonder.

"Not another word," said my father, in anger. "But I will read something to Mr. Iestyn Evans when I do see him. His father not cold, and putting this old nonsense in the paper. If a marriage has been arranged, I know nothing of it. I will be consulted if there is arranging to be done. Mr. Iestyn has got too many English ways. I will put a bit between his jaws before he is an hour older."

"Please to tell me who sent the paper," my mother said, and slapping her knee with each word, "and from where?"

"Owen," my father said, bending down to her. "Owen sent the paper from London. And he says will we let Angharad marry this fool, and love from both, home soon."

"Thank God my boys are safe," my mother said, "and thank God to have them home. When?"

"Not a word about it, the rascals," my father said, looking again at the writing. "Wait till Mr. Iestyn comes back."

"Leave it now, Gwil," my mother said. "If he had reasons, he had reasons."

"Am I the father of Angharad Morgan?" my father said, with fists, "or am I a marriage-broker?"

"Swanking, he was, Dada," Ianto said, "but no harm."

"Harm to me," my father said. "If Angharad is to be married, it shall be read in Chapel properly, and old papers after. But after, not before. Are we a lot of pagans, then, because a bit of a boy has no father to say yes and no?"

I was out in the back when I heard Angharad coming back with Iestyn, so I put my head from the door and gave her a whistle.

"Watch out, you Iestyn," I said, in a whisper, *"The Times* has come from London, and my father has got basins out for your blood."

"What is this, then?" Angharad asked Iestyn.

"Our engagement," Iestyn said. "Who has been busy-bodying?"

"Engagement?" Angharad said, with a frown up at him. "What have you been doing now, again?"

"O, my God," said Iestyn, "you will drive me crazy, between you. I announced our engagement in the Press in a proper and suitable manner. Have you any objection?"

"Yes," Angharad said, flat and quick. "Who are you to engage me without a word?"

"What are you talking about?" Iestyn said, and so surprised he could hardly say it. "Why the hell have I been coming up here all this time? Why have I been urging marriage on you for weeks?"

"Have I said yes?" Angharad asked him, freezing cold.

I think that was the only time in his life, or mine, that I felt sorry in my heart for Iestyn Evans.

He looked at her, and though his eyes were not to be seen, I could feel his look, so deep, so pleading, so woeful, so shaking to the senses, flying, and piling up through the darkness at her.

"Angharad," he said, as though a strangler was at work on him, "Angharad. Why are you so cruel to me?" And on his knees he fell, with his arms about her waist. "You must marry me. You must. You must. I love you, my darling. I love you."

"Get up, man," Angharad said, with knives, and her breath quick. "Will you make yourself a carpet for every fool to see? Go home, now. Come in two days and you shall have yes or no."

He got up and looked again, and the sounds of night were not loud enough to smother the silence of his fury.

"If you think you can treat me like this," he said, "you have made a mistake. There are plenty of other women in this world, and I can have my choice, any time I care to choose. Why have you kissed me if marriage was out of your mind?"

"I am Angharad Morgan," she said, and the river never ran colder. "Go to hell."

And she was gone before he could move, with the back door closing to rock the house.

"Damn all women to hell's everlasting depths," said Iestyn, and looked round as I blew out the lamp. "Have you got a loose tongue, Huw?"

"No," I said. "And if you want Angharad, say nothing of other women, and no showing off."

"The whole family the same," Iestyn said, and still wet about the eyes. "Never met such a crowd, from the youngest up. Does she ever see anything of that Gruffydd fellow?"

"Who am I to say?" I said. "Leave me, now. I am going to bed."

"Here is half a crown for you, Huw," he said, and put hand to pocket.

"Buy barley sugar for your little bay mare," I said, "and say who it is from. Good night, now."

"God damn," Iestyn said, and went round our back as though witches were at him with besoms.

Down at the little house next day I was busy planing lengths of walnut for the top of a writing-table, and Mr. Gruffydd was running a wheel to shape chair legs, when Angharad came in with tea and cake, no words, and pouring us out a cup each and coming with the plates.

"Well, Angharad," Mr. Gruffydd said, "how are you to-day?"

"Well, thank you," Angharad said.

"Good," said Mr. Gruffydd, and put cake in his mouth, and back to the wheel.

"Shall I talk to you in the next room when you have finished tea?" Angharad asked him as she used to ask my father for pennies to buy sweets, pretty, with big eyes, and a small smile.

"Now just," said Mr. Gruffydd, and got up, shaking wood shavings from his trews.

"Please to finish your tea first," Angharad said, and a crack coming to her voice.

"Come," said Mr. Gruffydd. "Huw, save your partner a cup of tea, yes?"

"Yes, sir," I said.

Mr. Gruffydd went to put his arm about her shoulders, but opened the door instead, and closed it behind him.

There is good it is to plane a good piece of wood with a sharp tool, and watch the grain coming better and with more shape with every peeling that curls from the blade. Mr. Gruffydd had his wood free from Daniel Thomas the Woodyard, because he had never missed a day to see Mrs. Thomas who had ridden her bed for years ever since a horse had bolted with her and tossed her on the cobbles of a farm. Good wood it was, too, and no better to be had, dark, with a reddish grain in the best shape I have ever seen, and dry and hard with age. Even the plane was giving it a polish, so I was having sweat to finish and go to polish it properly, for there is nothing to satisfy more than to see a high, shining smoothness coming to life under your hand, and to bend down to watch the sun lying upon it and enjoying himself.

I heard Angharad run from the house, and a little while passed, and Mr. Gruffydd came in, but I kept my eyes on the planing. The wheel started to turn, and stopped. Then it started again and went on a little bit, and stopped for longer. Then it started again twice as strong, and kept on, and it was still going when the light had gone and I put my tools in the chest.

"Well," I said, "I will go to my supper, now, sir, thank you."

"Thank you, Huw, my little one," Mr. Gruffydd said. "To-morrow again, is it?"

"Straight after school, sir," I said. "Good night, now."

"God bless you, my son," said Mr. Gruffydd, and I left him quiet before the wheel, on the floor, in darkness.

Chapter Twenty-Three

MR. GRUFFYDD read out the notice of the marriage of Angharad and Iestyn in Chapel the next Sunday, and when our family came out it was hours before we could come from there, for the people crowded to shake hands and kiss, and wish well, to my mother and father and Angharad and Iestyn, and Bronwen and Ceridwen and all my brothers, and even me.

"Well, Huw," Isaac Wynn said, and giving me a pat

on the head that with a bit more would have been a clout, "there is a lucky boy you are, indeed. A rich uncle, and a job all your life, eh?"

"I shall be down the colliery with my father," I said, and ready to give him a good hit on his old nose. "And not long to wait, either."

"O, tall talk from a short one, is it?" Isaac Wynn said, and staring, with the smile off his face.

"We will see when it comes true," I said.

"You are going to be another with those brothers of yours," he said, and shaking his head.

"That is all I want," I said, "so good-bye, now."

Then came the fuss, when Angharad and Iestyn started to choose where they would live, what they would put in the house, how they would dress for the wedding, and where they would have the service.

"Leave them," my father said, when my mother was in a temper with both of them for fighting over what each wanted and the other thought awful. "No business of ours. What business we had is finished. They have got to live in the house wherever it is, so keep from it, now. If you put a word in, and something is wrong in a couple of weeks' time, you will have sour looks, and little respect to the end of your days. So leave them."

"That Angharad," my mother said, and twisting her hands, "I will box her ears. Want this, take away that. Not this, that over there."

"I have noticed the young mistress," my father said, and a bit of a smile. "I seem to remember her mother with some want-this-take-away-that, too."

"Never as bad as that, I was," my mother said.

"I could tell a tale," said my father, up at the ceiling. "But no matter. One week of married life will cure her."

"Hisht, Gwil," my mother said.

"Well," said my father, "there was a radical change in someone else I know. And before the week was out, too."

"I am going in to Bron's," said my mother, and went out, nose high, and my father gave me a wink.

But indeed, it was making us silly to see them and hear them whenever they were in the house, and when Iestyn's aunt, who looked after him, came to see my mother, she said it was the same over there. She said that some nights he was so angry, that he would smash three and four pots to have ease of his temper, so she had packed the best pieces in the cellar till he found sense.

My mother wanted them to marry with Ceridwen and Blethyn to have both lots out of the way on the same day. But Iestyn was firm against it, and in that Angharad let him have his way. That was a surprise. Iestyn wanted to be married in the Chapel in London and then go to Paris and Berlin for a honeymoon. Angharad wanted to marry in London and then come straight back. Iestyn had his way. Angharad wanted to stay at Tyn-y-Coed, where his fathers had lived for six generations, a good big house, and full of splendid farmhouse furniture, but Iestyn wanted to sell it and build a house outside the town. Kiss and scratch, my mother called them, and so it was.

One night they came back to supper after a walk. Angharad was pale thunder, Iestyn with a pout.

"Mr. Morgan," he said, as soon as he was through the door, "a word with you in private, if you please."

"What is it, now again?" my father said, and got up from the chair clicking his tongue and nodding, and took Iestyn in the back.

My mother went on cooking, and I went on with my schoolwork. Angharad sat on the stool, looking in the fire, still with her cloak, and her hair hanging almost to the floor.

"What is it, now then, Angharad?" my mother said, as though it was no matter.

"Iestyn wants to take me away to-morrow to marry in London," Angharad said, low and so sad to make you stop thinking what you were doing.

My mother went on cooking as though she had heard nothing. Then she put the bakestone on to get hot, and wiped her hands, and turned to Angharad and knelt beside her to put her arms about her. And Angharad started to cry. O, broken in the heart, she cried.

"Hisht, my little one, hisht," my mother said, and rocking her as she did with Olwen. "There now, peach blossom mine. Dry the pretty eyes, is it?"

"Mama," Angharad wept, "I love him. Only him. But he sends me away."

"Hisht, hisht," my mother said, and frowning in the fire, with a hand pressing Angharad's head into her shoulder. Then I moved and she looked up, angry.

"Huw," she said, and sharp, "go from here, boy."

"Yes, Mama," I said.

But my father was in the back with Iestyn, Ianto and Davy in the front with some men from the union, and nowhere else in the house to go but upstairs to bed. But I wanted my supper, so down I went to Bron's, and found her sewing Ivor's working flannels.

"Well," she said, and the old smile, "what, then, with a face like green gooseberries with you?"

"Iestyn in the back with Dada," I said, "Angharad in the kitchen with Mama. No peace in the house."

"She will do all she can to make him break off," Bron said. "Poor Angharad, too. Still, there it is. Have you had supper?"

"No, indeed," I said. "And I am hungry."

"It is pity about you," Bron said, but joking. "Come you, and I will make you a basin of broth, is it?"

So we had supper together, for Ivor was on night shift, and lovely it was, too, only the leeks were a bit old, and the bacon was a little on the briny, and winter potatoes, of course, but still, with Bron to smile across the table, lovely.

"Bron," I said, and in a rush, not to have time to think to change my mind, "why would it do Nan Mardy good to see a shirt tail?"

Bronwen stared and stared with her spoon spilling soup, and then she lifted her chin in shouting laughter. She had a beautiful laugh, full and deep, and generous in tone, but I was coming restless before she wiped her eyes.

"Who told you?" she asked, and off she went again, eyes closed, mouth wide, teeth shining, on a higher note, as though she had just reached the best part of it, and me watching, ready to throw something, yet wanting to laugh with her.

"Where, boy, where?" she asked me again, wiping her eyes and swallowing and finishing her laugh with big breaths.

"Hwfa Williams," I said, and not wanting to say anything, now. "He said it would do her good. I want to know why."

"You will understand one day, Huw, my little one," she said. "Will you have more to eat?"

"I will have an answer to the question," I said.

She looked at me from one eye to another, but I could find no meaning in her face.

"Have you asked your father, Huw?" she asked me, very quiet.

"Yes," I said, "and he said to mind my business."

"I will speak to him," Bron said, and got up as though the matter was at an end.

"Why does everybody treat me like little Gareth?" I said, and got up, too. "Why will it do Nan Mardy good to look at a shirt tail? How do whores get money that should come to us?"

"Hisht, Huw," Bronwen said, with fright. "Where did you hear that?"

"From Ianto," I said, "but he told me he was sorry he said it in front of me."

"Huw," Bronwen said, and very kind, "go you home to bed, and have no worry about such things. As you grow older, so things will come plainer and your brain stronger to meet them."

"I will find out from Tegwen Beynon," I said. "She knows."

Bron was round the table and holding me by the collar in a moment.

"Huw," she said, stern and cold, "if you have words with that slut of a girl be careful to come nowhere near this house again. Now then, warning."

"I will, or I will be told," I said. "I will know or I will find out."

Bron put her arm round me and kissed my forehead.

"If I tell your father of this," she said, "he will strap you and you will go on your way just the same and God knows the harm. Have you asked Mr. Gruffydd?"

"I could," I said, "but I know my answer."

"If I knew I was doing right, I would tell you now," she said, "but you are a boy, and I might be wrong. I will think it over for a day, is it?"

"Right," I said. "Thank you, Bron."

"Good night, now," she said, and smiling her smile that was not a smile.

"Good night, Bron," I said, and kissed her quietly upon the mouth, and ran.

There is strange, and yet not strange, is the kiss. It is strange because it mixes silliness with tragedy, and yet not strange because there is good reason for it. There is shaking by the hand. That should be enough. Yet a shaking of hands is not enough to give a vent to all kinds of feeling.

The hand is too hard and too used to doing all things, with too little feeling and too far from the organs of taste and smell, and far from the brain, and the length of an arm from the heart. To rub a nose like the blacks, that we think is so silly, is better, but there is nothing good to the taste about the nose, only a piece of old bone pushing out of the face, and a nuisance in winter, but a friend before meals and in a garden, indeed. With the eyes we can do nothing, for if we come too near, they go crossed and everything comes twice to the sight without good from one or other.

There is nothing to be done with the ear, so back we come to the mouth, and we kiss with the mouth because it is part of the head and of the organs of taste and smell. It is temple of the voice, keeper of breath and its giving out, treasurer of tastes and succulences, and home of the noble tongue. And its portals are firm, yet soft, with a warmth, of a ripeness, unlike the rest of the face, rosy, and in women with a crinkling red tenderness, to the taste not in compare with the wild strawberry, yet if the taste of kisses went, and strawberries came the year round, half of joy would be gone from the world. There is no wonder to me that we kiss, for when mouth comes to mouth, in all its silliness, breath joins breath, and taste joins taste, warmth is enwarmed, and tongues commune in a soundless language, and those things are said that cannot find a shape, have a name, or know a life in the pitiful faults of speech.

So I kissed Bronwen for the first time, and I was sorry, and not sorry, afraid and yet brave with a gladness.

"Huw," Mr. Gruffydd said, next afternoon, "there was a matter you wanted to know from your sister-in-law yesterday. I am hurt to think you would go to anyone other than me for knowledge. And knowledge of that sort, Huw, is not to be imparted by any woman."

"I thought you would be angry with me, sir," I said, and blushing like a fool, and hot to think that Bron had told on me again.

"I am angry with you, now," he said, but with no anger in his voice. "If I am fit to instruct you in the Word of God, why am I unfitted to instruct you in the things of His natural goodness?"

"No, sir," I said, and saying it only because I could think

of nothing else, and hoping for a deep hole to come under my feet.

"Very well," he said, and still busy with the wheel. "There are some things you know, and some things you shall wait to know. Do you know the calculus?"

"No, sir," I said, "but I am learning."

"Good," he said, "one thing at a time. You cannot know until you have had time to learn, and impatience will gain nothing but confusion, is it?"

"Yes, sir," I said, and coming to be in a good sweat with the plane.

"Then first things first," he said. "There are men and women. But before that, they shall be boys and girls, and before that, babies, is it?"

"Yes, sir," I said.

"And before that?" Mr. Gruffydd asked me, "what?"

What, indeed. What, before babies. Nothing, I could think of.

"Nothing, sir," I said, "like in the beginning was the Word."

"Fair play, Huw, my little one," Mr. Gruffydd said. "You are having a good try. The Word was with God. And so with babies. Huw, there is an engine up in your back that Owen made. How did he make it? With hands, we know. But from the mind, before that, yes?"

"Yes, sir," I said.

"And babies are born from the mind, too, Huw," Mr. Gruffydd said. "From the mind of God. For they are little engines, but full of wonders, and a splendid mystery, for they are driven not by old oil, but by life itself, but instead to stay the same size as they were made, they grow and grow, day by day, to boy and girl, and then to men and women. There is a wonder for you, my son."

"But how do babies come, sir?" I asked him. "What is before babies?"

"Impatience," said Mr. Gruffydd. "Pity this is not the school of Pythagoras, for then you would be under a vow of silence for five years while your master taught you."

"I am sorry, sir," I said, and hoping for the hole again.

"Good," said Mr. Gruffydd. "Now then, as to babies. Man was born in the image of God, and God took Woman from the rib of Adam, is it?"

"Yes, sir," I said.

"So now there was Adam and Eve in the Garden," said

Mr. Gruffydd. "And what happened?"

"She sinned against the tree of knowledge," I said, "and gave him to eat of the apple, and they knew they were naked, and took fig leaves."

"Good," said Mr. Gruffydd, and going hard with the wheel. "What then?"

"Then came an Angel with a flaming sword," I said, "and sent them from the Garden."

"To earn by the sweat of their brows," said Mr. Gruffydd. "And what after?"

"Then Cain and Abel," I said, "and Abel was a good man, but Cain killed him."

"Wait," said Mr. Gruffydd. "Before to kill them, have them first. Adam and Eve we have got. Where did we have Cain and Abel?"

"From the Bible, sir," I said.

"But where from, to get in the Bible, boy?" Mr. Gruffydd asked me. "Adam was created, we know, and Eve from Adam. But where did Cain and Abel come from?"

"They were sons of Adam and Eve," I said.

"Good," said Mr. Gruffydd, and went to start on another leg. "They were the sons of Adam and Eve, and they were begotten, as the children of men and women have been begotten ever since. By a father and mother. Now, Huw, why is a man a father, and why is a woman a mother?"

"Because Adam is one, and Eve the other," I said.

"But why, I said," Mr. Gruffydd said, and looked up at me. "What makes a man a father? Wherein lies the difference? How do you tell a man from a woman, a father from a mother?"

"Well, sir," I said, "one is with moustache and trews, and the other with smoothness and skirts."

"Huw," Mr. Gruffydd said, "you are different on the outside from a girl, or you would be knitting instead of fighting, is it?"

"Yes, sir," I said.

"How, different?" Mr. Gruffydd asked me, going hard with the spindle.

"A girl is swollen in the chest," I said, "and we are not."

"And?" Mr. Gruffydd asked me.

"We are different below the waist," I said, "and girls are flat."

"Good," said Mr. Gruffydd. "Now then, what do you know of the womb? What is a womb, Huw?"

"It is in the Bible, sir," I said.

"Thus saith the Lord that made thee, and formed thee from the womb," said Mr. Gruffydd, from the Word, in his deep voice. "Engines from the mind of man, babies from the mind of God. But as engines must have a union between brains and hands, and then must come forth in the womb of silver-sand to have shape, so a union must come between a man and woman, and the baby comes forth with shape from the womb. Now, the iron-master made the womb of silver-sand for the engine parts to have shape, and Owen put them together. So God made the womb of warm flesh for the parts of the baby to have shape, and who put it together? The mother and father, is it?"

"Yes, sir," I said.

"And who is with the womb, of the two?" Mr. Gruffydd asked me.

I had a vision of Mrs. Beynon below me, with veins in her face and her hands tearing at the wall.

"The mother, sir," I said.

"Good," said Mr. Gruffydd, "so now we know that a man is father, and a woman is mother. He is father because he is different from her. She has a womb within her, and if it is the Will, a baby shall have shape and life. How?"

"From a union," I said.

"Now as to the union," Mr. Gruffydd said, in another voice, and as he would point the difference between the grains of two pieces of wood. "You have heard of the seed of man, Huw?"

"Yes, sir," I said.

"Good," he said. "There is wheat, and barley and corn. All seed. And you must sow to reap, is it?"

"Yes, sir," I said.

"So to have the baby in shape, there must be sown, first of all, the seed of man," said Mr. Gruffydd. "And it is sown in the womb. That is why men and women marry. Marriage is the union. Do you sow wheat out of season? Would you put seeds to earth in snow?"

"No, sir," I said.

"No," he said, "or you would be clapped in the mad-house, quick. There is a time and a season for all things. And the time of sowing the seed of man is at the time of marriage, not before. Never mind how impatient the farmer is to have a field of growing corn, he must wait for the season to sow, is it?"

"Yes, sir," I said.

"Yes," he said, "or be known for witlessness. So with man, Huw. The time of marriage is the time of the sowing."

The sun was on his way down the other side of the mountain, and against the orange and red of the sky on top, sheep were black, with rays of white light coming up from under them and lining their fleeces with hot gold.

"Well," said Mr. Gruffydd, "what more is there to know?"

"How is the seed sown, sir?" I asked him.

"How long have you had your mind on these things, Huw?" he asked me.

"A long time, sir," I said.

"Oh," he said, "supposing your mind was on food for as long, would I be in the right to call you a glutton? So in this matter. Be careful how you waste your time, or there might come a time to call you a wastrel, and an idler. Now you want to know how is the seed sown, is it?"

"Yes, sir," I said, "please."

"Very well," he said. "You said yourself that you are different on the outside from a girl. That is because you will grow to be a man, and at that time you will be guardian of the seed of man. Yes?"

"Where will I have it, sir?" I asked.

"Impatience, again," said Mr. Gruffydd. "You will have it within you, made from your own blood, and ready against the time of the sowing in those parts of you that are different from the girl. At the time of marriage, and not before, you will unify with the woman who will be your wife. And all things will follow."

"But how, unify, sir?" I asked, and having my voice from the top of my lungs, with trembling, for I felt heavy with knowledge, but greedy for more, and greed made heat within me.

"What does the word mean, Huw?" he asked, and stopped the wheel, for it was almost dark in the room, and even the shine was gone from the table-top.

"A joining," I said.

"It is exactly that," said Mr. Gruffydd. "That part of you that is outside is a link to the womb of the woman who is your wife, and through that link shall pour your seed, which is given by God, and willed to bear fruit of child by the Mind of God. So?"

"Is that all, sir?" I asked him, and worried, with no happiness.

"Is that all?" he said, and held up his hands. "What more, then?"

"Well, sir," I said, "I thought it was something more. Something terrible."

"It is terrible, Huw," said Mr. Gruffydd, and in quiet, with his hand on my head. "It is indeed terrible. Think, you. To have the responsibility of a life within you. Many lives. Think of the miseries and afflictions that can come to those lives beyond the span of your own. Think to have small children in your own likeness standing at your knee, and to know them as flesh of your flesh, blood of your blood, looking to you for guidance as you look to God the Father for yours. Can that be anything but terrible, in majesty and in beauty beyond words?"

"Yes, sir," I said. "But why do grown-ups say I am not to know, if that is all it is?"

"Well, Huw," Mr. Gruffydd said, and laughing now. "Shall it be shouted from the house-tops, then? Are there to be no proprieties? Do you undress in front of everybody in sight?"

"No, sir," I said.

"Then if you are careful of your own modesty," Mr. Gruffydd said, "think how much more so must we be modest about the business of birth. It is a responsibility that comes with age. Would you tell little Gareth about the workings of the engine?"

"No, sir," I said.

"Of course not," said Mr. Gruffydd. "He would like to know, no doubt, but his little brain would never grasp what you were saying. But in time to come, he will know as well you. Is it?"

"Yes, sir," I said.

"Because it will be simple to him," said Mr. Gruffydd, "for he will have reached the age of understanding. And he will say to you, then, is that all it is? And you shall say, that is all, my son, just as I say now to you. Well?"

"But why will it do Nan Mardy good to see the tail of a shirt?" I asked, and it was out before I could stop it.

"That is a low joke, Huw," Mr. Gruffydd said. "It is because she is an elderly woman who has had no husband,

and therefore no children. Hwfa meant she would be the better for a husband."

"How do you know about Hwfa, sir?" I asked him, and cold with surprise.

"There is little to be known about you that is unknown to me, Huw, my son," Mr. Gruffydd said. "Are you going to Dai Bando in the mornings, still?"

"Yes, sir," I said.

"Good," he said. "You will have good of it, but keep it to the mornings. Never let them have your time at night. No public houses, and no prize fights, is it?"

"No, sir," I said, with surprise. "There has never been talk of it, yet."

"Good," he said. "Home to your supper, now."

"Are you coming to-night, sir?" I asked him. "The place is always ready laid for you."

Mr. Gruffydd was quiet for moments, putting the tools back in his box, and pushing the wheel against the other wall.

"Give your good mother a kiss on the cheek," said Mr. Gruffydd, "and excuse me again to-night, please. Good night, now."

"Good night, sir," I said, and went out in the coming darkness with feelings that the world was upside down and the people in it all as silly as cuckoos. But now I understood why Bron had held from telling me, and I was grateful to her, and free of anger.

It was only a little time after that when Iestyn had his way with Angharad and took her to marry in London. Ianto and Davy went with them, but my father and mother stayed at home because they had wanted the wedding at our Chapel, and turned their faces from a marriage outside it. Ianto and Davy came back, and very quiet, with no news of London, and no talking about the journey. And from the looks on their faces, I knew better than to ask.

We got cards of Calais and Paris from Angharad, with a word or two, and a letter from Berlin that my mother and father read together, with my mother looking over my father's shoulder at the window one morning. Their faces were stiff and serious to start, lit white by the paper, but as my father read a page and turned his eyes to watch for my mother to finish, the stiffness passed and the seriousness failed, until, when they had finished, and were putting away their glasses, my mother patted down her apron, in thought, and looked at my father straight.

"Well," she said.

"It is all right with her, girl," my father said, and took her hand. "I told you. Settled down, she has, now."

"I hope," said my mother, through the window.

"Certain," said my father. "No worry. Wait till she will come home, and you shall see."

Chapter Twenty-Four

BUT IT WAS LONG AFTER that they came home, long after the weddings of Ceridwen and Blethyn and Davy and Wyn. Married together they were, in our Chapel one Saturday, the first day the snow had been off the ground for months. I remember, because if it had been snowing or slush underfoot I should have had to wear my school boots instead of my best, and they were too thick and out of keeping with my best suit of good grey tweed, and there is no sense to wear thick old boots with a good suit.

There is proud I was to go for my first suit made by hand. Before, of course, my mother had made my suits, or bought them from the shop, but there is no feeling to be had from a shop suit because there it is, made, and ready to hang on you. And hang it does, with lumps in the seat of the trews, and lumps under the arms, enough in the front to fold round you twice, the cuffs down to the tips of your fingers, and the trews too short to be long trews, and too long past the knee to be short trews. But you will wear what you are given, and you will be proud in it for two or three Sundays because it is new, but then the creases that show its newness go from it, and it is only a best suit again, and long on you, and bought big because you shall grow in it.

But to have a suit to your measure, with tape and chalk, eh, dear, there is a good feeling, indeed.

For a long time I had waited to have word from my father to go for my suit, but because Angharad and Iestyn went to London to marry, nothing was done. Then I got the word just before my brother said he would marry Wyn when Ceridwen married Blethyn, so that day I ran home from school with a purpose and straight down to Hwfa Williams and Old Twm.

"Master Morgan, a fitting," Hwfa said to Old Twm, as soon as I was through the door.

"Yes, yes," Old Twm said, and stitched faster to finish a little piece, and bit the cotton off, and stuck the needle in his waistcoat.

"Well," said Hwfa, with sweetness, and his little shoe-buttons fast on the big brass iron, "shall we have your bottom from the board, and a piece of chalk with you, if you please?"

"Gracious Goodness," said Old Twm, with the start of temper, and rolling over to come up on his hands and knees with grunts and stiffness, "am I fast on a winding wheel to come up with a bump every time some old fool is doing a bit of shouting, then?"

"I will thank you to hold the tongue," Hwfa said, coming to be red in the face, "and please to have your orders from me without the pleasure of your voice. Silence is golden."

"You are right, for once," Old Twm said, on his feet, and hands on hips to look at Hwfa, and as sweet in the voice. "The money you have lost in your time would close up the banks, indeed."

The shoe-buttons came to look at me for pity.

"All I am asking is for a bit of chalk," Hwfa said, to rend the heart. "What I am having would put marks against the names of saints."

"Chalk," said Old Twm, and very delicate in the voice, with a thin wedge of chalk on the palm of his hand. "Shall we see a master tailor using it on a good bit of cloth, now?"

Hwfa took the chalk with slowness, and his eyes all over the face of Old Twm all the time.

"You shall see a master man in his own shop," he said, every word of equal weight, "going about his business in ways that have gained a name for him wherever men speak of suits for men, and costumes for women, and outfits for riding to hounds, top coats and covert coat, cloaks and rain-cloaks, and all articles of attire to be made in cloth for all, old and young."

"Will we start now?" Old Twm asked him, very serious, and hands held up with the fingers loose and hanging down ready to start on anything, "because much longer of this and I will be smelling in my grave and the boy will grow whiskers to the knees."

"Peace, for the love of God," Hwfa said, and flying into a

rage, with his shoe-buttons sliding all over the shop, on me, on Old Twm, on the ceiling and on the floor. "If old Pharaoh could be had from the world to come he would see in you the seventh plague, indeed."

"Good," said Old Twm, and coming to slit the sleeve in my coat. "So exodus is only a matter of waiting, then, and you will be home safe to your tea in time for supper, Huw, my little one."

"Scissors," said Hwfa, and Old Twm had them in his hand as by magic.

Every man to his business, but indeed the craft of a tailor is beyond all doubt as noble and as secret as any in the world. To take a bolt of cloth and work with such simple tools as chalk, needle and thread, scissors and hot iron, and bring from them a suit to fit every little bump and crevice of the body, without ugliness, is a royal mystery indeed, and ancient beyond the knowledge of man, for all mankind has had joy to deck himself, right from the Beginning, and none shall say when that was.

"More in the shoulder," said Hwfa, making little marks with the chalk. "Up with the back."

Old Twm pulled up the cloth at the back only the smallest bit.

"Wait, wait," Hwfa shouted. "Will he have his collar over his ears, with you, you old fool, you? Down a bit. Down more. Wait. Wait."

"What, now, in the name of God?" asked Old Twm, with impatience, and fast losing sweetness.

"A coat I am making," Hwfa said, with froth, over my shoulder. "When it is trews I will let you know. Will you have the collar round his waist?"

"Nothing will surprise me in this place," Old Twm said. "There will be buttonholes in the bottoms of his trews before long. Collar a bit high in the back."

"I know, I know," said Hwfa. "Please to close the head."

"Close head, close sense," Old Twm said, "perhaps that is why."

Hwfa looked long at me as though he would cry, then he bit his lips, and still looking ready to cry, went to mark the front for buttons, but savage, and with quick side looks at the big shears on the table, as though ready to use them for a killing at the wink of an eye.

"Right sleeve short," said Old Twm, as though it were no business of anybody.

Hwfa took a big breath, and went to work on the left cuff.

"Right sleeve," said Old Twm, with a suck of a tooth.

Hwfa dropped his arms and closed his eyes. Then he opened them, looking as though the worries of the world were in his keeping, and went to work on my trews.

"Tighter at the waist," said Hwfa, "and higher, if it is no trouble to anybody in the shop."

"Shortness in the right sleeve," said Old Twm.

Hwfa started humming some tune of his own, and making little marks all over my trews with the chalk.

"There is pretty," said Old Twm, very serious.

"A journey of six months of Sundays and a good pair of feet," said Hwfa, almost in whispers, "would have to be had to find anything so pretty as you."

"So my mother said," Old Twm said, "and that sleeve of his is just below the bone of his elbow with him."

"Take off the coat, Huw, my little one," said Hwfa, with grandness. "A master tailor has no need to give a second look to anything. Come you Friday night and have it hot from the goose."

"O? He will give it to you himself, then," said Old Twm, going to sit. "And if you will find a leg of your trews hanging from your necks, and cuffs instead of flaps on your pockets, raise your eyes from my face, will you, please?"

"Yes," said Hwfa, flat, "in suffering and in pity, for he is the last of the Gadarene swine, and no more to come, thank God. Good night, now."

"Good night, Hwfa and Twm," I said, and off, with Hwfa hitting the goose in the iron holder to cover what Old Twm was saying to him.

. . . .

There is a day and a night we had when Davy and Wyn and Ceridwen and Blethyn were married, and no sleep the night before, either.

We were down at the Chapel, giving the hall next to it a bit of paint and a good scrub, and putting tables for the tea and cakes, and polishing chairs ready for the people on Saturday. My father, Ianto, Davy, Ceridwen, and Bron and me, and Mrs. Lewis and Mrs. Jones, our next-doors, and their boys and girls had been at it for hours and just getting the place to look in shape. Ivor was over the mountain conducting the big choir, and Mr. Gruffydd was up at a cottage where there was sickness, for I had chased a chicken in our back for him to take up, and nothing I hated more than killing one of our chickens, for I knew them and they knew me, and we were friends.

James Rowlands, one of the deacons, came in the hall from polishing the pulpit in Chapel, and held up a finger at my father.

"Visitors to see you," he said, "in the Chapel."

"Thank you, Jim, my little one," said my father. "Somebody about the weddings, I suppose?"

"Yes, I think," said James Rowlands. "But special. Come quick."

"Bring them in by here," said my father, on top of a ladder, with hammer and tacks for candle holders.

"Come in the Chapel, man," James said.

"No," said my father. "Ask them to have the goodness to come to me. I am at work."

"Right, you," said James, and out he went, leaving behind him the sharp smell of bees-wax and turpentine.

I was holding up the candles for my father to fit in when he was done with hammering. He finished nailing the last one in, and took the candles from me, but standing up on the top step again, he looked over at the door and almost fell from the ladder. A look as though witches had come to dance came to his face and the candles dropped from his hand, missing Bron by a hair, plump into the bucket to make a splash and puddle the floor, and Owen and Gwil were running to us, laughing, with their arms wide.

"Owen," my father shouted. "Gwilym, my little one. O, my sons."

Down the ladder he came with such a run that it fell from under him, but he jumped and landed and ran forward to meet them.

"Dada," Owen said, "there is good."

"How is Mama?" Gwilym said. "Bron, there is good you are looking, girl."

"Huw," said Owen, with smiles, "you have grown a good four inches."

"Long trews I am having," I said. "To-morrow."

"We have finished here," said my father. "Come, my sons. Home to your mother. She has waited long for this moment. Huw, see you all is well before to leave."

"Yes, Dada," I said.

So I helped Bron to do all that was wanted, and lock up,

and went up the Hill to have a cup of tea with her, for we had missed tea to work, and half-way up we met Mr. Gruffydd coming down, walking slowly, with his hat tipped over his eyes, and his hands deep in the pockets of his short coat.

"Owen and Gwil are back, excuse me, sir," I said, when we came together.

"Back?" said Mr. Gruffydd. "Who?"

"Owen and Gwil," I said. "Now just."

"Good," he said. "A happy night for your good mother. I will be glad to meet them to-morrow. Good night, Mrs. Morgan. Good night, my son."

"Come to the house, Mr. Gruffydd," Bron said, and looking up at him, "I have got shoulder of lamb."

"I have got work," said Mr. Gruffydd and smiling. "I must finish the furniture, eh, Huw? So excuse me. Good night, now."

"Eh, dear, dear," Bronwen said, when we had gone up a little way. "Poor Mr. Gruffydd, indeed."

"Why, then?" I asked her.

"O," Bronwen said, and took the stone from the door and pushed it shut, for the night was cold. By the time I had lit the lamps the kettle was jumping, but Bron was still quiet.

"Why 'O,' Bron?" I asked her. "Is something the matter with Mr. Gruffydd?"

"If I was single again," Bron said, "I think I would try to marry him, shame to me or not."

"Why?" I asked her.

"Why, why, why," Bron said, and laughing. "Always why, from the old man. Because of the look of him, boy."

"Well," I said, stupid as a brush, "I see nothing wrong with him, Bron. He is the same, to-day as yesterday."

"Empty he is, boy," Bron said. "Empty as a split pea pod, and it will come back on us, you shall see.

I remembered the afternoons, the wood, the tools, the foot-rule, the teas, and the smell of hot glue.

"Angharad, then," I said, "is it?"

"Tea," said Bronwen, "and no stains on the cloth if you please. O, Huw, think. To-morrow I will wear my new costume. There is good. I would go to sleep now and wake in time to put it on."

"And my long trews, too," I said.

"Yes," Bron said. "A man you are now."

She was looking at me, and smiling the old smile. And yet, while she smiled, and I smiled back, her mouth trembled and her smile began to go and in its going she came to blush, and her eyes changed, and her eyelids flickered shut. She was going redder and redder.

And I began to blush, though for what, I cannot say, and the cup and saucer shook in my fist, and the cup rattled, so I put it down, but still Bronwen was red, and still she sat, not moving, looking down into the sugar basin, and the silence grew so thick that perhaps a man might rest his weight against it and not make it break.

"Go now, then, Huw," she said, in a little voice that cracked to a whisper, in the throat.

So I went, and shut the back door quietly, and stood to look up at the mountain that was blacker than the darkness, but no blacker than the misery of questions in my mind. Nothing had been said, nothing done, to cause such a happening. Yet there I stood, looking up at the mountain to borrow some of his peace, with the wind lively about me, and coldness blowing through me to take the place of the heat I had just left.

But another heat was in me that now I felt, and putting my mind to this fresh burden, I found a risen newness pillared in my middle, yet, for all its newness, so much a part of me that no surprise I had, but only a quick, sharp, clear glorying that rose to a shouting might of song in every part of me, and I raised my arms and drew tight the muscles of my body, and as the blood within me thudded through my singing veins, a goldness opened wide before me, and I knew I had become of Men, a Man.

Then the goldness passed, the cold pierced through, and doubt came down blacker than before, and misery with it, for quickly, as the vision came, so it went, and I was cold, shamed, and afraid, watching the sounding darkness and wondering how men could go about their daily works, happy, having no care, thinking nothing of this mightiness within, mindful only of their bellies, their comforts, and their pockets.

And I wanted to be as I had been yesterday, a boy again, without the heaviness of doubt, this pressing fear, this new treachery that lifted to realms of singing gold, and in a little space, flung to pits of night.

Courage come to me from the height of the mountain, and with it came the dignity of manhood, and knowledge of the Tree of Life, for now I was a branch, running with the vital blood, waiting in the darkness of the Garden for some unknown Eve to tempt me with the apple of her beauty, that we might know our nakedness, and bring forth sons and daughters to magnify the Lord our God.

I saw behind me those who had gone, and before me, those who are to come. I looked back and saw my father, and his father, and all our fathers, and in front, to see my son, and his son, and the sons upon sons beyond.

And their eyes were my eyes.

As I felt, so they had felt, and were to feel, as then, so now, as to-morrow and for ever. Then I was not afraid, for I was in a long line that had no beginning, and no end, and the hand of his father grasped my father's hand, and his hand was in mine, and my unborn son took my right hand, and all, up and down the line that stretched from Time That Was, to Time That Is, and is not yet, raised their hands to show the link, and we found that we were one, born of Woman, Son of Man, had in the Image, fashioned in the Womb by the Will of God, the eternal Father.

I was of them, they were of me, and in me, and I in all of them.

"Huw," Ianto said, "why are you standing there, boy? Are you cracked?"

"No," I said. "Watching the mountain, I was."

"Well, come in and watch a couple of pots, will you?" he said. "The girls have gone from the house so we will have to do it or go starving."

"Where is Ceridwen, then?" I asked him.

"Getting married to-morrow," Ianto said, "and doing a bit of queening in the front room. Mama is in there, too, with the boys. And Bron has gone to meet Ivor."

"She was in the house, now just," I said.

"No," Ianto said. "I saw her go. All cloak and heels, she was, as though Ivor was king of Babylon. So we have got a tidy bit of work in the kitchen as an extra blessing, boy. To hell with the women. Never where you want them, or when."

So into the kitchen to do some washing up, and put big potatoes in the hot coals with cheese and butter to roast, and make hot a couple of pans for the small fry, and the saucepans for the potch. Then to lay the tables, a job I have never liked. I do like to sit at a table properly laid, for I think the sight of knives and forks in their places, with glasses and the good furniture of eating, gives something more to the appetite, for your fingers have an itch to be using them. And nothing more I hate than a table laid without care. Stains on a cloth, or wrinkles, or a knife not in the straight, a fork turned aside, a spoon put the wrong way up, will have my thoughts in a knot until they are put right. But I would rather scrub a floor than lay a table, with the fetch and carry of handfuls of cutlery, and piles of plates, and glasses, and cruets, and laying a cloth so that too much is not on one side and too little on the other, and the pulling this way and that until you are ready to roll it into a ball and push it in the fire, for my mother starched her cloths, and polished her tables, and laying a cloth became an exercise in patience almost coming to a waste of time, though worth the trouble when done.

Out to the back to mix the potch, then. All the vegetables were boiled slowly in their jackets, never allowed to bubble in boiling, for then the goodness is from them, and they are full of water, and a squash, tasteless to the mouth, without good smell, an offence to the eye, and an insult to the belly. Firm in the hand, skin them clean, and put them in a dish and mash with a heavy fork, with melted butter and the bruisings of mint, potatoes, swedes, carrots, parsnips, turnips and their tops, then chop small purple onions very fine, with a little head of parsley, and pick the leaves of small watercress from the stems, and mix together. The potch will be a creamy colour with something of pink, having a smell to tempt you to eat there and then, but wait until it has been in the hot oven for five minutes with a cover, so that the vegetables can mix in warm comfort together and become friendly, and the mint can go about his work, and for the cress to show his cunning, and for the goodness all about to soften the raw, ungentle nature of the onion.

By that time the small fry are bouncing together in the hot butter drips, and coming browner every moment like children in the sun, and shining with joy to smell so good. As soon as they are the right, deep colour of brown, and still without cracks of heat, when the small sausages are the same colour all round, give them a turn of the fingers of thyme and sage, just a turn of the fingers, mix the panful well, and put all on a big, blue willow pattern dish.

Bring the roast potatoes from the coals, and you will find the butter and cheese gone into them with as much pleasure as they will soon go into you, and rest them among green leaves of lettuce, and new radishes.

Now call everybody quickly to the table, and eat plenty.

There is good to see happy faces round a table full of good food. Indeed, for good sounds, I will put the song of knives and forks next to the song of man.

My mother was the last to sit, as usual, and the first to notice an empty plate or an idle knife and fork. Her eyes were all over, seeing all, missing nothing, and on her plate the smallest meal of any, yet quick to scold if a morsel was left, or a third helping refused by one of us.

"Did you have good dinners in London?" my mother asked Owen.

"No, Mama," Owen said. "We went to cook shops most of the days."

"Roast beef and mashed," Gwilym said, "with cabbage and Yorkshire, and jam pudding, cup of tea, sevenpence."

"Sevenpence?" my mother said, in a whisper. "Goodness me, boy, were you rolling in money?"

"No," Owen said, "but it is dear in London."

"Are you going back, Owen?" Ianto asked him.

"No, indeed," Owen said. "If Mama and Dada will have me back."

"This is home to you," my father said.

"Glad to have a good sleep, I will be," Gwilym said. "Nothing but night work the last month and no sleep last night or the night before."

"So what will you do, my sons?" my father asked.

"Down the pit," said Owen.

"Yes, yes," Gwilym said. "And happy to be back after that old tunnel."

"Working in a tunnel, Owen?" Ianto asked him. "Which one then?"

"They are making an underground railway for London," Owen said. "But no planning to it. They will make fools of themselves in time to come."

"I suppose you told a foreman that," my father said, loading his pipe and smiling.

"Owen was the foreman," Gwilym said, "and he told the surveyor."

"Eh, dear," my father said. "So you had the sack?"

"Not for that," Owen said. "He was rude to me, so I had to instruct him in courtesy."

"Ah," said my father, "then, it was, you had the sack, is it?"

"No," Gwilym said, "the surveyor had the sack. Owen

had a rise in his wages and a bigger gang. I had the sack."

"O," said my father, "you had the sack, did you? Why?"

"Wages and conditions for the men," said Gwilym, very hang-dog and talking to his plate. "I started a Union. They found out when we joined the Dockers parade, but I told them to go to hell. But one night I called a meeting after work, and the boss came in and I was sacked on the spot. So Owen left, too. No need. Then we saw Iestyn's notice about the wedding, and the bit in the paper about Davy and Wyn, and we said Home."

"John Burns and Cunninghame Graham are getting things done, then?" Davy asked.

"The best Union of the lot, now," Owen said. "And there is a man is John Burns. What is going on down here?"

"Anything but what is sense," Ianto said. "Sliding scale, that is all you will hear. The fools say that sliding scale wages allow them steady work. They cannot be got to look at figures. Nobody will look at the royalties going to butter-bellies and lordlings."

"Why not?" asked Owen. He was broader, blacker in the beard, shorter and curlier in the hair, but the same strong grey eye. "The men of the valleys are not fools."

"No," said Davy. "Not fools, but too damned well behaved."

"I will thank you not to use any language inside the house," my father said. "Please to remember that we made a bargain with the owners on sliding scale. It is for us to honour it. So be silent about your Union. Plenty of time for it when you find yourself cheated."

"Now, now," my mother said, "no more words. Did you go to Chapel in London, Owen?"

"Yes, indeed we did, Mama," Owen said. "Every single Sunday."

"Castle Street," Gwilym said, "and good too. The choir is singing before the Queen soon."

"There is beautiful," my mother said, and smiling at us, but not seeing any of us. "Singing before the good little Queen. I would think their voices might come to be like angels to sing for her. Pray day and night to be in good voice for her, I would."

"When is the Eisteddfod, now?" Owen asked.

"Six weeks," said my father. "Ivor is in with his choir."

"Choir?" Gwilym said, with big eyes. "Ivor? Since when, Dada?"

"Weeks, now," said my father. "And I shall look to see all of us standing in it, too. Davy is soloist."

"How many in the choir?" asked Gwilym, laughing. "If I will see Ivor waving a piece of stick, it will be my death. Twenty-five all told?"

"One thousand, three hundred and fifty male voices," my father said, and suddenly the room was still. "Such mightiness has not been heard since the Coming of the Dove."

"Bigger than Caradog?" Owen said, an I hummed in surprise. "We heard good choirs at Crystal Palace, too. But the tenors were no good."

"Tin trumpets," Gwilym said. "Mice could shout louder."

"Wait till you hear our tenors," my father said. "Gabriel have put aside his trumpet in shame."

"I will enjoy to open my lungs again," Owen said. "But where is Mr. Gruffydd?"

"Working," I said. "He will be glad to see you to-morrow, he told me to tell you."

"O," said Owen, and looked at my mother, and we were all quiet again.

"Dada," Gwilym said, "how is it Angharad came to marry young Evans? Was she senseless?"

"Why senseless?" my father said, in quiet, looking at his pipe, and my mother making a face at Gwilym and making it straight again when my father looked up at her.

"Well," Owen said, "he was always a lout."

"A purse-proud ninny, him," said Gwilym. "And no better for a bit of Oxford, either."

"He is your brother-in-law, now, at all events," said my father, "and Angharad has made a good marriage. She will never want, neither will her children."

"I hope he does something about his property when he comes back," Ianto said. "Old Evans could do what he did because he spoke his men's language. They will stand no nonsense from this one, though."

"There is a petition going in this week," said Davy.

"What is the use of a petition?" Owen asked, and a new note coming to his voice. "John Burns has shown you what to do. Worry the Government. Make a nuisance of yourself."

"And have six months of starvation for nothing but loss, and death to children," my father said. "Nonsense, boy. It do look very good in books, but hard on the mind and belly. Leave it, now."

"Will you starve for ever, one day, then, Dada?" Owen

said, and stern in the eye. "Markets are closing every day. Prices are rising. What will you do when they close the pits?"

"I will tell you when there is danger of it," my father said. "For the second time, leave it, now. Let us sing. I want to hear if London have taken the bells from your voices."

So Wyn went to the harp, and Ceridwen to the piano, and my mother and father sat in their chairs on each side of the fire, and we all had places about them.

And we sang.

Then the neighbours began to come in, front and back, and then Ivor and Bron came in, with cheers from everybody, and Owen trying to squeeze the life from her, and Gwilym looking in Ivor's pockets for his baton, and shouting from all for him to conduct us.

By that time we were so hot and so close together that there was no room for Wyn to play, so outside we all went, into the street, with chairs and stools.

A fine night it was, with the moon pulling silver skirts behind her to brush the top of the mountains, and the wind humble to have our voices and saying only a little bit himself to show he had one still, and the Valley waiting quietly for us to fill it with song.

Fill it we did, for hours, sitting in the street, with all the windows open and people leaning out to sing, and Ivor conducting from the top of a chair in the middle of the Hill. Sometimes you would see a few women go into the house, and a couple of minutes later come out with big teapots, and home brew in jugs, and others again would come out with bread and cheese and cake. But the singing never stopped, end one, start the other, till Wyn was coming to have blisters on the fingers from pulling the strings, and Davy took her from the stool and sat with his arm about her on our window sill, with her head on his shoulder and his coat on her knees.

Beautiful is the voice rising to the quiet of night. Nobody, now, to cough, or rattle paper, or come in late and make the noise of the devil with a chair or a dropped umbrella, and put heavy feet on loose boards.

Quietness, and blueness, and faces in white light where the moon smiles upon them, and darkness that moves where she does not. And in the quiet, O, hear the sweet, the gentle voice, those pretty sounds of many tones that live in the shivering strings of the harp. Wait now, for the slow pluck of deep chords, and feel them filling your heart and bring yourself to be ready against the coming of the swift, strong mounting, chanting melody that brings fire to the blood, and a command to raise up the voice that shall not be denied, and sing, hearing about you the sharp edge of clean notes struck in that moment when fingers touched the single string and the baton arm flew down.

Hear you, then, the voice of your brothers and sisters, deep as the seas, as timeless, as restless, and as fierce. Tenors spear the clouds with blades that had their keenness from the silversmiths of heaven. Baritones pour gold, and royal contralto mounts to reach the lowest note of garlanded soprano. And under all, basso profundo bends his mighty back to carry all wherever melody shall take them. Sing then, Son of Man, and know that in your voice Almighty God may find His dearest pleasure.

I felt Bronwen looking at me a couple of times outside there, but when I looked at her, even though I looked quickly, she always looked away and never once did she smile. But when I went in the house to help my mother with the teapots, I went to the cupboard and took out her cup and saucer and filled it to take to her, first of all.

"Tea, Bron," I said.

"O, Huw," she said, but in the voice of a stranger, "there is a good boy you are. Dying, I am, for this."

"What is the matter, Bron?" I asked her, in a whisper, and thankful for the singing all round us. "Did I say something or do anything to-night?"

She was in darkness, and the cup was big, covering her face, but I saw the moon put her finger on a tear, then she turned away from me.

"To-morrow, Huw," she said, in her own voice. "It was nothing."

But again I felt the foolish newness busy within me and I went from there, and did the work of two among the teapots, and helped with the little, pleasant kindnesses that my mother was busy to do of cutting bread and butter and spreading milk cheese, for old ladies with few teeth, and putting a hot poker with honey in home-brewed beer, for Old Mr. Jones, who wanted to sing but felt the cold, yet could not be pushed to go to his bed.

Most of the men on the Hill had a bit of sleep in chairs till early morning, but I went up the mountain with Ianto for mushrooms, and took a basketful back, with flowers for Ceridwen and Wyn, and some for my mother and Bron.

My father and Ivor, with Ianto and Davy, went down to the colliery to work the morning shift. As soon as they were gone, the real business of the day began. The house was cleaned from top to bottom, all the furniture was outside to be polished, clean curtains were hung and the knives and forks and spoons were given a shine. Then all the cooking started, with the neighbours helping, and I built fires in troughs outside to take the pots and tins overflowing from the stoves and grates.

Then we peeled potatoes and sliced vegetables, stripped chicken and duck, cut steaks and chops, sliced bacon and forked sausage until I was sick at the sight of food. Then we laid all the tables, and some of us went down to the Chapel hall to lay up down there for the Eisteddfod in the evening, and set chairs and hang curtains.

When the hooter went at noon we ran back up the Hill, and I put baths for my father and brothers out in the back, and put the buckets of hot water near, then I had a dip, and went upstairs to put on my long trews.

Well.

I wonder does anything feel better than to put on the first pair of long trews.

In this very room, here, where I am sitting, I took the paper from the suit, and pulled little bits of cotton from it, and held it up to feast upon it. Off with my clothes and into a clean shirt, with a stiff collar, and careful to tie my new white tie, that Bron had given me, in a wide knot, and pin it with my father's pin. On with the socks, new too, that Ceridwen had made for me, and then to work with the comb and water to have my hair with a parting, and flat.

Now for the suit. Pity that the coat and waistcoat cannot go on first, so that the trews can be saved till last, as you will eat potatoes and meat first, and save the new peas till the last. But there it is, trews first.

So, careful, not to spoil the crease, or get the ends on the floor, you balance to have one leg in and draw it on, and then the other, and stand to button them to the braces, and you feel the cloth covering your legs all round and down, and you look and see the creases falling sharp to the top of your foot. On with the best boots, polished to see your face, and careful in bending again to lace them. Then stand, feeling the trews bearing down upon the braces, and put on the waistcoat, and feel it snug about you, then on with the coat, nothing to fold over, no palmful of cuff, tight, but not too tight under the arms, and flaps all flat, and the collar rolling down to button over at the top.

Royal, royal is the feeling, to be standing in your good long trews, and well I understand the feeling of gentlemen with sashes round their middles and feathers in their hats. You are brave with glory, and with fear for none.

Up on the bed I got then, to try and see my trews in the little bit of glass. But it was too small and this little room was too dark, and I could only see some shining boot and a bit of turn-up. But I was feeling elegant, and that was enough for me. Even old Napoleon never felt so good, and when I went downstairs, very careful again, no Queen's Ambassador to the Court of the Tsar had more straightness in his back, or lift to his nose, or firmness to his feet, than I had.

I felt good inside and out, a feeling not to be had many times in your life, indeed.

Then my mother saw me.

She was just putting on her hat, with the pins ready to stick in.

Her eyes went big, and she opened her mouth to speak but no words came, and the pins dropped from her hands and the hat hung upon her head, with the veil caught in a comb at the back.

"Well," she said, and put her hands together, and with a smile that was nearly crying, "Huw, my little one. Who will tell you from a lord, then?"

"Is it fitting me, Mama?" I asked her, and going hot.

"Fit?" Mama said. "Like the green in trees. And I should think so, too. A sovereign and a bit it cost us for Hwfa. Do you like my costume, then, Huw?"

So I knew my mother felt about her costume as I felt about my suit, and I looked at it from the front and back to give it proper respect, though my mind was on what the boys and girls outside would say about me.

"Beautiful, Mama," I said, and she smiled again, very pretty.

In came Wyn and Ceridwen then, but not in their wedding dresses, and another turn round and look, and hand claps and kisses, and trying to tickle the backs of my legs, but I ran from them, and out in the back to meet my father.

"Well, well, Huw, my son," he said, and looking me up and down, and turning me about, and looking at the linings of the coat, and the buttonholing and the way the buttons had been stitched on, "Hwfa have done a creditable job, indeed. No pig fits his skin better."

"How do I look, Dada?" I said, a bit disappointed he had gone to look at the work instead of me.

"The same as yesterday, with long trews extra," my father said, flat. "Take your brothers' coats down to the field when you have had dinner, and remember the extra candles for the hall."

"Yes, Dada," I said, very thin.

So into the house again, and smelling the richness of new baked cake and bread crusty from the oven. But I was afraid to eat much in case to spill, so I was off down to the field with the coats long before the match started, and everybody poking fun and saying I was too proud to eat. And indeed, going down the Hill with the boys all staring and taking off my cap to the women, that is what I was, proud as proud, and glad to have something to do with my hands. But I could do nothing with my nose and mouth, for they were all shapes and twitching like the tail of a cow, until, long before I got to the field, I wished I was back in my old clothes with nothing to feel except hot or cold.

I was glad to be by myself on the field for a little bit and I went to find a good place to see the match, up on a mound half-way between the goal posts. There I put the coats, and sat down, with care again, and there is good to sit down with long trews and give the fronts a hitch so that the knees will be free of bag. It is almost a sign that you are a boy no longer, and then it is that you will think of a pipe and tobacco to round you off.

The other team came in a brake with four good horses and changed behind the hedge, with a couple of boys to tell girls to keep clear. By that time our team were leaving their houses and there is pretty to see their jerseys coming down the street, and prettier still when the other team ran on to have some kicking practice. Now the field was filling, with crowds of people coming down the Hill, and dog-carts and traps and gigs coming along the mountain road every minute, until the square was full of wheels, and the fields up the mountain full of grazing horses, with some of the men looking after them to earn an extra pint.

Ivor went on to referee and spin the coin, and when we won the end with the wind a big cheer went up, for the wind always dropped low toward sunset, so what there was of it, we would have for the first half.

A healthy sound is the tamp of the leather ball on short green grass and pleasant, indeed, to watch it rise, turning itself lazily, as though it were enjoying every moment of the trip up there, against blue sky, and coming down against the green, in a low curve right into the ready hands of a back.

A whistle from Ivor, and the captain on the other side takes his run and kicks, and as you watch the ball climb you see the teams running into position to meet one another underneath it.

A forward has it, but before he can so much as feel it properly, he is flat on his back, and the two sides are packing over him. A whistle from Ivor, and the first scrum, and shouts for Davy as he lifts his arms to bind his front men. In goes the ball, and the tight, straining muscles are working, eight against eight, to hold one another and then to push each other the length of the field. But the ball comes free behind the pack, and their fly-half has it, so fast that nobody knows till he is on his way toward our touch line with his three-quarters strung behind him and nothing but our full-back in his way. Shout, crowd, shout, with one voice that is long-drawn, deep, loud, and full of colour, rising now as the fly runs pell-mell and Cyfartha Lewis dances to meet him, and up on a rising note, for inches are between them, louder with the voice in an unwritten hymn to energy and bravery and strength among men.

But Cyfartha is like a fisherman's net. The fly has been too clever. He should have passed to his wing long ago, but he is greedy and wants the try himself, and on he goes, tries to sell a dummy, and how the crowd is laughing, now, for to sell a dummy to Cyfartha is to sell poison to a Borgia. The fly is down, and Cyfartha kicks the ball half-way down the field to our forwards, and has time to offer his hand to poor Mr. Fly, who is bringing himself to think what happened after the mountain fell on him.

And my father is laughing so much that his glasses are having trouble to settle on his nose. Owen and Gwilym are shouting for all they are worth, for Davy has the ball and his forwards are all round him to push through the enemy. Shoulders and knees are hard at work, men are going down, men stumble on top of them, fall headlong and are pinned by treading, plunging boots. Red and green jerseys are mixed with yellow and white, and mud is plenty on both. On, on, an inch, two inches, bodies heave against bodies, hands grab, legs are twisted, fall and crawl, push and squirm, on, on, there are the white posts about you, but red and green jerseys hide the line and form a wall that never shows a gap. On, yellow and white, pack up behind and keep close, pull the ball into the belly and shield it with your arms, down with your head, more shoulder from the back, keep closer at the sides, push now, push, push, push. A red and green down in front, another, who carries away a third. Another push now, and the ball is slipping from him. A hand has come from the press below and grasps with the strength of the drowning, but a wriggle to the side and a butt with the hip loosens it and on, on, half an inch more, with an ankle tight in the fist of red and green who lies beneath two yellow and white and only enough of sense and breath to hang on.

Down with the ball now, fall flat, with eight or nine on top of you, and there is the whistle.

The ball rests an inch over the line.

Then see the hats and caps go into the air, and hear a shouting that brings all the women to the doors up and down the Hill, and some to lean from the back windows.

Again the whistle, and Maldwyn Pugh looks up at the posts, makes his lucky sign, and takes his run at the ball that rests in its heeled mark, and kept there by the hand of Willie Rees, who lies full length in the mud with his face turned away, not to be blinded by the slop that will come when the boot leaves his hand empty.

Empty it is, and the ball on its way, and the crowd quiet, with the quiet that is louder than noise, when all eyes are on the same spot and all voices are tuned for the same shout.

The ball travels high, drops in a curve, turns twice. The crowd is on its way to a groan, but now the wind takes it in his arms and gives it a gentle push over the bar, no need for it, but sometimes the wind is a friend, and there it is.

We are a try and a goal, five points, to the good.

Red and green kicked the ball down to the line and as I watched it, I saw a handkerchief waving below there, and looked, and Ceinwen Phillips was looking at me and her teeth big and white and her eyes nearly closed, laughing red, with red and green ribbon in her hair, and a big bunch of red and green ribbon in her cloak, and her hair the colour of new hay long about her.

She came running toward me and I was in a mind to run

from her, for I had no wish to be seen with a girl, and I knew that my brothers would have plenty to say if they saw us together. But she was too close to me now, and nothing to do but smile and try to look as though I was glad she had seen me, instead of wishing her in the deserts of Egypt.

"Huw," she said, trying to hold her chest from troubling, "there is glad I am I came. My father and Mervyn brought me. There is a good team you have got. They say your brother will be in the international match this year."

"Too early yet," I said, knowing she was speaking only for the sake, "but he is playing well to-day, indeed."

"There is beautiful you look in your long trews," she said. "I was looking and looking. No, I said, he is just like Huw Morgan. But he is too grown up. A man, he is. Huw's big brother, I said, to myself, of course. And then I looked again when you were shouting now just, and I waved my handkerchief to make sure. There is funny."

"Yes," I said, and blushing, and my hands in the way again, and hoping there would be enough in the game to keep my brothers busy on it and not on me.

"There is hot I am," Ceinwen said, blowing. "Is there a drop of water to be had?"

"Plenty up at the houses," I said. "Hit on the door and ask."

"I am a stranger," she said, and pity coming to make soft her eyes. "And perhaps I might meet a man, too."

"Mervyn will take you," I said, pretending to watch the game, but watching my brothers from the sides of my eyes to see if they were turning round.

"He wants to see the match," she said. "I asked him, but he was nasty to me. And I am ready to drop, so dry I am."

"Drinking is bad for you when you are hot," I said. "Chew a bit of grass, girl."

"Am I an old sheep to chew grass?" Ceinwen said. "A drink I want, to take the cracks from my tongue. Three hours it took to come here, and no dinner before it, either. O, Huw, give me a little drink of water, is it?"

A man made of thick iron would have to melt like a candle to hear a woman in that voice, so small, so high in the throat, with something of baby, and yet all of woman. But I was afraid to be seen with her, for I was bound to have a roasting from the family, and my brothers would make life so hot to make of hell a bliss.

"Look," I said, "I have got my brothers' coats by here.

I will ask one of my other brothers to look after them, and while I am doing that, you go on over to the bridge beyond the Three Bells, and I will catch up, is it?"

"Where is the Three Bells?" she asked me, helpless again.

"O, to the devil, girl," I said. "Through the hedge and along the street to the right. Go, now."

"I know," she said, and pulling a good pout, "you are afraid to be seen with me. I will cry, then."

So out came her handkerchief and, indeed, she started to cry among all those people who knew me, and loud, too, with plenty of spit in the sobs.

"Hisht, girl, hisht," I said, ready to kill her if only to stop her from making a noise. "Will you have everybody to see you, now?"

"I want a drink of water," she was saying, through breaths and sniffs and gulps. "There is cruel you are."

O, and then my father turned, full of cheering, for Davy had gone through again, and with his mouth wide he saw me and looked at Ceinwen, and at that moment, off she went again, with her mouth drawn down, and her eyes closed, and her face to the skies. And me going from one foot to the other and an itch in my fingers to strangle.

"Only a little drop of water," she said, but only us two would know what she was saying, so full of chokes and coughs it was.

"Hisht," I said, "I will give you a drop of water. You shall swallow the river. But hisht, now, will you? Here is my father."

And here he was, very stern, looking at Ceinwen and then at me, as he came. And my brothers turning to see where he was going, and more people turning to see what they were looking at, and then a crowd looking and some of them coming closer, and Ceinwen having lovely times, and going off into a high pitch of moaning, with sniffs and to spare.

"Good God," my father said, "what have you done, then?"

"Nothing, Dada," I said. "She only asked for a drink of water."

"Drink of water?" my father said. "Will you lie to me?" He looked at Ceinwen and put his arm about her.

"There, there," he said. "Come on, now then. Tell me what he did."

"I want a drink of water," she said, with her head on his shoulder, and her fist fast on his collar. "No dinner, I had, and three hours to get here, and so hot. I asked him, but he said to chew grass."

"Well, Goodness Gracious, boy," my father said, "are you mad? Will you refuse a girl what you would be in a rush to do for a dog?"

"I had the coats to mind, Dada," I said, in the voice of a small fly.

"Coats, coats, coats," he said, and to burn the skin. "Have you got a tongue to ask one of us? Go, now, and take the young thing up to the house and ask your good mother to give her all she wants, and quick. The girl will go from here thinking we are all savages, indeed. Go, boy."

"Yes, Dada," I said. "Come on, Ceinwen."

"Ceinwen?" my father said. "Do you know her name, then?"

"Yes, Dada," I said. "She is in my school."

"And you let the girl perish for a drop of water?" my father said, and in such anger and surprise that there was little voice left in him. "Well, Devil throw smoke, I am in a good mind to tear that suit from your back, you rascal, you. You deserve the treatment of a bully. Wait till your mother hears this. Go from my sight."

I walked from there like a mongrel with my eyes on the grass, passing all the people who were looking at me, as though I had no notion they were there, and stepping a little longer than Ceinwen so that she had to run to catch up. Outside the field I stopped to wipe my forehead, and a full feeling was in me that made me careless of what else might happen, even if the sun fell in chips in the middle of the street.

"There is a bitch you are," I said to her.

She looked at me with a bit of a frown, and her eyes catching the sun with flecks of pale light coming and going, and her lashes still stuck together with tears. And she started to laugh. In the eyes, at first, to make you think she was going to cry more.

Then altogether, loud, with almost as many tears as her crying, and stuffing the handkerchief into her mouth, and pulling the cloak about her face, leaning against the wall for weakness.

"Your face," she was saying. "If you could see your face, now just. O, Huw, there is sorry I am you had trouble."

"Shut up," I said, "I have got some more to come next time my father sees me, never mind my brothers. Why did you cry? You could have had your old water."

"I was only acting," she said. "Not crying, I was. Acting. Was I good?"

I looked at her, and tried to see inside her, but it was like trying to look through a wain full of corn, with bits sticking in your face and the ends tickling your ears, and a weight on top of you and whispering all about you. Her eyes were full of many lights, greys and blacks and perhaps blues, but so quick to come and sudden to go, and would never be certain which you saw, or if you saw them at all. And as you looked, a dead feeling, of weight, and closeness, pressed upon you, and your eyes would slip down to her mouth and as you watched, you saw it moving within itself, crinkled, pink, and the tops of her teeth just showing and the tip of her tongue riding them. Then the soft pockets at the sides of her mouth would move upward and the crinkles would be gone, and teeth would show and the tongue slip out, palely, shining, a narrow fatness spreading a wet polish and going back to rest in comfort upon the tops of her teeth. Up, again, with the eyes, past tight-shut nostrils that widen as you look, up the straightness of nose to her eyes again, and more lights have come into them, with something of that mist that you will see over the heat of the fire, when all things are seen as though they moved under water. This, with the wind putting his fingers into her hair and pulling, and throwing up and catching, to let fall again.

"Was I, Huw?" she asked me, in whispers.

"Let us go to the house for water," I said, and turned from her, going quick up the Hill and glad to have cold wind in my face and ordinary things to look at.

My mother said nothing when I told her what my father had said, but she looked at Ceinwen with that little look that seemed to last for hours, and yet was only a little look, and she nodded when Ceinwen dropped a knee. But no smile from her.

If it is said that a girl is a small eater, perhaps Miss Ceinwen Phillips was left out of the reckoning. I am the last to wish any a small appetite, for good food deserves stern treatment, and nothing is better than to see plates coming empty and the clock taking the minutes and no notice taken of either.

But Ceinwen.

Well.

"Who is this old girl you have brought to the house, Huw?" my mother asked me and cutting a thick piece of ham jelly pie. "Is she eating for the winter to come?"

"Well, Mama," I said, and feeling disgraced, "she is a big girl, I suppose."

"Big girl," my mother said. "Hear it all."

"Greedy, she is," Bron said. "Did you see the way she had the apple pie?"

"She said it was too good to leave," I said.

"She was eating too fast to taste," said Bron. "You take her wherever you found her after this, and leave her. It will be hours before she will have her feet in comfort, so there is no danger to you. And come you home, straight. Is it?"

"Yes, Bron," I said, and went out to stand by Ceinwen.

"O, Huw," she said, and holding herself. "There is good. I will eat till my skin bursts."

"Water it was, you wanted," I said.

Ceinwen was rolling in comfort, taking crumbs from round her mouth with stretched tongue.

"I am fat with goodness," she said. "I will go and say thank you to your Mama, and I will ask her to come to us when she wants, is it? Then we will go back."

So she went inside to my mother, and I collected the empty dishes and set clean ones, and wiped the crumbs from her place.

"Well," she said, when she came out, "so there will be two weddings here to-day, then?"

"Yes," I said, "but you will be far from both."

"I have just been invited," she said, and doing her hair at the back. "I am going to wash dishes for a bit. So I will come back with you and see my Dada, and then come back, is it?"

So back we went to the field, but I was out of patience with her, and in no mind to watch the game because of it, so I was glad when the whistle went. Mr. Phillips went up to the house with her, and Mervyn went for the horse and trap to take it nearer to our back. I went to the Chapel hall, and put everything ready, happy to be by myself and walk in my long trews up and down the wooden floor.

I heard the wedding party come down and go in the Chapel, and the murmur of the crowd outside, then the singing, the laughing, the prayers, and more singing, with the crowd coming more and more noisy, and deacons going out to them to ask for quiet, and telling them to feel shame.

"Glad I am they are all strangers out there," James Rowlands said to me when he came in and bolted the door. "If they belonged to our Valley I would be ready to go to my grave for disgrace. Such conduct indeed, while two are being joined in sight of God."

"How long, now, Mr. Rowlands?" I asked him.

"Not long, my little one," he said. "They were beyond better or worse when I came from there. Two better couples I have never seen. Me and your poor father have not stopped to cry. Beautiful, indeed."

So up and down I went again, and very good it is to be with yourself in an empty room, to walk as you want, and say as you want, with no thought for what others may say or think.

The singing of the last hymn came through the noise outside and the crowd heard and joined in. The doors were opened in Chapel, and people began to come out, pushing everybody from the porch to let Davy and Wyn, and Blethyn and Ceridwen through. I was on a chair looking out of the window to watch them go, and indeed I will swear there were differences in our Davy and Ceridwen even in so short a while. It was in the smile they had, in the way they waved, in the way they stood and even in their walking. It was as though they had lost something, but found something better, and yet still ready to worry for what they had lost if only they could find out what it was.

Thomas the Carrier took them up the Hill in carriages with flowers and ribbons, and all the people in front pulling them with ropes, or crowding about and behind them, throwing flowers, singing different songs in any key to hand, shouting, and jumping up to try and catch a look from Davy, and people leaning far out of bedroom windows to shout, and wave, and throw more flowers, and fling toffees at the crowds under them, and the sun beginning to think of bed and his light going, and a fine dust rising from the road and powdering overhead.

"Well," Bron said, "where were you in Chapel, then?"

"I did the candles and set the fires in by there," I said. "Dada was angry with me, so I stayed in the quiet."

"Where is that old sow of a girl, with you?" she asked me, and taking off her cloak. "Have nothing to do with her, Huw. One look and I was finished."

"She is doing dishes up at the house," I said. "She was asked because she said she liked Mama's cooking."

"Then let her stay up by there till it is time to go," Bron said, "and you stay down here. Is it?"

"Yes," I said, "if I am with you."

"Plates," said Bron, "and in plenty, over by the cakes. And small spoons in the box by the cups and saucers, or they will drive us mad for a spoon, again."

"Why have you come from the house, Bron?" I asked her. "I thought you were going to have wedding tea with them."

"Mr. Gruffydd came up," Bron said. "And I saw him looking. The house was shouting full of Angharad, so I put my cloak on and said I had a headache."

So we went to work on the food and drink for the Eisteddfod, and when the other helpers began coming in they found there was little to do but sit down and eat again. But it was only a few minutes after that, and the choirs began to come in to take whole rows for themselves, and people putting hats and coats and pieces of paper on chairs, and others trying to push them off and put their own down on the sly, with words coming high and faces going red, and deacons pushing through the crowd with frowns to find the cause of the trouble and put all at peace again.

I had saved good places for my mother and the boys in the middle of the front row, so when they came I was proud to show them in. But I had forgotten Ceinwen and Mervyn and Mr. Phillips, and my mother said she would go back home rather than sit, with guests left standing. So Gwilym gave his seat to Mr. Phillips, and Mervyn sat on a couple of coats on the floor between his father and Owen, and my mother told me to take Ceinwen behind the tables to Bron and do a bit of helping.

So there I was with Ceinwen again, and as soon as we were out of the crowd and away from eyes, round in the back where we boiled the water, she put her hand in mine and put her arm round my neck.

"Go from me, girl," I said, and pushed her off.

"Be sweethearts, Huw," she said with pity, and soft. "Your brother and sister are married, see, and everybody happy excepting only us two. Nobody we have got, only an old father and mother, and brothers. Be sweethearts, Huw. Then we will have somebody. There is lovely."

"No," I said. "Soft, that is."

"Huw," she said, and put her arm round my neck again, and kissed me.

My mother kissed with dryness, a touching upon the cheek or forehead, an assurance that we were her own. Bron kissed softer, with more of crispness, and with a little sound in it, but always upon the cheek. My aunts kissed as hens take bits from the ground.

But Ceinwen kissed.

The softness of her mouth was a glory of surprise, and cool, not even warm, with an easiness of moisture, and the tip of her tongue making play in idle strolling, lazily, and yet full of life, and her weight lying heavily upon me, her hair falling about our faces, shutting out the light, and all other smells save that of her, that was the perfume of the broad, sweet lands of the living flesh, that rose from her, and covered her about and followed her as she walked.

Then my mouth was cold, empty, and she was looking down at me.

"How many girls have you kissed before?" she asked me, as she would ask to pass lettuce.

"None," I said, and going cold to go from her.

"Go on, boy," she said, and giving me a push. "There is an old liar you are."

"The water is boiling," I said, and pulling off the pots from the grids, and glad of plenty to do. "Go and tell Bron to have the tea ready."

"Are we sweethearts, Huw?" she asked me, in a high little voice, and her hands busy with ribbons on the front of her dress.

"No," I said. "Go from here."

"I will come for you again," she said, and meant, and went.

All through the evening and into the late of night, the singing went on, with children first, then boys and girls, then the men and women, and after the choirs. And all the time we were working to make tea and serve food, until it seemed that all the world had come to eat, and drink, and sing.

Only when the candles began to go, and the lamps had to be trimmed, did people begin to put on coats, and nod to one another, and look for children, and send somebody to harness the horse, and start to shake hands with everybody.

Of course, my mother and father were in the middle of a crowd, then, and another hour for saying good-bye, even though everybody knew they would see them in Chapel next morning. But thanks had to be said, though they might wait till morning, with still twenty miles to go behind the horse.

I went up to the field for Mr. Phillips' mare, breathing deep of the cold darkness, glad to be free of the noise, and closeness, and heat, of people. But when I undid the shackle and started to lead her away, I heard Ceinwen calling me from the bottom of the field, and stopped, hoping she would miss me in the darkness and go away. But she came slowly toward me, not calling now, but singing, softly, David of the White Rock, in contralto, deep, clear, and the wind bringing it to me as though he liked it and wanted me to hear.

"Huw," she said, only a little way off, and stopping, with no more of the song.

"Your father is waiting," I said, and went on down. She came on my other side and put an arm about my neck, leaning upon me, and pulling me to walk slower.

"Put your arm about me, Huw," she said, into my ear.

"Go on, girl," I said. "There is soft you are. Put my arm, indeed. Like a couple of fools."

I wonder what is it, that makes us speak so foolishly, and with so much hurt to those who would confer an honour or do us a pleasure if, perhaps, we think such honour or pleasure will cause the censure of others, or disturb that shifty creature called Conscience.

Yet Conscience is a nobleman, the best in us, and a friend.

I knew I wanted to put an arm about Ceinwen, and I knew that I was in heats to kiss her again, but the stupid spirit was in me to deny both, and in the denial, to hurt her, as though that hurt would do some good to me, and precious Conscience.

I was kept from telling the truth, and putting my arm about her with pleasure and a smile, and kissing her with willingness to enjoy, even though we were on a mountain side, in darkness, and as good as from by there to the moon away with all created tongues and eyes, and the acid of one, and the pricks of the other, and the malice and ignorance of both.

But the knowledge of them and their hurts made for fear

and made me a liar, in truth, in spirit, and in feeling, and I was dumb as a lout.

"O, Huw," Ceinwen said, and pulled me to stop, and stamped her foot, "I like to kiss. I want to kiss."

"Shut up, girl," I said, in discomfort, knowing well how I felt, and envious of her truthfulness, and shamed because of it, but still unwilling to come to the front in case she poked fun, and in case we were late and my father asked questions, but mostly because I wanted to feel better, with less on the conscience, than she.

We looked at one another for a minute, both of us in black shadow, able to see nothing only a black shape. Then she put an arm about me and held tight, and pulled me to her and kissed me, but this time her teeth bit through both my lips, and the pain made me struggle, trying to shout, but only a sound from the throat, and blood running warm and smooth and salt into my mouth.

"Now," she said, breathless, and putting me away, "next time, kiss. And no nonsense. Good night, now."

So I watched her run, and sucked at my lips, and climbed on the mare's back and rode down, laughing all the way, though for what, I cannot tell.

Funny it was to see her coolness when she said good night to us in the Square, and her straight back, and empty eyes, and the smile, and the folded hands, and the bend of head when her father cracked the whip and they started for home. She even made a little frown to Mervyn because he shouted to me.

Eh, dear, women.

But we help. Yes, indeed, we help. We only say we cannot understand them when we cannot understand our craven selves, cannot release ourselves from fear that ours is the first blame, cannot assume and hold our position as men, and must for shame, load them with the onus of the prime move in order that we may partake of the sin, and to hell with that word, too, and to assuage our delicate moral sense with nonsense about temptation, and Eve, and the frailness of mortal man. The truth is not in us, neither do we look for it, and we are cowards and not men. In the day of King Arthur, a man would fight to the death in honour of a woman, but in these days, those who will call themselves men will cower, even in their thoughts, at the prospect of having to reckon with the eyes and tongues of those warty bawds and pussy sluts who peddle oral filth.

Gossip.

Hear it all.

Gossip. Hear the sound of it.

Many a better noise has come from the back.

May all such end their days soonest, with cancers of the misused tongue and all the vitals, and perish with the special torments of the damned, and pass without hurry into Hell, and lie upon the hottest grid through all eternity, with water only an inch beyond reach and the green pastures of Paradise always clear in their sight.

I have no love for gossips.

It was gossip that sent Mr. Gruffydd from us, and gave me his gold watch, though I have never been able to look at it without thinking of the nagging evil that piles lies on lies with every second it marks.

Davy had shouldered his son, and Ceridwen had taught her twins to walk before Angharad came home again.

Chapter Twenty-Five

THERE HAD BEEN TROUBLE down at the Evans Colliery for months on end, but it was always settled by the manager and a man from Town, and then breaking out again, until everybody in the village was tired of it, and nobody would listen.

At first, Mr. Gruffydd did most of the talking for the men, for they trusted him. But sometimes they would doubt even him, and then they got worse in their doubts, and started employing a lawyer to put their case. Then another lawyer was called in, with the men having the hat round to pay the expenses and then more lawyers. But all of them together never did as much as Mr. Gruffydd did for nothing, but only the men's wives had the sense to see it, and one night they all went to Mr. Gruffydd after Chapel and asked him to see what he could do.

"What, then?" Mr. Gruffydd asked my father. "They want so much for the stone they are cutting to come at the coal, so much for water on the levels, so much for putting props, and a ballot for the best places. What am I to say?"

"We are having the same fight," my father said. "That

is why the Union is growing and sliding scale going from favour."

"What are you doing?" Mr. Gruffydd asked. "Then I shall know how to talk to the manager."

"I am in favour of a man from each colliery in all the valleys meeting the managers of all the collieries, and their owners," said my father. "Table the complaints, listen to the difficulties on the other side, and giving a bit and taking a bit, with fairness and fair play to all."

"Good," said Mr. Gruffydd. "I will try that."

But it was no good. The meeting was refused, the terms were refused, and the men struck work. Then they went back again. Then out again. Then nobody cared if they were in or out, and most of the best men got jobs in other collieries, and strangers came to the Valley and worked for the money that our men refused to take.

And Iestyn had his life threatened, and my mother wrote to Angharad, in London, to stop him from coming down. Even we got a bit of blame from some of the men just because Iestyn had married into our family.

Then Iestyn sold out to the owners of my father's colliery, and they said they would work it only when their levels went through underground and joined it, and so closed it, putting four hundred men from work.

Strikes we had had, and funerals, to keep men from work, but that was the first time we had ever had men standing in the street without work waiting for them.

"This is the beginning, Dada," Owen said. "You will see, now. Plenty of labour, fall in wages. Scarcity of labour, rise in wages. Watch, now."

"There is an agreement," my father said. "There is a minimum."

"The minimum," Owen said, "will be the minimum when these men are working. Four hundred men extra in this Valley, and others to join them in the other valleys. When all those men are back at work, there will be a new minimum."

"We shall see," said my father.

And a new minimum there was, too, for when a man complained, or spoke too loudly near the manager, he was put from work, and another taken in his place from the idle crowd at the pit head.

For less wages, always.

Some of the men went to work in other valleys, some

went to Sheffield, to Birmingham, or Middlebrough, some went even to the United States of America. And some stayed in the village.

And so we knew, for the first time, men without work, who kept from the workhouse only because it was too far away, or because their sons were earning, their relatives were kind, or their friends were charitable.

But even so, other men and their families were coming into the Valley and starting in the collieries for less money, or helping builders, or setting up little businesses in grocery, and tobacco, and newspapers, and cook shops, until the village had houses on both sides of the road round the mountain, on one side, and climbing up the mountain on the other. Two new streets of small houses were built behind the Square, and two more chapels, one for the Methodists, and one for the Calvinists, and the Roman Catholics put a church for the Irish over on the other side of the river.

Even with the trouble coming flying to meet us, we grew, and we were happy.

Ivor ran in one night with his face lit like a summer dawn, and so happy it was pleasure to see.

"Well," my mother said, and put down her needle and stretched her back.

"Read it, Dada," Ivor said, and gave a letter to my father.

"Well, Gracious Goodness, boy," my father said, and looked from the letter to my mother, staring wide, and with open mouth, and then back at the letter and up and again at the letter, until my mother was shifting as though sitting up in bed with crumbs under her.

"Will you drive me silly, then?" she said, with ice.

Even the kettle looked as though it were listening.

"It is a command," my father said, as though reading the Word. "A Royal Command. Good God!"

"A Royal Command?" said my mother, and her eyes going big, and her shoulders falling loose. "What, now?"

"Mr. Ivor Morgan," my father said, and sitting up, clearing his throat, "is commanded to appear before Her Majesty at Windsor Castle with chosen members of his choir."

"O," said my mother, long drawn and high, and almost ready to faint.

"Her Britannic Majesty," said my father, with tears

ready, and standing. "To sing before the Queen. My son. I never thought to see the beautiful day. Let us give thanks."

"Yes, indeed," said my mother, and down we all went on the knees.

"O Heavenly Father," my father said, with his hand in my mother's, and both clasped together, and looking up, "I give thanks from the heart to live this day."

"Yes," said my mother.

"I give thanks for my good son," said my father.

"Yes," my mother said, and rested her face against his shoulder.

"And for his good mother," my father said, "my blessing for thirty years. I give thanks for all I have, and I do give thanks for this new blessing. For you are Our Father, but we look to our Queen as our mother. Comfort her in her troubles, O God, and let her mighty worries trouble not more than she shall bear in her age. And let, I beseech you, power to soothe, and sweetness to lull, and spirit to encourage, be given to the voices that sing at her command that night. And may Ivor have strength to acquit himself with us with honour. Amen."

"Amen," said we all.

"Beth," my father said, eyes shining and red in the face, "bring out the beer. Huw, go for Mr. Gruffydd, and 'no' will not do for an answer. Open house, to-night."

Down I went for Mr. Gruffydd, and found him cooking supper, with a fork in one hand and a book in the other.

"The choir is going to sing for the Queen, Mr. Gruffydd," I said. "And Dada says please to come up. Open house."

"At last, then, Huw, my little one," he said, and smiled, and took off the dish. "I wondered how long it would be."

So up the Hill we went, and people leaving their houses, and men running up the mountain with paper and wood to light beacons to call the choir from their houses, and women gathered in groups to decide who should cut the food and who should prepare the drink, with windows opening and people shouting the news in the street, and children in night dress running about with nobody to tell them to go back to bed, and cheers for Mr. Gruffydd, and a couple for Ivor, and even a few for me.

No orders to anybody, no notices in print, no trumpets, no cannon to throw fire and give headaches to old ladies, yet everybody was going about with a job to do, and willingness to do it well, and if you had asked any of them why, they would have looked at you once, with their eyebrows up, and clicked their tongues and pushed you from the light.

The night shift were in their working clothes ready to go down and the afternoon shift were coming up the Hill, when the men of the choir began coming in from the other valleys, over the mountain, and round by the river. By wain and brake and cart and gig and dog-trap, and even in goat cars, they were coming, in anything that would move faster than they could run they came, and groups of them were walking over the mountain all round us, with lanterns and torches to light them, little flowers of light making a rolling dance all the way down, with song from all of them, and the wind going mad to choose which to carry, which to drop.

Now the Hill was packed full of people, with no spaces among the hats and faces all the way down, from top to bottom, and here and there a torch, a lamp, with candles along the window sills, and even some of the men sitting on the roofs and hanging down their legs. Loudly and happily rose their voices, with laughter as the people above swayed back on the people below, and women gave little screams when they thought they would be crushed, and men pushed out their elbows to take the weight from about them, with jokes and more laughing, and there, a quartet singing, and women joining in the harmony, and here, a man singing a verse, and about him people's faces set intent to pick up the first note of the chorus, and come in, then, like lions.

Then they saw Mr. Gruffydd in our front bedroom window, and instantly a roar, that hit across the ears, and kept on, even though he waved to them to be silent, for minute on minute, the roar, going quiet and coming bigger again, roar, roar, roar, with open mouths and wild happiness in the eyes, and then a big hush from hundreds, as though the wind had met his master, and then stillness.

Stillness.

Mr. Gruffydd turned to my father, and he blew the note on the reed pipe.

Ivor raised his finger, and from top of the Hill down to bottom men and women hummed softly to have the proper key, with sopranos going up to find the octave, and altos climbing, and tenors making silver and contraltos and baritones resting in comfort and basso down on the octave below, and the sound they all made was a life-time of loveliness, so solid, so warm, so deep, and yet so delicate. It will be no surprise to me if the flowers of the gardens of heaven are made from such sound. And O, to smell a smell as good to the nose as that sound sounds to the ear.

But even heaven could not be so beautiful, or we would all be drunk with beauty day and night, and no work done anywhere, and nobody to blame.

Drunk with beauty. There is lovely.

"God save the Queen," said Mr. Gruffydd, and made way in the window for Ivor.

Ivor held out his arms wide to us, with his first fingers up, and his mouth making an O, and his eyes nearly shut, to tell us to sing soft, and the crowd made little moves all the way from top to bottom, not in restlessness, but to find room for arms to have ease, for feet to be firm, for chests to give good breath, for chins to point, and for room to sing.

Down came Ivor's right arm, once, twice, and at its lowest point, "God Save Our Noble Queen," sang tenor, with stern quiet, "Long Live Our Noble Queen," sang tenor and soprano, "God Save Our Queen," sang tenor, soprano, and alto.

Now Ivor gathered himself, and took all our voices into his fingers and drew them tight, and the clarion note was struck in the slow, strong, marching tempo, and grandeur came to frighten as the voices mounted in mighty majesty.

"Send Her Victorious," said we all. "Happy And Glorious."

Now gather yourselves, O Men of the Valleys, now open the throat, higher with the chin, loud, loud as the trumpets of the Host, sound out, that even at Windsor it may be heard to rock the very stones.

"Long To Reign Over Us," we sang, and leaned on the last note, while tenor and soprano loosed their wings to fly up to the octave, and hold.

Now.

Up goes Ivor's right arm, fist clenched, and his left hand held out to us to implore. More power, greater volume, more mightiness, spread the chest, bring in the air with a savage pull and send the voice to hit the sky with force to smash the clouds.

"God Save Our Queen," we sang, and ended with a cheering they could hear over in the other valleys, and those down in the village who were out of sight of Ivor, went on singing, like an echo that fell asleep on the job and runs now with sleep in his eyes to catch up.

I went inside our house to take plates outside and found my father giving Clydach Howell the letter, but flat in the pages of a bound book of *Christian Heralds*.

"A frame of the best wood you will find, Clydach, my little one," my father said. "And I will have a crown set above it, see, and it shall hang on this wall all the days of my life."

"Leave it to me, Gwilym," said Clydach, serious, and carrying the book as though it was his pass through the Gates, "I will make a job of this to bring tears to the eyes, indeed to God. And no cost to you, either."

"Cost to me," said my father, "or no frame."

"We shall see," said Clydach. "I do know where there is a bit of mahogany that the old devil himself would be glad to have his old claws on, if he knew where to find it. For years I have wanted to see it put to good use, but there was not enough for a chair, and too much to spoil for a stool. But now, a frame. You shall see a bit of wood, now, Gwilym, my little one, aye, by God, you shall."

"Drink up," said my father, and round went the pots.

There is a night that was, with everybody going home in groups round the roads and over the mountain, with one group over here singing a line of a chorus, and listening for a group over there to sing the next, back and fore, till the sound fell in the depths of the miles between and the wind was too tired to do any more carrying.

And the mountain lying awake on his side, smiling in the quiet darkness, happy to have us about him.

"Huw," Ceinwen said, in the playtime, "where is this nightingale, with you?"

"Plenty on the mountain," I said, "these weeks, now."

"When am I going to hear them?" she asked me, and looking from the sides of her eyes, as though anything I said would be lies, so save breath to blow tea.

"When you come over in our Valley," I said.

"Right," she said. "The men are going to London for Saturday, so on Saturday afternoon I will come, is it?

Then we can stay up the mountain late, and I can come back any time I like with the trap."

No use to make an excuse, and I had given a promise, so there it was.

"You will have trouble with your father," I said.

"He will know nothing," she said, and winked, and I blushed like a fool.

We had talked little since the night of the weddings, and only a nod before school, for she was often late, and never in much of a temper in the mornings, and Mervyn was always near, so a note across the desk or a touch of the fingers as she passed, was all we had been able to have.

Whatever is said to the contrary, I am ready to swear that green and red lights are set in the brain, and you will have a flash of red when you are going into danger. The red inside me was set stone still at danger whenever I thought of Ceinwen. Why, I cannot say, but it was. I was sure something was going to happen.

And I have never been so right.

Only a few of us were kept on at our age to take examinations. Mr. Motshill had told us that he was determined to push us through University. Nine of us, there were, and Ceinwen one of us, for she was gifted, and no doubt about it. Years in her father's business, and making out bills, and doing sums, had made her first class in arithmetic, and she could quote Shakespeare till Christmas came again, so there was nothing wrong with her English.

We had an easier time than the other boys and girls who were leaving at fourteen, and some before that. Not easier in work, mind, for Mr. Motshill was strict, but in coming in and going out. Monitors, we were, but only to see that the boys and girls behaved themselves. But we let them do as they liked, and never once brought them up even for speaking Welsh in school.

Friday night, when the village turned out to see Ivor and the men from our Valley go over the mountain to sing for the Queen, was soft with rain, a little cold, and a lovely blue.

The brake they went in was covered with leeks, and the horses wore three white ostrich feathers in their head straps, and more leeks on their blinkers, and red blankets. A prouder team of horses you never saw, and no use to say that horses cannot tell when they are dressed for show, for if you had seen them, and their little dancings, and half a neigh, and a couple of coughs, and restless with the hoof, and swish with the tail, good gracious, it was so plain that they wanted you to look at them, and pat them, and make those sounds through the teeth that horses love to hear from friendly men.

Up with the boxes with the best clothes, first, then two casks of beer and crates of bottles from the Three Bells, to see them as far as Paddington Station, and parcels of food, and then the men climbed up, my father among the last, with Ivor.

Mr. Gruffydd had shaken hands with all of them, and every one of them had asked him again, making a hundred times, to go with them. But Mr. Gruffydd smiled and shook his head. He would not, for he had Chapel on Sunday, and sick to go to before that. So the choir he had started went to Windsor without him, with enough noise from everybody to sound like the departure of the Persian hordes.

All the way up the mountain we watched them, and then Mr. Gruffydd turned about and went to the little house with the sea-shell porch, with a nod and a smile for us, and a pat on the head for me.

"Breaking his heart," Bron said. "If he had the money, he would be with them."

"They could have passed the hat," I said.

Bron looked at me with pity to burn.

"For him?" she said, and said no more.

Chapter Twenty-Six

MR. GRUFFYDD had changed a little, but I think I was the only one in the village to know how much. He seemed tired, and yet restless, and somehow older, not with lines in the face, or white coming to his beard, but something dark in the eyes made him so. The furniture took a long time, for only I was working on it, and then with gaps of days. He had a lot of work to do, with more men coming to the Valley, and labour troubles to preside over, and meetings in Chapel. He was reading less, too. I could tell from the set of the books, and the length of the candles. As to the furniture, he would start to work, and then sit, staring, and then shake his head, and give me a bit of a smile, and get up and go out to make tea. But he came a lot more to our house, and sat by the fire for a long time, night after night, smoking his pipe, and my mother glad to have him and always sorry when he said good night.

I was sorry to tell him that I would not be working with him on Saturday afternoon, but he asked no questions, and only looked at me, and smoothed his hair, and nodded. And that was worse, for I felt bound to tell him what I was going to do, if only to put myself right with him, but I lacked the courage, for it sounded so silly. Please, Mr. Gruffydd, I must leave the polishing on Saturday because I am going with Ceinwen up the mountain to listen to the nightingales.

So I left him, and there seemed to be a hole in the air that nothing would fill.

Round the mountain, by the beeches, I met Ceinwen. After three o'clock, it was, with the afternoon just coming heavy, and the sun hot, with the wind gone to hide up in the trees at the mountain-top. She pulled up by the stone I was sitting on, and took out a couple of rugs and a red straw basket and handed them down to me.

"What is this for, then?" I asked her, dull that I was.

"To eat, boy," she said, and jumped down to unharness the mare. "Are we going to be up there all night with nothing in our bellies but old sounds and screeches?"

"All night?" I said, and hot with fear. "I have got choir practice at seven o'clock."

"Let seven o'clock come," Ceinwen said, and gave the mare a smack to send her up to the grass. "Help to push the trap in by here, now."

So we put the trap tidy, and I led the way, loaded like a donkey, up the mountain to the trees near where the nightingales sang. Ceinwen was in a dress striped in grey and white, with a white cap with flowers and cherries in the lace round the edges, and red velvet ribbons drawing her dress tight at the neck. Heavy in the chest and hip she was, but long from hip to the ground, and inches taller than me, of course, and from behind, more a woman than a girl.

And my danger light giving me flash, flash, flash, all the way up, and putting my tongue in a clamp.

In and out of the sunlight, under the shadows of the trees, into their coolnesses, where leaf mould was soft with richness and held a whispering of the smells of a hundred years of green that had grown and gone, through the lanes

of wild rose that were red with blown flower, up past the
flowering berry bushes, through the pasture that was high
to the knees, and clinging, and that hissed at us with every
step, up beyond the mossy rocks where the little firs made
curtseys, and up again, to the briars, and the oaks, and the
elms, where there was peace, and the sound of grasshoppers
striking their flints with impatience, and birds playing hide
and seek, and the sun blinding hot upon us, and the sky,
plain bright blue.

"Well," Ceinwen said, when I stopped.

"Not too near," I said, "or you will hear nothing."

"Let us have a bit of shade, then," she said. "I am
cooking."

We put down the rugs among the twisted legs of an oak,
and Ceinwen lay flat, puffing, with her handkerchief over
her face.

"How long to wait?" she asked me.

"Hours," I said.

"Good," she said, "I will sleep."

I watched an ant running over the oak's leg. On my back,
with my hands going dead under my head, I watched him,
so near to my eyes that he might have been as big as a
horse. Hard, shiny, and brittle, he was, with a good polish
on his back, and legs bent like wire. I wondered if he saw
me as I saw him, if he had the same feeling about his home
and his people as I had, and if he was as scornful of me
as I was of him. I have always wondered what is inside the
skull of an ant, and what is the feeling to be an ant, if it is
like the feeling to be a man, if he sees, and thinks, or
knows his friends, and calls them by name, and can be
happy.

This one looked to be in a hurry about something, and
then forgetting what it was, and stopping every couple of
steps to try and think what it was, and putting his feet in
his pockets to see if he had everything and going on a bit,
and turning back. Silly, it was, but no sillier than some of
us. Old Owen the Mill often stopped in the streets feeling
in his pockets for something and then sending a boy back
to the house to ask Mrs. Owen what he had forgotten, and
standing there empty in the face and scratching himself
till the boy came back, and often it was nothing at all.

So there was no blame to the ant, and I watched him for
a long time, seeing Ceinwen's shoes, with the dust half

wiped off by the grass, just beyond the edge of the oak's leg, and purposely lying still not to wake her.

Then I slept, and woke with Ceinwen shaking me, and shivering with cold I was, stiff and damp, and surprised by the darkness.

"O, Huw," she said, in a little voice, and her teeth chopping, "light a fire, or I will die of cold or freeze to the death or perish of fright. Not sure I am, which is best to come first."

"Wait you," I said, and put my hand in the squirrel's hole and pulled out pieces of bark and dry leaves. There is a fire I made, too, with stuff from under the briars that burnt with a yellow flame, and gave lovely warmth.

So we took the eating from the basket and I filled the little saucepan from the rill, and made tea to go with the pie.

"Did you cook this?" I asked her, for something to say.

"Well," she said, with big eyes, yellow from the fire, "who else? Is it poison?"

"No, no," I said. "You are a cook."

"Well, thank God, now," she said, with laugh. "I wondered when I made it what you would say. Not very good, it is. A bit heavy in the pastry and not enough thyme with the meat. Not good."

"Good," I said, "I like it, and I will have more."

"A flattery," she said, opening and closing her eyes slowly, and each time she opened them, making them bigger.

"If it was bad," I said, "I would leave it."

"Spoilt at home," she said. "There is a job your wife will have with you."

"Only as good as I get now," I said, "no more, no less."

"You would drive the girl mad," said Ceinwen, "and she would throw a couple of dishes at you, and you would smash every pot on the dresser with temper. If you did it to me I would wait for you to sleep, and kill you with one hit."

"There is no hope of that, anyway," I said, and went to cut more tart.

She was quiet for minutes, and the fire cracked his whip to send up sparks and I looked at her a couple of times, but she was watching the fire without seeing it, with her arms stiff behind her, and her head buried between her humped shoulders, and her feet pointing straight, one foot crossed over the other.

"There is good," she said, with quiet, "to marry and have a little house."

I said nothing.

"A little house of your own," she said, "like your brother and sister. A new little house, fresh with new paint, and your own furniture where you want to put it, and no old nonsense from anybody else."

Nothing from me, again.

"With a little bit of garden, and a couple of hens to scratch," she said, "and babies."

"It will be long before any old babies are near me," I said. "I have had a house full with our family."

"Different if they are yours, boy," she said, and laughing wide.

"Plenty of time to think about it, any rate," I said.

"Would you marry me, Huw?" she asked, very shy, with a look sideways, and a small voice.

"No," I said, "there is dull you are, girl. Not from school yet, and marry?"

"My mother married from school," she said, "and four of us, still home, and me the youngest, and like a sister instead of Mama. Let us be married, Huw, and have a little house, is it?"

"To hell, girl," I said. "I will have to earn before marrying."

"Come to work with my father," Ceinwen said, and came nearer. "Learn the business while you are working and have good wages, then we can marry and have our own little house, is it?"

"Look you," I said, "no more silliness, to-night. To hear the nightingales we came up here. So listen."

"Well, give me a kiss, then," she said.

"Go from here," I said, and put more tart in my mouth. "Nightingales, not marrying, or kissing."

"Speaking with the mouth full," she said. "There is manners for you."

"Leave me to eat in peace," I said.

"I wish I had cooked nothing," she said, and angry. "You would be starving."

"We would have gone from here the sooner, then," I said, and glad to have a change of subject.

"O, Huw," she said, and pulling her handkerchief from her belt, "there is nasty you are to me."

And she cried.

With her legs curling under her, and hidden in the whiteness of her dress, and her hair like new hay fallen about her and spreading on the grass, and the white handkerchief in both her hands pressed to her eyes almost hidden among her hair, and her voice coming in little swords of sound at the end of each breath, O, there is a soreness inside me now to remember Ceinwen as she cried up there on the mountain and the nightingales sang about us, and the firelight was bright upon her, for the fire is out, the nightingales are quiet, and she has gone.

The man is made of stone who will see a woman in her tears and keep voice and hands to himself. So I went to her, and put an arm about her, and took her hands from her face and kissed the salt from her cheeks, and she lay heavily upon me, shaking, but finished with tears.

"Listen," I said, "there are the nightingales for you."

Fat and sweet is the song of the nightingale. A good, full singer, he is. No pinching of the throat or nonsense with half-opened mouth, or shakiness through lack of breath.

A good big chest full of breath, him, and a chest to hold it, too, and up with his head, and open with his mouth, thinking it no shame to sing with the voice that God gave to him, and singing with fear for none, true on the note, sharp at the edge, loud, fat with tone, with a trill and a tremolo to make you frozen with wonderment to hear. A little bird, he is, with no colour to his feathers and no airs with him, either, but with a voice that a king might envy, and yet he asks for nothing, only room to sing. No bowing, no scrapes, no bending of the knee, or fat fees for Mr. Nightingale. A little bough, a couple of leaves, and nightfall, and you shall have your song with no payment other than the moments of your life while you listen. Such voices have the Cherubim.

Many sang for us that night, and long we sat to hear them, till ash was grey upon the fire, and the wind was waking to do his work for the day to come. Ceinwen was sleeping with her head heavy on my knees, and her breath coming soft, slow, and no sound.

There is beautiful is sleep, and to see somebody soft asleep. So still, and the hands so pretty with quiet, with sometimes a little sound in the breathing, or an instant tremble, and in the face a calmness of pink; and the mouth in an easy innocence of rest, and gentleness a scent in the air about them.

So Ceinwen slept as I watched, and she woke, eyes wide, empty for moments and then filling with memory, showing teeth in a smiling yawn and her eyes full with a sleepy smile.

"It is late," I said. "There will be trouble."

"O, Huw," she said, in a voice to melt stones, and stretched her arms far above her head and brought them slowly down to put about me, and her body went from soft to coiling steel under me, and we kissed, and she laughed in the middle of it, and clicked her teeth at me.

A gentle madness comes of kissing, yet even so gentle, there is hot wish to hurt, though only to delight. To bite, to hold with force, to press the mouth with fury, to show strength that is male to softness that is female. Yet while I lay beside her and she was smiling quiet to let me cup my palm about the mystery of warmth and firmness that pushed up the stripes of her dress into ploughed hills, and my fingers knew the satin slither of her flesh under the coarse topsoil of fabric, and brought wrinkles to her forehead and sweet wryness to her mouth when I squeezed the tender stalks, I saw yellow of a lamp shining on the green of bush below us, and sat, cold, and my heart going big inside me and beating to stop breath.

"Huw," Ceinwen said, and felt for my hands.

"They are after us," I said, and pulled the rugs in a pile, and started putting the dishes in the basket. The fire was low, barely red, and the drainings of tea spat it out with a blowing of ash. I had the basket and Ceinwen had the rugs, and I pushed her before me up toward the top of the mountain and away from the many lights, that we could see so plainly now, working up to us.

We went up in an arc, through bush and gorse, pasture and briar, over hedges, and through herds of cows, when Ceinwen feared and hid her face and gripped my arms to push me in front of her, and down the steepness through the trees and on to the road. Good it felt to have the feet on hard stones again.

"Stay here," I said, "I will catch the mare and bring the trap here."

She nodded, and I found her dearer to me in her helplessness and fear, and kissed her cheek, but she stared in front, with her knuckles to her face, and a paleness of fear lighting her eyes.

"O, Huw," she said, in whispers, "if they find me they will put me in jail."

"Jail, girl?" I said, and so surprised as to be in another world. "What for, then?"

"Or they will call me in Chapel," she said, and tears taking her breath.

"I will get the mare," I said. "We will build bridges when the river wets our feet. Wait, you."

Off I went, round the road, running on the grass, with the talk of the brook louder than my footfalls, to the place where we had left the trap, but I was heavy with fright long before I got there, for fires were alight there, and men's shadows black against them, and tobacco smoke going up above their heads like the ghosts of babies.

. . . .

The trap had been pulled out of the space by the side of the road with the shafts in the dust, and another trap, just the same, near it, and the mare and another tied to the branch of a tree near them.

I knew what had happened while I made my mind firm that Ceinwen would go free of hurt.

The mare had run home and told them.

What to do, now, what to do and quickly.

I wonder where the thoughts do come from that help you to do what you do, when seconds before your mind was an empty ache, and you watched it working, like somebody else inside of you, crooking its fingers in helpless search of a notion.

Out with the matches and closer to the horse. I untied him and turned him to face the fire down the road. Then I struck a match and held it for a moment against his hock, telling him in the spirit that I was sorry for the hurt, but Ceinwen was staring in the darkness down the road and thinking of faces and voices in Chapel, and away he went with screams in a storm of hoof and dust, and I fell backwards and pushed myself up, with dust and burnt hair sharp in the nose, and jumped for the mare's head to untie her and lead her to the trap.

The men were shouting to one another and the horse's

rump was orange in the fire-light, and then gone in the
darkness on the other side, and the men running up the
mountain to head him off when he turned the bend on the
other side.

Into the shafts with the mare, with cursing for the weight
of thought behind her careful hoofs, up with the shafts to
slip through the harness, a pulling of straps on one side and
a run round to the other, a tearing at the tangle of rein tied
through the brass rings on her back pad, a jump at the iron
step and the springiness of the trap under me, and off went
the mare with the flip of the reins to send her.

So glad I was to see the whiteness of the striped dress
in the darkness that I could have shouted to skim the bushes
from the mountain, but I pulled the mare almost to sit, and
jumped down to give the reins to Ceinwen and throw up
the rugs and basket after her.

"Five minutes' start, no more," I said. "Good-bye, now."

"I will love you while I live," she said, with trembling.
"See you Monday. Good-bye, now."

Queen of the Brythons never swung her war chariot with
more skill. The whip whispered and cracked, the mare
plunged with her fores, and gathered herself to open her
wings, and was still, caught in a moment of surprise to
find four hairy roots holding her to earth, and almost in
regret, threw up her head to see spaces that she might have
flown, drew the mighty muscles under her, and jumped
from sprung haunches to stretch-neck gallop, with Ceinwen
standing black against the sky bearing on the reins.

I waited until the hush of the trees was the loudest noise
to be heard, and went down to the river and walked round
through the fields, to the bridge by the Three Bells, and up
home. Nobody was in the streets, and no lights anywhere,
but I could see many a yellow spark up on the mountain.

I came in round our back and climbed the shed to get in
this window.

The candle was lit as soon as I was in, and the window
closed for me.

Ianto, Owen, and Gwilym were sitting on the beds that
used to be over there, in their clothes, with their hats and
coats on this chair by here.

"Well," Ianto said, straight in the face.

"Hullo," I said.

"Where have you been?" Owen asked me, serious.

"Up the mountain," I said, and a bit of pride coming.

"With who?" Ianto asked me, and looking at me with his head down and his eyes gone to points.

"My business," I said, with emptiness coming inside me.

"Ceinwen Phillips, is it?" Owen said.

"My business," I said.

"Listen to me, you fool," Ianto said, with a whisper that might have been a shout, so big a jump it made me give, "do you want the men of the other Valley round here to burn the village? Is it a fight you want to cause?"

"No, no," I said, and a coldness of surprise in me. "Who is going to burn the village, then?"

"Every man here is waiting for it to start," Owen said. "Not a man is in bed. Those lights have been on the mountain these hours. If you had been caught they would have skinned you."

"Would you have sat here to let them?" I asked Ianto.

"We only knew it was you when we came up here, now just," he said. "Frightened sick in case Mama found out, we were. Lucky for you she have gone to sleep with Bron for the night."

"Your supper is on the table," Gwil said. "Have it, and sleep, for the love of God."

"I will go and tell them to stop looking," I said.

"Have your supper," Ianto said, "before I will skin you myself. If you go to them now, there will be murder certain. We want to save Mama worry. Supper, quick."

So down I went, hang-dog, to mix a couple of tears with the mint sauce. But when I came back up here, my brothers had gone to warn everybody it was safe to go to bed, and the lights had gone from the mountain.

But before I went to sleep I lay again beside Ceinwen and cursed with blackness the men who had carried the lamp that took her from me, the mare that had run home to tell them, and the lack of thought that let her go to graze without a shackle, and so ended in cursing myself, a blessed state, indeed.

"Fifteen feet of rope," Ianto said to me next morning, "and a picket stake. That is what you are wanting. Good God, what is next, I wonder? A boy and a bit of a girl up on the mountain till all hours. No more, understand?"

"Why not?" I asked him, with a rebel shouting inside me.

"Because," he said, "if it happens again we will have four hundred men over here. Think fortune to yourself that nobody knew who was with her. You would be good for a box instead of Chapel this morning."

"Listening to nightingales, we were," I said.

"I know, boy," Ianto said. "I have done a bit myself."

Chapter Twenty-Seven

THE TALK OUTSIDE CHAPEL all that day was split between the choir coming home and the search on the mountain. Some of the men wanted a deputy to go round to the other Valley and find out what the trouble was, but Ianto and Owen spoke against it, saying it would be better to let it die its death in peace. I was going over myself to find out what had come to Ceinwen, but my mother had use for me all day long, preparing food and drink for the choir, and I lost my worry in the clatter of pots.

Long after midnight it was when we heard the bands coming over the mountain, and good to hear in the dark quiet. Nothing is better to the ear, and nothing to raise the spirits more, than the boom of the big drum and the rasping voice of brass and silver swelling and dying as the wind takes his breath.

The beacons had been lit a long time to tell us the men were coming, so we were all ready for them. My mother went to get her cloak as though The Trump had sounded and the last boat was leaving the quay for Paradise. Bron had been wearing hers for hours, bonnet and all. They knew it would take the men a good hour to reach the Square from up the top there, and only a minute for us to get to the same place, but never mind, cloak, bonnet, mittens, and bottle of something to warm, quick, no stopping, all hurry, all haste, as though hope of glory to come depended on their getting down to the Square without another moment's loss.

Out in the street we joined in with everybody else on the hill, all going down together, and as we passed the little house with the sea-shell porch, Mr. Gruffydd came out, and went to the middle of the street to conduct us. We were singing when the procession got inside the village, and singing still when the wain stopped by Mr. Gruffydd, and the band and choir all singing with us.

Then the shouting of cheers, and my father looking all round to find my mother, and she crying so much she could see nothing of him, and he crying so much, he could see nothing of her.

"Take me to him, my sons," my mother said, and Owen and I made a way through the crowd.

My father was standing against a flat wooden crate about four feet square and a foot deep, looking as though he had found all of Ophir's treasure.

Owen and Ianto lifted it down, and I helped them to carry it up to the house, and my father shouting to us to put it in our front till he came and to take care, or if we dropped it he would kill us twice. It took us a long time to get that old crate up the Hill, for there was a thickness of people going up and coming down, and stopping to talk, and asking the choir what Windsor was like, and if the Queen was in gold, and if they had their food from diamond plates, and those who stayed home trying to look as though they would give a fig to go to Windsor to see the Queen, and old Silas Tegid the Maltster saying that he had never enjoyed a Sunday more than that day, so peaceful it had been, such resolution had appeared in Chapel, so beautiful the weather. Foolish are such people, for the lie is in their faces, in their voices, in their smiles.

I went out in the back to get the tool-box ready to unpack the crate, and Bron came in with wet tears and put her arms about me to cry for a bit, and warm and full of softness she was.

"There is a fool I am," she said, "washed away with crying, but nobody knows why, not even me. The Queen has given Ivor a baton, and a picture of her. Signed with her own hand, Huw. With her own writing."

Shouts for the tool-box inside, then, and me going in with it, and hammering, and prising, and splintering to get the cover off, between my brothers and me, for whoever had nailed the crate was at pains to show that he had nails and to spare.

My father was on tacks all the time, with my mother trying to make him drink a drop of hot broth, and Mr. Gruffydd putting an arm on his shoulder, and the crowd all round and in the doorway and looking through the open window, counting the nails as we threw them out. Then we took the lid off, and bayonets could not have kept him back from pulling out the wool flock packing.

"Now then," he said, "has every one of us got a good pot of beer?"

"Yes," we all said, and up with them.

"Good," said my father, and pulled a couple of pegs from the inside of the crate, and opened wide his arms to lift out the picture, with a red brocade back, and a wide gilt frame, made, every inch of it, and singing to you, by a craftsman who loved his work.

My father turned it and put it to stand on the sideboard, with not even a whisper from my mother about scratches.

"Now then," he said, and without a voice, from pride and lifting the weight of it, and taking his glass from my mother, and the beer shaking out, "Beth, from the Queen of Britain to your son."

Head and shoulders in black and white, with the background gone to mist, and almost as she was on a penny, the noble Queen looked out across her Empire as untroubled as my mother. But that prow of a nose could have cut through any sea, that chin would keep the shake from a mouth half as firm again, and the trouble never came to light that would bring a flinch to those austere, yet tranquil, eyes. The hard disciplines of a thousand generations of greatness sat lightly upon her, and yet left their subtle marks in the squareness of her shoulders, and the carriage of her head.

And upon the head, the Crown, and under it, to enrich its maleness, the mark of woman, a veil.

"Victoria, R.I.," said my mother, with my father's finger pointing to the writing. "O, there is proud I am."

Up on tip-toe to kiss Ivor on the cheek, and Ivor trying to smile, but gulps having the better of it.

"Up high," said my father, "drink, and not a drop to be left. The Queen."

"The Queen," said we all, and throats making sounds of joy in their own language to have the beer go down.

"She is smaller even than you," my father said to my mother, and kissed her cheek.

"Go on, boy," my mother said, from the kiss, and in doubt.

"She is, Mama," Ivor said. "She came up to by here, with me."

"Did you see her close, then?" my mother asked him, with wonder.

"She shook hands," Ivor said, and holding out his hand, as though still in a dream.

"Gracious Goodness, boy," my mother said, in whispers. "You shook hands with the Queen?"

"Yes, Mama," Ivor said. "Ask."

"The Queen shook hands," my father said, "and she asked who trained the men to sing, and if they were all coal miners, and if they were comfortable in the Castle."

"And then she gave me a baton," Ivor said, "not herself, but she told me it would come, and one of the soldiers brought it to me."

"With his name," my father said, "and the day and where, and for what. And it shall go in a special case under the picture on that wall. Beautiful, it is."

And beautiful it was. Of ivory, with silver and gold inlays, and a gold plate with the inscription on, and resting comfortable in red plush, in a long leather case of black crocodile, with two little silver hooks to close it.

Long it was before the house was quiet that night. Hundreds of people came in to see the picture, stepping on tip-toe to come in, not to make a mess, and standing to look with big eyes, and "Ehs" and "Ohs" from them all. And my mother sitting, like a queen herself, and all the women telling her what a credit Ivor was to the family, and what a time she would have in the morning when she washed the floor. But my mother would have washed the valley, and whitewashed the skies above it, for the happiness of those few hours.

That was one of the few nights I ever saw my father drunk, and then only on beer that others pressed upon him. And no man shall refuse a good drink of beer offered in good feeling. So when the boys carried him back, my mother only looked at him and smiled, and clicked her tongue, and sent them upstairs with him. If a man cannot get drunk on the night his eldest son comes back home with his hand warm from the touch of a queen, and her picture making the house into a shrine for pilgrims, well, Goodness Gracious, let us all go into the earth, and be quick about it.

Drunk again, he was, on the night our Davy scored a try against Scotland at Cardiff Arms Park, but so was the whole Valley. There was another night to remember, with my father dancing in the middle of the street wearing Davy's red jersey over his coat, and so much dried mud on it you could barely see the the crest. And Davy carried on the shoulders up and down the street time and time again. Everybody in the Valley got drunk that night, and if tea had been beer, the women would have been on the floor, too, for it was Open House all over the village and Davy was king of the world.

I made a glass case for that jersey, and another one for the cap. The jersey was put to hang opposite the picture of the Queen in our front, and Davy had the cap for himself. It was always a pleasure to see my father smoke his pipe in our front when somebody called, for there he was, like a king, with rare treasures all round him, conscious of it, and proud of it.

And there was a night when he got drunk because of me.

Only four of us were left in the special class at school by the time examinations were due to start. All the rest had left to go to work. There was John Dafydd, Llewelyn Rhys, and Emrys Tudor, with me in the little room next to Mr. Motshill's study. It had been a storeroom, but he had it cleaned out for us, and there we worked under him, or studied by ourselves.

Ceinwen had left after that Sunday without a word or sound. I saw her a couple of times with her father, in the coalyard, but we never spoke for we had no chance, and her eyes, although they gave me welcome and sore good-bye, warned me to give no sign that I knew her. So I knew there had been hard trouble there, and I was sorry for my part in it. And yet not sorry. For I often thought of her, and think now, of her warmth, and softnesses, and the dearnesses that women have that are so sweet to man. Mervyn had no notion that I had been with Ceinwen and I never told him. So I could only ask him questions that had to go all round the world before coming to the matter, and answers to that kind of question are never any use, so I stopped to ask them.

So four of us worked in that little room, and then went home to more work, and all day Sunday, too, except when we went to Chapel.

But the other boys had it harder than me, for I was strong in English, and thankful for it. I knew the great Dr. Johnson from his friend Mr. Boswell. There is a friend for you. To sit down and rack the brain to remember every word, and then the glad toil to write it all down. I am thankful to Mr. Boswell for many a peaceful hour, indeed. There is a marvel, hundreds of years after the spirit has gone to new life, that men will bless a name that once had flesh, and laughed, and had good food, and loved to hear good talk.

But the great Dr. Johnson was one in a century, and I count myself honoured to have tasted the wine of his speech, even though put to my mouth through the goodness of his friend. For that Englishman is not to be read with the eyes alone, but read out, as with the Word, with a good voice, and a rolling of the tongue, so that the rich taste of magnificent English may come to the ears and go to the head, like the perfumes of the Magi, or like the best of beer, home brewed and long in the cask.

Never will I forget the night my father read out the great man's letter to the Earl of Chesterfield.

We sat still when he put down the book, and the room was still, as though in fear, and the very air seemed filled again with the stinging silence there might have been in that house off Fleet Street, on the night when a quill scratched, and eyes looked down at the writing with that calmness and distant cold that comes of prodigious fury long pent and gone to freeze in a dark corner of the mind, yet always kept alive by prodding memory in the volatile spirits of dignity, and now loosed as from the topmost heights of Olympus, each word a laden fire-boat, each sentence a joy of craft, the whole a glory of art, this mere rebuke of a lordling, written by the hand that through long, hungry years, had wielded its golden sickle in the chartless wilderness of Words.

"If Ellis the Post brought me a letter like that with my name on it," my father said, with his eyes in slits, "I would go down from the house and come back feet first and blue as the drowned."

"There is a temper that old Earl was in," Gwilym said, with a long face, and far away. "I will bet he smashed every pot and stick in the house. And so would I. And send out for more, too."

So with Dr. Johnson and John Stuart Mill, and Spencer, and William Shakespeare, and Chaucer, and Milton, and John Bunyan, and others of that royal company of bards, thanks to my father and Mr. Gruffydd, I was acquainted, more than plenty of other boys, and thus had a lasting benefit in school.

English grammar and composition is difficult even for

the English, but worse and worse for a Welsh boy. He speaks, reads, writes, and he thinks in Welsh, at home, in the street, and in Chapel, and when he reads English he will understand it in Welsh, and when he speaks English, he will pronounce the words with pain and using crutches. So stupid are the English, who build schools for the Welsh, and insist, on pain of punishment, that English is to be spoken, and yet, for all their insistence, never give one lesson in the pronouncing and enunciation of the spoken word.

And Good God in Heaven, if you cannot read English aloud and in the English of the King, half the beauty is taken from you. O, and what pity, to hear a noble tongue chewed, and besmirched, and belittled by such monkeys in the form of men as our Mr. Jonas-Sessions. Poor Elijah. Even of you I can think with pity now, for you are in dust these years, and thank God.

I will remember that morning, even in the vineyards of Paradise, when Mr. Motshill sent me from the school for the last time, and so left a blank on the wall where the board should have gone with my name upon it in gold.

I was walking in the playground with James Dafydd, and we were quoting from *King Lear* to have it strong in our minds for the examination.

The lilac tree in the garden next door was lighting its lamps with blue coming to purple, and primroses, with faces of the innocent, were still fresh in the moss on top of the wall.

I heard crying in the infants' school, as though a child had fallen, and the voice came nearer and fell flat upon the air as a small girl came through the door and walked a couple of steps toward us, and stopped, with her hands, that were dimpled in the knuckles, and with bracelets of fatness about the wrists, spread before her face for shame.

In a pinafore starched to stiffness and shining with the weight of her mother's iron, with red socks fallen to nothing in the smallest clogs you ever saw, bright with polish, and gay as poetry with little studs of brass all round the soles, and a bit of ribbon in her hair, and with sobs to rend the heavens and shake her little bit of ribbon off.

About her neck a piece of new cord, and from the cord, a board that hung to her shins and cut her as she walked. Chalked on the board, in the fist of Mr. Elijah Jonas-Sessions, "I must not speak Welsh in school."

And Mr. Jonas coming to stand in the porch with Miss Cash and smile, with his hands in his pockets.

And the board dragged her down, for she was small, an infant, and the cord rasped the flesh of her neck, and there were marks upon her shins where the edge of the board had cut. Loud she cried, with a rise and fall in the tone, holding her breath until you wanted to breathe for her, with her tongue between her teeth and spit falling helpless, and in her eyes the big tears of a child who is in hurt, and has shame, and is frightened.

But as I went to her, and she looked up at me as though fearing something more to hurt her, I saw her eyes, that were the eyes of one not long from the cot and the tears that ran and shone in the sunlight swelled to crystal in mine, and in my blindness I saw, as through the mist of a morning, the grass upon a field torn, and a spewing forth of earth and stones, and men coming to stand before me who wore their steel as I wear tweed, in ease and comfort, and their swords were bright. And I heard a note in the infant voice as of trumpets sounding for battle, and drums beat, and men were shouting, chariots raced and dragon banners streamed, and bowmen plucked strings while steel spoke in the ranks and lance heads glittered in the sun.

And battle lust was in me, with blood running red about my feet and my hands red with it, and slippery, and the smell of it hot near me.

Then the mist went thin, and I saw Mr. Motshill looking at me, white, with his tie out, and pulling his side-whiskers, and Mrs. Motshill behind him holding a jug. I found that I was dripping wet and my throat raw with shouting. And a policeman looking at me, sitting beside me, with his helmet on the floor, one side of his moustache bent down and his hair untidy with him. Blood on my fists, not much, drying, it was.

"Having his sense, he is, now," the policeman said. I often saw him in town.

"Morgan," said Mr. Motshill, kind, but doubtful. "Do you hear me?"

"Yes, sir," I said, and sat.

"I suppose you know what you did?" Mr. Motshill asked me.

"No, sir," I said, and fright coming grey about me. "What, then?"

"You have nearly killed Mr. Jonas-Sessions, you wicked boy," Mrs. Motshill said.

"Not as bad as that," said the policeman, "but tidy, I will admit."

"Am I going to jail, sir?" I asked Mr. Motshill.

"That will depend on Mr. Jonas," Mr. Motshill said. "Do you feel well enough to go home?"

"Yes, sir," I said.

"Then go," said Mr. Motshill, tired, and making a move with his hand to Mrs. Motshill, "I shall write to your father when I have seen Mr. Jonas."

"Thank you, sir," I said.

"Come you, my son," said the policeman, and put on his helmet, and saw his moustache in the glass of the picture, and pulled a face in shock, giving the dying end a good pull to put all straight again.

Down the street I went with the policeman, with crowds about the gate to see me go, but I saw only their feet.

"What did I do to him?" I asked the policeman when we had got almost to the bridge.

"Tidy," the policeman said. "If I never move another step from by here. A couple of fat eyes, I will be bound and still picking up his teeth. When I pulled you off, you were at him on the floor."

"What do you think I will have for it?" I asked him, and in fear for his answer.

"Nothing," he said, and smiled. "And when Mrs. Stephens tells her old man what his little daughter have had round her neck, I will be wanted again."

"Will he die?" I asked him.

"Die, man?" he said, and a good laugh. "Good God, you have got to put poison down to kill rats, boy. No, no. A warning that is all. But I thought they had stopped to use the cribban. I had my knuckles hit bloody for talking Welsh in school, but no matter."

"So did my father," I said. "It was the cribban, round her little neck. I went mad, I think."

"No worry, and no matter," said the policeman. "Off home, and mind that temper and those fists. They are ripe to have you in trouble. Good-bye, now."

"Good-bye," I said.

That night all the family were round the table, and Mr. Motshill's letter in front of my father, brought by Ellis the Post after tea.

"It is my fault in the first place," my father said, and very sad. "I told him to fight, so there is it. But it is still disgrace."

"No disgrace to leave the old place," my mother said, "I have had my mind against it from the start."

"Expelled from school is disgrace," my father said. "Right or wrong, disgrace. And I had thought to have him a solicitor at the least."

"He can still take the examinations," Ivor said. "It says there is nothing to stop him."

"Send him to school in Town," Davy said. "He can find good lodgings."

"There are no good lodgings to be had on the earth," my mother said, "except only at home. So now then."

"Let him take the examinations," Owen said, "and see how he comes out. Then decide."

"The decision is to be made to-night," my father said, "and then kept. No use to go from month to month. I want him to go in the law or doctoring or something good. He has got a brain, so nothing is to stop him, there."

"Ask him what he would like," Bron said, looking at me.

"Well," said my father.

"I will go down the colliery with you," I said to him. "No examination and no doctoring and no law."

"Now then, for you," said my mother.

"Better for you to be silent," said my father. "Be guided, Huw."

"The colliery," I said, feeling the weight and points of all their eyes, and a window opening inside me, "I will cut coal."

"Just like the others," said my father, "obstinate and stupid. You will take the examination, boy, and pass it. University, then, and a good try for some respectable job, not coal cutting."

"What is not respectable about coal cutting?" my mother said, and her glasses coming off in a sign of trouble. "Are you and his brothers a lot of old jail-birds, then?"

"O, Beth," said my father, with tiredness closing his eyes, "leave it, now. I want the boy to have the best. I want him to have a life that is free of the foolishness we are having. Where he can be his own master in decency and quiet, and not pull one, pull the other, master and men, all the time."

"If he will grow to be a man as good as you and his

good brothers," my mother said, "I will rest happy in the grave. Since when have you fallen out of love with the colliery?"

"Beth, Beth," my father said, and anger coming, "I am thinking of the boy. It was different in our time. There was good money and fairness and fair play for all. Not like now. And I was never a scholar. He is. And he should put good gifts to good use. What use to take brain down a coal mine?"

"O," said my mother, sweet with ice, "so you are all a lot of old monkeys going from the house, then? No brains at all. Well, well. And I am keeping a madhouse here. And I am mad, too, I do suppose. And only one with sense in the family, and him sent from a school I would think twice to keep pigs in."

"Beth," my father said, "it is his future I am worried for. Why should he be a miner if he can be something else?"

"Why not?" my mother said. "There are men as good underground as on top, and perhaps a bit better. If he wants to be a doctor, good. If he wants to be a solicitor, good. If he wants to be something else, good. And if he wants to go to the collieries with his Dada, I will kiss him, and say good."

"He shall have himself to blame," said my father, and looking at me. "And if I will hear a word of complaining from him, I will hit him to the ground."

"The colliery, Dada," I said, "I will work."

"Good, my little one," my mother said.

"That is the settler, then," my father said, and opened his hands wide. "He shall wait till there is an opening. Then work."

"Good," said my mother.

"Good," said my father, "I am going to get drunk."

And while my mother cried, he went.

Mr. Gruffydd said nothing to me, for a wonder, about being expelled. Not a single word. He only nodded his head, and looked up at the mountain.

"Have you said you were sorry to Mr. Jonas?" he asked me.

"No, sir," I said, and surprised, for it was the last thing in the world I would do.

"Then go and say so," said Mr. Gruffydd, "and then come down to the house, is it?"

"Yes, sir," I said.

"Good," he said.

So back over the mountain I went, into the other valley and found Mr. Jonas' address from the caretaker.

"Are you going over there to finish off the job?" he said.

"No," I said, "only to say I am sorry."

"Useless," he said, and shaking his head, and scratching his leg. "You will never get back in his good books by saying you are sorry."

"Not for the sake of good books," I said, and ready to go home straight and say nothing.

"Then what use to say sorry?" he asked, smiling with no laugh in it. "A waste of time, good shoe leather, and no sense. To him, anyhow."

"I will say I am sorry," I said, "without advice."

"You will end with a rope," he shouted after me, all down the street, and I could hear him telling people who I was.

There was a heaviness upon me as I thought of Time To Come, and I wondered if Mr. Gruffydd had been a prophet when he said I would end on the gallows, for here was another of the same opinion. Strange it is to think of Time To Come. I thought then, as I walked through the streets of red brick houses to find Mrs. Jonas, of Time To Come. I tried to think what I would be, and what I would be doing in ten, and twenty, and thirty and forty years. But here I am, sitting on a bed, and still thinking of Time To Come, and still as wise.

You never saw a house fit anybody as his house fitted Mr. Jonas. Of smooth red brick, it was, built solid, and new, the colour of raw beef, without a blemish. A front door with splendid bit of graining with brown and yellow paints, six little windows of stained glass in the top half, a letter-box that was a yawn of brass, and in Church Script on the fanlight, with the letters pushed up a bit to have room, Briercliffe. A window that swole out of the house on the ground floor, with lace curtains, and a flat window, then, over the door.

And for the first time I noticed that the front doors were all shut, right down the street, even though it was a hot day.

I knocked, and the door opened with a noise to make you hold your teeth, and Mrs. Jonas looked at me with her eyebrows up.

"Good afternoon," I said, "I am Huw Morgan from the school."

"Come to ask after Mr. Jonas-Sessions, is it?" she said, and very kind, but serious. "Please to tell them he is still bad and very sore with him, but soon well again, I hope."

"I have come to say I am sorry," I said, and watched a year of different feelings come into her face and pass. Her hair was in a small knot on top of her head and curving up from her face. A white blouse with a high neck and a brooch, and a black skirt that pushed the hall mats out of place when she walked.

She looked, and I looked.

Then she took a good breath, and let it go.

"Come in," she said, and held the door wider.

In I went, and again the noise from the door, and a push, and another good push, till it was shut.

The smell inside, with curtains drawn and doors shut, was a bit like Chapel with helpings of cabbage, Irish stew, yellow soap, and the breathings of many hangings of cloth and pots of growing leaves, well soaked.

"Wait here," she said, and went upstairs like the wind among grass, and opened a door on the landing. I heard Mr. Jonas sharp in the voice, then quieter. She spoke for minutes, and waited, and I waited, and the house waited, and the door made noises in its sleep.

Then she came out and leaned over the stairs.

"Come you," she said, "only for a minute, and a privilege, mind."

So up I went, with seas running wild in my belly and hitting the breath out of me. Inside the small room, dark with pulled curtains, and warm on the face, a fan of crinkled paper in the fire-place, window shut, smells of carbolic and used bedclothes and hot breath gone cool, and vinegar.

Mr. Jonas was sitting up with a bandage about his eyes and a muffler round his mouth, a nightcap on his head and a sticking-plaster on his right-hand knuckles, that he lifted for Mrs. Jonas to close the door.

"Well," he said, "I suppose you want a pardon, do you?"

"Yes," I said. "I am sorry for what I did, Mr. Jonas."

"Not a bit of use to me," he said. "You deserved expulsion, and I insisted on it or I would have prosecuted you. Lick my boots and you shall have no pardon from me or word to Mr. Motshill, either."

"Not a pardon I want," I said, "only to say I am sorry."

"Look here," he said, "I know your sort too well. Humbugs. A vice with all of you. You humbug yourselves and you humbug others. But I know you. And I am sick of you. Damned lot of cant."

"I am sorry," I said, for there was shaking in his voice not good to hear, and the voice not strong as usual.

"Sorry, my God," he said. "A hundred yards from the house and everybody in town will hear you neighing. I had you brought up here just to tell you what I thought of you, you gutter-bred rat. Now get out."

He could have said anything to me and I would have said nothing back. I was so filled with surprise to be called a humbug.

"Why am I a humbug, Mr. Jonas?" I asked him.

He was looking at me from under the bandage, with his head up. I could just see blue hurt flesh, and I was sorrier than ever.

"Why?" he said, and sent breath from his nose with impatience. "As an illustration, your school record. You deliberately tried to ruin my name with Mr. Motshill, and since the devil is kind to his own, you were quite successful for a time. For a time. It may be some consolation to you to know that I shall be teaching Standard Six again when I return."

"But why am I a humbug?" I asked him.

"Because you pretend to be what you are not," he said, and in a temper to take the voice from him. "But why should I expect anything else? After all, look at your background. As I told Mr. Motshill, why be surprised? Coal miners. Living like hogs, with nothing in life but beer and bruisers and using the Chapel as a blind. Welsh. Good God, what a tribe."

"But why am I a humbug, Mr. Jonas?" I asked him again.

"Get out," he said, "you make a murderous attack on me presumably because I check the use of jargon in school, and yet you have the audacity to question me in English. Simon-pure humbug."

"You started in English," I said, "I thought you never spoke Welsh or I would speak it to you."

"Look here, Morgan," he said, and shifting on his elbow, as though he would throw me out as soon as finished, "there is no reason why I should talk to you like this, and God knows why I should do it. But I want to tell you this before you go. Welsh never was a language, but only a crude means of communication, between tribes of barbarians stinking of woad. If you want to do yourself some good, stop troubling your tongue with it."

"Oh," I said, and nothing else I could think of, except my mother and father and Bron.

"Yes," he said, "oh, English. The language of the Queen and all nobility. Welsh. Good God Almighty, the very word is given to robbers on race-courses."

"But you are Welsh, Mr. Jonas," I said.

"I had the misfortune to be born in the country," he said.

"No mistake about that," I said, and standing. "Welsh is in your voice and in your speech, too, and hatred will never change them for you."

"Get out," he said, "get out at once."

"I wish I could have the tongue of Dr. Johnson," I said, "only for a minute. I would hit you harder than I have with fists. You would never rise from your bed. I would strike you dumb and paralyse you. I am not sorry for what I did. I wish I had done more. I only came because Mr. Gruffydd asked me to."

"Ruth," he was shouting. "Ruthie."

"Live in hell," I said, "and when you are dead, go there."

I was down the stairs quick, and Mrs. Jonas picking up her skirts to come up.

"What did you do to him?" she said, and pulled me by the arm.

"Nothing," I said. "Only told him to live in hell."

"What right have you got to tell a man to live in hell?" she asked me and ready to fly at my face with her shaking fingers, "you wicked devil, you, putting him in pain and then telling him to live in hell. Go you and live there before I will kill you."

"Ruth who, were you, before to marry?" I asked her, and her mouth that was open to say more closed again, and her eyes emptied, looking from side to side in wonder, and a hand went to her cheek, and I felt the heat going from her.

"Morgan," she said, in a small voice of surprise. "Ruth Morgan, I was. Why, then?"

"Good," I said, and went from the house, with noise at the door again, and laughing all the way down the street.

Elijah was right that time, for I was neighing still, up on top of the mountain.

"He was mistaken," Mr. Gruffydd said, when I told him. "Welsh, they call us, from the Saxon word waelisc, meaning a foreigner. About the race-course, I cannot tell you. But if some of our fathers were a bit ready with their hands and quick in the legs the English must blame themselves. Perhaps most of them never heard of the laws they made against us. You cannot blame ignorant men. You might as well kick a dog for not wishing good morning."

"Why did Mr. Jonas call me a humbug, then?" I asked him.

"Sticks and stones shall break my bones," said Mr. Gruffydd, "Mr. Jonas should look home. Never trouble with people who call names, Huw. They are the infantile, the half-grown. And a man has got to have an inner knowledge and experience of the science of humbug before to honour another with the term. Remember, Huw. Be still, and know that I am God. Worry about nothing, especially the tongues of others."

"Why do you worry, Mr. Gruffydd?" I asked him, and hot with sorrow as soon as it was out. His eyes carried loads of darkness, and he saw with tiredness, and with patience that was willed, but not felt.

He looked down at me with something of a smile, something of a frown, something of hurt, and surprise, too, as though I had put out a foot to trip him.

"Worry, my son?" he said, with quiet. "I am not worried now and I never have or will. You must learn to tell worry from thought, and thought from prayer. Sometimes a light will go from your life, Huw, and your life becomes a prayer, till you are strong enough to stand under the weight of your own thought again."

"Yes, sir," I said, and willing to run from there, "I am sorry I said it to you."

"Do you find a difference in me, Huw?" he asked me, and his eyes coming to watch mine a little sideways, as though to make sure I was going to tell truth.

"Yes, sir," I said.

"How, then?" he asked me, eyes still.

"You are heavier in your talk," I said, "not so much smile, not so much interest, and not much of gladness, either. And nothing for the furniture."

He turned from me to look up the mountain, and I was

stricken with terror, in the quiet little street, with only two of us in it, down there by the side-door of the Chapel where a little path went dusty to the river, and the top of the water full of ragged windows giving light, and me in the midst of a fight that I could neither see nor hear, and yet shaken by its tumult, and its wounds.

"I have failed in my duty, then, my little one, is it?" Mr. Gruffydd asked me, after moments and moments.

"No, sir," I said, and ready to spill my blood for him. "No, sir, indeed. Only saying that you are a bit different from old times."

"Eh, dear, Huw," he said, and put his hand behind him and touched my shoulder, "go from me, now, and come in the morning for a start on the furniture, is it? We will finish it with a couple of good days' work."

"Yes, sir," I said, and went from him with misery.

Chapter Twenty-Eight

IESTYN'S SISTER was in the house when I went in, and I knew from my mother's face that there was trouble, though a stranger would never have seen it. Blodwen was dark in the skin, with black hair and round brown eyes, looking at you always as though you stood down at the bottom of the garden. A calmness was in her, and she sat still, back straight, with her hands folded and her feet almost under the chair. She spoke English nearly always, but plainly, for she went to school in London, and then to Paris, and I suppose the teachers there stood no old nonsense from anybody.

"Well, Huw," she said, and smiling very pretty, too. "How are you?"

"Well, thank you," I said. "How are you?"

"Impossible to feel better," she said. "I wondered whether you would bring the harp to Tyn-y-Coed to-night for me?"

"Yes," I said.

"Good," she said, and smiled again, but I knew from the way my mother was standing that I was one too many in the room, so out I went and down to Bron's to pack the harp.

I told Bron about Mrs. Jonas and she clicked her tongue.

"I was at school with her," Bron said. "Is Blodwen still with your Mama?"

"Yes," I said.

"More trouble, then," Bron said. "Angharad will be home here before long, you will see. Drunken swine, he is."

"Who, Bron?" I asked her.

"Never mind," she said.

Then it was that I understood the looks and nods and words here and there, when Angharad and Iestyn were spoken about in the house. It made me feel quite empty inside to think of Angharad having trouble, but there was nothing I could do, and I knew from the look of Bron that not another word would come from her, even with hot pincers.

So up with the harp and over the mountain to Tyn-y-Coed, and a lovely walk with plenty of stops, and a little hum from the harp every time I put her down.

A good big house was Tyn-y-Coed, built in the time of the second George on the house that came from before Elizabeth. The old part was still there, on one side, with chimneys of brick, and laid beautiful. Big windows on two floors, the rest of the house, and a big porch with pillars that went narrower toward the top. All of it was in white with green shutters, and all the farm buildings whitewashed and kept spotless. A lovely bit of property, it was, with trees to shade it and gardens front and back, brown cows in the pasture, black and white and brown chickens in the yard, geese and ducks white by the pond, and turkeys sitting on the gate by the stables.

Blodwen was there before me and standing at the door, with the houseman to take the harp from me.

"Come and take tea, Huw," she said, with her face in the green shadow of trees. "Wash in the little room."

So I went in to have tea, and very good, too. I liked that big room at Tyn-y-Coed. It was high, and the windows big and plenty of them, planned in a day when men thought spaciously and lived graciously, and had a love for good work. A look at the ceiling would have shown you that, never mind the furniture. And as for the fireplace, you would think it shame to burn coal there, so pretty it was, of white marble, simple, and so easy in its curves, and straightnesses, and flutings, that it was pleasure distilled to pass the hands over it, and think of the steadfast mind that carved it into shape.

Blodwen always had a little laugh at me when I went to Tyn-y-Coed, but it was a gentle laugh, and with sympathy, because I told her why I liked to put my hands on work that had been blessed by good minds and the passing of time.

"Would you like to come and live here, Huw?" she asked me, when we were having wheat cakes.

"No," I said. "If it was my house, yes."

"Supposing I asked you to?" she said.

"No," I said. "I shall be working soon."

"Must you?" she asked me, and looked at me straight, and her eyes were very brown. "There are plenty of pieces of furniture that need repairs. And I think that furniture you made for Mr. Gruffydd is simply lovely. Come and work here, Huw."

"I said I would work with my father," I said, and the face of Isaac Wynn coming to harden me.

"Oh, dear," she said, and breathed sharp, "I hate to think of you going down the pits. I hated my father going down, and I shall always be glad that Iestyn sold his interests."

"He put four hundred men from work, too," I said.

She looked at me, and tapped a teaspoon gently on her saucer as though she would be saying something in a moment to take the butter from the toast. Then she put the teaspoon down, and gave her nose a dab with a piece of lace that was never in this life a handkerchief.

"You speak like your brother, Owen," she said.

"Good," I said.

"Has he had any more news about his patents?" she asked me, as though it was of no interest.

"No," I said, "but a gentleman from America is coming to see him next week. Going to buy it, he is."

"Oh," she said, and a look in the teapot. "Is he going over there, do you know?"

"Perhaps," I said, "if he can get somebody to do his union work for him."

"Why he bothers with that nonsense is more than I shall ever be able to understand," she said, with impatience. "It can never be a union in the sense of the word."

"More than fifty thousand members," I said, "and growing every week."

"How do you know?" she asked me.

"I write the letters to London," I said, "ever since it

started. And if Owen goes, Ianto or Davy will be there to take it to the top. We will join with Monmouth soon, and then the Dockers, and the Firemen."

She sat quietly for minutes, hands folded, feet almost under the chair, a mauve shadow in the coming darkness, and the fire giving reddish light to her cheek, and eyes of red to silver.

"I heard him speak the other night," she said.

"Over the mountain?" I asked her, and surprised, too.

"Yes," she said, and I will swear she was blushing, because her voice was low, with a hem of whisper. "We went over together."

So that was why Owen was ready for three meetings in one night, with Ianto and Davy and he to take one each.

"I suppose he has plenty of friends?" she asked me, and in a sudden moment I knew she was warmer towards me, though there was no change in her, only her voice. As though a wall had fallen somewhere without a sound.

"Yes," I said, but taking care. "Plenty, indeed. In all the valleys. He could be drunk every night."

"Does he drink?" she asked me, with fright, quick.

"No," I said, "not a drop. Tea and water, Owen. Sometimes a drop of my mother's beer."

She seemed to go lower in the chair.

"I suppose, with a lot of brothers," she said, "young ladies abound? Have some more tea, Huw, please. Try this cake?"

"Tea, yes, please," I said, and handed my cup. "Cake, no, thank you. I have had plenty and very good, too. No young ladies."

"Oh," she said, "but of course, you men always say no, when you should be saying yes."

"No young ladies," I said, and firm. "They are a nuisance. Some, anyway."

"Am I a nuisance, Huw?" she asked me, and laughing.

"No," I said, "I like you. So does Owen."

"How do you know?" she asked me, very small.

"Would he go with you over the mountain or two steps anywhere else?" I said. "No, indeed."

Orange came to light the wall outside in the passage, and Mrs. Nicholas came in with a couple of sticks of candles, wide and round in her black dress with a silver chain and many keys rattling, and the candles making her hold up her head and her face like a gold sun with sparks in her eyes.

"Sitting in darkness," she said, in a fat voice, and scolding. "There is silly you are, Miss Blodwen. In darkness with a young man. Dear, dear. Every tongue in the Valley will chat."

"Let them," said Blodwen. "Do you mind, Huw?"

"No, indeed," I said, "but I would like to catch them."

"Catch them?" Mrs. Nicholas said, and lighting more candles. "Only go in any shop, or listen in the market. Like fleas in a poorhouse bed. Ach y fi."

"Nicky," Blodwen said, "I believe you are as bad as the rest."

"Well, indeed, Miss Blodwen," Mrs. Nicholas said, voice gone deep with shame, "there is a thing to say to your Nicky, indeed. Twenty years ago I would have had you over my knee for that, and no Nicky, please, Nicky, please."

"I still believe you can gossip with the best," Blodwen said. "Eight for supper to-night, Nicky."

"Oh," said Mrs. Nicholas, a bit sulky, "eight, is it, Miss Blodwen? Master Huw is staying, too, then, is he?"

"No," said Blodwen. "There will be another."

"Mr. Owen Morgan," Mrs. Nicholas said, with a nod not to be argued with, up and with the candle-holders, and going to the door with quick steps.

"Nicky," Blodwen said, and coming to be angry. "You jump to conclusions. Eight to supper. That will be all."

"Yes, Miss Blodwen," said Mrs. Nicholas, and turning round in the doorway, "Mr. Parry, Mr. Owen Jones, Mrs. Owen Jones, Mrs. Davies, Mrs. Griffiths, and Miss Griffiths, and you." She turned round and went to go out.

"And Mr. Owen Morgan," she said, over the shoulder, and the doorway was empty.

"That woman becomes more and more impossible," Blodwen said, "she takes advantage. Of course, Owen will be miles away."

"He was pressing his best suit, anyhow," I said, "and particular about a shirt this morning, before the shift went down."

"Huw," she said, with quiet, and warmth in her face, but cold serious. "Tell nobody, will you?"

"Eyes open," I said, remembering Cyfartha, "mouth shut."

And that was how I went so much to Tyn-y-Coed. Every piece of the furniture that wanted repairs, I did in my spare time. And made a suite of my own, too, but that was after.

I saw Mr. Gruffydd looking at me many times in those few days I worked with him before I started in the colliery. I saw his face in a shining, pink rub on the polish of the sideboard panels when he was looking at me behind my back. When I looked round at him he always looked away. At first, I wondered. Then I feared. But as one day went to two, and the looks got less, and the talk dropped to one or two words about the thickness of the polish, and the weather, and how hot the plates were for dinner, I started to wonder again, until I was on tacks to ask him what was the matter. For it is discomfort's own essence to be near a man and to feel him in torture of misery, to feel with him the very pain of the misery, and yet to be unable to help.

Little Olwen was bringing our tea down to us, and I used to go out and stand in the porch to watch her all the way up the Hill again, and give her a wave when she turned round. So she turned round every other step, and I had to wave or she would have been there yet. It always took a good long time to wave her home, and the tea nearly cold when I got in to it.

"She is very much like Angharad," Mr. Gruffydd said.

"Yes," I said. "When she grows, nobody will know the difference."

"Twenty years' time," he said.

What is there, in the mention of Time To Come, that is so quick to wrench at the heart, to inflict a pain in the senses that is like the run of a sword, I wonder. Perhaps we feel our youngness taken from us without the soothe of sliding years, and the pains of age that come to stand unseen beside us and grow more solid as the minutes pass, are with us solid on the instant, and we sense them, but when we try to assess them, they are back again in their places down in Time To Come, ready to meet us coming.

Or does the mention of it, I wonder, drive a wedge under that tight-shut door, just enough to let in a thin smell of the steamings we shall live through before those who know us can go about with long faces to say we are dead. Sad, sad is the thought that we are in for a hiding in every round, and no chance to hit back, no hope of a win, fighting blind against a champion of champions, who plays with you on the end of a poking left, and in the last round puts you down with a right cross to kill.

There is something of sickness in the thought that you shall make up your mind to enjoy your hiding, and the consolation is only that you will never know the tasting of defeat. For while they are taking your clay from the ring, you are up and starting your fight somewhere else.

I heard the blood in Mr. Gruffydd's voice, and searched libraries of words in hot seconds of emptiness only to give him comfort.

"Long time, sir," I said.

"I shall be an old man," he said.

"Yes, sir," I said.

"Old," said Mr. Gruffydd, "and nothing done."

"You have done much," I said, with a loud voice, to try and make up for want of words just before. "Chapel, and sick, and everything, sir."

"And everything," he said, and laughed. "Thank you, Huw. Eh, dear. I thought when I was a young man that I would conquer the world with truth. I thought I would lead an army greater than Alexander ever dreamed of, not to conquer nations, but to liberate mankind. With truth. With the golden sound of the Word. But only a few heard the trumpet. Only a few understood. The rest of them put on black and sat in Chapel."

"Is it wrong to do that, then, Mr. Gruffydd?" I asked him, and surprised out of voice.

"Why do you go to Chapel, Huw?" he asked me, still going on with his work.

"Because," I said, and then I stopped. Why, indeed?

"Yes," he said, and smiling. "Because you want to? Because you like coming? Because your mother and father come? Because your friends are there? Because it is proper to do on Sunday? Because there is nothing else to do? Because you like the singing? To hear me preach? Or because you would fear a visitation of fire during the week if you stayed away? Are you brought by fear or by love?"

"I'm a bit surprised, sir," I said, and indeed, I was dry with it.

"The questioning of habit is fruitful of surprise," Mr. Gruffydd said. "Would you fear a bolt of fire on your head, or some other dire punishment if you stayed away from Chapel without permission?"

"I would a bit, sir, I think," I said.

"So would most of them," Mr. Gruffydd said. "So they are brought to dress in black and flock to Chapel through fear. Horrible, superstitious fear. The vengeance of the Lord. The justice of God. They forget the love of Jesus Christ. They disregard His sacrifice. Death, fear, flames, horror and black clothes."

"I have never heard you preach against any of them, sir," I said to him.

"No, Huw," he said. "This people draweth nigh unto me with their mouth, and honoureth me with their lips, but their heart is far from me."

"What shall we do, sir?" I asked him.

"O, Huw, my little one," he said, and standing, putting the cloth from him, "what am I to say? Who am I to preach to other men? My sins are as great. Greater."

And he went from the house, and I saw him tramping the road to the mountain with weary quickness and my feelings were under his feet.

Chapter Twenty-Nine

IVOR CAME OFF THE DAY SHIFT and told me to get ready to go to work the next morning with him. I was in sweats with excitement to get my clothes ready, but nobody said a word in the house. Not a word. But the way they all said nothing, said more than if they had all climbed up on the roof to shout it over the Valley.

Next morning at quarter to seven I called for him, and my mother came with me as far as the door, but with no more fuss than if I had been going to school. I had my can, and my side pocket was heavy with five candles.

"Ready?" Ivor asked me, and Bron gave him his can.

"Yes," I said.

"Well," said my mother. "Another one off, then."

"Yes, Mama," I said.

"Good-bye, now," she said, and kissed me.

"Good-bye, Mama," I said.

"Ivor," my mother said, "look after him, now."

"Yes, Mama," he said. "Good-bye. And good-bye, Bron."

"Good-bye," said Bron, and a touch of a kiss for me.

And off we went, and my mother going quickly inside.

All the way down the Hill I had good mornings from the boys and girls, all looking at me with smiles as though to say wait, you, and you shall know you are alive in a couple of minutes. To the men, of course, I was only another boy starting to work, so only a few of them nodded, or gave me a tap on the back.

But going on to the pithead I had the same feelings as when I was in the boxing ring just before the fight was on. Something moving in the belly, and heat in the head, and lightness.

Dai Bando and Cyfartha were coming running to get in the cage when Ivor turned to go in, and me after him, looking back and hoping they would reach us in time. The cage was a box made of thick planks, bolted together on a steel frame, and the planks black with years of use, and the floor inches in dust, and sounding like a big drum.

Dai and Cyfartha squeezed in before the gateman locked up, and Dai saw me looking at him through the elbows of the man in front.

"O," he said, and short with breath, "you, is it? A bit of work, now then?"

"Yes," I said.

And the ground fell from underfoot, and we dropped, with a scream from the wind, into darkness, so dark that you thought you saw lights, and your knees were loose and bent.

Hundreds of times I went down, but I never got over the drop of the cage.

For moments you would swear you were blind. Then terror put sharp teeth in you.

For hour after hour we seemed to be there, waiting, and the air growing cold, but still dark, black, worse than night, and our feet barely touching the falling floor, until it felt as though we were standing in the middle of midnight with our knees bent ready to jump into morning.

Then the scream dropped and dropped, and the floor came firmer to the feet, the air was warmer and carried with it the salty stench of raw coal, and light came to us, and breath and savour of life to me, and gratitude, hotter than fire in me, for the gift of sight.

"Come you," said Ivor, when the gateman opened up.

I followed him through the arched brick of the pit bottom parting, and down the main heading that was noisy with trains, and the singing of men working on them. The main heading was only wide enough for the trams to pass, with clearance for walking on both sides, and about nine feet high with lamps every few feet to give dirty yellow light.

We walked a good long way among crowds of other men until Ivor turned up a little hole in the wall, bent double.

"Come on," he said, and smiling, "mind your head."

Up this pitch-black little tunnel we crawled, head almost to knees, and then Ivor stopped, and threw his pick down.

"Right," he said, and his voice coming like a roar in the dark. "Light your candles, and I will show you what is next."

So off with our coats and waistcoats and shirts, and I lit a couple of candles and stuck them, in their iron holders, into the prop. There was so little air that the flames went to six inches with them, and pretty indeed.

"Now then," Ivor said, "I will cut the coal, and you will push the lumps down the chute. Then go down and load all you find down there into my tram, is it?"

"Yes, Ivor," I said.

"Right," he said, and his pick punched deep into the seam.

So I started to work.

Ivor was a good workman, quick with his pick, untiring, and stopping only to move slag that fell when the coal was loosed. When he stopped, I stopped, but not to stop altogether, for we banked the slag against the sides and packed it tight to act as a prop for the roof.

For hour after sweating hour, bent double, standing straight only when we were flat on our backs, we worked down there, with the dust of coal settling on us with a light touch that you could feel, as though the coal was putting fingers on you to warn you that he was only feeling you, now, but he would have you down there, underneath him, one day soon when you were looking the other way. I used to look at the shining black strip in the orange light of our two candles, and think to myself that this might be the mourning band of the earth, and us taking it from her to burn, and she looking at us with half-shut eyes, waiting to have a reckoning. But there was always a fear in me, down there, that I never lost.

I always seemed to hear a voice in the heavy quiet,

beyond the punch, punch, punch of Ivor's pick, and the rolling echoes of coal sliding down the chute. And I always thought I saw a face in the glitter of the coal face, and never mind how much Ivor cut from it, it always seemed to be there.

The muscles of the belly might feel to be tearing apart long before the end of the day, so bent we were. Ivor would kneel, lie on his side, stand sideways and bent, or on his back, with sweat making his skin into black silk, but never a pause, never a stop, till it was time for eating, or for a swill of tea to take dust from the throat.

I knew well, even on the first day, where Dai Bando had those muscles in the belly.

And, O, what joy to come up in the cool air of night after hot hours in the light of candles, light that crawled with dust that sometimes shone. Then I knew, and knew with thanksgiving, why we sat on doorsteps when the sun was out. Only to be quiet, and rest aches, looking at clean light, feeling the blessing of the sun, free, for a couple of hours, from the creeping touch of the fingers of coal.

Up the Hill, among the crowds on the shift, and passing boys I knew without a nod from them, and surprised, until I remembered the top skin of coal dust that covered me from head to foot and hid me from them.

But I felt a man in real truth, to be coming up among that crowd of men, sharing their tiredness, blacked by the same dust, knowing the sounds and the sights of the colliery as they did, thinking with the same mind, of them, with them, a part of them.

I bathed with Ivor in Bron's back, for there were more than enough in ours already.

There is good to see the tubs ready and the buckets all lined up, steaming. Off with the clothes and leave them where they fall. One bucket over you to take off the worst, then a rub of soap, another bucket, more soap. Now you will see a bit of yourself, but the hands, and especially those little lines in the balls of the fingers, are hopeless. You shall scrub and scrub, but Mr. Coal will lie there and laugh at you. A good friend to man is water, indeed, but never friendlier than when he is running down your back, chasing coal dust off with a stick of soap.

Into the tub, then, to rub a white lather all over you and

duck under the water, holding breath to feel the gentleness all round you, close as your own skin.

"Well," said Bron, when I came up, "how is the old man, then?"

"Good," I said, and keeping as much of myself under the tub edge as I could.

"Come you," she said, and rolling her sleeves. "You are black down the back."

And she took the brush and scrubbed my shoulders, and then lathered with her hands and swilled water over me, till I was glad I was me and not the floor of her kitchen. A worker was Bron.

"Have I got skin left by there?" I asked her, "because if I have, there is a miracle again."

"Skin you have got," she said, "but no pattern, thanks to me."

Then Ivor came in, and bathed while I dried, and when I was dressed Bron came in again to scrub him, and I went down to the house.

"Well," said my mother, with a frown and a smile, "you are ready for your dinner, are you?"

"Yes, Mama," I said.

"Did you have it hard, my little one?" she asked me.

"No, Mama," I said.

"Good," she said. "Sit, now, and eat plenty."

When my father came in he pulled me by the ear and smiled at me.

"Solicitor's office, to-morrow, eh?" he said. "No more colliery, is it?"

"Colliery will do, Dada," I said.

"You will find out," he said. "There is plenty of time, and plenty of coal."

And in the years that passed, I found out, indeed.

I suppose I had been working a couple of months when I had a letter from Ceinwen, not from Ellis, but from a driver of one of her father's coal carts. She asked me to meet her the next Saturday afternoon in the same place as that last time, by the milestone. She must have known how our shifts worked, too, and I found out that she had made it her business to know.

I had almost forgotten her. But then she came back to me fifty times as strong, and I never went to sleep without thinking of her, and wishing hot for Saturday.

But before that Saturday, Owen had a telegram from

London and I helped him to pack his engine while Gwilym packed the tools, and then went to the station with them to see them on the train.

"Two to Paddington Station, please," Owen said, and not a hair out of place.

"Paddington?" the booker said, with big eyes. "London, is it?"

"Yes," said Owen, one eyebrow down and the other one up, and looking as though foot-long cigars would drop from his pockets any moment.

"Good God," said the booker. "Off, now, again?"

"Yes," said Owen, and scratching something off his cuff.

"Are you going with the volunteers?" the booker asked.

"What volunteers?" asked Owen.

"South Africa," the booker said. "Those old Boers are hitting the eyes out of them, out there."

"No odds to us," Gwilym said. "Old Roberts will have them, and quick. Business, us."

"Oh?" the booker said. "A bit of business, is it? What, now?"

"Ours," said Owen. "And two tickets to Paddington, with your permission."

"No offence," the booker said. "Only asking a civil question, I was."

"And having a civil answer," Gwilym said. "Two tickets to bloody Paddington, and quick."

We were walking up and down the platform like three lords for hours before the train came in, letting everybody see the Paddington labels on the bag, and looking at them very superior because they were only going a bit down the line, but we were off to London. I wished I was going, too, but I had quite as much of the game as my brothers, and perhaps more, for when the train went, I was able to wave to them till they turned the bend, and everybody looking at me when I went, and saying to each other that I was one of the Morgan boys and two of my brothers just off to London. There is a lovely music in the saying of the word.

But I had a letter in my pocket from Owen to Blodwen, to be given to her in secret. Only messengers of princes know how to feel so important as I felt that day.

Over to Tyn-y-Coed I went, and in to find Mrs. Nicholas putting asters in the copper jug on the hall table.

"Well," she said, with something of sourness.

"Miss Evans, please," I said.

"She have gone from the house," she said, and started to hum.

"I will wait," I said.

"Not with those boots on this floor," she said. "It is with polish for the feet of gentry. Kitchen round the back."

"I will be in front," I said, and went out.

I saw Blodwen coming round the house with flowers in her arms, and with gloves and shears straight from the garden. There is pretty she looked in her big hat with flowers and roses, and red and yellow, in a bunch in her arms.

"Huw," she said, and stopping, bent forward a bit, with a big smile. "What a pleasant surprise."

"Owen has gone to London," I said, with quiet, so that any ears in the house might burst, but no matter. "Say nothing. He gave me this letter, and he said for you to say nothing, nothing to anybody."

She gave me the flowers to hold, and opened the letter as though it was a job she could have done without. But then she read, and smiles came back twice as strong, and even some pink toward the end.

"O, Huw," she said, with laugh, "how glad I am. Tell your mother, will you, that I shall be in London on Monday? A sudden call."

"Good," I said.

"And tell her," she said, and the smile had gone, "if nobody else has, that Iestyn sails for South Africa in three weeks."

"Is he a soldier, then?" I asked her, and nearly dead with surprise.

"Gracious, no," she said. "Something to do with coal for the Navy. Now then, tea for Huw."

"Yes, indeed," I said, "and then back, quick. Night shift, me."

"I have sworn to have you out of that pit, Huw," she said. "And before you are much older. We shall see."

We did, too.

But not as Blodwen thought, bless her heart.

"Yes," my mother said, when I told her what Blodwen had said, "Angharad is coming home while he is away. Say nothing outside."

Chapter Thirty

CEINWEN, then, on Saturday afternoon, and me in my best brown tweed, with a buttonhole of rose, red, with a smell like the mists of Paradise.

Here comes the trap, the old one, with the paint worn off, and grey with the weather, and the old mare smiling and lifting her big knees as awkwardly as ever she did.

And Ceinwen.

Standing up, waving the whip, in a dress of blue, and a long blue coat, and a big hat sitting on top of a rick of new hay. No plaits. No hair hanging loose. Up.

A woman.

But still the smile, and still the eyes, and O, still the kiss.

"Huw," she said, and her face as though with a light inside it, and her voice coming fresh as from a thousand miles away, "there is grown you are, boy."

"Your hair is up," I said.

"This long time," she said. "Let us hide the trap, quickly."

"And tie the mare," I said. "No more slipping home to tell stories."

"I nearly had my death through her," she said.

"Did you have trouble that night?" I asked her.

"Trouble?" she said. "Good God, boy, I was strapped till I was in bed for days. But they never found out about you."

"I was coming over to see your father," I said, with shame to put me in the ground.

"Good job you stayed home," she said. "He had a gun waiting for you. Do you know why I asked you to meet me to-day?"

"No," I said. "Why?"

"I want you to take me to the Town Hall for the acting," she said, and looking at me with her head down, with her eyes only just to be seen under the brim of her hat, with that in them to make me have my breath short, and turn quickly away.

"What acting?" I asked her, and going up in front of her so that she should not see my face.

"The acting, boy," she said. "The actors are coming to the Town Hall for two nights. I will never be allowed to mention the word in the house, never mind to go by myself.

Mervyn would faint if I asked him and perhaps tell my father. Then he would lock me in. And if I went by myself, perhaps they would stone me in the street."

"Why do you want to go?" I asked her.

"O, Huw," she said, and came close to me, like a little girl, with a pouting, and her eyes blinking, but slow, and opening them wide, wide, to show them big and grey, of a deep greyness, with a blessing of softness and something of tears and a smile far down.

I turned from her, with the hammers striking the white hot steel in my middle, and a fire withering my spine and sending tears to my eyes, with reason perished and sense gone, and only sight left, but crippled, so that the greens of trees and grass were a mixing of green without shape, and in the ears, only the turmoil of my blood, and from far away, her voice. You live within yourself as king when you become a man.

"I want to be an actress," she said.

"Why?" I asked her, and put reins about my voice.

"Because I want it," she said. "No, why, only I want it. I am sick to the heart with the coal yard and hands black with coal. I want to be an actress."

"There will be no place at home for you when you go," I said.

"No matter," she said. "Not a tear would come if I never saw them again."

"You will have a hard life," I said. "And wicked people, too."

"If Mr. Irving is wicked," she said, "I will be wicked, too."

"Who is he?" I asked her.

"Good God, boy," she said, as though the mountain was going from under us, "who is he? They are going mad to see him up there."

"Where?" I asked her.

"In London," she said.

"Are you going to London?" I asked her, and hoping with cold hope that she would say no.

"Yes," she said. "In time to come. They will come to the stage door for me, too. With flowers."

"When is the acting?" I asked her, hoping again that I would be safe in work down below.

"Next Wednesday and Thursday, seven o'clock, four-pence, sixpence, and a shilling," she said. "And you will be in time, so no good to say you are working. I have got a list of your shifts."

"O," I said, "making sure, were you?"

"I made well sure," she said, and laughing. "Will you come? Say yes, Huw."

How to say no, when she was saying yes in that voice, would tax the will of a shift of prophets. No use to struggle for there was a laziness coming heavily upon me, and all I wanted to do was stretch my muscles and lie near to breathe her scent, to be near her mouth, in reach of the softness of her.

"Yes," I said.

"O, Huw," she said, and put an arm slowly about my neck and pulled me down to kiss me, with strength that was savage, and sounds were in her throat, and round movements tormented her body, and the grip of her fingers left bruises for days to come. And I had a madness hot within me that was of the mouth and the fingers and the middle. No man shall know what gods are working in him, then.

The mouth reaches for newer fruit that seems to be near, but never to be tasted. The fingers are intent on searchings to soft places, but the senses are too far from their tips and impatient of their fumblings. And at the middle where the arrow steel is forged, there is a ruination of heat that seems to know, within itself, that coolness will come only in the hotter blood of woman. There is itch to find the pool, twistings to be free to search, momental miracles of rich anointments, sweet splendours of immersion, and an urgency of writhings to be nearer, and deeper, and closer. In that kissing of the bloods there is a crowding of sense, when breathing is forgotten, muscle turns to stone, and the spinal branch bends in the bowman's hand as the singing string is pulled to speed the arrow.

And in its flight it reaches to a rarer height than can be found in earth. An anthem rages as a storm, with chanting in poetries that never knew a tongue, and loud, strange music, and crackling fires of primal colours burst behind the sight-blind eyes and myriads of blazing moons rise up to spin for ages in a new-born golden universe of frankincense and myrrh.

Then the tight-drawn branch is weak, for the string has sung its song, and breath comes back to empty lungs and a trembling to the limbs. Your eyes see plainly. The trees are green, just the same as they were. No change has come. No bolts of fire. No angels with a flaming sword. Yet this it was that left the Garden to weeds. I had eaten of the Tree. Eve was still warm under me.

Yet still no bolt, no fire, no swords.

Only the song of a thrush, and the smell of green, and the peace of the mountain side.

And Ceinwen, lying quiet, with a trembling when she reached for breath, and making sounds, then, like the fingers of the wind through the high notes of the harp, with tears passing softly from the corners of her eyes, and her hair, fallen among the grass in bright, curving coils that shone.

She opened her eyes and looked up at me, and she sighed a little bit, and a breath got caught on the crag of a sob, and she swallowed deep to be rid of it.

"O, Huw," she said, and put limp arms about me. "Sweetheart mine, what did you do?"

"I loved you," I said.

"Glad I am I never knew," she said. "Oh, glad I am the first is you. There will never be another. Sweetheart mine, only you."

"Peach blossom," I said, and kissed her, and sat, to look down in the Valley.

How green was my Valley that day, too, green and bright in the sun.

"Half-past six, Wednesday," she said, when the mare was in the shafts and stamping.

"Right," I said. "By the side of the Town Hall."

She put the whip in her left hand and looked at me, and O, there was a dear shyness in her that I had never seen before. Innocent you were, my Ceinwen, and innocent you always were. You only were a woman.

"Well?" I said.

She looked down the road.

"Have you lost respect?" she asked me, with a smallness of voice.

I looked at the back of her head, and saw the pale, loose plaits of hair tucked underneath her hat, with stray ends hanging down to the collar, and the sun making the net shine and silvering her veil, and the lobe of her ear red and fat, and dust upon her shoulders. A warmth sang out of her, and in her untidiness, and dustiness, and the bend of head and the little fist upon the whip, I found her dear, dear to me.

"Respect for what?" I asked her.

"For me," she said.

"Why?" I asked her.

"Well," she said, "because you loved me."

What shall a man say, to give a woman ease of mind in so sad a place, is something hard to think of.

"Look," I said, "if I could claw the soul from my body you should stamp on it with nails and no sound from me. What is respect? Shall I touch my cap to you?"

"But I am wicked?" she asked me, with tears coming.

"God knows," I said. "And nothing has been said from by there."

"But, Huw," she said, "do you think of me the same as you thought before?"

"O, Ceinwen," I said, and kissed her with little kisses, "am I a rat with green teeth, then? The minutes will go slow till half-past six on Wednesday. With you, I have seen and heard beyond this life. Shall I think less or more of you because of it?"

"More," she said, very pretty. "Please, please, please."

"More," I said.

"Good-bye, now," she said, and up in the trap.

"Good-bye," I said.

"O, Huw," she said, and sat, hopeless.

"What, now?" I asked her.

"The coal yard," she said. "Come and give me another good big kiss to last, is it?"

Up I went in the springy trap, and if I never move from by here, I kissed her to leave a mark.

"Mm," she said. "Good-bye, now."

"Good-bye," I said.

A lovely smile, and a crack of the whip, and a moving of blue in a blowing of dust.

Home, in a dream lived backwards, me.

Time moved on the end of Ivor's pick all day on Wednesday. Punch, punch, punch, said the pick, and I was savage glad to send the lumps roaring down the chute, hasty to slide down in the smelly darkness and lift coal with the strength of giants into the trams, and push them loaded along the rails and off. Every lump was a few moments nearer her, every tram minutes less, each punch of the pick like the tick of a clock, every lump out of the seam a foot nearer to her in a tunnel of time. But a long, long old day, indeed.

But on top of the mountain, in my best grey suit, picking a few little flowers for her, I remembered nothing of it, but I sang to make the birds sit quiet and tip their heads and lift an eye. Good manners have the birds. If you are happy and your voice goes high in a song, they will find seats to be near, and no noise in the finding, and quietness till you have done.

The Town Hall was called Town Hall only because it was the only hall in the town. Of bricks, but without thought. Many a farmer would have thought it shame to have it for a barn. Good for the breeding of rats, the sticking of notices, and the sittings of justices.

Ceinwen held my hand tight when we went in, and I was careful to have two shilling ones near the door, in case. We waited till the place was full, but even then, we only went to our seats when the caretaker put out the lamps, just before the curtain was dragged open, and stuck, another drag, and stuck again, and a wait, and quiet coming, and somebody behind the stage whispering that there was always this bloody palaver with the rag, and another good pull, and then we were off, and Ceinwen squeezing her shoulders from happiness.

Shakespeare we had, from members of the company, all doing a bit from the plays. Hamlet had a cold in his nose, and so did Richard, and Macbeth, and Shylock. I am willing to swear the same man played them all. But very good. Ophelia was fat, and so was Cordelia, and Lady Macbeth, and Portia. But very good, too. And pretty, but a bit fat. If she worked in a colliery God knows how she would have a bath. A good sit in the river, I expect.

Plenty of clapping from the front for a small girl who played Juliet, and then put on grey hair and spoke the lines of the old nurse. Roars of laughing, even when he was saying nothing, for Falstaff, who was having trouble with a pillow stuffed underneath his tunic. I could see the stripes on it.

Then a drama, by the entire company, Falstaff said to us, of actors straight from Drury Lane and the Grand Theatre, Milan, and any doubts of his veracity, please to see the management, and thanking us for our kind attention and beg to remain our most obliged, and respectful. His name was Mr. Raymonde Ffoulkes.

"There is elegant," Ceinwen said, in whispers, and near to a faint with joy to be there, but so serious she felt with the acting, that she might have been in Chapel.

We got into something, then, about a lighthouse, and everybody going mad because no light was in it, and a big ship coming home from Cape Town, full of wounded soldiers and beautiful nurses. Falstaff was the lighthouse keeper and Ophelia was his daughter, she in long tails of hair that she pulled with grief, or whatever it was, and he with his hand to his forehead, and stamping up and down to put the candles out in the stage lights, and a long taper coming from the sides, each time, to light them up again. We would have had more interest if we could have had a look at the lighthouse or the ship, but they were out in the sides, and we had to think we saw the villain in the rowing boat. He had put the light out, Falstaff said, because his half-brother, who had been wounded in the war, was coming home to claim his inheritance, but if he drowned, there would be only one claimant to the title and estates. So out went the light, and quick, no matter about wounded soldiers and a fig for beautiful nurses.

Then Falstaff went for the Royal Navy.

Swimming.

Then the villain came on, spitting on his hands from rowing, and wiping sweat from the work, and shivering in the storm, never mind that I had to loose my hand from Ceinwen's because they were so wet with hotness. Hissing we were, and holloaing to blow him back in the water again, but never mind, what did he do but pitch in to Ophelia and give her a couple of good ones and put her out, and every man in the hall on his feet with his coat half off, and ready to go up there and pick marrow hot from his hip bones. And Ophelia lying flat in the middle of the stage like a bundle of washing.

"I would like him to do that to me," Ceinwen said, with sweetness and close in my ear, "only just once. I would kick the drums from his ears, son of the devil's own dam, he is."

But then, before the Royal Navy had chance to show himself, there was sound of a hymn from outside, and a hitting on doors, and shouts, with alleluias and swearing mixed, with a hushing of hishts from those in the hall, and scrapings of feet and scoldings of chairs, but the hymn was louder, from hundreds, and the shouts not to be denied.

"Come you," I said, and pulled Ceinwen out into the lobby.

"O, Huw," she said, "is it more trouble for me?"

"For me, too," I said. "Wait you."

In the little hall Falstaff was sweeping coppers and silver into a leather bag and very quick about it, too. The double doors were rocking under kicks and the pressure of shoulders. The shutters in two windows were having the attentions of crowbars and one of them burst as Falstaff flew back along the passage to the back of the stage, with holes in both his stockings and a slipper that flapped.

"Come on," I said, "follow him down the passage. I will stay and see nobody comes after you."

She kissed me, a moment, nothing, the blowing of a feather, not even the opening of a bud in the time of man. Yet in that moment I lived again our time together, but though I saw and felt the things of earth so clearly, that other world that I had seen, that other music I had heard, that universe that I had created of myself, that was my own, was far, far beyond me, and I yearned to know it, and have it again, wide and strange and beautiful, about me.

Off she went, and I turned to watch the door.

Then I saw Dai Bando and Cyfartha Lewis coming out in the hall, and looking at the door that was bulging now, and cracking in the panels. With them were other men, all crowding out to see what the noise was about.

"Dai," I said, and touched his arm. "How about the back way?"

"Well, indeed to God," he said, and smiling to show his tooth, "there is good to see you, boy. Have you been having a pennyworth of this rum shanks in by here?"

"Yes," I said, "what is the crowd outside for?"

"Chapel," he said. "There was a hell of a row because they let the actors have this place. The chapels were holding special prayer meetings to-night against it. Raising hell out there, look. Eh, Cyfartha?"

"And likely to be a tidy bit more in by here, Dai, my little one," Cyfartha said, and buttoning back his cuffs. "So I will clear my decks, like that one in by there."

"Let us go through the back," I said.

"I am going out the front," Dai said, and pulled his

bowler hat on tight. "I have paid money like a Christian. I went in and sat like two Christians and I am going out, as I came in, through the front, like a Christian. Eh, Cyfartha?"

"Christians, both, Dai," Cyfartha said. "Front, us."

"Will I come with you?" I asked Dai, with planks falling from the door and faces to be seen outside.

"Come on, boy," Dai said. "Come between us. When my right is busy with a chin, please to put the good toe of your boot to their shins, eh, Cyfartha?"

"But gentle, Huw," Cyfartha said, and very solemn. "Gentle, not to hurt. If you break a bone, see, a weight it is to the conscience. A pity, indeed."

"Ready now," said Dai, and buttoning his coat, and a coldness coming to make his eyes pale. Frightening to see, for I remembered the muscle that in clothes looked nothing.

Then they were in, pressed headlong by the crowd outside, and a shout went up from inside and out, and faces were on top of us, hot and red, with staring eyes, and mouths wide with shouting about hell and sinners and the devil.

Dai's fists swung one, two, and two men fell sideways, senseless, under the feet of the crowd. Cyfartha hit his lovely long left flat upon the nose of a tall young man in a square bowler hat. The hat went to the roof. I never saw where the tall young man went. A fat blackcoat with ginger side whiskers had a fist in Dai's coat collar. Dai's head came up sharp under blackcoat's jaw, and I saw it slip out of place. Brown cap had come to fist Dai a good one on the ear. I kicked for touch in the middle of his shin and as his teeth clicked in pain, Dai's elbow came up to knock a couple out.

Then the lamp fell as a billet of wood hit it, and we were in raging darkness.

A hand gripped me like the Devil's tongs, and carried me in a forward rush to the door where the sky showed lighter than the darkness of the lobby. Black heads were moving there with crowds more down the steps outside, but with Dai on one side, and Cyfartha on the other, using heads and elbows, fists, knees, and boots, with screams of pain and sharp flat hits of fists on flesh, and gross knocks of boots on bones, and the grunts of strength used full, we came to cooler air, but still squeezed close in the shouting crowd, and having their breath in the face, and the smell of them with tobacco and sweat.

"Heads down, Dai," Cyfartha shouted, and they bound an arm about one another, and I eeled in between their shoulders, and heads down, they went through that crowd like flame through paper, and me treading on the bodies, and even on the faces, of those who would have stood to block the way.

Full tilt we went into a husting of crates they had put there to have speeches on. The table and chair went over and the crates started to go over, for the crowd was dense and going back and back from the press of men shoving a way out of the hall.

We were crushed against the rocking crates, but Cyfartha pulled himself up on the top of one and held it down, and put down a hand to help me, but somebody came toward him with a stool raised high to smash on his head and I shouted. I saw Cyfartha turn and duck as I fell back among the crowd, and when I stood up again, he was helping Dai to have a footing, and then he came for me.

That was when the policemen came. I was up beside Cyfartha when I saw the silver spikes shining in their helmets. Dai saw them, too, and hit the sergeant a half-arm left that put him out flat, falling to the pavement, feet flying all shapes, and as the second went to hit him with his truncheon, a hook caught him in the round comfort of belly, and his mouth flew apart, and he fell in among the shouting crowd. Cyfartha had done something to the third one, and the fourth jumped down out of harm.

But now police were clearing the crowd and Dai saw a danger of more jail and hooked his thumb at Cyfartha, and laid hold of me.

"Come on," he shouted. "Through a shop and out through the back way. Quick."

But I thought of Ceinwen and slipped away from Dai to the clearing space between me and the hall.

"See you to-morrow, Dai," I shouted, and jumped down, running fast for the side-door and missing a rush of men by inches. It was dark up there and no light, but the door was open and I went in.

Two little rooms there were, but both empty, both warm from the bodies of those who had lived a little of their lives there, and from the candles that had marked the time in fallen grease.

Then a match was struck, and I saw the caretaker, with the green baize of his apron torn down the middle, and looking as though the least I would be was a wizard, with a skull, and snakes coming from the eyes.

"Who is it?" he said, and shaking to churn butter. "Dammo, man, you are standing like stiff from the coffin. Speak, man."

"Have you seen anybody here to-night?" I asked him. There is silly are the things you say in times like that.

"Seen anybody?" he asked me. "Well, I will go to my death. Have I seen anybody? The whole five valleys have been in by here, hitting hell out of one another all night. Seen anybody? Is there anybody living who stayed home?"

"I am sorry," I said, "I was looking for a young girl."

"More shame to you," he said, and lighting a bit of candle in a hole in the wall. "Young girls this time of night?"

"She ran down this way when the fighting started," I said.

"O," he said, and impatient with anger, "no time to talk about old girls. Have you seen my hall? A cattle pen, and a good week to clean it. I would like to have had my boots in the chops of a few of them."

"Did you see a girl," I asked him, "with fair hair? Young she was, and with a smile."

"O," he said, and pinched his eyes to sharpness, "a sweet-heart, is it?"

I nodded to him.

"Yes," he said, and nodding with his lips tight, "I remember. Mrs. Prettyjohn took her with her. They went in the coach."

"Where did they go?" I asked him, and a coldness busy in me.

"Wherever they went," he said, "and a riddance to rubbish, so help me senseless. No more actors here. None, from to-night. I have had a gut's full and brimming. Good night, now."

"Good night," I said, and went.

Eh, dear. How cold it was over the mountain that night, inside and out.

And a light in the kitchen, and the back door open, when I got home.

"That you, Huw?" my father called, from the kitchen, and I stopped dead.

"Yes, Dada," I said.

"Come you here," he said, and I went in, closing and bolting the door, and taking plenty of time, wondering what had happened to put that note in his voice.

"Have you been to the acting to-night?" he asked me, when I was in and standing before him.

"Yes, Dada," I said.

"You would disgrace your mother and me in such a manner?" my father said, and thin with anger.

"No disgrace, Dada," I said.

"Disgrace," he said. "You dare to come home here, stinking with the smell and touch of them, and your brains polluted by their filth? Think shame to yourself."

"But, Dada," I said, "only Shakespeare they did. No pollution."

"Pollution of Satan," my father said. "Shall you have anything else from such a sink of corruption? Whores, cotqueans, and dandiprats to spread their wares before you? Think shame, Huw Morgan."

"I think shame that you should think of me like that, Dada," I said.

"I am glad to see a glimmer of decency in you, then," my father said. "A splendid thing, to be stopped in the street by such as the son of Abishai Elias and told my son is in with bawds and toerags."

"I will see him later," I said.

"You will please to go outside and bathe from head to foot, first," my father said, "and then you shall come inside and pray for the good of your soul. And if you go to such a den again, and I come to know of it, I will have you outside with the fists. Remember."

"Yes, Dada," I said.

"Bathe," he said.

And I bathed.

Frozen I was, and paining with cold where the wind put his sharp old fingers through cracks and dug at me, and not even warm when I was dry, so the prayer was chopped in bits by restless teeth, and all my sense was in my pair of aching feet.

A beautiful ending to a day I had wished for with rich longing.

Longings, indeed.

When Owen sent a telegram to say he was off to America with Gwilym, I longed to be with them. But when he wrote to say he had married Blodwen Evans, I longed for Ceinwen, to be married to her.

That was a morning, with my mother crying and my father trying to tell her they had meant no harm marrying in a registrar's office.

"Just as good and binding as Chapel," my father said.

"They could have come home," my mother said. "We are not good enough."

"O, nonsense, girl," my father said. "Business, see, and sailing to America takes the time. He is a man in business now, with his own life to make. And no man is happy who is without a good wife."

"No good wives in an old office," my mother said, and tears to fill pots.

"Go on with you, girl," my father said. "London is big, and the days are short. He could have done much worse than marry her in an office."

"Hisht, Gwilym," my mother said. "What he did was only a bit above worst."

But she was quiet for days to come, and even the lilies of the valley from Blodwen's bouquet, that she sent in a parcel, helped nothing. She was angry, and in pain, that her two boys should go away all the way to London and America, and no proper good-bye. And then to be married on top of that, again.

"I said good-bye to them for London," she said, "not America."

"Good-bye is good-bye," my father said.

"There is good-bye, and good-bye," my mother said. "Would I send my two good boys all the way to America with only an old kiss and a couple of beef sandwiches and a bit of old cake? Good-bye, there is, and good-bye. And I was denied to say it. And I am their Mama."

"Good letters from them both," my father said. "And from Blodwen it was lovely, indeed. A joy to read it."

"You shall have your joy and welcome," my mother said. "You are easy to be satisfied. A bit of old paper with pen and ink, and no matter if all your boys go down the Hill and off. Did I go to bed, and come from there with paper and ink, then?"

"Hisht, girl," my father said, and coming to be red. "Have quiet, now, is it?"

"The day will come when you shall always find me quiet," my mother said. "I hope you will have proper good-bye, indeed."

"O, Beth," my father said, and going to her. "There is a nasty thing to say to me. It will come easier for you when Angharad comes home. Let it be quick."

Yes, let it be quick. Then, let the memory be quick to go.

Chapter Thirty-One

SHE WAS CHANGED beyond the knowing, our Angharad.

But I knew how she had been only when I saw her as she was.

She was at Tyn-y-Coed, as mistress there, but never coming up to us. Never.

The trap came over for my mother one Monday morning, and the groom gave her a letter. She read it, and gave it to my father for him to read while she went up to dress, dry in the eyes, but sharp in her movements as though to live at all was a test of patience.

Bron came in to do the house and cook for us, and when my mother had gone, my father took his bucket up the mountain, and Bron clicked her tongue.

"Trouble, trouble," she said. "Poor Angharad."

"Why should Mama go over all that way?" I said. "Is Angharad tired in the legs?"

"Not a word against Angharad will I stand to hear," Bron said, and down went the kettle to spurt spitting steam on the oven top. "A good sweet girl and no pleasure in life."

"She is living in Tyn-y-Coed," I said.

"She should have been living in Gorphwysfa these years," Bron said, and I went quiet in surprise, for she had never been so direct before.

Gorphwysfa was the little house with the sea-shell porch.

"I wonder does Mr. Gruffydd know she is back?" I asked her.

"He will know soon enough," she said. "There are tongues in plenty to tell him."

We were on afternoon shift that week, so there was no chance for me to go over to see Angharad, though my mother brought me back a set of pens and a book by Mr.

Dickens, with her kind love. There is a lovely book it was, too, called *Martin Chuzzlewit*. I will have Mr. Dickens in with the others led by Dr. Johnson. I had his Mr. Pick-wick later on. Eh, there is funny. I had my mother in fits, downstairs here, telling her about Snodgrass, and that other fool, old Winkle. And that fat old lump of a boy in the wheel-barrow, and Sam Weller with his v's for w's.

But when I went to Tyn-y-Coed, the first day I had a chance, I was so stricken with the look of Angharad that I could barely speak with sense.

White was in her hair, plain, even in the shadow of the room.

A starvation of light in her eyes. A deadness, that not even her smile took the cross from. A withering of the low notes in her voice, so that her laugh was thin alto where before it had been rich contralto and a joyul sound to hear. A fretting of the fingers, she had, and the coming and going of an untidy little frown between her eyes, that made three ragged little lines there, like the crippled foot of a crow, so strange to her, for she had once been so still, so sure, so much at peace, yet all the time so quick with life.

"Well, Huw," she said, when I kissed her cheek.

"Well," I said.

And we looked.

Her hair was done all round her head, very pretty, with a small hat with flowers of blue. A blouse with pleats down the front of silk the colour of the yellow wallflower, and a long skirt darker, with a wide belt of blue the same as her hat, with a big oval silver buckle. And a little watch with a gold bow up by her heart, and one ring. A wedding ring.

This girl used to wash pots in our back, and scrub the kitchen floor, and tickle my father's neck for pennies and run down the Hill like a boy.

This girl.

This woman.

Angharad.

"I look ill and I should take care of myself," she said. "Everybody coming in the house says so. So you say it, and I will rest quiet again."

"It is inside you," I said.

And we looked again.

"There is big you have grown, Huw," she said, with a

move of the mouth and a look through the window, in a voice that had weights upon it.

"You have been away long," I said. "Do you remember when you used to give me a few little sweets to go to Sunday School?"

"Huw, my little one," she said, and tears were pink and shining. "And I used to have them back from you in class. Yes, I remember. There is shame."

"Not shame," I said. "You liked a couple of sweets."

Now she was crying, but no move of her face. Just only crying.

She put an arm about my shoulders, but she was looking through the window and her body was stiff, straight, no bending, no breaking, as though she shared a tiredness with me, as a traveller leans against a milestone that takes a little more from a long road.

Then she shook her head and shut her eyes tight, and wiped them as though they were in the head of an enemy.

"A fool I am," she said. "Sit, Huw, and have to eat."

She went across the room to the bell like the old Angharad, and gave it a pull to set bells ringing in the forests of Russia.

"Now then," she said. "A bit of sense, for a change. Huw, you are coming from that old pit."

So much like my mother that I laughed out loud.

"Eh," she said, and a good smile, "there is lovely to hear a laugh, too."

"Come over to the house, girl," I said. "You shall hear plenty, and have a few, too."

"I shall never come to the house, again, Huw," she said, and I knew from the way she said it, without feeling, an opening of the mouth with one word after another on a string, all the same size and weight, that it was no use to ask why. A wasting of time.

Then Mrs. Nicholas came in with the tray and the girl behind her with another tray.

"Now then, Mrs. Evans," she said, in her fat voice, and a smile about the nose, and sideways with the eyes. "Tea, is it?"

"Thank you, Nicholas," Angharad said, but different, like Blodwen, but even better. "Leave it. I will pour."

"O," said Mrs. Nicholas, "you will pour, Mrs. Evans, is it? Of course, I have always had the pouring to do for other ladies. Thumbs off the plates, Enid."

And Enid got a knock with the keys over the back of the hand and sucked it, quick.

"That will do, Nicholas," Angharad said. "Not so handy with those keys, or I will have them from you. And I will pour."

"Yes, Mrs. Evans," Mrs. Nicholas said, and made a little knee, with still the smile about her nose, "a new mistress is like new sheets, yes? Little bit stiff, but washings to come."

And out she went, in her roundness, and fatness, and blackness, and starting to hum at the door.

"A bitch, that one," I said.

"Pedigree," Angharad said, firm and sure. "I am sour to be near her."

"Send her away," I said.

"She has been with the Evans family for forty-seven years, sixty times every day she will tell you," Angharad said. "I could never do it with a good heart. And she has done nothing to deserve it. The house is beautiful, and not a turn of the hand from me. Up all hours, she is, and very kind with a cup of tea, or smelling salts, and a cushion. But I could scream when she comes anywhere near me."

"A bitch," I said.

"A bitch," said Angharad, and we laughed.

"How are all the boys and girls we used to know?" she asked me. But I knew from the look of her, and the voice, that the question she wanted to ask was screaming itself red inside her.

"Good," I said. "Eunice and Eiluned Jenkins are married. Eunice is at home, and Eiluned has gone to London, to keep a dairy. Maldwyn Hughes has gone to be a doctor. Rhys Howell is in a solicitor's office in Town and sending home ten shillings a week. Madog Powys is in the tinplate works over the mountain. Owen got him there. Tegwen Beynon is married to Merddyn Jones' son, and up at the farm."

What use to go on, when she was asking no questions. She was waiting for me to say it for her.

"And Mr. Gruffydd is still first up and last to bed," I said, and bending to put my plate on the floor not to see her face. But I saw her hand. "And he can still be heard from one end of the Valley to the other, too, and no strain."

Quiet.

So quiet that you might even think you could hear the flowers having their little drops to drink.

So quiet, that to crack a biscuit between the teeth, would seem as bad as making a noise in Chapel.

"How is he, Huw?" she asked me.

As though her lips were dry, and she wanted a drink of water.

"Not as he was," I said, and on purpose.

Her eyes came big, and points were in them, sharp.

"What is the matter with him?" she said. "Is he ill?"

"Inside," I said. "In his eyes and voice. Like you."

She got up and stood with a hand on the mantelpiece, and looked across the top of my head at the window. Nothing was in her face, but her eyes were terrible, terrible, terrible.

"Go from here," she said.

And I went.

Straight to Mr. Guffydd I went, in the little house with the sea-shell porch, and found him reading in the room where we so often had shared tea. The furniture was a pleasure to see, now all in place, with a good carpet made by Old Mrs. Gethin and her daughter up at the farm by the waterfall on top of the mountain.

"Mr. Gruffydd," I said, "am I disturbing?"

"Come you in, my little one," he said, and a smile.

"Angharad is at Tyn-y-Coed," I said.

He closed the book, slow, with steady hands.

"Yes," he said.

"She is with sickness," I said.

"Has she had a doctor?" he asked me, and something new in the voice.

"No," I said. "Sickness of heart, it is."

He put his hands flat on the table, and stood quickly, and his hands left greyness on the shine of the table top.

"I can do nothing, Huw," he said.

"You are a preacher, sir," I said. "Come unto me all ye that are weary."

"O, Huw," he said.

Then there was quiet again, and while it was quiet, and while he stood with the knuckles of his fists together, I went.

It was weeks after that when my mother told me that Angharad wanted to see me. I had told my mother what had happened, every word, and she had said not a word. Not even a click of the tongue. But I had special little bits for tea for long after.

I found her in the kitchen garden having beans from the scarlet runners. Long green walls of them, there were, and Angharad in white among them.

"Well," I said, behind her.

She gave me half a look over her shoulder, with her hands busy with the beans over her head, and letting them drop into the basket without looking.

"Well," she said, "there is a stranger you are."

Gentle, with smiles, and her voice a bit lost among the leaves, and a good colour, from pulling at the beans with her arms up.

There was a wall between us, of a stickiness, not to be seen, with steps on both sides, but neither of us able to move our legs. Kind strangers, we were.

"Yes," I said, "will I help you?"

"I am finished," she said. "Let us go in the house."

Down by the currant bushes she stopped to see if fly was in them, but when she had looked at a couple of leaves she stood straight again.

"I am sorry I was nasty to you, Huw," she said, with quickness, and some shake in the voice, and looking at the bush.

"Not nasty," I said, and without comfort, and wanting to run.

"Nasty," she said, with more of strength, and quieter, as though she felt, with me, the size of my hands, and my shame for them. They were everywhere but right. "I could have killed myself when you had gone. Nasty I have been, to a lot of people, and no fault of theirs. I was sorry, Huw, and I am sorry now."

"It is nothing, girl," I said, and more uncomfortable, and redder than she was coming to be. There is a fool you feel when somebody is saying they are sorry for doing something to you. It is worse than if you had done something yourself. So you are having the worst of it twice, start and finish.

"Shall we kiss?" she asked me, and pulling her hat down with both hands, shy as a wren, and very gentle.

"Yes," I said, and kissed her chin, but she kissed me solid.

Then she blew out her breath with fat cheeks.

"Well, dammo," she said. "It is out, at last, then."

"What, now?" I asked her.

"Saying I was sorry," she said, and with a laugh. "Practising for weeks I have been, boy. And nothing I said, I was going to say."

"No need for it," I said.

"Yes," she said, "there was. Come you, let us have a chase round the garden, is it? Last one to the greenhouse has got bugs."

Off we went, and me keeping just behind her, and she with her skirts bunched in her hands, running as though glory to come was down there, and laughing up into the sky, and stopping at last because her hat was coming off, and the hat-pins pulling her plaits loose.

"O," she was laughing, and swallowing air, and holding her chest, and pulling out hat-pins and hair-pins. "There is good, Huw."

"Yes," I said. "Good, indeed."

She looked down at the pins in her hands, and the wind blew about her hair, and she was quiet.

The smells of the garden were rising warm about us, of turned earth down by the strawberry beds, and the songs of the currant bushes, and a good fatness of syrup from the apple trees, with bitter freshness of dahlias flowing on the top. And the wind happy to carry it on his head with a little whistle, like a butcher boy with a good big baron for somebody.

She looked at me, looked down again, turned the hat-pins, looked down the path and watched a little blue butterfly, down at the pins, up at me, down again. Up and down, again. Up and down. Up.

"Thank you, Huw," she said, and looking from one eye to the other.

"It was nothing," I said.

Down at the pins again.

"No," she said, and tears ready. "It was nothing. O, Huw. You were the only one. Nobody else cared. You told him."

And crying to break the heart in bits. Coming to stand softly against me and lean, and shake, and the hat-pins sticking in me, and a bumble bee having a good look at both of us.

"Come on, girl," I said. "Nothing to cry for, is it? All over, now."

"First cry," she said. "Never before. That is why. All over. Thank God."

And off again, worse than ever. But not in pain. A scent from her, from a bottle, that went deep.

"Finish, now then," I said, "is it?"

So up with a good breath, and a smile coming, and a good blow on my handkerchief.

"Eh, dear," she said. "I am like an old baby."

"I expect there will be a new one in the house when I go back," I said.

"Poor Bron," she said. "Let us pick fruit for her."

So back over the mountain I went with a couple of bushel baskets full of blessings from the bushes and trees, and when I was home, I was an uncle again.

A boy, Taliesin, they called him.

Ivor was so proud that night.

And dead within the month.

We were on night shift and going up to our stall, and I had stopped to have a better grip of the pick. I heard a crack, as though stone had been struck.

Ivor called in the darkness, but I never heard what he said.

The roof fell on top of him.

And I was standing there looking up into a black storm.

Helpless, as the rock fell, and splintered, and dust flew to blind and strangle.

Nothing to do but go back, hearing quietness coming quietly among the falls of echoes.

"Are you right, Morgan?" Rhys was shouting, with a candle in front of his face, and his hand round it.

"My brother is under the rock," I said.

"Blood of Christ, boy," he said, "have your head sewn, quick. Picks up, and stop work."

And men passed me one to another till I was out, and they were pressing forward, with picks hitting at the rock, and lumps being passed from hand to hand, as I had been.

They found him, but he came up in his coffin, screwed down ready.

Bron sat in the corner chair for days, still, looking through the doorway, no tears, no frown, nothing of fear. Just sitting quietly and looking.

Chapter Thirty-Two

"Give one," my father said, while he was nursing Taliesin, "and take the other. The Lord giveth and the Lord taketh away."

"Go in to that girl in by there," my mother said, "and say it to her. She will have an answer for you. Or perhaps I will save you trouble."

"Hisht now, Beth," my father said. "Kindle not the wrath."

"To hell with the wrath," my mother said. "And I said it plain to be heard."

Mr. Gruffydd used to come up and sit with her, and sometimes take her to Tyn-y-Coed for the afternoon. But it was long before we began to see the old Bron we had known.

I went back underground with Davy, in his colliery, a little farther away than my father's, only a few days after Ivor had gone. Then Davy went to London about the Union, and I went in the blacksmith's shop as a helper.

One day I came back in the afternoon with a bit of a burn and my mother went down to borrow linseed oil from Bron, and came back with her.

"This old boy of mine is always cutting and burning," my mother said.

"A good old boy, he is, fair play," Bron said, and pouring oil.

"Soft words swell the head," my mother said. "I am sorry in the heart that I spoke for you to go down the colliery, my little one. Sorry in the heart."

"Why, Mama?" I asked her. "Only small, these are. Other men have them, and no notice."

"Other men are other men," said my mother. "But my boys are my boys. A good glass of buttermilk, now then, is it?"

"Yes, please, Mama," I said. "And a bit of Bron's short-cake."

"O," said my mother, with her mouth like a little button-hole, "so your Mama's shortcake is to be given to the hens, is it?"

"No, Mama," I said, "shortcake day is to-morrow with us, but to-day with Bron."

"Only bread I made to-day," Bron said, with a smile that was only stretching the mouth. "Nobody to eat it, only Gareth and me, and we would rather have currant bread."

Silence came to burst among us. We were like rock, not moving. And Ivor was large about the place, putting his boots on, and telling my mother how flat the tenors were singing in the second choir, and humming a bit to show her.

And my mother standing, holding her chest with her hands that were all of bone, and looking sideways through the window, and her eye, that I could see, shining.

Bron went to the door and leaned against the jamb, with a hand flat upon the wall inside.

"O, Mama, my little one," she said, in a voice that should have been eased with many tears, "I am lonely without him. I put his boots and clothes ready every night. But they are there, still, in the morning. O, Mama, there is lonely I am."

My mother stood for minutes after Bron had gone.

"Huw," she said, "I will have Bron to live here, if she will come."

"She will never come, Mama," I said. "One mistress in a house."

"Then you shall go down there and live, then," my mother said, and sharp to move and off with her apron. "I will go down now, and find out if she will have you. She have got to cook and mend for somebody, and give comfort for somebody. So till the proper time have gone, and she do find another husband, you will do."

"Another husband, Mama?" I asked her, and O God, the world was flying to pieces and black with a new hate that came to drop heavy about me like a fall of rock. A new kind of hatred, I felt. A jealousy, and an envy, and a refusal in blood to see another man beside Bronwen. A newness of vision I found, that made me deny another man to have life in the world of moons beside Bronwen. Clean house, cook, sew, darn, all those things that women do in their daily lives for men, all those things, she might do for another man. But give him passage to the mightiness of song, and the strange poetries, and the noise of harp and timbrel, and a place in golden skies with the spinning of many moons, no. The anointment at the well, the immersion in the living, richer Jordan, the warmer baptism, the glory of enunciation, no.

No.

And a hatred came to be red inside me, to keep the no, no.

I was the sentinel, the vigilant.

And yet I had no wish to be with Bron as I had been with Ceinwen. With Bron was her own world that she had kept for Ivor, and I was the stranger at the gates, and no desire in me to enter in.

Then I knew, and felt, the loneliness of Bron. For I was lonely for the world of Ceinwen, the world that was mine and hers, that we had found together. That Garden of Worlds, where stood an Angel with flaming sword to see that we had only a momentary moment of its beauty, and sent us forth again, with shaking breaths and blind eyes and weakness in the limbs to live in desolation jewelled sharp with the memory.

"Another husband," my mother said. "Yes, boy. She is young. No wages going in the house. She has got years of beauty yet. And too proud to ask help. Of course, another husband. Quick, too."

"I will go and see her," I said.

I went down to her, and found her sitting in the corner chair, still looking through the door.

"Bron," I said, "would you have me in the house to live?"

She looked up as though I had been speaking another language.

"And have my wages," I said.

"Your home is with Mama," she said with quiet, but kind, as though giving excuses to herself. For there was light behind her eyes.

"My home is wherever I am," I said.

"Your Mama will be bruised in the heart," she said.

"Mama, it was, who said it first," I said.

"From pity," Bronwen said.

"Not pity," I said. "Sense. If you put clothes night and morning, let them be my clothes."

"I am not a cook like Mama," she said, going weak in the voice.

"You are a cook of cooks," I said, "but Mama has years of cooking more than you, that is all."

"It will make trouble in the family," she said, looking round the kitchen to see if things to say were hiding behind the teapot, or behind the plates on the dresser, or the copper pots on the mantelpiece.

"Trouble, yes," I said. "If you say no. I will feel shamed to have been forward, and Mama will think I am not good enough for you."

Quiet, and if things to say were hiding, they were careful not to be seen.

She looked through the doorway again, but now her hands were putting tucks in her apron. I went over the tiles with my boots sighing in the sand, and shut the door with a swing, and put my back to it, and she looked at me with the smile that was not a smile.

"Yes or no?" I asked her.

"Yes," she said, with calm, and starting the chair to rock.

"Good," I said, "I will get my bed."

So up to this room I came, and rolled up the mattress I am sitting on now, and slid it through the window, and then the bedstead. Downstairs, then, to take them up to the little room like this one in Bron's house, that was empty. Back to fetch my clothes, and back again to give good-bye to my mother.

"Well," she said.

"Well," I said.

"Off again, then," she said.

"I will come plenty of times, Mama," I said.

"Right, you," she said. "And supper every night, is it?"

"Yes, Mama," I said.

"Good-bye, now, then," my mother said, dry.

"Good-bye, Mama," I said, and kissed her, and went.

Quiet, those first few months were, with Bronwen. There was a line drawn between us that was plain as though put there fresh with chalk every day. From each side of that line we lived, and spoke, and smiled. Not as strangers, for we knew each other too well. We knew when we laughed that we were not having all the laugh, that it was not wide, or deep, or high enough, that the best part of it was on each side of the line, kept back. We knew when we talked together that we were not talking with all of us, but only that bit of us that others would see and know as Bronwen and Huw Morgan. If we came near each other we were like hedgehogs with spines to keep away, though we never showed it. But we knew it. The air between us was hot with a hotness that only the two of us could feel.

Our laughing was false with a falseness that only we could hear. Our talk was empty, of food, and the colour of Taliesin's cheeks, and the darkness so early in the evenings. But we know why we were talking emptily, and why we never looked at each other.

We were gently afraid of each other, though without fear, and with nothing of fright. We were afraid only in the spirit and delicacy of being afraid, of the same nature of afraidness that blood horses feel when a hand is placed upon them, and they shake under the skin from tail to muzzle.

A fear of the touch, whether from speech, eyes, or body.

And only because we knew of another world, that could be reached in a moment, and felt for a moment, and gone in only a momentary moment.

In these months I knew why Eve took leaves, and why they hid from one another, and I realised the magnitude of the curse that sent them from the Garden to work by the sweat of the brow, out of that glory, one to cut coal in a crawling of dust, the other to stand at a sink and scar her wrists with scum from greasy dishes.

Strange it is that you will live from day to day for months and months, and nothing to happen except getting up and working and going to bed. Then a little thing happens and you watch it grow about you, with terror, and to take the burden a little from you, you try to pretend you are in a dream.

Chapter Thirty-Three

DAVY was a long time in London, with not much to show except knowledge of what was going on in the Unions up there, and sending reports down to our branch. I did most of the letter writing, and I was able to see the Union having strength as from the flow of my pen.

Every week new members by the hundred, and every week more and more voices shouting for action against the owners. Shorter working hours, more money, ballots for places where the seam was richest, closing the collieries against outside labour, all had their champions, and all ready to fight.

Ianto had been speaking night after night for weeks, not for action against the owners, but against the Government.

Mr. Gruffydd was with him, there. They wanted to stop the royalties paid to landlords, especially those paid on every ton coming from under pastureland, that paid rent above, and a royalty below only because the main heading ran under it.

"They will charge royalty on the air above it, next," Ianto said. "No royalties, none, and our own trucks and engines, and railway staff, and a rental to the railway companies for the use of their tracks all over the country. Then a fleet of coalers of our own to take it out to the world. But out to the world only when every fire-place in the country has got a splendid fire, every scuttle full, and every cellar loaded."

"Who is to own all this?" my father asked him, and with steady pulling on his pipe, and looking at the end of his slipper.

"The people," Ianto said, in quiet, and pale, with a flame. "Only the people. God made the earth for Man, not for some of the men."

"Where will you have the money to buy it, my son?" my father asked him, still steady with the pipe.

"God made the coal, Dada," Ianto said. "But Man makes the money. Pity, indeed, if God put His hand down through the clouds and gave us all a bill for the riches He made for us and gave to us, free. What would happen, I wonder?"

"It is beyond me, Ianto," my father said, and knocked out a full pipe in his worry. "There seems to be truth in what you say, indeed. But the Bible and God are not in the business of the pit. Only ledgers and Mammon. You will have it hard, my son. Hard, indeed."

"Good," Ianto said. "It is only when men forget to fight for right that they fail. There are plenty to fight for wrong. We will finish with the sliding scale first, anyway. That will be a start."

Night after night, all over the valleys, men met in hundreds to argue about the sliding scale. Older men, like my father, who had earned a handful of sovereigns for a week's work, were blaming the younger men for the difference, and blind to argument. And they clung to the sliding scale because it was at least a living.

Then Ianto was discharged from the colliery with Will Thomas and Mostyn Marudydd, all three of them Union workers.

Men wanted to drop tools there and then, but Ianto kept

them in. He wanted no hungry children on his conscience, he said.

For weeks the three of them went about the pits to have work, but no, even though they were skilled men, there were no places for them.

"They have sharpened their knives for you," my father said. "You will never work in the collieries again while you live."

"Right you," Ianto said, "I will go over to the ironworks tomorrow."

"Is the Union too poor to pay you whole time?" my father asked him.

"What I do for the Union," Ianto said, "is from the heart. Will you have it said of me that I skulked into a job I made for myself?"

"But Ianto, my little one," my father said, "somebody has got to do the job and be paid for it."

"Good," said Ianto, "but not me."

So over to the ironworks he went, and had a job labouring in the furnaces, and coming back at night to work by the lamp. Four miles there, and four miles back, and a twelve-hour day in between. A bath, and his dinner, and more work with the pen, or with the voice.

I was still with the blacksmith, but doing jobs underground for most of the time, on trams that broke down, and blunted tools, and on all the little jobs that heat and a hammer will mend.

I found little joy in working with iron, for it had no will of its own. A pump on the bellows, a heat blown pale, and out comes your iron like a slave, ready to be hit in any shape you please. In wood, you must work with care, and respect, and love. For wood has soul and spirit, and is not at the mercy of triflers. One slip of your chisel in carelessness or ignorance, one shave too many with your plane, and your work is ruined, and fit only for burning.

But with iron, you shall beat and beat, and only an angriness of sparks, like the spitting of a toad to answer you, and if you make a mistake, back on the fire with it, a leaning on the bellows, and here it is again, poor spiritless stuff, ready to be beaten again.

I went often to Town to fetch iron in strips from the forge there, when we were low in stock, and held up on a job.

I was over there one market day, in the afternoon, in my

working clothes and black from the pit and feeling shamed
to be walking among the people in case I spoilt their good
clothes.

The forge was near to the market hall, so that the
farmers could pull up in the square to unload, and trot their
horses over to be shod where they could keep an eye out
for customers who might be waiting at their stalls to buy.

So the forge was always a busy place, on market day,
full of laughing and voices, and the grunting of bellows,
and the hot whispers of fires, and the silver count of hammers beating out the strokes for sweating sledge-hammer
men and the stamping of horses, a dull knocking of nails in
hoofs, the fall of files on stone, impatient breath of iron
drowned in the cooling tank, and sharp to the nose with
the frying of hoof as the new blue shoe was fitted.

And outside, the little blue trap from Tyn-y-Coed, filled
at the back with baskets, and inside the forge, the bay
mare, with her off hind stretched and held between the
knees of the smith.

I was looking at her and laughing to see the look in her
eyes, whether to kick or not, when I heard a voice I knew
well.

"New shoes again," Mrs. Nicholas was saying, with the
smile carved about her nose, to a farmer and his wife from
the next valley. "But only to be expected, see. Out all day,
she is."

"Are you having much work at Tyn-y-Coed, then, Mrs.
Nicholas, my little one?" the farmer's wife asked her.

"Work never stopping," said Mrs. Nicholas, and picking
the fingers of her gloves. "Come one, come the other, from
morning till night."

"Entertaining, young Mrs. Evans is, now I suppose?" the
farmer said. "Old Evans kept them away."

"It will never surprise me to see the poor master rise up
white from his grave one of these days," Mrs. Nicholas said.
"Only the gravestone is keeping him down there now, I
will swear."

"Gracious goodness, Mrs. Nicholas, my little one," the
farmer's wife said, "what for, now then?"

"What for?" Mrs. Nicholas said, with her hands up, and
her eyes up, and the suffering of eternity in her voice.
"What is going on in the house, of course. Are you standing there in your good little clothes and saying to my face
you are knowing nothing about it?"

"No," said the farmer, and taking out his pipe, with his eyebrows up, and his wife coming closer, and both leaning forward. "What, now then?"

"The only ones in the Five Valleys," Mrs. Nicholas said, in grief. "Nobody else, only you."

"Good God, Mrs. Nicholas," the farmer said, and looked at his wife, and they pulled a mouth at each other, and looked again at Mrs. Nicholas as though she held their hopes at the Bar. "What, now then?"

"Not for me to say," Mrs. Nicholas said, and a shaking of the head, and a look at the floor, as though she saw Old Evans lying there in his winding sheet, "only the housekeeper I am, and forty-seven years, with odd, in the family, and living to curse the day."

"Well, well," the farmer said, "there is terrible it is, whatever it is, is it?"

"Terrible, Mr. Davies, my little one?" Mrs. Nicholas said, with stiffness, through a closed mouth, and a straightening of the back, and eyes gone dull to think of a word, "Not the word. A collier's daughter, Mrs. Davies, my little one, using best china and lace tea cloths every day of the week. And that is only a bit of it. Fancy me, you know. A ride in the trap, if you please, with a preacher every day."

"With a preacher, Mrs. Nicholas?" Mrs. Davies said, in whispers.

"Who is he, then?" Mr. Davies asked her, with his hair in crawls with him.

"Who?" Mrs. Nicholas said. "Who is in the house every night till all hours? Who, are you asking? Who, then? I am in bed, with my candle out."

Mrs. Nicholas looked about, but took no notice of me, for I was black, and turned into rock, and she bent to them and whispered, and I saw spit from her speech bright in the air, and as she spoke, their mouths and eyes became round with smiling horror.

"Eh," Mr. Davies said.

"O, Gracious God in Heaven," said Mrs. Davies, in whispers, as though a fireball was to be expected then and there.

"Yes," said Mrs. Nicholas, and fat from duty done, "and how do I know he goes from the house at night?"

The three of them looked at one another, and devils danced about them.

"And her poor boy of a husband out in Cape Town," Mr. Davies said, "bleeding for his country."

"Wait you, Mr. Davies," Mrs. Nicholas said, with her eyes shut as though her life were going from her, and holding up her finger to make the sign of writing with a pen, "only wait, you."

"Well done," said Mr. Davies, in Chapel voice, from the chest, and with sternness, "thou good and faithful servant."

"Yes, indeed, Mrs. Nicholas, my little one," said Mrs. Davies in a voice that the least Mrs. Nicholas had done was to save them all from the gallows. "Suffering you are, now, but reward to come, is it?"

"O, I hope, I hope," said Mrs. Nicholas, and a handkerchief coming to help with the tears. "Poor, poor little Master Iestyn. A slut from a coal mine fouling his home, and him thousands of miles away. O, dear, dear. Ach y fi."

"Ach y fi, indeed," Mrs. Davies said, and a pinkness of the face to be from there and meet others. "In His keeping, you are, Mrs. Nicholas, my little one."

I had to go from there then, blind and dumb, job forgotten, nothing in me. Empty, I went, without even a word to Mrs. Nicholas. Yet, feeling nothing, I could have killed her with no thought of to-morrow, but only sickness to touch the fat wrinkles of her neck. But instead, I had the sense to go.

To Bronwen I went, and found her wiping Taliesin after his bath.

"Well," she said, "there is early you are, boy. No bath is ready for you yet or anything."

"No matter," I said, and I told her, and her face was white as the towel when I finished.

"Eh," she said, with tiredness, and closing her eyes, and holding Taliesin close to her and lifting her head. "I do hope from my soul that the tongues of people will be slower to hurt when my sons are grown to men, indeed. What good are they having for it?"

"What are we to do?" I asked her.

"Tell Angharad," she said, as though there was no argument.

"It will kill her," I said.

"Better to come from us," she said. "If that woman have written to Iestyn he will be writing soon or perhaps coming home. That would be worse for her."

"Is it true, then?" I asked her. "Is Mr. Gruffydd going over there till all hours?"

"Do I know?" she asked me, with straightness, and stopping to tie Taliesin's napkin. "Is it business of mine? Are you questioning it?"

"No," I said, and lost inside me. "But I thought it was all lies."

"That is not the point," Bron said, "their business is their business. Nothing to do with us, you, me, or anybody else on earth."

"But, Bron," I said, "he is a preacher."

"And a man," Bron said, "and Angharad is a woman. Well?"

"Is it right, then, Bron?" I asked her. "She is another man's wife."

She held Taliesin up and kissed him so that her mouth made a lovely roundness in his fat little cheeks and he laughed just like a hen, with his breath coming backwards.

"How have you been looking at me these months?" she asked me, quick from the kiss, with quietness, and with something of tears.

I looked down at my hands and saw the veins swollen in the blackness of grime, and I knew a shame that had the edge of a razor cutting deep into me with a hurt that made me want to scream.

"There is shamed I am, Bron," I said.

"Shamed?" she said, and pushed breath from her nose with a sound of impatience, "of being a man? Or being found out?"

"No," I said, and the razor doing beautiful work inside me, "to give you extra trouble in the mind."

"You are talking nonsense, boy," she said, and a kiss for Taliesin again. "Go you and bathe. Then some dinner, and we will talk again."

While I was having dinner, Bron was upstairs changing into her best, so when she was ready I had finished.

"Now then," she said, "will you go to Mr. Gruffydd while I go to Angharad? Or will I go to Mr. Gruffydd?"

"You go to Angharad," I said. "If I have my eyes on that black bitch I will strangle her. But how shall I tell Mr. Gruffydd is something beyond me."

"Say it out," Bron said. "Just say. Then it is for him."

"Right you," I said.

"Good-bye, now," she said, and came closer and

smoothed back my hair, and smiled at me with her teeth
and her eyes in slits with shine in them. "O, Huw, there is
a nasty bump you have had, too. Did you think I was
blind, boy?"

"No," I said, "I knew you knew, but I thought no matter as long as nothing was said."

She laughed out loud, and a lovely laugh had Bron, deep
and from the chest.

"There is a funny old boy you are," she said. "We will
talk more when I come back, is it?"

"Yes," I said, and feeling worse than ever, shamed and
angry, and sore in a place I could feel but could not touch,
as though I had fallen with my brains on a gravel path,
and scraped the skin off.

"See Mr. Gruffydd before you see Mama," Bron said,
"or she will see by your face that something is sour with
you and have it out of you, every word. Good-bye, now."

"Good-bye," I said, and we looked at each other, and I
tried to keep from smiling at her, to show that I was feeling serious, but nobody could see her eyes like that and
keep trouble inside them.

So I smiled, and Bron laughed again, with gentleness,
and quietly shut the door.

I sat there till the light had gone, thinking about Bronwen and me, with still the soreness, and plenty of sourness,
and some of the shame. But the smile kept coming back
and spoiling it. I was coming to be in a sweat of anger with
myself for being such a fool as to tell Bronwen that I had
thought all would be well if nothing was said, and worse
still, to remember her voice when she asked me how I had
been looking at her. I thought shame to have been such an
animal. I called myself low names and whipped myself
raw, in thought, and tried to think of some punishment fit
for me.

But the smile kept coming back and spoiling it.

Bron knew.

And she laughed about it.

There is strange, that only a little problem of your own
will take your mind far from a tragedy belonging to others.
I had forgotten Angharad and Mr. Gruffydd, and only
Gareth crying upstairs, and waking Taliesin, made me
think of Bronwen's errand, and so brought me to think of
mine.

So off I went, down the hill at a trot, and round the back of the little house with the sea-shell porch.

"Well, Huw," Mr. Gruffydd said, and just pulling down his cuffs, and his face fresh and a bit pale from a wash, with his hat and coat and some books ready on the table, and his slippers pigeon-toed by the chair.

"Mr. Gruffydd," I said, "I have got something to tell you."

"Will it wait, Huw?" he asked me, and smiling. "I am late now, see."

"To Tyn-y-Coed you are going, sir?" I asked him.

"Yes," he said, and turned his back to put on his coat, and I knew from the bend of his back that he was ready against attack, and for some reason feeling an anger.

"That is what I have come for, sir," I said.

"For what?" he asked me, and cold, and still with his back to me.

So I told him.

Not a move from him all the time. Only standing in the candlelight, with his back to me and his hands fast in the collar of his coat.

"O," he said, as though I had told him that rain was starting, "at last then, eh, Huw?"

"Yes, sir," I said.

"Next," he said, "what to do? Angharad must be protected."

"You shall do that only by strangling Mrs. Nicholas," I said.

"You cannot stop people from talking, Huw," Mr. Gruffydd said, and still without feeling in his voice, still with his back to me, "nor shall you stop them thinking. They are products of a faulty environment. And faults are what you shall expect."

"What shall you do, sir?" I asked him.

"Leave me, now, my little one," he said, "I will think about it."

"Good night, sir," I said.

But he was quiet when I went from there, and still standing with his back to the door when I passed the window.

The village was still when I went back home after a walk along the river. Not a light anywhere, except at the pit. I had thought to clear my head, but the walk made me feel worse than before, and I found pain alive in me to walk up the hill.

Even in the time I had been to work, change had come to the river, to the streets, and even to the shape of the village. The river had been built on all the way down to the path that led up to the Chapel, and the walls of new engine sheds were built flush with the banks, so that the bilge spewed into the stream, and the sound of them all, one after the other, like a sickness.

The new streets were much narrower than ours, and the front doors opened straight on to the street, no garden, no flowers, no bit of green to bless you coming in or going out. No backyard, either, and not even a blade of grass for a garden. And every house in a street full of houses, on both sides, exactly the same as its neighbour, with not a brick difference. And all of them jammed tight together, with not an inch of air between them.

Four new slag heaps had been started, with their cable tips running to the top of the mountain, so that the slag dropped on to the green pasture and found a level down among the trees. A big beech, that I had climbed not long before, now reached out of a smoking heap like the hand of a spirit entombed.

There was a light in the kitchen when I got back, and my heart was lifted to see it.

Bron was sitting in the chair, sewing, and the kettle jumping on the hob, and the cat leaning his chin on his front paw and opening only one eye for me, and a good smell of onion soup to kiss the nose.

"Up still?" I said, but not looking at her.

"We were going to talk," she said, with smile in her voice, "so I stayed. Did you see Mr. Gruffydd?"

"Yes, he only said you cannot stop people from talking and thinking," I said. "He is going to think about it."

"Angharad is off back to London, first train," Bron said.

"Was she angry?" I asked her.

"No," Bron said. "She knew about it."

"She knew?" I said.

"Has she been living all her life here, and no sense?" Bron said.

"But did she let Mr. Gruffydd go there and go there all this time and no word?" I asked her.

"Do you think Mr. Gruffydd knew nothing?" she said, and busy with plates.

"Then what use to tell them, or worry for even a moment?" I asked her, and feeling wronged to the heart.

"Have what there is to be had while there is time," she said, and put a bowl of soup in front of me. "They have done harm to nobody."

"But he is a preacher and she is Mrs. Iestyn Evans," I said. "Surely it is wrong, Bron?"

"Why?" Bron asked. "Why is it wrong for Mr. Gruffydd to see Angharad?"

"Well," I said, and steam from the soup wetting my face, and glad to make it an excuse to pull out my handkerchief to have a good wipe to have time to think.

"Yes, well?" Bron said, with sharpness, and the knife half-way through the loaf. "Shall I say? Because your mind is like those beauties down by there. Like Mrs. Nicholas. A fine brother you are. And a fine one to talk. Strangle her, you wanted. Strangle yourself for a change."

"Well, Bron," I said, "there is nasty you are. Only asking why, I was."

"Is Mr. Gruffydd to be treated any different from other men only because he is a preacher?" she asked me, and angry. "Is he any less a man? Has he fewer rights?"

"But with another man's wife, I am saying," I said, and ready to break the house to pieces in temper.

"With another man's wife, what?" Bron said, in a voice to put ice to hang from the stove. "Harm to who, if he talks to her, and she has benefit from his company?"

"No harm," I said.

"Then?" she asked me, with the smile that was not a smile.

"O, to hell," I said. "It is none of my business."

You should have heard Bron laughing. In fits and helpless, trying to cut bread, but too weak to hold the knife.

"Eh, dear, dear," she said, and wiping the tears, "there is a silly old boy you are, man."

"Why am I silly?" I asked her, and trying to smile, but finding it hard to work against the soreness.

"Because you are doing what Mr. Gruffydd has been doing," she said, "and sleeping in the house, too. Would you like others to talk about you?"

Well. Like sunlight coming to blind.

"Nobody could say anything about me or you either," I said. "I would only like to hear them."

"You shall, before long," she said, certain as bricks.

"Well, Bron," I said, "I will go, then."

"You shall stay," she said. "Let them talk, with their minds like a cess, and mouths like pots, with them. And think well about yourself before to talk of others. I told you this afternoon about the way you looked at me. Think of it a little more, and ask is it right before to ask questions of others."

So I sat like a dog with hurts after a good kicking, and went to bed, feeling the weight of her eyes, and her smile warm in the room, but not looking at her and unwilling to smile back.

Chapter Thirty-Four

ANGHARAD went to London, and Ceridwen went to stay with her, with the children, for a time. My mother went up there for a month, and indeed, from the fuss you would think the south pole was only the next stop from where she was going.

How quiet is the house when the mistress has gone.

You walk in, and the same smell is a comfort to you, the air on your cheek has the same feel, the fire makes the same noise, the china plates on the dresser shelves laugh at you as they always did, and the clock is still as loud as he always was with his heels on the road of Time.

But a warmness is missing, a briskness, that moved as soon as the latch was lifted, and those sounds that followed, the rattle of the teacaddy, the crunch of the lid, the chime of spoons in saucers, the poking of the fire, and the hot hurry of scalding water upon tea leaves, are gone, too.

"Good God," my father said, "nobody shall know how I miss your mother. Sweetness have gone from life, indeed. The first time to be without her for thirty-nine years. Eh, dear. I am lost without my good Beth."

So I often saw my father writing under the lamp, scratching his head to find something to write about, even telling her that the handle had come off the kettle, and about Gareth cutting a lump out of the door with my chisel, with pages about Taliesin, of course.

There is strange to see a man quiet in his own world, and searching it for jewels to give his queen. I often wondered how my father saw his world, and wished I could be sitting inside him only for a minute, while he was writing to my mother.

Her letters to him were on one page, and written big to fill up room. Without fail, she had to hurry to catch the post and remained his loving Elizabeth Morgan.

And he always cried when he read them to us.

I went back to work with only a good swearing from the smith, and a couple of weeks later I was sent underground again with a place of my own and a boy to work with me. Twelve years old, he was, and a good little boy, but a bit young for the job, so I had more work to do.

He was filling the tram at the bottom of the holding one Saturday morning, and I was up at the face piling slag. I heard shouting down on the main, and I thought he might have been run over, so down I went bent double, sliding on coal all the way.

Fighting, he was, with a bigger boy, and having a hiding, but fair play to him, standing up and giving some good ones when he had chance.

"Come on," I said, "working for me, you are."

"I am sorry, Huw," he said, and dropped his hands, but the other one put a hard right into his ear that sent him flat.

Well, well.

One good smack on the side of his head sent him over a pile of coal.

"Manners," I said. "Lacking in your family, evidently."

"O," said one of the men, who had been looking on, "since when has your family come so good, then?"

"Please to keep shut your mouth about my family," I said.

"You keep family matters out of your talk, then," Evan John said. "A lot to talk about, you have, with a sister whoring after every preacher in the district, and a married woman."

I broke two of his ribs with a right, I broke his nose with my left, and I left his face only when I felt his jaw smash under my fist.

Then I went back to work.

When I got out of the cage on the pit-top the assistant manager beckoned me.

"The police want you," he said.

"Good," I said. "Where?"

"In the office," he said.

So I followed him into the office and a sergeant of police came from behind the door and tapped me on the shoulder.

"Huw Morgan?" he said.

"Yes," I said.

"Assault and battery," he said.

"Will I have a bath before you lock me up?" I asked him.

"Not locking you up," he said. "You will be summoned first."

"Shall I go?" I asked him.

"Warning," he said. "Keep in the house."

"You are discharged from the colliery, Morgan," the manager said. "You Morgans have been a nuisance here for years."

Home I went, and bathed, and sat down to dinner.

Bron put the plate in front of me, and then looked.

I could see her blue dress and a bit of apron from the side of my eye.

"What did you do to the backs of your hands?" she asked me, as though a hand were over her mouth.

"If he had been a single man," I said, "I would have killed him. He spoke of Angharad."

"O, Huw," she said, and sat beside me. "What, then?"

"I am due for a summons from the police," I said, "and I am put from work."

We were quiet together. Then she put a hand on my shoulder.

"Eat your dinner," she said.

Only a little while after, there were footsteps in our back with no scraping of the heel, quick, clean, solid, belonging to somebody with a duty to be done and no time.

"Mr. Gruffydd," Bron said, and ran to put chairs straight, give the table cloth a smooth, and poke the fire.

"Huw," he said, and big and dark in the doorway, "you have had trouble."

"Yes, sir," I said, and standing, for his face was white, with a redness in his eyes.

"Over my name," he said, "and your sister's?"

I said nothing.

"I am shamed," he said, tired, but with anger shaking him. "Shamed. It will be worse in the court-house."

"I think no matter of them or the court-house," I said.

"Mr. Elias will see to it that you do," Mr. Gruffydd said.

"Mr. Elias?" I said, and with surprise.

"Mr. Abishai Elias pressed the charge through his son," he said, "or there would have been no summons. Evan John's father is his shopman."

"I will wait for it," I said.

"I am going away," Mr. Gruffydd said, and sat down slowly. "I am going from the Valley. They dare not say anything to me, but I see it in their eyes. Some of them, anyway. I am wrong to stay here from stubbornness. I should have gone long ago."

With the weariness of a beaten man, and his eyes at the mat, and his hat turning in his fingers, and his hair falling down to cover his face, and his shoulders a curving width of wrinkled black. Bron, with her apron to her eyes.

Me, cold.

"I am sorry, sir," I said.

"I will see your good father," he said.

And he went, while I looked at the flames behind the bars of the fire, and thought of nothing, only the curving yellow sharpness of them, and the deep mourn of Bron's tears beside me.

"Well, Huw," my father said, "what, then?"

"I will go in carpentering," I said.

"What is happening to us?" he said, quietly, with thought. "It is terrible, with us. Ivor, Ianto, Davy, Angharad, you. What your poor mother will say, I will never tell you. Now, Mr. Gruffydd."

"Have you tried to keep him back, Dada?" I asked him.

My father pointed his pipe up at the mountain.

"Go you," he said, "and push that one by there out of its place. To Patagonia he is going, and in Patagonia he will land one of these days. So make fast your mind."

My mother came home while I was over the mountain buying wood. When I went in the house she was still in her bonnet sitting on the rocking-chair in Bron's, and nursing Taliesin, with a towel over her black silk to save trouble.

"Well," she said, when I kissed her. "More, now then?"

"Yes, Mama," I said.

"When is the summons?" she asked me, as though she was asking when was Wednesday.

"Day after to-morrow," I said.

"Are you afraid?" she asked me, and looking at me straight.

"No," I said.

"Good," she said. "I brought back a London hat for you special."

"Thank you, Mama," I said. "How is Angharad?"

"Going to Cape Town," she said, and lifted Taliesin to kiss him and keep the shake from her chin.

Chapter Thirty-Five

So IN MY LONDON HAT, and best tweed, off I went to the court-house, with my father and Mr. Gruffydd on each side of me in Thomas the Carrier's best trap, and people to watch us go all the way down the hill and through the village, without a smile or wave.

All the way over the mountain, slag heaps were like the backs of buried animals rising as from the Pit. Living trees were buried in them, and in some, gorse was growing with its lamps alight, and grass was trying to be green wherever the wind would let it rest in peace.

"Will there be any of the Valley left free of slag?" I said to my father.

"It was never allowed in my young days," my father said. "Laziness and bad workmanship, and cheapness, my son. But I am thinking more of you coming to be free. The slag is there, and nothing to be done about it."

"We have got a good solicitor for you, Huw," Mr. Gruffydd said, "so there is plenty of chance for you."

"I am not worried," I said, and strange, I was not. I had been feeling that strangeness in the belly as though a window was open down there, only to think of the court-house, and police, and a judge, and worst of all, of prison and bars.

But Bron had given me my hat before I left, and stood by the door to kiss me good-bye.

"Good-bye," she said.

We looked at one another, deep, deep we looked. And with suddenness I knew her loneliness, her grief, her wanting for Ivor, that she never showed by word or look. Women have their own braveries, their own mighty courageousness that is of woman, and not to be compared with the courage shown by man.

In that moment when I was full of thought for myself, with winds in chorus through the window in my belly, Bronwen had pity upon me, and in her pity, lost for only a little minute the shield of her courage, and I saw deep into her eyes and felt the emptiness behind there, and heard the voice calling in the silence, and felt the tears she wept when all of us were sleeping.

So shamed I was, that I wanted to drop down there and kiss her feet.

Well I know why the old ones put camel hair upon themselves and used the whip.

"O, Bron," I said, "only now I know."

Her face cracked in front of my eyes, and I could not bear to look.

Up at the mountain I looked, to the green, the blueness up there on top, to feel his hardness under my feet and his strong breath cold upon me, and then to pray for some of his peace, while Bronwen bled beside me.

"I am not afraid any more, Bron, my little one," I said, "but I am glad this came if only to know this. If I come back, I come back. And if I stay there, I stay. But back or stay, I am not afraid. I am only shamed. Good-bye, Bron."

I put my arm about the gentle warmth of her, and in her tears and softness, with lavender reaching into me to tear with claws, I kissed her cheek with a brother's kiss, and left her with my window tight shut and ready for the deaths of War. The bowmen at Agincourt were not colder to choose a shaft than I was to pull a bit of mignonette to wear in my buttonhole.

So into the trap and off, and with figs to everybody.

The court-house I never noticed. I had that feeling in me that you will have when a cut is to be stitched, or a burn to be scraped, when the doctor is threading the needle or honing his little knife. It is a blunting of feeling that you put upon yourself, after you have prayed for the strength to keep your mouth shut and be held from the shame of being a coward. As though you slept while you stood awake.

For long we sat on forms outside among crowds of people I knew. I smiled at them, and that was all.

Then, Evan John came to me, with his youngest brother to talk for him, for his chin was in thick bandage, and his eyes still swollen and sore with cuts.

"Huw," Dafydd John said, "Evan wants to say this is no doing of his. He is going in court only because he have been summonsed. He will say nothing."

"Thank you, Evan," I said.

"And he is sorry you had a fight and please to shake hands," Dafydd said.

"I am sorry, too, Evan," I said. "We have always been good friends. But I had to do it, see."

Evan shook hands and nodded a little bit, but even so such a nod gave him pain and he frowned, and smiled with his eyes.

"No case, then," Mr. Gruffydd said.

"Self-defence, if the colliery prosecutes," our solicitor said. "That will be our defence. The only danger to us will be the witnesses they call."

Mr. Esdras Daniels was a small man with a long moustache that curled right down to his chin, and then came back up again with another twist, like two broken circles, tight, both of them, with pomade. His hair was flat to his head and polished across his skull to hide the pinkness. Little black eyes he had, that looked at you as a shopman looks at you for size, but Mr. Daniels was measuring you for a bill to item, six and eightpence, with stamp, five shillings, and witness fee with expenses, and begged leave to remain your most humble and obedient servant, in copperplate script and a blur of purple ink.

"Morgan," a man in a black gown shouted, from a face that had its colour from a handling of pots. I passed by him while his mouth was slack, and knew.

Four old men on the bench up at the back, and that one on the end there, Abishai Elias.

"Up in the box," somebody said to me, and I went to a little space behind three sides of wood, while everybody shuffled feet and spoke in low voices, and book-covers flapped on desk-tops, just like school when the teacher has gone out for a moment.

I will never know to this day how the man who asked me to raise the Testament said the oath. In one long word he said it, and I gave him back my notion of what he said, only by relying on the sound it made to my ear, and repeating it. If I said the oath, it was not in my language, but nobody shall tell me that it was in English.

I swear by Almighty God.

Terror, there is, in the words.

Yet, in his mouth, and in mine, nothing, only a mess of oral sloth, shameful even from a baby.

After that, I went back in my sleep, again, and I was up

on the mountain with Dai Bando and Cyfartha, and with Shani down by the school, and with Ceinwen at the acting, anywhere with anybody, but firm in my mind not to make sense of the talk that I could hear going on all round me.

Only when I saw my father's hands on the back of the seat in front of him, and the shouting whiteness of Mr. Gruffydd's face, then, I opened my ears.

The other solicitor was talking to the Justices, and very graceful with a pencil between his fingers, with his little fingers like women will use them on teacups when somebody important is visiting.

"We apologize for having brought the case to court," he was saying, "but in the circumstances my client thought it necessary in the interests of justice. That our witnesses have decided not to testify is, I think, a tribute to the defendant's prowess. It is known that he is a crony of prize-fighters and others of the same kidney."

Mr. Esdras Daniels got up very quiet and bent forward to the Bench with a smile made by queen bees.

"Your Honour," he said, "is this preamble strictly necessary?"

"My friend must allow me to acquaint the court," Mr. Pritchard said and smiling to chide angels, "of the circumstances which force us to withdraw the summons, thus causing a great deal of inconvenience, and avoidable delay in a much-overworked court."

"Proceed, Mr. Pritchard," said one of the old men, and four heads nodded in a line.

"There is little more to be said," Mr. Pritchard said, with a shaking of the head, and speaking in the throat as though his breakfast was troubling him, "the unfortunate affair, as I have said, was caused by a reference to the defendant's sister, a married woman, and a well-known preacher. Doubtless the defendant felt himself obliged to defend the woman's name, and did so with savage cruelty, taking the law into his own hands, instead of calling upon the Law to come to his aid, and in a proper manner, demanding satisfaction in the High Court with a writ for slander, to be issued by the woman, or her absent husband, or by the preacher concerned. This was not done, nor has it been done. And to-day, through the intractability of witnesses, I am forced to ask the Court for permission to withdraw."

"I submit," said Mr. Esdras Daniels, up on his feet, and speaking as though he had just drunk deep of The Wrath, "that my client, and other innocent people, have been subjected to heaping indignities."

A tap with the hammer from the Bench.

"Dismissed," said the old voice, "no indignities, only shame. Shame, indeed. Dismissed. And not sure if we are right to dismiss, either."

Another man sitting below the four of them stood on his chair to talk to them quietly, while noise in court of boot and voice came louder. Mr. Daniels and Mr. Pritchard were having a little talk together, very happy, too, and a little laugh to finish, before to tie papers and give to a man with a sack behind them.

A tap with the hammer, and quietness.

"Dismiss," said the old man. "Next case."

"Outside," said the man in the gown to me, and out I went through crowds of staring faces.

Straight out to the trap, with my father and Mr. Gruffydd up in their seats, waiting.

"Home for the love of God," said my father, and Thomas whipped up.

Back into the wide greenness of the Valley we went, and not a sound all the way, with that feeling about as that you will have when a man has had a hurt and keeps a little smile on the mouth in case you look at him.

"Thank you, Thomas, my little one," my father said, when we were home.

"Nothing, man, nothing," Thomas said. "Good-bye now."

No word or look for Mr. Gruffydd, before he whipped up down the Hill.

"Will you come in for dinner, sir?" my father asked him, but looking at the house. I was looking at the cork lining inside my London hat.

Mr. Gruffydd put his hand on my father's shoulder and turned about, and went from us.

"O, God," my father said, with tears. "Come you in, and shut the doors, my son."

For the first time, our front door was shut tight in the daytime.

James Rowlands came round our back after dinner, and stood in the doorway. In his best, he was, with a straightness of face.

"Gwilym," he said, "meeting of deacons."

"O," said my father, "when, now then?"

"Now just," said James. "Are you coming?"

"Yes," my father said.

My mother was watching them both, in quiet, pale, with brightness in the eyes, but not of smiles.

"Well," my father said to her, and looked at her.

"Well," my mother said to him, and looked at him.

In that quietness they were speaking their own language, with their eyes, with the way they stood, with what they put into the air about them, each knowing what the other was saying, and having strength one from the other, for they had been learning through forty years of being together, and their minds were one.

"Good-bye, now," said my father.

My mother nodded, and he went.

That night, when I came home after a meeting with Ianto, Bron was waiting with my dinner.

"Mr. Gruffydd has been put from the Chapel," she said. "The deacons said he was unfit. Seven votes to three."

"Plenty more chapels," I said.

"Dada is leaving," she said.

"So am I," I said.

"And me," said Bronwen. "We will have a Split."

"With Mr. Gruffydd to preach and bring everybody from the Chapel," I said. "Leave the deacons by themselves."

"He is going in a sailing ship to Patagonia at the end of the month," she said. "He asked them to let him stay till then. But they said he was unclean. Mr. Isaac Wynn."

"What did Dada say?" I asked her, but not looking.

"Mr. Isaac Wynn is with vinegar plasters," she said, and trimming her words as with shears, "and your good father had a bit of an eye from somewhere."

"Good," I said. "Where is Mr. Gruffydd?"

"I took supper down to him, now just," she said. "He was putting sacking about the furniture. Ordered out by to-morrow, he is."

Ice threw itself upon me with redness.

The clock marched and marched and marched.

"I will go down to him," I said.

"To-morrow," Bron said, and put a hand on my head. "His supper is in that basket. No supper in Gethsemane, he said."

Chapter Thirty-Six

I WAS DOWN AT GORPHWYSFA early next morning, but Mr. Gruffydd was up and washed, and reading, when I knocked. The house was empty in sound, with roped bales and crates along the walls of the passage, and more piled in the middle of the room.

"Well, Huw," he said, with calmness, and no different from any other time, "I am glad you have come."

"Thank you, sir," I said. "You have done everything, then, and nothing I can do for you. I am sorry."

"There is, my little one," he said, and smiling. "A great service you may do for me. Will you?"

Well.

You shall only look, and try to move the stones.

He turned his back and went to look through the window.

"Do you remember the daffodils, my little one?" he said, and his voice with the lowness of wind from the north-east. "Mentor and pupil, we have been. But friends always. This furniture, that we made together, I want you to take to Tyn-y-Coed. I promised it."

Quietness again, and birds beginning to shout in the garden.

"I was wrong to call this room Gethsemane," he said, "I sullied the name. Blind and selfish and foolish, we are, at such times. We did that work with love in this room. We were happy here. Nothing wrong with the Garden, only me."

A blackbird putting loops and twists in his voice outside, and thrushes shouting in the grass, and blueness coming to the sky.

"I am only sorry to go, with nothing done," he said. "Sorry for nothing else. The idle tongues, the meannesses, the poverty of mind, are as much my fault as anybody's. Perhaps there will be good work to be done where I am going."

Ellis going by, and Mari the mare wanting a nail in her shoe.

"I am going this morning," he said, and Mari dancing among the deeps of his voice. "This watch my father gave me when I entered the Ministry. I would like to give you more. Take it, Huw. It has marked time that I loved."

Warm from his pocket in my hand, the smoothness of gold and glass.

"No need for us to shake hands," he said, and his voice riding winds and seas, and his back black in front of me. "We will live in the minds of each other, Huw, my little one. Good-bye, with love."

I went from there. With blood on my chin I went from there.

Up on the mountain I went, and stayed there with my face in the grass till the sun was hot on my back.

When I went down, Gorphwysfa was empty.

Place of Rest, well named.

The village was like a place of the dead for days afterward. People walked as though the skies might open and pour fire. Children were kept from the streets. A quietness was upon us.

My father was like a man in his sleep, but he had the sense to pay rent for a stable and buy paint and whitewash to clean it. We were down there every day till Sunday scrubbing and painting.

On Sunday morning we went to Chapel just the same. We said good mornings to the same people and passed them on the Hill as we had always done. But we turned to the right at the bottom of the Hill and went in to the stable, that was our new Chapel, and my father read the lessons.

The Split, we were.

Ten of us.

And for three-quarters of an hour we sat in silence, and the voice of Mr. Gruffydd, wherever he was, filled us again with courage, and with hope of a better world.

And his watch was in my hand, warm as when he gave it to me.

"Are you with us here this morning, Mr. Gruffydd?" my father said, with my mother's hand in his. "Lifting up our eyes to the hills, we are, see. As you said, so we do. Forever. God bless you. Yes. And, O God, give ease to the sore hearts this day. Amen."

"Amen," said we all.

"Let us sing a good hymn," my father said. "Let us

give our voices a good bit of work, now, before they will wash away."

So we sang, and I seemed to hear Mr. Gruffydd's basso as you will hear it from a choir, only to be heard if you bend your ear and listen well, and only then, if you know what to listen for.

As months went to winter, the Split came to have nearly a hundred people, and we bought the stables between us, and worked on it to make it a fitting place for the reading of The Book. Night after night we were down there, carving seats, and woodwork for the pulpit, and making doors, and paving the floor, until it was pleasure to go in there.

Even Dai Bando and Cyfartha helped with the masonry, for Dai could lay stones with the best, and no help needed to lift them, either.

"Huw," he said, one night, "come with us on Saturday, is it? Benefit for Cyfartha it is, and we want extra seconds. You have never been before. Eh, Cyfartha?"

"For a favour," Cyfartha said. "Dai is fighting, see."

"Dai?" I said, and in surprise, for he was coming to fifty in years, and a bit short in the lungs on top of the mountain, too.

"Needle match," Cyfartha said. "I am timekeeper. Willie Lewis is one second we can trust, see, and you are the other. Will you come?"

"If it is benefit for Cyfartha," I said, "I will come. What is the needle for?"

"Talking too loud," Dai said. "Big Shoni, it was. In the Three Bells."

But Big Shoni was taller, and broader even than Dai, a man with a loud voice who punched little men and drank their beer. Many times he had been hit across the head with pick-handles to teach him, but he was not the kind to learn. So many were afraid of him, and even in the colliery they kept friends, and gave him good places where he could fill trams with least trouble.

"Where will you fight?" I asked him.

"Over the mountain," Dai said.

"I will be with you," I said.

Chapter Thirty-Seven

I TOLD BRON where I was going, for I liked to be in the house early to tell the boys stories before to go to bed, and it was a long walk home, so I knew I would be early if I got in the house with daylight.

"Well," she said, with thinking, "as long as you will be safe, go, you."

"I will be safe, Bron," I said. "Sorry I am, not to tell them their story. But two on Monday, is it?"

"With a couple of sweets," she said.

Happy we were, in that little house, happy, indeed.

There had never been a word between Bron and me since the morning I had told her how shamed I was, and that feeling of shiver between us had gone, too. We were as though one, neither man nor woman, safe, solid, at peace.

There is strange to go from the quiet of home to a place where men go to enjoy themselves with sport. A change, they call it, and a change it is, indeed.

I had never been to a prize-fight before, so it was a life in another world, and a world I can rest quiet to see burnt.

The air was a stink of blueness, sharp with the heat of bodies, and with the weight of puddled beer drying into boards that never knew soap and water, and soured with tobacco spit.

Black and grey they huddled on benches, the sportsmen, with their faces red in rows, regular as match heads, one behind the other, every mouth wide, every eye wild, and their voices mixed in a thickness of sound, an untidiness of raw tone, without good thought or sense.

Born in the image of God, they were, every one of them, and some loving woman having pains of the damned to bring them forth, to sit there with their mouths open, like calves under the net in the market-place.

Enjoying themselves.

"Dai," I said, "I would go from here quick, if you and Cyfartha had another second."

"What is the matter, man?" Dai asked me, and bending to my ear, for the shouting was senseless.

"It is shame to bring good lungs in here," I said, "more shame to fight only to please these. There are better grazing in the fields."

"Sport this is," Dai said, in such surprise that you would laugh to see, "boxing, man. Do you want it in bloody Chapel, now then?"

"These men are in blood for money," I said. "To hell with it."

"To hell with you, too," Dai said. "Eh, Cyfartha?"

"Would you fight free, Huw?" Cyfartha asked me.

"Every morning for years with you," I said. "No money, and better sport than this. I will have a man in blood if there is a matter between us. But not for money. And not for these cattle, either."

"Let them hear you," Dai said.

"To hell with them," I said. "Am I afraid of worse than cattle?"

Dai looked at Cyfartha with pity and hopelessness.

"A second, mind you," he said. "Fighting two, I will be, to-night. Big Shoni and him, eh, Cyfartha?"

Cyfartha spat a full ten feet.

Two men were in the ring, tops bare, and belts about their trews. Small gloves they wore, but worse than the bare fist to punch, for the leather was frayed and it cut the skin.

I looked at the floor, for both of them were punching the life from each other, hit one, hit the other, no science, no brains, nothing, only fists landing flat on flesh to fetch blood bubbling, and bruises red.

A rare pleasure, indeed, and a sport, and please to hear the cattle bawling.

A boxer would have put both in their graves, and a riddance.

What is there in the spirit of man to make him earn his money by crushing the bones and drawing the blood of another, I shall never know.

I was sick to sit there, with that sound about me that stained the air when a Man sweated on a cross, and blood spurted upon the walls of Roman arenas, and flames took flesh from the legs of silent men.

Here with us still, the same sound, changeless.

"Come you," Cyfartha said, "our corner, this one by here. Bucket and bottle up there, quick."

You should have seen Big Shoni.

Six foot of him, solid, with muscle thick under fat, and smooth, without a hair on him. Big jaws he had, that seemed to come out of his chest without help of a neck, and his bald head coming to a point, like an egg, with scars across it, and little dents that were full of shadow. His eyes, it was, that gave fright, for they shone yellow in any light, and looking across at us, they seemed to be jewels of the devil put there to kill spirit.

"God is my life," Willie Lewis said to me, in whispers, "Old Dai must be from his senses to put foot in the ring. Look at that one, by there."

"Big he is," I said. "But Dai knows where to hit."

"I hope," Willie said, and meant. "If that one hits Dai, we will bury him on the way back. If you are having my opinion, see, old Dai have picked himself a burden, here."

"Bucket and bottle?" Dai said, and pulling on the ropes to come in, with a coat over his shoulders, and his legs in clean white breeches and stocking, with soft shoes.

"All here," I said.

He looked square at me while he rubbed his hands dry from the pickling tub. Each knuckle was like a little rock with him, and each hand bigger than both of mine, brown now, from the pickle that hardened them. Fists to put fear in you, especially with those pale eyes that watched you, without a blink from slits that never opened. Deadly, they were, with courage that knew nothing of doubt, little of worry, and less of powers beyond. A man whose world was fixed inside the things he knew, with the things he had done and seen, and having seen and done, he knew, and knowing, was unafraid, without desire to question further, or wish to have a reason.

"Cattle, then?" he said to me, in his high little voice.

"Look at them," I said, "only waiting to see you in blood. Hear them, then."

"Shouting for a win, they are," he said. "What is the matter with that?"

"Plenty," I said. "If you had friends here they would be stopping you, not shouting for a win. And friends of his would be sorry to see him having disgrace to fight a man half his weight."

"Me, half his weight?" Dai said. "What the hell do I care? I will hit him out in two rounds."

"Hear the cattle, then," I said.

"Men, they are," Dai said. "Come to see sport, man. What is wrong, Huw? Are you having fogs in the brains, with you? A good boy, I thought you, and hoping to see you earn a few sovereigns for yourself."

"Never," I said. "No money buys my blood, or pays me to take it from somebody else. Fight, yes. Prize-fight, no. Prostitution, it is."

Cyfartha rang his bell, then, and boots were busy on the floor to show impatience, and the cattle were shouting ready to be milked of lust to see pain plain on the faces of others, and bruises blemish the white polish of other flesh, and blood sticky about fists and chests and floor, and red and thick from crushed nose, and cut eyes, and broken mouths.

Eliel John, landlord of the Post Horn, with a belly curving almost to the knees, and thick in the moustache, was pushed up on the outside boards of the ring, and held on to a corner post, looking about the cattle with an eye soft with spirits, tearful with fellowship.

"Gentlemen," he said, and pulled home a breath to straighten himself, knowing himself at last to be an importance, and feeling inside himself a desire to show forth the qualities of dignity that oratory demands. "I am known to you all as a sportsman, I am hoping. Yes?"

"Yes," the crowd shouted, and other things.

"It is my proud duty, to-night, in this hall," he said, with a slow sweeping of his grey bowler hat, "where I am known to you all, every one of you, Eliel John, me, and my father, Enoch John, before me, always at the Post Horn, and no man have ever come in for a drink, thirsty and gone away empty, if no money to pay. Eliel John, me, and friends we are, all of us, and I would stand to the face of the devil and tell him. I love you all and you all love me."

"Yes," the crowd shouted, and some rudeness, too.

"So in this hall to-night, we are, all of us, good ones all, and working for our money," said Eliel John, coming to cry and his mouth like a cut in a ball under pressure from a thumb. "No thanks to anybody, only our work, and us. They can all go to hell, and I will fight anybody who says not."

His grey bowler hat fell from his hand, and he almost fell from the ring, but the arms propping his bottom saved him, and finding support there, he thought himself back in his seat, and sat, and more men had to come to help the others, with clapping and shouting from everybody, and Eliel looking about with tears, and bending his head left and right to give thanks, as though throned.

Then Cyfartha rang the bell again, and shouted to

Eliel to call the names for the fight. It took Eliel seconds to know he had forgotten what he had stood up to say, so Cyfartha went to shout in his ear, and the cattle were shouting to be heard in the south.

"Gentlemen," Eliel said, still sitting, "twenty-five rounds. Dai Bando, Shoni Mawr. A needle, it is, with a prize from the hat, and give plenty. Ten to one I am giving on Shoni to win."

The arms under him were tired and he sat back too heavily, and down he went on top of half a dozen as sober as he, with a shouting of laughing from all. Only two got up. Eliel was out, twenty stone of him, and not a breath in him, lying over three men with his mouth open and his face gone dark.

Cyfartha rang again, and Dai went out to touch Shoni's hand, stepping away to square up, with smoke coming from the oil lamps above them, and light having it hard to come through the shifting blueness to do its orange work upon them.

Shoni's yellow eyes were fast on Dai's. Bent in the legs and flat on his feet he went round and round, fists high, and moving only a bit. Dai was moving with his body, and sliding, one foot flat, up on the toes with the other.

Shoni's left straightened to show a ball of muscle behind his shoulder, but Dai's head moved, and his right shoulder swung forward to dig a hole in Shoni's fatness, and his left came over Shoni's shoulder to fill his eyes.

Nothing to be heard in the noise of voices.

Dai was following Shoni, moving slowly, watching.

Shoni was blinking one yellow eye, for the other was lost in tears and blood, with flesh swelling above and below. Dai's left straightened in a one, two, three, as quick as you could see, all on Shoni's nose.

Shoni swung his right and even in all the noise I heard it crack on Dai's head among his grey bristles, and Dai bent under it, as with the stroke of a hammer.

Shoni saw a hole in Dai's guard just below the jaw, and pulled back to brace himself, but in the moment even when his muscles were tight to pack behind the punch, Dai's left hit him full upon the mouth to take him off balance, and as he fell back, a right hook had him neat on the chin and the ring shook as he fell flat.

Dai came back to us for a lift of the bottle, and stood looking at Shoni's pair of men trying to put life in him.

But Dai's punching had done its work well. His shoulders, next to me, were like pale walls of stone shaped smooth by hammer and chisel into roundnesses, and lengths of broad cord, all of it hot, living muscle, yet hard to believe, even so close to the eyes.

All the time the cattle bawled, and money spoke from fist to fist in bets. Then Shoni was on his feet, dripping with water, and his face a mash of blood and bruise, one yellow eye alight, and fists up ready.

Cyfartha rang the bell again.

In went Dai, quickly, working over on Shoni's blind side, but Shoni had taken the advice from his men and stood his full six foot, far from Dai's left, out of danger from his right. They looked at each other for moments, still waiting, thinking what to do, while the cattle nosed the empty manger and tramped and called in greedy rage.

Dai knelt, not quite to the floor, but to have spring in his knees, and came up, left straight from the shoulder, both feet off the ground, seeming for a moment to hang in the air, legs wide apart, body upright, left fist in Shoni's bruises, right pulled back ready for the cross.

But Shoni took the left with only a shake of the head, and as Dai landed on his toes, a short right caught him on the jaw and hit him three paces off, flat, and looking to be out.

Willie ran with the bucket and I with the bottle. Willie made a knee and pulled him upright while I pulled his mouth open to push the bottle neck inside. Dai opened his eyes, but no light was in them, and he looked round him as one who wakes from sleep.

"Up, Dai," Willie was shouting, "up, man. You have got him, Dai, my little one. Keep on your feet. Leave flying to the angels, man. Got him, you have. Go in and kill."

But Dai never heard a word, I am sure. I was giving him the towel as fast as I could and watching for life to come back in his eyes. Life there was, but strange, as from far away, without light.

Without a ring from Cyfartha, and no word from one of us, Dai pushed Willie away from him and stood, pulling at his trews and hitting one fist into the other, ready.

We ran to the corner as the bell rang but before we were there they were into one another, and I turned, with fear to look.

Dai was bleeding from the mouth, and a right had

smashed his nose as I turned my head. Shoni was all shoulders, with his fists swinging from bent, tight arms, and as the fists landed, blood flew. Dai was standing with his head down, bent from the waist, with his fists against his chest, doing nothing.

Then he shook from top to toe, and turned to the side, trying to see through the blood that blinded him, but Shoni sent in a hook that had him on his heels with his hands going out to find something solid to hold.

Now hear the cattle.

Shoni looked at his corner and something of a smile came to change the look of his head, for he was happy, and ready to enjoy the rest of it with the cattle, taking his time, choosing the places to put his punches, in no hurry to come to the finish, for he knew, and the cattle knew, that Dai would stay down only when sense had left him. So from then on, see, good sport.

But Dai put out a hand and touched Shoni's forearm. Only a touch, only enough to tell him that he was touching Shoni's right forearm, and to give a marker where his head would be. As I watched him in wonder, his right swung over Shoni's shoulder, and the knuckles grazed Shoni's only good eye, cutting flesh away as though with a razor, leaving the bone white and filling, then, with blood, and Dai sending in a left to follow that missed by inches.

Shoni bent away with his hands to his face and blood dripping through his fingers. Dai came toward him, left arm out, not with a fist, but with fingers stretched to feel. Again he touched Shoni's shoulder, and quickly the fingers felt his face, and again the right came over, landing fair upon the muscle of the jaw, and Shoni went over sideways through the ropes.

I was in the ring and over to Dai before he had dropped his hands, but behind him, I went, for the eyes were still with nothing in them, and the fingers trembling to feel for Shoni's flesh, and the right arm ready with its ram of pain.

"Dai," I shouted, close in his ear, "Dai. It is Huw. Drop your hands. It is finished."

"Finished?" he said, and coming to look at me. "Am I out, then?"

"No, no," I said, and busy with the bottle. "Spit now, Dai. You have won, man."

He spat, and his only tooth fell out in a froth of blood, and hopped across the boards.

Cyfartha came running to push me yards, taking Dai by the shoulders and holding him close.

"Dai," he was crying, with tears, "Dai. Cyfartha, I am, my little one."

Dai's hands patted Cyfartha, with the short thicknesses of his fingers held apart, as they might have beaten against the breast of his mother.

"Will we carry him?" I asked Cyfartha.

"Yes," he said. "Let us have him home, quick."

"Did I give a good fight?" Dai said, and looking up at the roof.

"You had him out," Willie said. "Still out, he is."

"Good," Dai said, and quiet as a cat, with the life of him hot behind his quietness. "Something have come to my eyes, Cyfartha."

But Cyfartha was crying against the corner post, so Willie and me joined hands to carry Dai to our stool, and empty a couple of buckets over him.

A journey not to be forgotten, that one over the mountain, after the fight, and Dai with a hand on my shoulder, blinded now by spirits to take away the pain, and Cyfartha quiet drunk and savage against the world.

With the whiteness of the moon cold upon us we went, but I was colder to think of the mind behind me that kept a hand fast on my shoulder with the grip of one in fear of the Pit.

"I will have him," Cyfartha said, when we got in sight of the village.

"Let me see you safe home," Willie said, but fearing, and his eyes big.

"I am with eyes," Cyfartha said, savage in the voice, and ready to hit. "Go from here."

"Good night, now," I said. "I will see you to-morrow morning."

"Go to hell," Cyfartha said. "You will see to-morrow. Shall Dai?"

So home Willie and me went, and Cyfartha holding Dai to him and talking to him as a mother.

·   ·   ·   ·   ·   ·   ·

Everybody said Dai's blindness was punishment for his wicked ways, and because I was there, I was thought to be part of a scheme, planned by God, in His mercy, to teach sinners a lesson in the workings of the Will.

Of course, the Split was blamed too, and we lost nearly twenty people who feared that something might be happening to them for staying away from a proper house of prayer to go and pray in an old stable.

Cyfartha took Dai to Cardiff to see a doctor, but some gentle little thing at the back of his eyes had been ruined by the punch, and though he came to see more and more as the weeks went, he never saw his share again.

So between them, with their savings, they bought the Three Bells, and lived there, Dai to serve all day, Cyfartha working his shift as usual and helping behind the flap at night.

Only once, in all their years together, Dai left his chair in the bar to go out and down to the mine with his working clothes on.

Once, only once.

A time to live again, indeed.

Chapter Thirty-Eight

I DID WELL in those years I had as master carpenter. From all over the Valley they came to me for doors and frames and solid works in wood. Our back at Bron's, and behind here, was like a woodyard at one time. Four men I had, and a couple of boys, to learn, in the end.

I think we were happy, then.

I wonder is happiness only an essence of good living, that you shall taste only once or twice while you live, and then go on living with the taste in your mouth, and wishing you had the fullness of it solid between your teeth, like a good meal that you have tasted and cherished, and look back in your mind to eat again.

Two men were after Bron with flowers and sweets. Matthew Harries and Gomer James were a couple of good men, indeed, and now that I think of them, it was something to the credit of Bron to have two like them after her, though we never thought so at the time, of course.

How strange is the way we live.

Bron and me had lived in that house for years, until the boys had grown out of stockings, before we had a single serious talk.

Ever after that time when I went to court we had been deep friends, but whenever the talk seemed to be nearing

rocks, I went from the room or thought to speak of something else.

Firm I made my mind not to be cause of more worry to
her, and firm I was.

Bron was firm, too, in her own way, and because I was
working hard, and the boys took her time, there were only
a few minutes in all those weeks of days, when we were
alone together and quiet enough to be able to think.

It is only then, when there is time to let the mind play
free, that trouble comes to you. Even in the middle of
sawing a plank, I often thought of Ceinwen, but she had
gone and nobody knew where. Many times I went over to
see Mervyn, but he knew nothing, and seemed shamed to
speak of her. Then they went to open a coalyard somewhere and nothing was left of the family, so all I could
have of Cienwen was in my mind, and I kept her there as
men keep libraries of rare books, seldom to be touched but
happy to know you have got.

Then came the night when Matt Harries asked Bron to
marry him.

I came home from supper with my mother and found
Bron in the rocking-chair, sewing forgotten, looking at the
door, for as I opened it she looked straight at me.

"Well," I said.

"Well," she said.

"No supper to-night, then?" I asked her, for the table
was with flowers.

"Supper in plenty," she said, and smiled shy. "How
would you like Mrs. Bronwen Harries?"

Now that the question was with me flat, I had feelings
of ease to think that I could see her go with nothing only
sorrow, for she seemed to have my youngness with her,
and all my earliness, that it was pain to lose. No longer
had I jealousy, for I knew that the world of Bron was not
my world, that it would be a foreign place, and I a
stranger, unhappy there.

"If you like him better than Gomer," I said. "Good."

"Would you be glad to send me off, Huw?" she asked
me, but with nothing in her voice.

"No," I said, and busy with a thread in the tablecloth,
"I will be sorry to see you beside any other man, though."

"Why?" she asked me.

"It seems wrong for another man to have life near you,"
I said, "or to be busy in your mind for another."

"Why?" she asked again, but with warmness coming in her voice.

But it is beyond the reach of man to tell why, and so I felt, then.

For as men have fists and heads to defend themselves, so women have a gentleness of silence about them, a barrier built of things of the spirit, of pain, of quiet, of helplessness, of grace, of all that is beautiful and womanly an equal part, given to them because they are women in defense of their womanness. And this barrier a man will find against him to turn aside his male attack, keep his arms pinned, stop his mouth, cool his eyes, reduce his heat and restrain his idle imaginings. This barrier it is that women who are women keep always at a height, coming from behind it only when, with knowledge and in light, they trust. You shall see it in their eyes.

And I knew that Bronwen trusted me at my word, but Matthew Harries she trusted as a man. The two were different, and the difference caused me hurt, and yet was a loveliness in itself, for there is honour in a trusting upon the word alone, and a strange delight in thinking that only a word will hold so much in check.

"You are Bronwen," I said. "No other reasons."

"The law is against us marrying," Bron said, with quiet.

I looked at her, and found her eyes full of the shinings of tears and her head on the side, gently, as though she would bless me, and her mouth soft, to shake, and her hands tight together in her lap.

"Long we have been together, Bron," I said, "and God love the dear day. But never mind about the law, it would be wrong. You are not for me as wife, and I am not for you."

"So I knew," she said, with tears, "but you are sweet comfort to me only to have you near. Like Ivor you are, see, and in you I see him. In your voice I hear him. Your eyes are like his. You put your boots on as he did. Tie your tie. Put your hair."

Then I knew that there can be sin in the world, and sin so vile that words will not dishonour themselves by coming forward to describe it.

I had thought our silence, our feeling to be the same, born of the same fear, a fear of touch that might lead to union.

But now I was filled with ashes to know that Bron had been keeping the barrier at its strongest only to turn me aside, for she had known what was in my mind, and had suffered it only because in me she saw my brother, and the likenesses were dear to her, and she longed for them, and was brave, without fear, ready to withstand what was really me only to have those little things in me that were in the likeness of Ivor.

O, the love of woman is a glorious thing, and strange in its ways of work.

I thought of her looking at me tying my boots, and seeing Ivor, and watching me do my hair, and seeing Ivor, and hearing me sing, and the pains of knives in her to think of Ivor, and all the time she looked and watched in hungriness, I had thought her to be thinking as I was.

Sin, a blackness of sin, to be thrown in a cess of disgust. Iscariot and his rope were near me as I sat there that night.

"Bron," I said, and not seeing her, "you know why I was shamed?"

"Yes," she said, with her smile that was not a smile. "But no harm."

"Why?" I asked her. "Supposing I had been a fool?"

She looked into the fire and there was quietness, except the kettle whistling to tell us that he was too hot, and please to take him off, or he would burst and rust the stove. So I took him off, and knelt beside Bron, with warmth for her, but with coolness in me, and strange, restful it was, to take her hand and feel for her only the love of the heart.

"Well," she said, soft, and with regret, but with smiling that was half of crying, "I suppose I would have been a fool, too."

"For Ivor's sake?" I said.

"Who is to know?" she said. "For Ivor, yes, to think him back again. But I was sorry for you, too. So lonely. And always so kind to me. It is a little thing to do for some."

"Then why did you know it would be wrong to marry?" I asked her, in wonder.

"O," Bron said, and moved her head, "Ivor was strong, I suppose. And I was afraid. Eleven years older than you, I am. You are young. And you think beyond me."

"But why afraid?" I said.

She looked at me with calmness, and I saw my mother in her.

"Have you been with a girl, Huw?" she asked me.

"Yes," I said.

"Who?" she asked me, and looking again in the fire.

I was quiet, for I was unready to break the peace of the world I had found up on the mountain.

"Ceinwen Phillips," she said, as though I had answered. I said nothing.

"O, Huw," she said, and put her arm about me. "There is sorry I am."

"Why?" I asked her.

"Why, why, why," she said, and with laugh. "All your life, why. This time because it is pain to think of innocence in ruin."

"But I found it beautiful beyond life," I said.

"Yes," she said, and smiled, and O, to see Bronwen smile. "Beautiful, indeed. Ivor said the same to me."

"That is why we cannot marry," I said, and stood up. "Ivor found his world with you. Shall I bring strangeness to you, and trample where he lives still? Let the law be wise."

"But, Huw," she said, with something of hurt, "what is this world Ivor had, then?"

"The one we find with a woman," I said, but in shame to speak of it, because in words it sounded foolish. Ordinary things like teapots may be talked about because we know them and they are solid under the hand. But to talk of the world that is hidden in every woman is a journey of pain, for the words are not in use to tell of it, and to use the words that are is only a hopping on uneven crutches.

"What world is it, Huw?" she asked me, and sat up straight to hear.

"O, Bron," I said, "I only know it is with me. Only for a little we live, and feel ourselves truly alive, with truth, then the Angel with a flaming sword comes to slash us out. Beauty and music, there is. I am a fool."

"No, indeed," she said, and gentle. "But I also have a world, is it? And I will have whoever I say to share it. Ivor it was, first, because I said Ivor and nobody else. You, it would have been second, if I had said yes. But neither of you if I had said no."

So Bronwen showed me more of the strength of woman,

which is stronger than fists and muscles and male shoutings. For now, instead of thinking about her as guardian of a world denied to me, and foreign to me because it belonged to another, I was made to think of her in truth and verity as owner and possessor, with right of denial and sanction over all, as equal sharer, and with right to say who and when, according to her will and none other.

And she was bigger in my eyes, with more of respect, for she had responsibility and I had none. Her strength had kept me from her, her will had prevented me, her spirit had triumphed. Mine was the emptiness of one who waits at gates locked beyond his vision, flattering himself that he waits at an open fairway out of respect, not to disturb, and then, essaying entry, marches forward with boldness only to break his nose upon the unseen steel.

The world I had shared with Ceinwen was as much her own as mine, and the world Ivor had known was Bronwen's as much as his. It was a death to me to think of Ceinwen as possessor, and with right to allow another man to share.

But if I had the right to think of the world with Bron, there was no reason to deny the right to Ceinwen of sharing with another man.

I died, but I lived again.

"Huw," Bronwen said, "did you think of children?"

"What children?" I asked her, as though pulled from darkness.

"Children," Bron said, and gentle, watching me as though with pity. "Ivor had two sons."

Still I was dense, for there are times when the mind is far away, and words are only a tracing of sound, meaningless.

"Gareth and Taliesin," I said, "and fine boys, indeed. They would laugh to have me for a father, or even fosterfather."

"But supposing you were a father, Huw," she said, "what, then?"

So surprised I was that she laughed at me.

"Do you expect to find this world of yours," she asked me, "without to become a father?"

"O God, Bron," I said, and a coldness coming to make me shake and freeze inside the brain. I could feel the pinch of whiteness in my face, and in my ears the voice of Mr. Gruffydd. "Ceinwein."

She looked at me straight, and the lines in her forehead and above her eyes smoothed out as though a hand had passed across.

"Have you heard?" she asked me.

"I have asked plenty of times," I said, and with soreness in the throat, "but she has gone. I never once thought. Never once these years. There is a swine I am. There is a swine."

"But just now, see, a world of beauty and music," she said, "then, a swine."

"A responsibility," I said, hearing a deep voice, "in beauty and majesty beyond words."

"Mr. Gruffydd," she said, simple, quick.

"He told me," I said, "and I forgot. Witlessness, he said. Good God, Bron, what is the matter with us that we act like fools instead of men?"

"The beauty and music," she said, and looking in the fire again. "It is a call, Huw. And some are not strong."

"Do you feel it, Bron?" I asked her.

She smiled at the fire, and was quiet, and her fingers turned and turned her wedding ring.

"Yes," she said.

I looked at the kettle, to have rest from the mysteries piling one on the other, for he was black with work, and puffing fat cheeks, ready to go about his business any moment of the day, with a will and always at his best, wanting only a drop of water, a little fire, and he would boil and blow and spit like a good one.

I envied him his simple life, and then was ashamed again, for I was a man, with responsibility, though with little thought for it, and he only a kettle, yet doing his job and living his life, a kettle, nothing but a kettle, born in the image of a kettle, pretending to be nothing else, and on his mark every moment, to carry out his responsibilities as a kettle.

But I was born in the image of God, a man, creator, with power of life and death, a father, blessed with the gift of the seed of Adam, a sower of seed, to bring forth generations of new lives.

This I was, and envying a kettle.

"There is strange to talk like this," she said. "I would have blushed to burn a little while ago. Now it is nothing. But glad I am your mother is from here. She would think little of me, indeed."

"I will think more of you," I said, and kissed her cheek, "and you will marry Matt Harries, is it?"

"I will think," she said, and got up to get the tea caddy. "The boys will have nothing to do with him. And so kind to them he is, too."

"Jealous, they are," I said.

She looked sideways at me, smiling, and then I was coming to blush again, and ready to hit my head on the door for being such a fool.

"Are you jealous, Huw?" she asked me.

"No," I said.

"Sure?" she asked me.

"Sure," I said, for I could feel Ivor warm about us, and all round Bron, and the thought of him steady beside her filled me high with pity. For gone though he might be, she still was blessed by him, for he was about her, near to her, part of her, with her in and out of sleep, and to think of putting a kiss upon her, then, with anything more than the love of the heart was a hollowing, deep disgust.

"How do you know?" she asked, with a bit of hurt, as though I was not giving her respect. "Am I ugly, then?"

"O, Bron," I said, and went to her, but she turned her back, that was straight as boards, slim, a perfection of rest for a right arm, "not ugly, only sacred, you are. So plain it is now. How could I be jealous? If I was a fool with you, what would be the end? I would cut my throat from shame."

"Why would you be a fool, and where is the shame?" she asked me, cold, resting her hands on the caddy, and staring wide at me. "Am I somebody from the gutter?"

I looked at her for long, trying to find the words, but they sounded so hurtful that I feared to open my mouth.

"Look, Bron," I said. "One man, one woman, is it?"

"Yes," she said, but ready to say no.

"Ivor and you," I said. "He has gone, but you are here. Yet, for me, he is still with you. You and he are one. To see you is to see him. To touch you is to touch him. To think of you is to think of him. He is about you like lavender. His hands touched you, his mouth kissed you. He was with you and used your flesh for his sons. Where is there place for me?"

"But, Good God in Heaven," Bronwen said, and whiter than I had ever seen her, and staring to put you in fear, "am I a belonging, then? Bronwen Morgan I am, but the

Morgan only because I said so. Ivor is still Ivor with me, and our sons upstairs to tell you so. But what right have you to make me property? Am I an old den of house, then, with a sign outside? Stop to think like a fool, man, and have a cup of tea."

Well.

I shut my mouth, and had my cup of tea, silent, thinking, watching Bron, but unwilling to talk again, for it was like a tangling of ropes that one moment you think you have got straight, and the next is a despair of knots to try patience and drive you mad. I think I felt a bit of hurt, too, that my fine feelings had been kicked in the ash tub, where they belonged, no doubt.

"I will marry nobody," Bron said, with quiet. "And that will settle it. But no more nonsense, is it?"

"No," I said.

"Good," she said, and lit her candle. "Good night, now."

"Good night," I said.

I sat, and she went upstairs lightly as she always had, and across the landing to the front bedroom.

For the first time I heard the key turn stiff and sore in the door.

Dai Bando never hit a man harder.

Eh, dear.

For long after that, the feeling was between us again, but this time not happily as it had been before, but with more of resentment, until I thought I would have to leave the house only to have peace for us both.

A horrible feeling, it is, to know you are a burden in body and spirit to somebody dear to you.

Matt Harries cured it, and quick.

Fair hair, he had, curly, and parted with neatness, and a good moustache the colour of his hair, always pulled tidy but never greasy. A good grey eye, he had, too, that looked at you straight and with deepness not to be denied.

"Huw," he said, one day out in the back here, "shall I say something?"

"What, now?" I said, and into my pockets for a bit of pencil.

He was handling a chip of mahogany, pulling bits off, and watching the wind have them.

"You will have to hold the temper," he said, and the greyness of his eyes sober upon me.

"What, then?" I asked him, and stood to face him.

"Bronwen," he said, but quiet, as though in shame to say the name.

"Well?" I said, coming to be impatient.

"There is talk," he said, with tongs pulling the words from him.

"O," I said. "For what?"

"You," he said, and a spinning quietness came to draw tight about us.

"Me, what?" I asked him, but somebody else talking.

"You and Bron," he said, but with pleading and softly. "I know it is all lies, Huw. But there you are. They say Gomer and me are out because you are in."

"Who have you heard?" I asked him.

"My mother told me," Matt said, "and she had it in the market weeks and weeks since. She was out of patience with me, and it came out, sudden, see."

There is blind we are at times in our lives, sometimes over years and years.

How I could have imagined Bron and me could live in the same house day in and day out for years on end, both of us grown, with only two boys in the house beside us, and go free of the evil of people's minds, well, there, I cannot tell.

I must have been mad all the time.

For people with little sewage systems in their minds are only waiting for a man to live in the same house as a woman, and then starts the stench, and the bigger the system, the more the stench, until it is wonder that they are not rotten from the poison, and ready for their graves.

"Keep your ears open," I said, "and I will keep mine. And if he is a man, Christ help him. If it is a woman, we shall see."

I went straight and told Bron, and she smiled, a bit at first, and then, full on her face, the old, old smile that only Bron could smile.

"I knew, boy," she said. "For months. Years."

"You knew?" I asked her, "and no word to me?"

"Did I want a murder, then?" she said, and laughing. "No, boy. Let them talk. They are not even worth spit."

"You are worth more than spit to me," I said.

"What harm?" she said. "I am still as I was. You are still as you were. Talk, that is all it is. Nothing more to do, so talk."

"Let me catch anybody," I said. "I will tear the tongues from their throats."

"Leave it, now," she said, and a hand on my arm, very pretty in the eyes.

So I kissed her, and went out, and up on top of the mountain to have peace, for I had a grudge that was savage with heat against everybody, and only up on top there, where it was green, and high, and blue, and quiet, with only the winds to come at you, was a place of rest, where the unkindness of man for man could be forgotten, and I could wait for God to send calm and wisdom, and O, a blessed ease.

Chapter Thirty-Nine

UP THERE IT WAS, on that day, that I knew teeth of fear.

I was coming back, empty of anger, and ready to let tongues have their way, when I saw men working to put up tipping piers from the colliery to the top of the mountain directly behind our house, and all the other houses on the Hill.

"Good day, Lewis," I said to the foreman. "What is this, then?"

"Slag tip," he said. "Up the top here."

"But it will roll down on top of us," I said.

"In time to come, I suppose," he said, but not taking much notice. "Years, yet."

"Years?" I said. "They have got no right. Those are our homes down there."

"Go on, man," he said. "Where the hell will the slag go, then? If you want to work, the slag must come out. If it comes out it must have a place to go. So there, you, and here it is."

No use to blame him.

Useless to curse the men, or their work, or the steel struts they were bolting together to carry deadness to the mountain.

I went to see my father, but he only nodded and wiped his glasses.

"Yes," he said.

"We must do something, Dada," I said. "Quick."

"What?" he asked me, with quiet. "The slag must go somewhere. They can only do the best they can. If they keep it underground as they used to do, it will have to come from the wages of the men. While they are piling slag, they cannot be cutting coal. One of the two. So the mountain it is, for the sake of wages."

"Who sold the land?" I asked him. "Jones the Chapel?"

"No," he said, "he sold it long ago."

"Who, then?" I asked him. "If we know we might get him to sell to all of us on the Hill."

My father smiled and scratched his head.

"Go and see Abishai Elias," he said. "He is the owner. Or was. It belongs to the colliery, now. So does all the mountain land, excepting only our land on the Hill."

"A hiding without a fight," I said.

"Yes," my father said. "For the women and children. Leave it, my son."

I almost hated my father, then, but I saw what he was afraid of doing and I had sympathy, for however hard we fought, we must be beaten by empty bellies. The rights of man are poor things beside the eyes of hungry children. Their hurts are keener than the soreness of injustice.

But then Davy had more trouble, and our minds were busy with him until he was out of it. By that time the tip was built and working, and we could only look up at it with our hands on our hips and curse it, and hope for the hate of Satan to fall on old Elias.

Davy had been back only a few weeks when it happened. My father had spoken for him to start work in his pit, and down he went, gladly, and Wyn was happier than she had been for years, for she was tired of going from one place to another, and wanted a home, and for once in his life he listened to her.

One morning I met him coming up the Hill off the night shift, and even under his dust I could see his anger.

"What, now?" I asked him.

"They have paid me short," he said. "Working to the waist in water all week, with the boy, and short to-day."

"How about the minimum?" I asked him.

"They said no," he said. "But I will have a reckoning."

He was not allowed to join the shift on Monday because he had written a letter to the manager.

"Right," said my father. "Let us have a solicitor, and put them in Court. Or the men will come out and more trouble."

Over the mountain we went, and found a solicitor, a

young man, not very happy to take the case because he had thoughts for the future, and he knew, and we knew, that the colliery could starve him out.

"Right you are," he said. "Leave it to me."

We left it, and the days and weeks went, with appearances in Court before justices, and commissioners for oaths, and swearings of affidavits, and all the drawn-out painfulness of law cases.

And money going out, and going out, and going out.

"Never mind, my son," my father said to Davy. "If it costs the last sovereign, the last stick, and the last brick of this house, we will have them before a Judge. And all their slipperiness shall not avail them in the day of judgment. There was a bargain struck, and they shall keep it as we have done."

The day of the hearing came, and notices were given to Davy with the arms of the King upon them.

"At last," my father said, and pointed with his pipe to the arms. "Here is a sign, see. As the devil loves the cross, so do rogues love this. Now you shall see another bolting of swine."

But when we got to the court our solicitor was standing in the front, in the big hall that was dark with the rain outside, waiting for us with impatience, and shaking in the hands with anxiousness.

"Settle with them," he said, almost in whispers, and looking about to see if any were listening. "Be sensible, Mr. Morgan. They are powerful. They can take the case as far as the House of Lords if they want to, and break you on the way."

My father's fists struck into Mr. Vaughan to hold him by the coat as a hawk strikes into a mouse.

"Look," he said, with splinters of glass in his voice, and his eyes two inches from the little green onions of Mr. Vaughan, "we have come here for a hearing after months. House of Lords or House of God, go in by there and start to make your case, before I will take the bones piecemeal from your carcass.

"Yes, sir," said Mr. Vaughan, and swallowed a small town, and picked up his papers, and went in, with little steps, like a girl going to meet her other mother for the first time.

A good, big place, the Court, with a smell of books, and ink made from powder, and soft coal smoke.

Up on the high place was the Judge with a robe of blue and red, and grey hair to his shoulders very tidy, and looking as though he was willing to go to his grave before to hear any more of the silliness of men.

Our case was called among the first, and a solicitor stood up to put the colliery case. Detail after detail was read out of Davy's past life, about his activity as a firebrand, and his discharge, and the generosity of the colliery in having him back again through the good offices of his father.

"What has this to do with the claim?" the Judge asked, as though clean sand had just been dusted on the floor of his mouth.

Eh, dear.

The question had everybody in fits down in front, with whispers and frowns, and little men running on tiptoe with pieces of paper one to another, and the Judge looking at the end of his pen over the top of his spectacles.

"My clients claim," the solicitor said, "that there is no basis for a claim. The man was paid the wage that he received, which we admit is below the minimum wage, because in the manager's estimation he was incompetent. That estimation will be borne out by witnesses."

If you had seen my father's face.

Davy sat stone-still, arms folded, as man after man we knew well, went into the witness box and swore that Davy was an incompetent workman. And him sitting there, watching them.

And Mr. Vaughan doing nothing, except a bit of a smile here and there to the solicitor on the colliery side.

"Might we hear the claimant?" the Judge asked into the air, to nobody, as though he spoke to hear his voice.

More running down in front, and Mr. Vaughan looking far from happy when he looked at Davy to take his place in the little box near the Judge.

"How are you going to prove to the Court's satisfaction," the Judge said, direct at Davy, and I thought, with something of kindness, "that you are, in fact, a competent workman, and entitled to be paid the minimum wage allotted to that class of man?"

Davy looked very good in his best black suit, indeed.

"I have been working since I was twelve, Your Honour," he said.

The Judge's greyness shook quickly from side to side, and his glasses flashed in the light of the lamps.

"You may have worked for fifty years," he said, "but still be lacking in competency. How can you prove your claim?"

My father gave me a dig with his elbow that almost took me from the world with fright.

"The dockets," he said, in whispers, with fire burning high in his eyes. "The dockets, man. Where are they, with you?"

Thank God for a lifetime of tidiness and order in the home, for every pay docket we had ever had was on the file, all of us, from the first week's pay we had ever drawn.

I stood up with the files heavy in my arms, and Davy's eyes came off the Judge to look at me, for he had seen my movement, and all in Court heard me make a way through the benches toward the front.

"What is this man doing?" the Judge asked.

"My brother, Your Honour," Davy said. "With proof of competency. Those are the amounts I have drawn every week since I started work."

One docket after another the Judge turned over, and for quiet minutes there was only the voice of crispness in paper to be heard.

Then the Judge looked at Davy, and down at the solicitor.

"Can anybody tell me," he said, "how a man can earn three and four times, and even more than six times, as much as the amount of this claim, over a period of years in the same colliery, and still be held as an incompetent workman?"

No answer from anybody, but the air going to shrivel about us.

"Apparently not," said the Judge. "In my view, on evidence provided by the company in its own pay dockets, the plaintiff establishes beyond doubt that he is a competent workman, and therefore is entitled to receive the minimum wage as provided under the agreement. The claim is allowed, with costs."

I am only sorry that we were not allowed to shake the Judge's hand, and then dance on the desks.

It was late before we had supper that night, for people were coming from all the other valleys to cheer my father and Davy, and shake their hands, and call them true men. My mother stood to watch, holding her chest with one hand and putting tucks in her apron with the other, pretending to smile.

She knew, and my father knew, that there were two sides to every face.

"Make your minds firm," my father said to us, while my mother and Olwen were washing up. "To-day is the last of us in this Valley. If I am spared, I have got a couple more years' work, and then finish, me. Ianto is in iron, and Huw is in wood. What will you do, Davy, my son?"

"I will have my share of the box, Dada," Davy said, "and I will go to New Zealand. Wyn's father will come with us."

"You could go to your good brothers in the United States," my father said, but with weakness in his voice, for he knew his answer.

"New Zealand," Davy said, with nothing in his voice or face.

"Not charity, my son," my father said. "But I will be happy to know you are close together. They are your brothers."

"New Zealand, Dada," Davy said.

"Good," said my father.

"Dada," Ianto said, "I am going too, I am sorry to say."

In the dark pane of the window I saw my father shut his eyes.

"You too, Ianto, my son?" he said, with stiffness. "To New Zealand, then?"

"No, Dada," Ianto said, and looking up at Davy's jersey, "to Germany. There is a German over at the works there, now, and he says I could have a better job with him. So I will go. There is nothing in front of me here."

"Say nothing to your Mama," my father said. "Let this day be over, first."

We sat still, looking at the floor, and the walls, and the furniture, but not at one another, and we dare not look at my father, for he was fighting rivers.

"Shall we read a chapter, my sons?" he asked us, in a little while, and Davy was up quick to fetch the Book.

"What shall we have, Dada?" he said, with the thickness of guilt and black leather ready on his knee, and his fingers hooked in the pages.

"Isaiah, fifty-five," my father said. "Ho, every one that

thirsteth, come ye to the waters, and he that hath no
money, come ye, buy and eat. Yea, come, buy wine and
milk without money and without price."

And while Davy read, my mother came to sit by my
father, and Olwen sat on the floor with her arm on his
knee, and her face on her arm, and his hand was on her
head nearly hidden in her hair, and his other hand lay
in my mother's lap, with her hands tight about it.

Chapter Forty

IANTO AND DAVY went away together, for Ianto knew
that two good-byes would be hard on my mother, and
Germany sounded just as far as New Zealand to her.

I crated all Davy's furniture, and made boxes with
baize linings for the crockery, but it was a job of sadness
for me. Every tap of the hammer seemed to send him
farther away.

One morning they stood before my mother with their
coats on their arms and their hats in their hands, and
the clock telling them to leave home.

"Well," my mother said, and took off her apron to
show her best black silk.

"Well, Mama," Ianto said, and smiling a big one, but
having it hard with his voice.

"Off, now, again then?" my mother said, smiling too,
with her hands busy to puff the sleeves of her dress.

"Yes, Mama," Ianto said and rubbing his hat with the
cuff of his coat, though Olwen had brushed it to smoothness only a minute before.

"And you, Davy," Mama said, with her hands quiet.

"Yes, Mama," Davy said, and putting another knot in
his parcel of sandwiches and cake, looking at nobody.

"Will you write?" Mama asked them, high.

But they said nothing, and I looked out of the door and
down the Hill.

The kitchen was full of the speech of my mother's eyes,
but quiet except for the clock.

"Well," my father said. "Shall we have a move?"

More quiet, and Olwen coming to cry.

"Good-bye, Mama," Ianto said.

"Good-bye, Mama," said Davy.

But my mother had no good-bye for them, but only the

sound of her kiss, the little sound her kisses made, that were dry upon the cheek.

Ianto went first, and Davy after, and then my father, and the people on the Hill looked up at the mountain, and down at the pit, but not at them when they waved good-byes, for Ianto had his arm about Davy's shoulder, and my father was standing in the middle of the street giving them a start, and a chance to button their coats.

My mother went to sit on the stool by the fire with the work-basket close to her feet. She never mended socks before the peace of the afternoon, but she could never sit still and do nothing, so while her good boys went from her she sat to think of them, but I never saw her so round in the shoulders or slower to thread a needle.

And Olwen piled the breakfast plates as though it was their fault her brothers were off down the Hill.

With my atlas I tried to show my mother where her children had gone. I drew pencil lines from us to Owen and Gwilym across the Atlantic, and to Angharad down there in Cape Town, and to Davy in New Zealand, and to Ianto in Germany.

She looked at the page with her head back as though it had a smell, and sideways with the eyes, holding the book with loose fingers, not anxious to see, distrustful of what she saw, and ready to stop her ears against what I was telling her. She wanted to listen to nothing, and see nothing that might bring to her more coldness of the heart than their going had given her.

For she thought of them all as she thought of Ceridwen, only just over the mountain, to be seen any time of the day with only a good walk there and back.

"What is this old spider, now then?" she asked me, and not even putting on her glasses to see.

"One line from us to Owen and Gwil," I said, pointing it for her. "Down here to Angharad. Over there to Ianto, and down by here to Davy and Wyn. You are like the Mother of a star, Mama. From this house, shining all that way across the continents and oceans."

"All that way," my mother said. "Goodness gracious, boy, how far, then, if they can have it all on a little piece of paper?"

"Only a map, it is, Beth," my father said, and a wink

to me to be quiet. "A picture, see, to show you where they are."

"They are in the house," my mother said, flat. "And no old pictures, and spiders with a pencil, if you please."

"Yes, my lovely girl," my father said, and I put my atlas away.

It was a blessing that Ianto and Davy went then, for they would have been in trouble sure if they had waited for the end of the year.

"It is coming, Huw," my father said, as a man will look at a rain cloud and wonder if there is time to go back for his coat. "This time it will be worse than ever. I have told your mother to prepare for a bad winter. But thank God your good brothers are from here. I was always worried from my life in case they landed in jail."

I think my mother was glad, too, for that fear had always been near to her, and perhaps the relief that they had gone from the Valley in peace helped her in her dark days, when she was quiet, without words for us, and short with Olwen, and we knew that she mourned.

Bron was a help at those times, for we never dared to say a word, but Bron could put an arm about her and tickle her, and make a good cup of tea, and put her in a chair, with talk about the boys and Angharad till the tears dropped and she smiled to remember, and then she was right for another couple of weeks.

So the weeks went, but day by day the trouble was coming to be worse. Where there was one meeting, now there were a dozen, and not only at night but in the afternoons too, and toward the end, in the mornings.

It was the subject-matter of the meetings that made me worry. Before, in the time of Mr. Gruffydd and my brothers, the meetings were called for a purpose and were orderly, with a subject defined and a vote to be taken on a show of hands.

But then it seemed that anybody who could talk was sure of a hearing, whatever might be coming from his mouth, sense or not, and it was a surprise to me, that men I knew to be as hard in the head as the bole of an oak, would stand to listen.

I was busy in my shop in the back yard from morning till night, making doors and window-frames and tables and chairs. I started small to have the time to work up a stock, so that I could use my time, later on, to make good furniture and perhaps panelling.

Orders I had in plenty, though I would never touch coffins, and in that, lost many a fat job and thought it no matter. I never saw a reason for putting noble wood and good work about deadness and dropping it down a little pit.

So, busy with my own job, I had little time to notice what was going on outside, and when I did, and worried, my work covered the worry and I forgot in the joy of using my shining tools, and thus the shock was greater.

One Saturday Bronwen had a birthday and I thought I would take her to Town for an outing and buy something new in a box for her. We left the boys with my mother and took Olwen with us.

Well, well.

There is a time we had.

There is good to take somebody you love on a trip to Town, for a smile is happy on the face, and even a little joke will bring a good laugh, but one with salt will have you in stitches.

O, and a royal feeling it is to spend money without caring, and a prince I was that day. So between laughter and princeliness I had my day and lived it well, and found it much to my liking.

People were stopping in the street to look at Bronwen and Olwen.

"What is the matter then, Huw?" Bron asked me, with big eyes, and a little voice. "Dress, or what, is wrong with us?"

"Nothing wrong, girl," I said and feeling in my pride to be three of me, and twice as high. "Lovelier than Pharaoh's daughters, you are, see. So go you, now."

"Go on with you, boy," Bron said, pretending a frost of impatience, but a smile in the making behind her eyes, and watching people to see if Olwen was having more of the looks. If she had seen a man looking at her, she would have turned her nose to the skies and so put him in a bruise of blushes, but if she had seen him looking at Olwen she would have been hurt, and wondering if she had a bit of soot on her nose or too many years.

A good, good laugh I had, to see them playing the game

of Woman. A pretty game it is too, and men having quite
as much of the fun when they have the courage to use their
eyes. Women love to be looked at, though they will deny
it with an oath, and men, the fools, will look up, look
down, and blind themselves and have humped backs with
looking at the pavement, or have twists in the neck from
looking at something on either side, only not to look, or
be thought looking at a woman. There is senseless, there is
stupid and there is dull.

For please to tell me what is better to look at than a
lovely woman, and I will come from my dinner to see.
And all women, never mind who, or what, have a loveliness
of their own, so who will say that we must cover our eyes
and see nothing only stones and sky, is one without good
sense and feeling, an ingrate for the gift of vision, and
barely half a man.

Bronwen walked in front of me looking up at first-floor
windows in the street, knowing only that eyes were on her,
and coming to be a pincushion full of the spikes of sight.

"I have got a name," she said, when I told her not to
mind the stares. "So please to mind your affairs. How
would I feel if I looked at a shop and a man spoke?"

"Would you have time to feel?" I asked her. "And
would he?"

"Trouble then," she said, "and an end in a police-station.
Leave it now. I will look when I want to, and when I
want to, I shall look."

Strange that women always trouble for the worst that
never happens. Not a man of all the hundreds we saw that
day would have dared to say a word to her, even if she had
looked back at him, for there was an air about Bronwen
that shouted a warning to fools, that was plainer than a
written sign.

Too conscious of her womanhood she was, and ready to
spoil her day by worrying over it.

"There is silly you are, girl," I said to her. "No matter
about tongues at home, but only old eyes here, and you
are running up a street with no enjoyment of it."

"I have yet to hear the words," she said. "But these
looks I can feel. Change places only for a minute."

"With gladness," I said. "Only to give you comfort.
They are looking because you are a new wonder, not
often to be seen, and they will think of you in years to

come. So you will live in many places at once, and always in beauty. Are you thankful?"

"No," she said, and then I saw that she was, but denying it because she was playing the game of Woman.

Olwen was looking at Bron in hope that soon a slackness would come to her steps so that we might look at the shops, for about us were the things of dreams and all of an afternoon was in front of us.

But Bronwen was used to the village street, and the eyes of those who knew her, so I knew we had perhaps an hour of discomfort to live through before she grew less tender of herself and more a part of the crowding streams of people, the dusty street of many sounds, and the noise of horses by the hundred, with more traps and carts and carriages than we had ever seen in all our lives before.

There is strange to walk in a town. Something is strange in the faces of people who live all their lives in a town. For their lives are full of the clock and their eyes are blind with seeing so many wonders, and they have no pleasure of expectation or prettiness of wish. Good things are heaped in the windows all round them, but their pockets are empty, and thus they suffer in their minds, for where they would own, now they must wish, and wishes denied soon turn to a lust that shows itself in the face. Too much to see, day after day, and too much noise for peace, and too little time in a round of the clock to sit by themselves, and think.

At last we had ease of eyes when we reached the arcades and went in to the lighted quietness of those winding streets of glass, full of thanks to the man who thought of them, and happy to be there.

I had splendid minutes in a bookshop while Bron and Olwen were buying presents in the shops for women.

O, there is lovely to feel a book, a good book, firm in the hand, for its fatness holds rich promise, and you are hot inside to think of good hours to come.

I would willingly have stayed there till the bolts were itching to be shot, but Bron came in and took me by the arm, with her mouth tight, and pulled me gently to the door.

"Old books, again," she said. "And two out here to march up and down while you are rubbing your old nose up and down pages."

"Let us buy a couple of books for the boys," I said, for the book-seller was looking at me as though I owed him money.

"A couple of testaments," Bron said, quick, for the shop was full of them.

"Go on, girl," I said. "They have got testaments to spare. A book to read, I mean. Would they thank me behind my back for a testament?"

"A little Prayer Book and hymn book in a case," Bron said, "there is pretty."

"Have it yourself," I said. "Something to make them shout to have. A couple of good books. Something worth taking back from Town."

So I bought *Ivanhoe* and *Treasure Island,* after a serious talk with the bookseller, a good little man with loose teeth and plenty to say, and all of it sense, and a few good dips into both of them myself, until Bronwen started to tap her foot, with her mouth screwed up on one side, and Olwen looking so sour to make miracles of sweetness out of little green apples.

"An outing for me, is it?" Bron asked me, in a voice to bring snow. "Come you, now then. Let us find another bookshop and I will go to live in it. Books, good God, and the shops will be shut in only another minute."

But when we had drunk a cup of tea she felt better, and the world was good when we went in the market, and Olwen was even humming.

Long, wide, and high, under an arch of glass, with the sun strong about us and stalls very tidy and full of good things, and voices coming happily from hundreds in a deep sighing sound that echoed in warmth, and a lovely smell made of many smells, of mint and cabbage and celery, and cured bacon and hams, and toffee and flannels and leather and cheeses, and paraffin oil, and flowers.

There is gladdening to see many kinds of flowers in long lines, standing brave in buckets and boxes, with reds and yellows and blues and purples and whites with a slenderness of green in among them, and coming closer, to put the nose into a bucket full of red roses, cold with freshness to make the smell keener and so drive it deeper into the head, as with nails of honey.

Out we went with arms full of flowers, and parcels of cheeses and a black ham, with a couple of bolts of flannel, two pairs of solid boots for the boys and a hand-worked apron for my mother, and both my pockets crammed with toffee, and our faces paining with big lumps that tasted lovely.

Then we bought dolls for Ceridwen's little girls and a boat and an engine for the boys, and saucepans in copper for my mother, and a set of jelly moulds for Bron. I waited outside a woman's shop while Bron was fitting herself with a dress, and Olwen was having a coat, but when they came out they were stiff with parcels, and short in breath with buying, but if they had spent a million sovereigns, they could not have had more happiness in their eyes, and my heart could not have known more lightness, or I would have been off the earth and drinking the skies.

We were loaded like packmen ready for months in the mountains when we went to the station, and we sang all the way back home, and when Thomas met us, he sang, too.

Down at the turn in the road, just before the rise that led into the Valley, we saw hundreds of lamps, and Thomas clicked his tongue with impatience.

"Talking, still," he said. "They have been grinding their tongues since this afternoon. Wonder there is any left in the Valley."

"What, now?" I asked him, and surprised.

"They are coming out," he said.

"I will get down," I said. "I will hear what is being said."

"No trouble, now, Huw," Bron said, and trying to pull me back. "Better for you to come home, straight, with us."

"Stop the trap, Thomas," I said and I went down to the meeting.

A stranger was talking about capital and labour with the names of Marx and Hegel thrown in as candied peel is put in a cake. Mr. Marx was made to sound like a newly risen Christ and Mr. Hegel as a John the Baptist, with gold flowing easily between them, endless as the waters of Jordan, ready for all to gather by the capful.

I listened to him for minutes, but there was too much noise about me to hear all he said, for the men were arguing among themselves and in places there were fights. Red revolution and anarchy was what the speaker wanted, with a red flag to fly over all, and everybody equal.

If I had found in myself the voice of a bull I could not have made myself heard, and I was sick in my heart, too, and without spirit to make the effort.

So I walked home in the darkness, leaving behind me the noise of them until the bulk of the slag heap shut it out, and for only once in my life I was grateful to slag.

It was pain to me that men could be so blind, but it was greater pain to know that my brothers and Mr. Gruffydd, and the brave ones of early days, had all been forgotten in a crazyness of thought that made more of the notions of foreigners than the principles of Our Fathers.

I was in a heat of worry to know what to do, whether to go back there and speak to them, or let them go in the company of foreigners, to have a lesson.

Down by the dead river I was, with slag rising up behind me, and a roughness of stone under foot where years ago the trout had come to wait for flies.

I stood still in the cool quiet, looking up at the blackness of the mountain, hearing only the north-east wind busy with his comb in the grass, and my eyes came to be wide, and sight was pinned to a place in the night, and waters returned to the river.

The sky became a sudden gold, and the mountain was of silver, and the river ran free and wide as a sea in a brilliance of precious stones. All about the mountain-top was a sparkling of unsheathed steel, and I saw, with a loftiness of fear, that a host of men were standing there looking into the Valley, and armour was shining on head and breast, and colours were gay on shields, and hands were clasped on the hilts of swords that pointed into the ground.

I was dull with wonder and drowned in a dream, but fear soon went in a bright tiredness of feeling, and I had strength and wit to wish that I could go closer to see their faces, and hear their voices, and know the sound of their speech.

Somewhere beyond the steadfast ranks, a trumpet sang a rich male song, and a thousand banners were raised as one, and swords went up in a burnish of flame, and steel heels clashed together.

A drum spoke up in a single flourish and the banners began to move, and a golden dust was rising from the marching ranks, shining about their helmets, reaching nearly to the ribbons and flowers that hung from the banner tops.

Then all the winds of Heaven ran to join hands and bend a shoulder, to bring down to me the sound of a noble hymn that was heavy with the perfume of Time That Has Gone.

The glittering multitudes were singing most mightily, and my heart was in blood to hear a Voice that I knew.

The Men of the Valley were marching again.

My Fathers were singing up there.

Loud, triumphant, the anthem rose, and I knew, in some deep place within, that in the royal music was a prayer to lift up my spirit, to be of good cheer, to keep the faith, that Death is only an end to the things that are made of clay, and to fight, without heed of wounds, all that brings death to the Spirit, with Glory to the Eternal Father, for ever, Amen.

Trumpets sang again and drum-beats carried the marching feet across the golden sky, and the banners were held in the arms of the winds to show the crimson dragons, and at the head, a throng of steel was bright, about the Cross and Crown.

They passed from me and I was coming to stand in the darkness again, and my eyes were heavy and filled with the sands of staring, and I thought I could still hear the Voice behind the voice of the wind.

I went slowly up the road to the village, and lifted my cap to the house with the sea-shell porch, and up, slower still, to our house.

"There is a time you have been, boy," my mother said, and smiling more than I had seen in months. "Did you have trouble?"

"No, Mama," I said.

"Is there something the matter, my little one?" she asked me, with a hand on my arm.

"Only what I heard at the meeting, Mama," I said.

"What, now?" my father asked me.

"Revolution," I said. "I wonder what would the boys say if they could hear."

"Leave it," my father said, and blowing through the stem of his pipe, "they will be tired of it. Revolution, indeed, and not enough sense among them all to turn a tap."

"O," my mother said, with impatience. "Let us have peace from them for one night, will you? Come and look at the beautiful presents, and then supper."

But I had seen too much that night, so the little things

we had bought that made my mother smile for pleasure were nothing to me, though I tried hard not to show it.

I gave Bron her present in a box when we were back home. A brooch, set with a garnet, on a lover's knot of gold.

"O," she said, and her eyes were with light, and I saw that her mouth was soft for me, but there was nothing in me to answer her, for the Voice seemed to have taken my strength.

"I will put it on your best silk," I said, and lines came swift to her face, and in my mind I cursed myself, for her best silk had always been Ivor's favourite, so I had said the wrong, wrong thing again, and worse, as though on purpose, to knock that light from her eyes and softness from her mouth.

"Thank you," she said, and went quickly to light the candles.

I stood in the kitchen while she went upstairs with no good night for me, but I knew she was quiet because of tears.

For minutes, I stood there, burning as in a fire, to go to her and kiss her, and beg forgiveness for a thoughtless fool, but I still could hear the voices on the mountain, and I sat in quiet to listen.

And again the key turned in the door.

Next morning men were running up the Hill to shout that they were out on strike in the next valley.

My mother gave my father little looks all the time we were having breakfast, but he said nothing, and looked nothing, but she knew.

Bronwen had gone early to Tyn-y-Coed with Olwen to give the house a polish, but before she left I had made her a cup of tea, and pinned the brooch on the inside of her apron.

No words, only a cup of tea, and a pinning, and a kiss, and such a lovely smile, and off, and I sawed a plank that was eight feet long without a single rest, so good I felt.

That afternoon, Olwen came to me running, with tears dried on her face.

"Huw," she said, "the strikers in the other valley are marching round the mountain. They made fun of me and Bron because of Iestyn."

"You will have to go over the mountain, then," I said,

and-angry to think some lout had made them unhappy, and wishing to have him close to my fist. "I will show you a good way to-morrow."

"They said we would be stopped going near Tyn-y-Coed again," she said. "Nasty things, they said. They were going to have the clothes off us."

"About the first, we will see," I said. "As to the second, I will pray to be near."

My father came back that night, and on his face a blankness of spirit.

"Out, again," he said. "Nothing to be done."

"How are the men such fools?" I asked him. "They have had lesson after lesson."

"A few words of the right sort," my father said, "a bit of flattery, a couple of words to have sympathy, and then some fighting talk, and most of them are like sheep for the slaughter. Those who are not can be accused of cowardice, or of knuckling to the owners. You know them."

Yes, I knew them, and loved them, and was sorry to the heart for them.

"What now?" my mother said.

"Sit down and wait," my father said. "No use to talk. Too many are at it with no notion why. I will rest my tongue until I am asked, or till the time is ripe to do a bit of good."

"Well, Dada," I said, "surely this is the time for us to go out and speak to them?"

My father put his hand steady on my shoulder, and looked at me greyly in the eye, without a blink.

"My son," he said, "your good brothers are from home only through speaking to them, and for them. They warned them enough not to strike. They saw its uselessness, at the last, as I have seen it these years past. Speaking to them now is a waste of breath. They are drunk with unreason. Leave them."

Chapter Forty-One

I WENT DOWN TO THE VILLAGE that night to the Three Bells, to fit shutters over the windows.

Dai was in bad spirits and so was Cyfartha, for a strike meant a stoppage of trade and a piling of debt. Cyfartha had come out with his shift, and he had been having both edges of Dai's tongue since he put foot over the step.

"Red flags," Dai said, with bubbles in his voice. "By God, I would give them red flags, indeed. Only to have my bloody eyes right, and I would show a couple of them, indeed to Christ. Eh, Cyfartha?"

"O, Dai," Cyfartha said, and shameful to soak in the sawdust, "I am sorry, dear Jesus, I am sorry. But could I stay on my own to cut coal and nobody to push the trams, and the horses idle?"

"I have told you, yes," Dai said. "I would see them in hell's good blazing before to take orders from them. Pounds and pounds we have lost through strikes. What gain, please to tell me, now, where you are standing, what gain? Nothing, not one halfpenny, eh, Cyfartha?"

"No, no," Cyfartha said, and a swallow of beer as though to wash away his sins, and then looking into the glass, "but damn me everlasting, Dai, they all came up, I tell you. Only me and the boy down there if we had stayed."

"Stay till you rot, then," Dai said, "but think for yourself. Do any of them know what they are out for? Some for a price on the five-foot seam, and some for ballots on places, and some for a price on cutting stone. Instead to have it solid on the table among them all. Everybody pull, pull, pull. And every pull a different one, and the owners sitting fat to laugh at us all for fools. Eh, Cyfartha?"

"Too tired for talking, I am, Dai, my little one," Cyfartha said. "Put my mouth to a barrel I will, and sleep drunk for a couple of days. That is the best for me."

"If they would listen to your good father, Huw," Dai said, in sorrow, "instead of these who think with heads of parsley. Shocking, to make the eyes run."

"The sportsmen, these are," I said. "The cattle."

"I am ready to pole-axe a couple, then," Dai said. "Are the shutters right, with you?"

"Solid as the house," I said. "Are you afraid of trouble?"

Dai looked round the bar, first, and then put his head to my ear.

"They have sworn to flood the pits this time," he said, with whispers. "If I will catch one to open his mouth to say so, I will hit his teeth to mix with his brains. But sly, they are, see. Nobody do know where the orders are coming from. I heard it in the bar, here, but only in talk. Ears open, mouth shut, Huw, my little one, and if you come to know, tell me. Only tell me, eh, Cyfartha?"

"I will hold him gentle by the tail for you to hit, Dai," Cyfartha said.

"And I will hit him to leave the tail in your hand," Dai said. "Shall we have a little walk over the mountain to-morrow, Huw?"

"Yes," I said. "We will go to Tyn-y-Coed to meet my sisters. Some of them were careless in their language to them and they were frightened they would put hands on them because of Iestyn."

Dai looked at me, mouth loose, waiting for words to come, and his eyes went wide from me to Cyfartha, and back to me, and his fists coming open and shut.

"Your good sisters?" he said, and red coming all over his head, and water to the eyes. "Well, for the love of God, what are we coming to, now then? Huw, me and you to do a bit of watching to-morrow night, and Cyfartha and a few good boys a few yards behind. Eh, Cyfartha?"

"Not too far, Dai," Cyfartha said, "in case to have a bit of trouble, and me not there to have the pleasure."

"Pleasure it will be," Dai said, and hit his fist on the bar counter with force to crack planks. "Only please to let me see one eye too many on them, and I will hit him, by God, to make them sink a shaft to pull him out of the mountain. Eh, Cyfartha?"

"There is cruel you are, Dai, my little one," Cyfartha said, and very solemn, too. "If you will hit him a bit harder, see, he will come out the other side and walk home, and no trouble to anybody."

James Rowlands came in, with a shortness of breath and a face full of bad news.

"Mr. Winston Churchill is sending soldiers up here," he said, and his asthma having him sore.

"Who the hell is he, then, with you?" Dai said.

"Home Secretary," James Rowlands said, and having his pint from Cyfartha very grateful, "in London."

"Is he somebody, then?" Dai said, as wise as before.

"I think," James Rowlands said, through the drink.

"Soldiers," Dai said, with quiet. "English soldiers, I suppose?"

"Would they be fools, and send Welsh?" James Rowlands asked him.

"The only fools here," Dai said, "are us. But English soldiers, eh, Cyfartha?"

"Trouble," Cyfartha said.

"Eyes or no eyes," Dai said, "I will be in it. Bloody English soldiers, indeed. To hell with them, eh, Cyfartha?"

"To hell, Dai, my little one, to hell," Cyfartha said.

Only a couple of days later, when they were both serving soldiers of the West Riding Regiment and some Munster Fusiliers with all the beer they could drink, and not a pennypiece in payment:

"Well," I said to Dai, "a good one, you are. To hell with the English soldiers, then? With beer to cool them down there, is it?"

"O," he said, and coming a bit red. "Good boys, they are, see. No harm in them, and swearing very tidy about coming here, too. Couple of officers up in the front room, and saying worse than the men, eh, Cyfartha?"

"Educated they are," Cyfartha said. "No trouble from these down here. They are only having a few pence a day pay, and nothing extra for a black eye."

In all the other valleys there was trouble and to spare, with baton charges, and fights between pickets and blacklegs. But in our Valley, although the men were in the streets all day, nothing more than shouting was going on.

Again the mark of shoulders rubbing in idleness was coming plain to be seen, all along the walls in the main street, telling of the thousands wasting the rich moments of their lives, with the earth offering them an abundance just beneath their feet, and given free to them, by God.

Well, well.

If ever I will have the privilege to meet God the Father face to face, I will ask did He laugh, or did He cry, when He saw and heard what we were doing down here, with a concern that runs itself, and given to us free.

Wonder to me He has never put a fist through the clouds to squash us flat. Or perhaps, like the good Dr. Johnson, His time will come, and then it will hurt all the more. I am in shivers to think of the Day.

The Day of Reckoning.

I think that perhaps no bad trouble would have come close to us if a policeman had not taken it upon himself in his sweetness of dignity to hit a half-wit with his stick.

Old Sami Canal Water, we called the half-wit, because

his mother made ginger beer that he sold at the pit-tops, and a poor living indeed, but they owed nobody and kept from the rates.

The men were coming back from a meeting and I was up on the banking waiting for my father, and I saw a policeman galloping his mare and shouting to the men to make way.

Some of them ran up the banking in fear of the mare's hoofs, but those further away started to shout and some of them lined up to stop him.

Old Sami Canal Water was running from one side of the street to the other, lost, screaming in fear, and beating his hands together, and the bottles falling from his basket to burst white and splashing in the road, and with each burst, a scream from him, and trying to pick up the broken bits, and the mare coming at him stretch-neck.

And almost under her forelegs another bottle burst, and she reared, and Sami fell, clawing at her, with only the whites of his eyes showing, and the policeman raised his stick and brought it down on Sami's head with the sound of a spoon on a boiled egg.

War.

Anything in blue, with silver buttons, from that day on, was an enemy.

That policeman, who knew Sami, and all of us, was no stranger. But if he had a mother, she was hard put to know her son that night. He went over the bank, quick, and his mare was behind the Three Bells for weeks after, well fed, and fat, ownerless.

That night, more than a thousand men attacked the colliery to have the blood of the police in the boiler-house.

But they were not all our men. There were strangers among them, who seemed to be giving the orders, and I could hear somebody calling to put the pumps from work and flood the pit, so I was off, quick, to find Dai and Cyfartha.

"Right," said Dai. "Call the boys, Cyfartha."

Off down to the pit-top we went, in pitch darkness, about twenty of us, and round the back, away from the road where all the men were shouting.

Glass was smashed in the windows of the offices, and stones were hitting like hail against the walls of the power house.

"What will they gain, the fools?" Dai said, with his hand on my shoulder. "Give them a shout in the winding-house, Cyfartha."

So Cyfartha and a couple of us lifted a shout to Iorweth and the door opened a crack to show his face behind the lantern, but he saw there were many of us and shut it again, so we had more shouting to do, and at last we were in.

Iorweth had been in the winding-house with his shift mates for days, sleeping there, afraid to go home in case the men set about him for a blackleg.

"We want a look through a window, quiet," Dai said, "only to see the happy little man with most to say, outside there. Then we will have him. Iorweth, my little one, and you shall come home with us in peace, and I will sleep in your house, is it?"

"Thank you, Dai," Iorweth said, too tired to smile. "Glad I will be, indeed. Go you."

So up we went to the windows, carefully, not to have a stone in the eye, and looked out on the crowd. Big windows of many small panes they were, to have light for the engineers busy on the big wheel.

The crowd stretched up the banking toward the village, packed tight, and all their faces white in the light of flares. Shouting they were, and young men in front with armfuls of stones, throwing for bets, to see who could smash most panes.

"There he is," Cyfartha said. "I see him."

He was pointing to a small group, standing away from the crowd, with a man in a bowler hat in the middle, doing a lot of talking.

"Me and you, Dai," Cyfartha said, and jùmped down. "Only me and you."

"Good," Dai said, and off with jacket and cap. "Take my arm and let go when I am near to him, eh, Cyfartha?"

"Come you, Dai, my little one," Cyfartha said, and out they went, hand in hand.

They came in the light only when they were a few yards from the group, and when the crowd saw them, they all cheered, for not one of them could mistake the broad, squat bandiness of Dai, with Cyfartha's straightness beside him.

Straight to the group they went, and then.

O, and then.

The quick, upward passage of Dai's white forearms, the flash of his fists, and the swinging swiftness of Cyfartha beside him. One after another, the men went on the ground, flat, arms flying apart, faces white one moment, out the next, and no sound coming to us because of the crowd.

Then the two of them walked back with their hands in their pockets with a pile on the ground behind them, and men crowding about to see what harm had been done.

"A mongrel," Dai said, coming in. "That one in the bowler. I heard him swearing."

"Iorweth back home, now then," Cyfartha said.

"Look, Dai," Iorweth said, "will we go across and help with the fires? The pumps will stop, if not."

"Come you," Dai said, and over to the boiler-house we went, but when the crowd saw us going they threw stones again, but too far away to hit us.

The manager was in the boiler-house, tired too, with some policemen playing cards, and a couple of his clerks ready to cry with tiredness, trying to stoke the fires, and making a clerk's job of it.

"Come from there," Cyfartha said, and pulled a slice from one of them. "Into your coat and ready for home. A couple of us will stay on here, and you have rest."

"Are you men unionists?" the manager asked us.

"Yes," I said.

"Good God," he said, and surprised even in his tiredness, "Morgan."

"But the boilers will be giving steam to-morrow," I said, "Morgan or not."

"I am grateful," he said.

"Who is for home," Dai said, "go home," and went, and left Cyfartha and a couple of us, with the policemen playing cards, in the heat of the boiler-house.

At six o'clock in the morning, with frost coming to shine in the light, we saw Bron, all by herself, bent under a basket, hurrying across the pit-top, and calling my name.

"Well, indeed to God," Cyfartha said, with his mouth full of the breakfast she had brought, "a woman I will thank God to have met."

"Are you coming home, Huw?" Bronwen asked me.

"When the reliefs come," I said, and having it cheerful with bacon and eggs.

"No getting in trouble, now then," she said, and standing with her arm about me.

"Trouble?" I said. "And you coming down here alone? Stay in the house, Bron, my sweetheart, and keep Olwen and the boys in, too. The crowd is with madness."

"Right, you," she said. "Come with me to the street, is it?"

So to the street I went, and Cyfartha watching, but the village was without workmen, empty, and the houses coming sharp with morning light.

Lovely was Bronwen that morning, with the cold to put a redness of flowers in her cheeks and her eyes with dear blueness soft for me, and tearful, from the poking fingers of the south-east wind, that was busy about us with mischief.

There is a wholeness about a woman, of shape, and sound, and colour, and taste, and smell, a quietness that is her, that you will want to hold tightly to you, all, every little bit, without words, in peace, for jealousy for the things that escape the clumsiness of your arms. So you feel when you love.

So I felt for Bronwen, but I never told her.

"Well," she said, when we had stood for a minute, and me trying to think of something to say, and her looking up the street, and at me with a bit of a smile, and up at the Hill again.

"Well," I said, "remember what I said about coming out of the house. And please to say thank you to Mama for breakfast."

"Yes," she said, soft, a little girl having orders for behaviour at a Sunday School treat.

"If old Malachi Edwards wants his chairs," I said, "he will have to wait. I will be here till the finish."

"Yes," she said. "No home, to-night, then?"

"We will see," I said.

"Good," she said, and smiling. "Good-bye, now."

"Good-bye," I said.

We looked deep at one another again.

O, where is the harm to love any woman who looks as Bron looked, then?"

For her womanness is a blessing about her, and you are tender to put hands upon her and kiss, not with lust, but with the joy of one returning to a lost one.

But there is a binding and trying in the mind and conscience, keeping you from lifting as much as a finger, and those strictures were tight round me, to make me dumb and keep me still.

And she half turned away, and turned to me again as though I had spoken and her eyes with darker colours of blue, now, and seeming to be heavy with a happy concern for me, and her mouth open to ask a question, but then she smiled her smile that was not a smile, and closed her mouth to tight roundness that was of Eve, and then smiled a big, big smile to thaw the frost right down the Valley.

"What now?" I asked her.

"Nothing," she said. "Only good-bye."

And up the Hill she went, straight, flat in the back, with a clean, quick step without a scrape of the heel, and half-way up a turn to me, and a wave, and the air coming to smile about her.

Chapter Forty-Two

CYFARTHA looked kindly at me when I went back.

"Breakfast for the gentleman," he said, "wherever he is. A good one that. If I had met her young, I would have hit you to hell out of it."

"Two of us to fight, then," I said, "my brother and me."

"Yes," he said, and he looked a bit strange, as though he had said the wrong word.

I wish I had taken more notice, then.

But the fires wanted notice, and the police were waking, so I forgot.

Day after day we were in the pump-room, and my father bringing food to us in the morning, and Dai coming at night, with reliefs.

Every hour the crowd got more dangerous, for the leaders could do nothing, the owners would do nothing, the Government did nothing, and in the meantime, the soldiers marched up and down in handfuls, and the police walked about in fifties, and having it stiff wherever they showed their heads, and windows were smashed and shops were looted, and honest men were stopped from doing what they had a mind to do, by gangs of boys, who had been given eight years of free education, and were still unable to use their minds.

They were outside all day, shouting, throwing, and you must live in front of it to know the sadness of it.

Cattle, to be herded, as with dogs, from gate to gate.

One afternoon we heard a bigger shout outside, and ran to the door to unlock it.

Olwen was trying to fight her way through to us, and with hands on her to tear her cloak and grip her hair.

Out we went with firebars and slices, and into the cattle, and see them run, with a couple on the ground to have a lesson.

"There is a fool of a girl, you are," I said.

"The horses," she was crying, "the horses."

"What, the horses?" I asked her, and ready to hit.

"They are down there in the stables," she said, with tears thick, "hungry and thirsty, they are."

"Good God," Cyfartha said, "forgotten them, I had."

"Howell has been trying to have a truce to bring them all to the surface," she said. "They are nearly all up in the other pits, but not here. Dada has just come home from a meeting to tell us, so down I came quick."

"Cyfartha," I said, "I will ask the cattle for help."

"Good," he said. "I will have the cage up the top, ready."

Out I went to the crowd, and stones coming to breathe past me.

"Listen," I shouted to them, "the ponies are down there and nobody to give them comfort. Who will come to help?"

"Let them stay," somebody shouted. "Nobody is troubling for us."

But, fair play, the cattle had a voice of pity, and it was deep. Then men began to come forward, and when I had twenty, I had enough. Over to the pit-top we went, and down in the cage.

Well, if you had seen the little horses when they saw us. Like children, they were, ready to sit down at a party, and with just as much noise. All the lights were out down there, and candles were all we had, but the ponies were so full with joy that they pushed against us with their noses, and rubbed their necks, and so put our candles out, and swearing coming high, then, to find matches and light up again.

But the ponies knew the way to the cages, like cats, for darkness was friendly to them, and up we went, cage after cage of them, and all shouting to be going on top to grass.

Eh, dear.

If you had seen those ponies running when we let them

loose. Blind they were, but they knew that the mountain had only kindness for them and nothing for them to trip on or trap to bring them low.

If only we could all have been as happy.

My father was going from one pit to another in the district to inspect underground and taking his life as a gift to do it for men were ready to kill anybody going to work for the owners.

I knew my father had gone down the pit that had been Iestyn's, for he had told me he was going that morning, and to expect him to come up our shaft after a walk right the way through underground. The pumps were keeping the water down as far as we knew, for the gauges showed normal, but he wanted to be sure.

So, while the cattle were shouting and throwing, and leaders on both sides were arguing and being offended, and men were worrying about such matters as wives and children, my father was underground, with rats and flood-water, and darkness for companions, with his eyes sharp for danger to the livelihood of men.

We heard nothing from him all day, and the afternoon went dark for evening, and still nothing.

"Huw," Cyfartha said, "come you here, boy."

He was over by the gauges, looking up at the glass, with his piece of waste to his mouth.

"Well?" I said, and looked at the level.

The black was rising, to tell of water in the pit, and more than the pumps could send out.

"I am going down," Cyfartha said, and lines in his face. "There is fouling down there."

"And my father," I said.

"Perhaps he came up the other end," Cyfartha said. "Give me an hour."

"Right," I said, and we shook hands, and I went to the winding-house to tell Iorweth to lower the cage, then over to the crowd that was waiting for police to show themselves.

"The pit is flooding," I shouted to them. "Any volunteers to go down?"

But the men who wanted to come were afraid in case they were beaten in the streets later, or had their homes wrecked while they were down.

"You are cutting your own throats," I said to them. "If

the strike ends to-morrow you will have weeks of waiting while they take water from the levels. More waiting, more idleness, more going without."

"Come closer," somebody shouted, "and we will cut your throat and send your guts to Churchill."

More shouting from the crowd, and a move forward, with stones falling. Nothing could be done with them.

I went back to the boiler-house.

I knew that my mother would be worrying up at home, and I thought with shame of the days I had been in the boiler-house with not a word to her, but only by messages in other mouths. Of all other things we think, but seldom of the comfort of our mothers.

So I waited until police reliefs came, and while the crowd was busy with them, I ran down the banking to the river bed and up as far as the village, at the back of the Three Bells, and in through the side door.

"Dai," I said, "Cyfartha has gone down by himself to see if there is flooding."

"O?" he said, and went on playing patience. "Is there news of your good father yet?"

"No," I said, "I am going up to the house to see my mother, now just. Perhaps Cyfartha has met trouble, Dai."

"My respects to your good mother," he said, "and call in here on the way back, is it? I will have a couple of the boys here."

"Right," I said, and I could hear him shouting half-way up the Hill.

Fire-light was red on our curtains in the back, but Bron's kitchen was dark, no smoke was coming from the chimney, and Gareth's wooden engine was hiding its colours in the evening by the back door. That was strange, for the engine should have been inside long before, and the wash-house full of smells for supper, and Bron singing in the kitchen.

You know a loneliness and a quiet at such times.

"Mama," I said, half-way through our back, "are you here?"

"Where else, then?" she asked me, from my father's chair by the fire. "Is he with you?"

"No," I said, and knew that she meant my father and was in terror for him, though in her voice was a slow care-lessness that she had put there to try and assure herself and blind me. But I knew when I kissed her, and felt her shaking. And she was sitting in darkness, in my father's chair.

"Will you have to eat, my little one?" she asked me, and that was wrong, too, for she had made no move before to ask.

"No, Mama," I said, "only come up for a kiss, I have."

"Your Dada has been gone since this morning, Huw," she said, and I put an arm about her, and O, a pity that was a century of fire passed through me to feel her littleness, and to think of the men and women who had taken life from out of her.

"Yes, Mama," I said. "So you are sitting in the dark to wait."

"No," she said, and staring wide in the fire, "I was in the wash-house peeling potatoes, and Ivor came."

The kitchen went black about me, and my jaws were tight with fear for her and for myself.

"You have worried too much, Mama," I said, but not in the voice that I knew.

"Do I know my own son?" my mother asked me, with quiet, and with a certainty of utterance that silenced me. "Ivor, I saw, and I smiled at him, and he smiled at me, and nodded his head."

The plates on the dresser laughed in the fire-light and the wind put his lips to the chimney-pot and blew a little tune.

My mother looked at me and tried to smile, but her face was slack with weakness, and her mouth kept pulling in jerks that were ugly.

"I wonder what has come to your Dada?" she said, and her voice was like her mouth.

"I am going down now to see," I said, and got up. "Is Bronwen out?"

"She is down at Iestyn's pit," my mother said. "She went with Olwen, this afternoon, to take dry clothes for him."

"But he was coming up through our shaft," I said.

"He was too long underground," she said, "so they went to Iestyn's pit in case he came back up there. The crowd was too big down the bottom, here."

"They should never have left the house," I said.

"It was something for them to do," she said, and then she was crying, but not with tears.

"Mama," I said, "no more thinking like this, is it? You

are in darkness and frightened. Come you, now. A light, and a cup of tea, quick."

"Leave me," she said, and I never heard her sterner. "Go to your father."

"Yes, Mama," I said, and kissed her, and went from the house, and ran down the Hill to the Three Bells.

Dai was with the boys all in their working clothes and Dai's cleaner than any, sharp with creases from the cupboard shelves, and tight for him. They all had a glass and Dai gave me one that was three fingers deep with brandy.

"Come you, Huw," he said, "a health. To two good ones underground. Drink with love."

We drank, and Dai seemed to have drunk only tea, but I was still coughing when we were down among the crowd at the pit-top, with Dai holding my arm, and fisting with his right, and the rest of us using picks and shovels to have a clear way. Over to the cage we went, with police making a baton charge from the boiler-house to keep the crowd from us.

"Have anybody come up?" Dai asked the sergeant.

"No," the sergeant said, "and the water-gauge is still rising in there."

"Right," said Dai, and holding on to me until we were in the cage, "there is good to be in my clothes, and ready for work again. Not a button to meet on my trews, see, and string to keep me tidy round the middle. I have got a belly like a sow through sitting to swill in that old bar."

The cage swung gently, not quite on the bottom level, for the water was up to the waist, and we stopped it where it would rest dry, and jumped, one by one, into a black stillness of quiet ice, walking through to the pumps as though chained at the ankles. One of the pumps was damaged, but the other looked to be sound, and we started to work on them till the engineers gave a signal up to the surface.

Good, it was, to hear the voice of them, and to know that the waters were beaten.

"They had a good try, whoever it was," the engineer said. "No time to finish, thank God in His Goodness. There must have been more than a couple."

"Cyfartha must have caught somebody at it," Dai said. "You will find the rat in the water, here. But where is Cyfartha?"

"I wonder did he chase the others?" Gomer said.

"No surprise to me," Dai said. "Let us find him. You have got the eyes. Come, you."

So into the main we went, with candles high, and splashing at the rats, with water to the chest in places, and to the knees later. Then we came to the trouble.

The roof had fallen. Props had been weakened, and the pressure of water had torn away cogs as though made of paper.

"O, God," Dai said, and feeling the rock with his hands, "is he under this?"

"Is my father?" I said, and seeing my mother plain beside me.

"Come on," Dai said, "into it."

Into it, yes, into it.

With fright chewing holes in me, and my mouth dry, and trembling, I went at it with the pick, and Dai doing the work of three beside me.

We had to smash through that dead weight of stone and clay, and carry it rock by rock and spadeful by spadeful out of our way, knowing that somewhere inside it my father or Cyfartha might be lying hurt, or dying, or dead.

As we worked we prayed, and between the prayers, we cursed the heavy, dead, stupid hardness of the stone and the thick, lifeless clay, and then prayed each time we strained to lever a bit of rock that some sign would be given to us that we were near.

But we had to work carefully for the roof was soft and with low rumbles to warn us that more would come down on top of us if we put a pick too far or a shovel too high. When we tired, others took our places, and when they were dropping, three more, until our turn came again, but all the time we were taking rocks away, or piling clay and muck. To the knees in water, and bent, for there was only four feet of head room and knowing we must work fast, but held back because of the danger of a fall to make our work a waste of time.

The candles began to go, and a man went back for more, and something to drink, for we were dying down there, so hot it was, so filled with dust, and a scum of dust thick on the water, and mud to the calves, and water rising fast as we worked downwards.

Dai was thick with mud, and throwing rocks from him

as fast as he could have his hands on them, with a curse for each one, and his mouth in a wide line of hate, and his eyes mad through shining black muck, using the pick now, and nobody able to go near because of its bite, and throwing it down to pull out more rock, and to toss it behind him, careless where it went as long as it was not in front.

Hour after hour we were down there, and with every yard, air getting colder and stiffening us, and the water rising to freeze us about the waist, until life was only a dig, and a pull, and a carry and drop, and a crawl back, and a dig and a pull and carry and drop, and a crawl back again.

And muscle screaming please to rest, if only to straighten the shouting back, or stretch the torn palms of the hands.

But Dai Bando was up in front there, burrowing without a stop, working in darkness, feeling for rock with his hands, no sound only the sobs of his breath, and in his crouched back, a mightiness of threat to any who stayed even to hitch his trews.

Then Dai shouted, a high whisper of a shout, that sent ants crawling up my head.

"Cyfartha," he was shouting, "here is his coat, see."

"Up in a stall road," I said, for we had worked close to the wall and the coat was in the hole going up to the right.

"Clear the main, or the stall road?" Dai said.

Everybody stopped work.

If we went on up the main, we might be leaving Cyfartha and perhaps my father up in the stall road.

If we worked up the stall road they might be dying in the main in front of us.

I believe God the Father knows how you feel at such a time and sends a sign.

We had a sign, then.

We heard Cyfartha's pick hitting a signal on a rock.

Up in the stall road.

If we had gone on working, we should never have heard.

And Dai, who had never been in Chapel to pray since a boy, hit his hands together, and fell on his knees in the muck, crying like a woman.

"O God," he said, "with thanks I am, for this gift to me. Cyfartha is the blood of my heart. Have my eyes and my arms. I am thankful. In Jesus Christ. Amen."

"Amen," said we all.

"Give me the bloody pick," Dai said, with new life. "Stand away now."

And the pick swung and struck as though he had just started.

"Mind the roof, Dai," Gomer said, in fear, for the pick was driving deep, and the stone above us was growling.

"To hell with the roof," Dai said, like an animal, "God is with us, and bloody near time, too."

Behind us we heard men coming, and saw lanterns, with the manager and more of the men behind him.

"Right," he said, "you men can go to the surface. I am proud of you."

But Dai went on picking and pulling, and none of us stopped.

"Come on," he said, with sharpness, "these men are fresh."

"I will crush him in pieces," Dai screamed, up in the narrow tunnel, "I will have Cyfartha from here. Tell him to go to bloody hell, with him."

And the manager knew, and the rock came back, and back, and Dai went up, and up, lying full length now, and a man behind, full length, and behind him, another, full length, passing rock and muck behind, one to another, with the roof touching our backs, and our bellies in blood from stones and black heat that was pain to breathe, about us.

And Dai screamed again, a sound of terror, and of triumph, dulled by the tunnel and the heat and footage.

"Cyfartha," he was screaming, "Cyfartha. Back out."

"Back out," Gomer said, in front of me, and his boot soles came close to my face to bruise.

"Back out," I said, to Willie, behind me, and I slid back, taking my rock with me.

"Back out," Willie said, to his hind man.

Out of the heading we crawled, and Gomer coming to fall in a faint in the water, and then Dai.

If the Devil rises from the Pit as Dai came from the tunnel, a few of us are booked to die a second death with fear.

Black, and naked, and with lumps of mud stuck to his head and shoulders, and all of him shaking with strength that has gone weak, he shone wet in the lantern lights, and his eyes framed with pink, sightless with tears, and his mouth wide to the roof to breathe.

And in his arms Cyfartha, black, too, and still.

"Is my father up there?" I asked him.

"Up there," Cyfartha said, but only just. "I was after him."

"I will take Cyfartha to the top," Dai said, "and back, then, for your father."

"I am going in," I said.

"I love you as a son," Dai said. "Go you."

So up I went, and as far as Dai had gone, in a little chamber of rock, and more rock piled in front again.

"Dada," I shouted, "are you near me?"

I hit my pick on stone and listened.

Only the growling up above, and voices from behind in the tunnel.

So on I went again, pick and pull, pick and pull and wasting more time getting the rock back, and scooping mud, and trying to shovel.

And then I found him.

Up against the coal face, he was, in a clearance that the stone had not quite filled.

I put my candle on a rock, and crawled to him, and he saw me, and smiled.

He was lying down, with his head on a pillow of rock, on a bed of rock, with sheets and bedclothes of rock to cover him to the neck, and I saw that if I moved only one bit, the roof would fall in.

He saw it, too, and his head shook, gently, and his eyes closed.

He knew there were others in the tunnel.

I crawled beside him, and pulled away the stone from under his head, and rested him in my lap.

"Willie," I said, "tell them to send props, quick."

I heard them passing the message down, and Willie trying to pull away enough rock to come in beside me.

"Mind, Willie," I said, "the roof will fall."

"Have you found him?" Willie asked me, and scraping through the dust.

"Yes," I said, and no heart to say more.

My father moved his head, and I looked down at him, sideways to me, and tried to think what I could do to ease him, only for him to have a breath.

But the Earth bore down in mightiness, and above the Earth, I thought of houses sitting in quiet under the sun, and men roaming the streets to lose voice, breath, and blood, and children dancing in play, and women cleaning house, and good smells in our kitchen, all of them adding more to my father's counter-pane. There is patience in the Earth to allow us to go into her, and dig, and hurt with tunnels and shafts, and if we put back the flesh we have torn from her and so make good what we have weakened, she is content to let us bleed her. But when we take, and leave her weak where we have taken, she has a soreness, and an anger that we should be so cruel to her and so thoughtless of her comfort. So she waits for us, and finding us, bears down, and bearing down, makes us a part of her, flesh of her flesh, with our clay in place of the clay we thoughtlessly have shovelled away.

I looked Above for help, and prayed for one sweet breath for him, but I knew as I prayed that I asked too much, for how were all those tons to be moved in a moment, and if they were, what more hurt might be done to others.

Afraid I was, to put my hands with tenderness upon his face, for my touch, though with the love of the heart, might be an extra hurt, another weighing, for they were with dirt and cuts, and ugly with work that was senseless, not good to put before his eyes, for they were the hands of the Earth that held him.

His eyes were swelling from his head with pain and his mouth was wide, closing only a little as with weakness, and then opening wide again, and his tongue standing forth as a stump, moveless, dry, thick with dust.

And as the blood ran from his mouth and nose, and redness ran from his eyes, I saw the shining smile in them, that came from a brightness inside him, and I was filled with bitter pride that he was my father, fighting still, and unafraid.

His head trembled, and pressed against me as he made straight the trunk of his spine and called upon his Fathers, and my lap was filling with his blood, and I saw the rocks above him moving, moving, but only a little. And then they settled back, and he was still, but his eyes were yet beacons, burning upon the mountain-top of his Spirit.

I shut my eyes and thought of him at my side, my hand

in his, trying to match his stride as I walked with him up the mountain above us, and I saw the splashings of water on his muscled whiteness as he stood in the bath, and the lamplight on his hands over the seat of the chair as he knelt in prayer at Chapel.

Air rushed from his throat and blew dust from his tongue, and I heard his voice, and in that strange noise I could hear, as from far away, the Voice of the Men of the Valley singing a plain amen.

So I closed his eyes and shut his jaw, and held him tight to me, and his bristles were sharp in my cuts, and I was heavy with love for him, as he had been, and with sadness to know him gone.

"We can move the rocks now, Willie," I said.

"O Christ, Huw," Willie said, "is he out, then?"

"Yes," I said, and feeling warmth passing from between my hands, "my Dada is dead."

"Hard luck, Huw, my little one," Willie said, and coming to cry. "Hard old bloody luck, indeed. Good little man, he was."

.   .   .   .

My mother sat in the rocking-chair with her hands bound in her apron, and looked through the open doorway up at the mountain-top.

"God could have had him a hundred ways," she said, and tears burning white in her eyes, "but He had to have him like that. A beetle under the foot."

"He went easy, Mama," I said.

"Yes," she said, and laughed without a smile. "I saw him. Easy, indeed. Beautiful, he was, and ready to come before the Glory. Did you see his little hands? If I set foot in Chapel again, it will be in my box, and knowing nothing of it. O, Gwil, Gwil, there is empty I am without you, my little one. Sweet love of my heart, there is empty."

Well.

.   .   .   .

It is strange that the Mind will forget so much, and yet hold a picture of flowers that have been dead for thirty years and more.

I remember the flowers that were on our window-sill while my mother was talking that morning, and I can see the water dripping from a crack in the red pot on the end, for Bronwen was standing there, with her face in deep, dull gold from the sun on the drawn blind.

Thirty years ago, but as fresh, and as near as Now.

No bitterness is in me, to think of my time like this. Huw Morgan, I am, and happy inside myself, but sorry for what is outside, for there I have failed to leave my mark, though not alone, indeed.

An age of goodness I knew, and badness too, mind, but more of good than bad, I will swear. At least we knew good food, and good work, and goodness in men and women.

But you have gone now, all of you, that were so beautiful when you were quick with life. Yet not gone, for you are still a living truth inside my mind. So how are you dead, my brothers and sisters, and all of you, when you live with me as surely as I live myself?

Shall we say that good Dr. Johnson is dead, when his dear friend Mr. Boswell brings him to thunder and thump before your very eyes? Is Socrates dead, then, when I hear the gold of his voice?

Are my friends all dead, then, and their voices a glory in my ears?

No, and I will stand to say no, and no, again.

In blood, I say no.

Is Ceinwen dead, then, and her beauty dear beside me again, and her eyes with jewels for me, and my arms hurting with the grip of her fingers?

Is Bronwen dead, who showed me the truth of the love of woman? Is she dead, who proved to me that the strength of woman is stronger than the strength of fists, and muscles, and the male shoutings of men?

Did my father die under the coal? But, God in heaven, he is down there now, dancing in the street with Davy's red jersey over his coat, and coming, in a moment, to smoke his pipe in the front room and pat my mother's hand, and look, and O, the heat of his pride, at the picture of a Queen, given by the hand of a Queen, in the Palace of a Queen, to his eldest son, whose baton lifted voices in music fit for a Queen to hear.

Is Mr. Gruffydd dead, him, that one of rock and flame, who was friend and mentor, who gave me his watch that was all in the world he had, because he loved me? Is he

dead, and the tears still wet on my face and my voice cutting through rocks in my throats for minutes while I tried
to say good-bye, and, O God, the words were shy to come,
and I went from him wordless, in tears and with blood.

Is he dead?

For if he is, then I am dead, and we are dead, and all of
sense a mockery.

How green was my Valley, then, and the Valley of them
that have gone.